Orkneyjar
(Orkney)

HORÐALAND

North Sea

Æbbercurnig
Bebbanburg
† Lindisfarnae
† Werceworthe
† Uuiremutha
Eoforwic

BRITAIN

iscay

Quentovic

Aachen
(Aix-la-Chapelle)

LANDS OF THE FRANKS

SEPTIMANIA

Papia

Banbalūnah
(Pamplona)

L U S

Garundah (Girona)

Roma

Balansiya (Valencia)

ROMAN SEA

(MEDITERRANEAN SEA)

IFRIQIYA

Praise for

MATTHEW HARFFY

'Harffy is a master of the Dark Age thriller...
A Time for Swords is a bold opening to yet another
enthralling series. It promises to be one heck of a ride.'
Theodore Brun, author of *A Mighty Dawn*

'Terrific white-knuckle action, absolutely gripping storytelling...
Can't wait for the next one. Highly recommended!'
Angus Donald, author of *Robin Hood and the Caliph's Gold*

'A breathless charge through Dark Ages intrigues and infight-
ing that brings the period to savage, bloody life. Masterful.'
Anthony Riches, author of the Empire series

'Nothing less than superb... The tale is fast paced
and violence lurks on every page.'
Historical Novel Society

'Harffy's writing just gets better and better... He is really
proving himself the rightful heir to Gemmell's crown.'
Jemahl Evans, author of *The Last Roundhead*

'A tale that rings like sword song in the reader's mind.
Harffy knows his genre inside out.'
Giles Kristian, author of *Camelot*

'Top class adventure writing, with action that
moves as fast and keen as a whetted blade.'
Ian Breckon, author of *Battle Song*

BY MATTHEW HARFFY

A Time for Swords series

A Time for Swords
A Night of Flames
A Day of Reckoning

Bernicia Chronicles

The Serpent Sword
The Cross and the Curse
Blood and Blade
Killer of Kings
Warrior of Woden
Storm of Steel
Fortress of Fury
For Lord and Land
Forest of Foes
Kin of Cain (short story)

Other novels

Wolf of Wessex

A DAY OF RECKONING

MATTHEW HARFFY

An Aries Book

First published in the UK in 2023 by Head of Zeus,
part of Bloomsbury Publishing Plc

9 7 5 3 2 4 6 8

A catalogue record for this book is available from the British Library.

ISBN (HB): 9781804548547
ISBN (E): 9781804548578

Cover design: Ben Prior/Head of Zeus

Printed and bound in Great Britain by
CPI Group (UK) Ltd, Croydon CR0 4YY

Head of Zeus
First Floor East
5–8 Hardwick Street
London EC1R 4RG

WWW.HEADOFZEUS.COM

A Day of Reckoning
is for Steven A. McKay.
Great author and partner in podcasting.

A DAY OF RECKONING

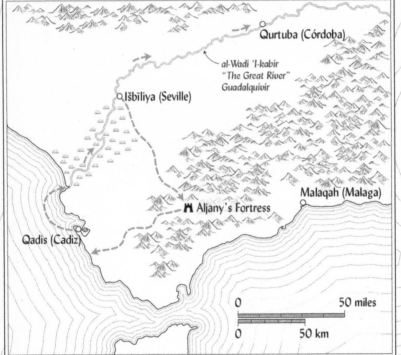

Qurtuba (Córdoba)

al-Wadi 'l-kabír
"The Great River"
Guadalquivír

Išbíliya (Seville)

Malaqah (Malaga)

Ⱶ Aljany's Fortress

Qadis (Cadiz)

0   50 miles

0   50 km

N

Bay of

ATLANTIC OCEAN

A L - A N D

Toledo

Qadis (Cadiz)

Ⱶ Aljany's
Fortress

Legend

○   Settlements

Ⱶ   Fortresses

✝   Holy sites

– – –   Hunlaf's route

·········   Hunlaf's previous route

0   400 miles

0   400 km

For the Lord thy God is a consuming fire, even a jealous God.

Deuteronomy 4, verse 24

For, behold, the Lord will come with fire, and with his chariots like a whirlwind, to render his anger with fury, and his rebuke with flames of fire.

Isaiah 66, verse 15

Place Names

Early medieval place names vary according to time, language, dialect and the scribe who was writing. I have not followed a strict convention when choosing the spelling to use for a given place. In most cases, I have chosen the name I believe to be the closest to that used in the late eighth century, but like the scribes of all those centuries ago, I have taken artistic licence at times, and, when unsure, merely selected the one I liked most.

Some of the place names also occur in my Bernicia Chronicles novels with different spellings. This is intentional to denote that this is not part of that series and also to indicate the passage of time and the changes to language that occur over the centuries.

Æbbercurnig	Abercorn, Scotland
al-Andalus	The Muslim-ruled area of the Iberian Peninsula
al-Wadi 'l-kabir	"The Great River". Guadalquivir River
ar-Raqqah	Raqqa, Syria
Balansiya	Valencia, Spain
Banbalūnah	Pamplona, Spain
Bebbanburg	Bamburgh
Byzantion	Constantinople (Istanbul)
Danapr	The Dnieper
Dark Sea	Black Sea

Eoforwic	York
Ġarundaḧ	Girona, Spain
Hálogaland	Hålogaland, Norway
Họrðaland	Hordaland, Norway
Ifriqiya	Area comprising what is today Tunisia, western Libya and eastern Algeria
Išbīliya	Seville, Spain
Lindisfarnae	Lindisfarne
Madīnat as-Salām	The City of Peace, Baghdad, Iraq
Malaqah	Malaga, Spain
Oguz il	"Oguz Land". Turkic state located in an area between the coasts of the Caspian and Aral Seas
Orkneyjar	Orkney Islands
Papia	Pavia, Italy
Qadis	Cadiz, Spain
Quentovic	Frankish trading settlement. The town no longer exists, but is thought to have been situated near the mouth of the Canche River
Qurtuba	Córdoba, Spain
Roma	Rome
Roman Sea	Old Arabic term for the Mediterranean Sea
Rygjafylki	Rogaland, Norway
Septimania	Visigothic kingdom in modern-day southern France that roughly corresponds to the former administrative region of Languedoc-Roussillon (now part of Occitanie)
Ubbanford	Norham
Uuir, River	River Wear
Uuiremutha	Monkwearmouth
Werceworthe	Warkworth
Yafah	Jaffa, Israel

One

I feel stronger today than I have for months. I am yet old and frail, and I can still feel the scratching at my guts from whatever ailment torments my earthly body, but it has only been a day since I completed the second annal of my life's story and I sit once more, encaustum mixed, a fresh sheet of vellum before me and a newly cut quill in my gnarled hand, ready to continue the tale of my life and of those who travelled alongside me across the known world so many years ago.

Nobody can understand the ways of the Lord. In His infinite wisdom He chose this morning to end a life, taking a soul into heaven. I know I should mourn the loss, but I cannot find it within me to weep. With this particular death I can continue my work without resistance. It would be wrong of me to say that I am gleeful that a man has died, but it would be a lie if I were to say I am truly sorry. I have committed enough sins in my long life without adding to them by telling untruths of the dead.

I am certain now that God has given me this reprieve so that I may complete my writings. And I dare not tarry. There are many more stories to tell. Other adventures and escapades with which my life has been cursed. Or perhaps it would be better to say I have been blessed by them, for I have seen so much that my mind is like a dusty library, row upon row of places, people and events I have witnessed. I would tell of Roma, Oguz il, Ifriqiya, the Holy Land, and of how I travelled the length of the wide Danapr and crossed the Dark Sea to the greatest city on earth, Byzantion.

I am eager to write of all these things and more, but when I set aside my quill yesterday, I was exhausted, my soul weary and filled with sorrow after recounting the events in Hǫrðaland and Rygjafylki. To write of those events was to tread the dark pathways of memories I had wished never to revisit. And yet walk them I did, seeing again the faces of those whom I had slain and those who had died at the hands of the madman we found there far in the north where the summer sun barely sets. I knew not whether I would have the strength to scribe more of my story, and, even if I was able, I worried that Abbot Criba, who despised me, would discover what I had been about all these months and forbid me to continue. Worse, I could well imagine that when he found that he had been openly disobeyed; that I was not working on a copy of the *Vita Sancti Wilfrithi*, he would fly into a rage and destroy my work. At first he might baulk at the cost of losing the expensive parchment, but there was too much of my life's story already written to be erased by knife or pumice stone, so I was sure that in the end Criba would resort to throwing my work onto a fire. In his rage he would create a pyre of my memories.

That thought haunted me, like the voices of those whose lives I have taken, whispering to me in the darkness of my cell. Then, yesterday, no sooner had I set aside my pen, Criba sent word that Coenric and I were to visit him in his chamber immediately after Vespers. He had not come to my room or spoken with me for many weeks and I could think of no reason for his summons except that he had surely found out about my work and now sought to berate me for my disobedience.

I had imagined his pinched, sneering face as he ordered the destruction of the writing I had laboured over this past year. I prayed that I might be able to convince him otherwise.

I also prayed for the strength to accept the abbot's command, whatever that might be. Though my body is weak, in many ways I am still the warrior who struck Ljósberari's head from his shoulders. That same pride and rage still resides within my now fragile frame. I am a God-fearing man and I have eschewed violence for many years, but I feared that if the abbot should threaten to undo my work, I might not be able to stay my hand.

And so it was that as the familiar words of the Vespers prayers washed over me, I asked the Lord silently for guidance, that He might grant me wisdom in the meeting with the abbot. I had been too infirm to attend services with the brothers for several weeks, but I made the effort yesterday evening. When I looked up at the abbot as he led us through the office, his eyes met mine. I was taken aback. There was real hatred there. I knew Criba loathed me and disapproved of my past, and there was a malevolent triumph in his glare that spoke louder than any words he had ever uttered. If I had been in any doubt of Criba's intentions, the glowering disdain in his gaze told me I was right to fear the abbot's wrath.

"I will see both of you in my chamber immediately," he hissed the moment that Vespers was over.

I made a show of tottering slowly.

"We will be there as quickly as my old legs allow, father," I said, leaning on Coenric for support, even though these last few weeks I had regained some strength and was able to walk short distances unaided. My deception and this small victory pleased me. I kept my expression meek.

Criba's face flushed and he hesitated, perhaps wondering if he should walk with us. "Do not keep me waiting," he snapped, sweeping away, cheeks dark with emotion.

"Does he know?" whispered Coenric.

"I can think of no other explanation," I replied, scanning the faces of the gathered monks. Most nodded in welcome, but a few – those ambitious men who were closest to Criba – looked away too quickly. Perhaps they knew what awaited us.

"Come," I said, giving Coenric's shoulder a squeeze. "No evil has ever been lessened by waiting. Let us get this over with."

There was no answer to our knock at Criba's chamber. The flicker of expensive beeswax candles and the ruddy light of a fire shone from beneath the door. Outside, the wind gusted and a driving rain began to fall. I shivered. Winter is coming, and no matter how defiant I am, I am still an old man and I craved the warmth I knew awaited us inside Criba's room. I was seldom permitted more than a small fire of twigs, but I knew Criba liked to keep his own hearth stoked. At the very least I could warm my bones beside his blazing fire, while he chastised me. I knocked again.

Silence.

I pulled the door open.

There, on the small rug that had been a gift from the mynsterfæder of Æbbercurnig, lay Criba. I knew at once he was quite dead. His limbs were tangled, his legs buckled awkwardly beneath him, like a dropped puppet. He must have died instantly. His eyes stared at us unblinking, the light from the fire and the candles dancing in the quickly drying orbs.

Beside me Coenric gasped.

The warmth of the room rolled through the doorway and enveloped us. For an instant I was tempted to push Coenric into the chamber so that we could enjoy the fire for a while. But then I realised how that would look and how, as all of the brothers knew there was no love lost between the abbot and I, they might jump to the conclusion that I had helped him on his way to our heavenly Father's side. My past was no secret.

They all knew I was capable of murder. I had killed dozens of men in my youth.

Leofstan always said that God works in mysterious ways. I understood in that moment, standing there and looking down at Criba's corpse, that God must want me to complete my writing. A feeling of elation washed through me, but I did not smile. To grin would be unwise and whatever God's plan was, I doubted He wished for me to revel in the death of the abbot.

"He's... he's..." stammered Coenric. Looking at the boy, I saw his face was the colour of whey. He was shaking terribly. His eyes were wide and glimmering with unshed tears. The sight of death did not shock me. It is easy to forget that the life I have led is unusual. Of course, my life is all I have known, but Coenric was not much more than a child, and he had lived a sheltered existence since he came here to the minster. There have been no Norse raids in his short life, and the only exposure to battles and blood were in the scratched accounts of my adventures.

He looked like he might puke, so I pulled him round to look at me.

"Go and fetch Brother Godstan," I said, speaking firmly. Godstan was one of the older monks and would be a safe pair of hands to deal with this situation. He was not ambitious and grasping like some of the others and had never fawned over Criba, seeking his approval and hoping for advancement. Everybody respected Godstan and they would listen to his words once tidings of the abbot's death got out.

Coenric stared at me as if he no longer understood Englisc. I shook his shoulders.

"Do you hear me?"

He started to look back at Criba's ungainly, unmoving form.

"Look at me, not him," I snapped, some of my youthful vigour returning in that moment of crisis. His eyes flicked back to mine. "Go for Brother Godstan. Tell nobody what has happened here. Not even Godstan, just tell him he is to come at once. Do you understand?"

He nodded uncertainly.

"Good. Now go."

I shoved him out of the chamber and pulled the door shut behind him. There were several fresh logs on the fire that blazed in the hearth. I wondered whether Criba had placed them there just before dying. His position implied that he might have been turning away from the fire when he fell. I stepped closer to his crumpled shape, searching for signs of violence. There was no blood that I could see. My nose wrinkled as I smelt the distinctive scent of death. Criba's bowels had voided and the pungent stench of shit pervaded the warm air of the room. I did not expect to find any signs of a struggle. Criba had only been out of my sight for a short time as we made our way to his chamber. It seemed to me most likely that he had merely dropped dead. His face had been dark and choleric after Vespers and I felt a small, unchristian thrill that his anger at me might have been the cause of his death.

I was sitting on a stool before the fire when I heard footsteps outside. The door was pulled open and Coenric, still pale, ushered in Godstan. He was a solid man, short in stature but with broad shoulders and strong, farmer's hands. I had always liked him. He acknowledged me with a nod.

"Don't just stand there, boy," he said. "You're letting all the warmth out, and it wouldn't do to let any of the other brothers see Abbot Criba like this."

Coenric swallowed, stepped into the room and pulled the door closed. He pressed his back to the timber, so as to be as far from the corpse as possible. He must have told Godstan about Criba, for the old monk did not seem perturbed by what he found in the chamber.

He made the sign of the rood over his chest and knelt down

beside the abbot's cooling body. He grimaced as his knees popped.

"You found him like this?"

"We haven't touched him," I said.

Reaching out, he closed the abbot's eyes. I half-expected them to snap open again. I have seen such before and it is unnerving to behold, and what with Criba being such a cantankerous old goat, I would have thought it the kind of thing he would do. However, his eyes remained mercifully shut. Coenric relaxed almost imperceptibly. He was muttering the Pater Noster under his breath, but it seemed to me that some of his colour had returned to his cheeks.

"It would appear that the Lord has called our spiritual father to his bosom. There is no sign of what has caused his demise, but when the Almighty summons the faithful to His side in heaven, there is nothing to be done. I have seen this before. A man's body just gives up, and his soul departs."

"That's what it looked like to me," I said. I didn't add that I had seen more than my share of violent deaths to recognise when someone has been killed by blade or arrow.

Godstan arranged the abbot with his hands over his chest as if in prayer. With difficulty, he straightened Criba's legs, tugging and pulling until they came free from beneath the dead man's bulk. The abbot's hands flopped to the rug either side of his still form. Sighing, Godstan replaced them on Criba's chest, taking the time to interlace the fingers so that they would not again become dislodged. With a groan, he pushed himself to his feet.

"I must tell the rest of the brethren the sad news of our father's passing. I think you have done enough, Hunlaf. You should go back to your quarters to rest. You too, Coenric. You look as though you might swoon at any moment."

"Thank you," I said, thinking again of Leofstan and how

God works in the strangest ways. "Who do you think will become the abbot now?"

Godstan scratched behind his right ear.

"It is hard to say," he said. "You know as well as I that there are several possible candidates. Men who show goodness of life and wisdom in teaching. But the process of choosing our next father will take time. The brethren will decide, but first we must send word to the bishop. And we must mourn and pray for Abbot Criba. It could be several weeks until the new abbot is appointed."

"Of course," I said, keeping my face sombre despite the joy I felt at his words. I rose with difficulty, needing to reach for Coenric for support. The boy stepped into the room, closer than he would have wished to the corpse of the man who had ruled the minster ever since he became a novice.

As we opened the door, Godstan spoke, making us halt.

"I know you have been working on a copy of the *Life of Saint Wilfrid*," he said.

I looked at him sharply. I could not be certain, but it seemed to me that there was a twinkle in his eye. I said nothing.

"What better way of honouring our late father," he went on, "than continuing with the work he commissioned you to perform? If I were you, I would apply myself with all diligence to the task. Perhaps you will be able to complete it before the new abbot is installed."

And so here I am, the day after Abbot Criba's death, taking up quill and ink once more. The rain has blown over in the night, leaving the land bright and clean. Through the open window I can hear the sound of the brethren singing praises for Criba's soul. I feel the slightest pang of shame that I am not with them, performing my Christian duty. But then I think of the bitter tyrant of a man who lies in state in the chapel and decide there are more than enough voices raised in prayer and song for the abbot. I have more pressing matters to attend and it is surely God's will that I should continue to commit my story to vellum that it might be read by those who come after me.

In the night, while the brethren wept and wailed for the abbot, I pondered the point from which I should pick up my story. The wind buffeted the minster and the draughts that blew under my door and through the shutters carried the chill of death. I shivered beneath my thin blanket, knowing that I will follow Criba all too soon. There are so many adventures yet for me to recount, but the abbot's passing has further reminded me of the fleeting nature of our time on this earth.

If I am only given enough days to finish one more tale I feel it should be that of *The Treasure of Life*. The book had entered my life the day before the Norsemen first descended on Lindisfarnae like wolves on defenceless lambs. The teachings in the book had driven Scomric beyond all reason, turning him into the murderous Ljósberari.

It could also be said that the book was the cause of Leofstan's death. My own obsession with the tome would lead to the spilling of much more blood. I will pay for the lives I have taken when I face the Lord at the Day of Judgement. But for now, God in His wisdom has granted me the time to complete the story of *The Treasure of Life*, and so I once again gird myself against the pain of peering back into the past, where that accursed tome held sway over me, calling me southward as if with a siren's song.

Since first seeing the book, its presence loomed in my mind like a shadow. That shadow had also been cast over those who travelled with me, their lives becoming as inextricably entwined with mine as the weft and the warp of a cloak. Their faces rise up out of memory now. Lithe Gwawrddur, moving with the grace of a cat. Drosten, his dour face lined with blue swirling Pictish paintings. Hereward, who was quick to jest, but deadly and dependable in battle. Runolf Ragnarsson, the enigmatic Norse giant who had blessed me with his friendship. And Ahmad, the dark-skinned thrall, whose knowledge and learning had shown me the way to the book.

All of these, and many more, journeyed with me in search of *The Treasure of Life*. And yet there was one other, without whom we would not have experienced our adventures or seen the shores of distant lands. Runolf knew this traveller better than any other, for it had been fashioned by his hand and it responded to his touch like a lover.

Brymsteda. Sea steed. It was the sleekest and fastest ship any of us had ever seen, and it bore us over far-flung oceans as easily as a young stallion carries a child over rolling grassland.

I have decided where I should return to my tale. It is aboard *Brymsteda*, as we skimmed the surf of dark seas off the coast of Hispania. The sail of a ship had risen out of the morning fret, and the Imazighen corsairs who manned it had not yet understood that *Brymsteda* was no fat merchant vessel to be plundered by pirate dogs.

Two

The ship emerged rapidly, sliding out of the sea mist that had cloaked the world during the night. With the rising of the sun, a breeze had picked up and it was this wind that had begun to shred the mist, exposing the approaching vessel.

Runolf cursed. No ship would normally get so close without being seen, but this was no normal morning. At dusk, Runolf had intended to find a secluded cove where we would camp for the night, but the mist had shrouded the sea with such speed that it had made it impossible for us to sail close to the land for fear of tearing *Brymsteda*'s hull on the rocks that dotted the coast.

At the sudden apparition of the ship, Runolf began barking orders and the crews of each of *Brymsteda*'s sections roused themselves and quickly began to follow the commands of their crew leader.

Most of us first joined Alf's Midship crew, heaving on the halliard to pull aloft the heavy sail. The great expanse of wool began to catch the slight breath of wind that came with the dawn.

Scurfa, in charge of the Aft crew to which I belonged, was quickly on his feet and tugging at the sheets.

"Adjust the braces there," he said to me. I did not need to

be told twice. There had been a time when I was unsure of what I needed to do when at sea, but that had been two years earlier. Now it was second nature to me and I set to the task of shortening the port-side brace, knowing what was required from a quick glance at the rigging and listening to Runolf's shouted orders. All along *Brymsteda*'s sleek length, the other crews were hurrying to do what was needed.

I finished securing the brace and looked eastward. The sun was bright through the haze, causing the approaching ship's shadow to float like an ominous spirit in the mist. The sounds of shouts in a strange tongue echoed over the waves and I could just make out the shapes of sailors on the other vessel, rushing and bustling about like ants whose nest has been kicked. It seemed they had been as surprised by us as we had by them.

I shivered, my breath steaming in the air before me, and as ever I marvelled at how cold it could get at sea when on the lands we were passing I knew it would soon be as sweltering as the hottest of summer days in Northumbria.

"By Þórr's hammer," shouted Runolf from the steerboard, "untangle that rigging."

I followed his gaze and saw that the Drag crew were in trouble. A couple of lines had become snagged as the sail was adjusted to catch the wind. Pendrad and Oslaf, warriors both, but now, like me, competent sailors, were struggling to free one of the ropes, while Revna, Runolf's daughter, was working at the other. Her golden hair fell about her face and she didn't so much as look up at me when I hurried to help her.

"Hold that," she snapped, thrusting a damp rope into my hand.

I did as she asked and watched as her deft fingers worked at the tangle of hemp ropes. Some of the sailors had protested when Revna had joined the crew. A ship was no place for a young woman, they said. Runolf had been adamant. He would not countenance leaving his daughter behind. "I have trained her in the ways of battle and sailing," he'd said, "and she is a match for most men at both."

Watching her expertly working the lines, there was no doubt she could handle herself at sea. Her white teeth bit into her lower lip as was her way when concentrating. My closeness to her almost drove me to distraction and I cursed myself for a fool. She was a beauty, of that there was no question, and all of the men aboard looked on her fondly, but everyone knew not to seek anything but friendship with her. Runolf was not a forgiving man and I recalled what he had done to Chlotar, the Frank who had sullied Revna in Ljósberari's domain.

I had been careful to hide my desire for Revna, and she had never given me any indication that she felt anything toward me. There were many available women in the world, and since we had returned from Rygjafylki, I had wasted no opportunity to seek out their company, but still I secretly yearned for Revna.

"Give me that," she said, interrupting my thoughts. When I didn't respond immediately, she growled in a way that reminded me of her father and snapped her fingers. I gave her the rope. In moments, the rigging was fixed and the sail bellied out with the freshening breeze.

Revna waved to her father and turned away from me without a word of thanks.

I made my way back to the Aft section, where I was greeted by Gersine with a grin. He was the only person I had confided in about my feelings for Revna. I wished I had never made the mistake of telling him. He had seen the interaction between us and shook his head.

"We should have left you in Uuiremutha," I said. He chuckled. The truth was that I was glad of his company. We were close in age and where he had once idolised me, he had faced his own share of hardships now and looked on me as an equal.

"I miss my mother, and even my father," he said with a

lopsided smile, "but I do not rightly know how we can ever return to Uuiremutha."

I sniffed. There was nothing much to say. He was right, of course. His father, Lord Mancas, might forgive his son, but he would hardly be likely to forgive me, or the rest of the crew.

"Shall we arm ourselves?" I called out towards the stern of the ship, where Runolf leant on the tiller.

"No need," Runolf shouted back, his gold-flecked red hair and beard swirling about his face in the rising wind. "*Brymsteda* will outrun those whoresons. See how they hurry to set their sail. But that ship wallows like a pregnant mule. They'll never catch us."

I was surprised he had not altered our course to intercept the ship. Runolf never shied from a fight and we had some thirty men aboard. All were able to swing a blade, and together we had fought many a sea battle in the last two years. While Wihtgar and the shipwrights of Northumbria had set about building more vessels like *Brymsteda*, we had been tasked with patrolling the waters of the North Sea whale road. Sometimes we would chase away solitary ships that tempted their luck in defiance of the trade agreements in place between Rygjafylki and our kingdom. At other times, we would confront ships from the lands of the Picts, when they made the mistake of thinking it would be easier to attack the shores of Northumbria from the sea than to carry out their cattle raids on foot. We taught them the error of their ways with tenacity, sea-skill and cold steel.

This small ship coming out of the mist with the rising sun at its back did not look to be a match for us and I wondered at Runolf's decision as the wind filled our sail and the deck canted beneath my feet. Then I saw the small man at Runolf's side and I understood. Giso wore simple robes, similar to those of a monk or a priest, yet he was neither. The dark-haired man saw me looking in his direction and inclined his head in recognition. Giso was an emissary from the court of the Frankish king, Carolus. What his business was in al-Andalus was a mystery to us, but I presumed he would rather arrive at his destination without a pitched battle with an uncertain outcome.

I looked back at the approaching ship. Several of the men aboard had manned oars and they were beginning to pull in quick strokes, adding their strength to the power of the wind in the sail. But the ship was still moving languidly, and cresting a rolling wave I could see that Runolf was right. We were already pulling away, and even without unshipping our own long oars, it would not be long until we had left the other ship far behind.

I felt a slight disappointment. It had been weeks since last I had tested my skill with a sword. I had grown to love the sensation of abandon I felt in battle. Sometimes, in dark moments when sleep would not claim me and I lay awake, my head filled with too many thoughts, I wondered if Leofstan would recognise the man I had become since his death. I craved the surge of power that came with violence and killing. I neglected my prayers and no longer observed the offices, or attended mass. I could barely recall the last time I had confessed my sins. By then, I felt that my offences were too many to speak of. I was often drunk. I bedded any woman who showed an interest in me, and I took pleasure in beating men who confronted me, and revelled in killing my enemies.

But despite indulging all of these base desires, I was no fool. We were finally, after nearly two years, sailing south in search of the book that had caused me so much misery, and I recognised that there was no reason to jeopardise the chance that I might be able to lay my hands on that tome and to study the teachings within it, even if they were heretical. Leofstan had once told me it was only a book, that the words within it could hold no magic. I was sure he was right, but I hoped that by reading and understanding what lay within the pages of *The Treasure of Life*, I could comprehend what madness had gripped Scomric. Perhaps understanding what had happened to the monk, might help me to forgive his actions, and maybe, if I could do that, I would be able to put the horrors of the past behind me.

"You should pray with me for fair seas and good winds."

Startled at the voice close to my ear, I turned to see Giso. The small man had an unpleasant tendency of creeping up on me.

"I do not wish to pray," I said.

A gust of wind further tattered the thinning mist. The sail billowed, causing the rigging and the mast to creak. *Brymsteda*'s speed increased and I grasped a stay to steady myself.

"It seems the Lord does not require our prayers," Giso said, smiling. He knew of my past in the brethren of Werceworthe, and his constant requests to pray needled me. I was a monk no longer and this pious Frankish messenger seemed to do nothing but ask to pray and worship the Lord with me. He glanced at the pirate ship, that was already more than a spear's throw distant. "We will leave these corsairs behind and be on our way without any costly bloodshed."

I grunted, not wanting to give him the satisfaction of agreeing with him. Whatever secret mission Giso was on, his master had also expressed an interest in the book that I sought. Our shared goal would gain nothing from a skirmish with pirates.

I turned away from him and thought back to when I had first met Giso, and how we both came to be here in these southern waters.

Three

We had first encountered Giso a fortnight before, at Aachen in the court of the great King Carolus of the Franks. It was not the first time we had visited the Frankish lands. *Brymsteda* was King Æthelred's prize ship and he liked to show it off, so on more than one occasion we had carried messages, dignitaries and even some trade goods, between the courts of Northumbria and Frankia. But we had never before been invited into the palace halls of Aachen. This time we had been given the task of carrying gifts and missives to Carolus and also to Alhwin, the Englisc scholar, holy man and counsellor of the monarch. It was Alhwin who had wished to see us.

Æthelred's orders had come to us from Lord Mancas. After we had delivered the messages, we were to await responses. We had been content to do so in the barracks at Aachen.

The Frankish guards were hospitable enough. It had been raining constantly, and we sat huddled around braziers of burning wood, playing dice and knuckle bones. Better to be inside in the warm than at sea in such weather. The Frankish wine was good, and there were several women in the environs of the palace who would share a man's blankets in exchange for one of the king of the Franks' newly minted silver *denarius* coins, and in many cases for much less than that.

We were in the barracks when the elderly servant came for us. The servant was grey-haired and scowling, his lips pursed as if he had a bitter taste in his mouth. Perhaps he believed the task of requesting our company for his master was beneath him. He found us placing bets on a game of knuckle bones between Gwawrddur and a huge Frank, whose meaty hands were surprisingly fast and nimble.

All of us who sailed with Gwawrddur had expected the Welshman to win easily, but now it had come down to the deciding toss of the bones, and a crowd had formed around the two men. There was a lot of silver riding on the throw, and a hush fell over us in anticipation.

The burly Frank went first, dropping only one of the small pig bones. Nobody made a sound as Gwawrddur prepared himself. With lightning speed, he threw the bones at the exact moment that the servant cleared his throat and spoke in a loud voice as if announcing an arrival in a lord's hall.

"You are summoned to an audience with the Most Reverend Alhwin."

Gwawrddur, distracted by the sudden voice, fumbled and missed two of the bones. The Franks cheered, clapping their man on the back. *Brymsteda*'s crew groaned and turned angrily to the servant whose interruption had caused our man to lose, costing us dearly.

The servant made no show of remorse, or even that he understood what had happened.

"If you would follow me," he said.

"Did you say, Alhwin?" I asked.

"Yes." He looked me up and down. "Hunlaf?" I nodded. "I have orders to bring you to my master, along with the Norseman, Runolf, the Welshman, Gwawrddur, the Pict, Drosten, Hereward, the Northumbrian, and Ahmad, the Moor."

I was astounded that Alhwin knew of us by name. He was almost legendary. The library he had helped to create in Eoforwic was said to be the most extensive collection of books in Christendom, and there was talk of him creating a library to rival it in Frankia. I had wished to meet him, or at least to be allowed to study his books, on the previous occasions when we had visited Aachen, but my requests had always met with a firm refusal. I wondered if this was how he had heard of me, but the fact that he asked for several of us by name made me wonder. That he included Ahmad, Mancas' thrall, made me suspect the summons had something to do with our adventures in the lands of the Norse and my search for *The Treasure of Life*, though how he would have come by such knowledge was beyond me.

I was confused, but excited as we followed the sombre servant through the courtyards and gardens of the palace. The others were angry, grumbling at their losses and unimpressed by my open-eyed excitement at the prospect of meeting the famed scholar and perhaps getting a chance to see his vast collection of writings. The servant walked quickly through the drizzle, over rain-slick cobbles, past the shadowed shapes of hedges and shrubs and the patrician gaze of several sculptures whose drenched faces appeared to be crying as they looked down on us. There was a feeling of great wealth in the halls of Aachen, but more than that there was a sensation of power. Carolus had no need to demonstrate his influence with gaudy displays; he had conquered the lands of the Saxons and Langobards, putting all who opposed him to the sword. His authority was not in question.

The rain soaked my cloak and kirtle. I shivered, thinking of the power that resided in the inhabitants of these buildings and the men who walked these gardens. The men we had been playing games of chance with served King Carolus. He owned everything I could see and his dominions stretched over much of the world. He was renowned for his Christian piety, his ambition and military prowess, and his ruthlessness.

And Alhwin was his most trusted counsellor.

My companions' mood had not improved as we walked through the rain, but perhaps they too wondered at the summons by one of the most influential men in the world, for when the servant ushered us into the cavernous hall deep within the palace complex, Runolf nudged me.

"Trouble?" he asked. He whispered, but his rumbling voice carried into the shadowed recesses of the hall.

"No trouble at all," replied a voice from the far end of the building. There were windows at intervals along the walls, but the day was dark and little light permeated the space. I peered into the gloom, but could only make out a shadowy form sitting at a writing desk. The man stood and beckoned for us to approach.

"You can leave your wet cloaks with Heribert," he said. "Come. I have a fine wine from Papia and the fire is warm."

Beside me, the servant removed his own cloak and shook out the rain with a snapping of cloth. The loud sound echoed in the hall and made me tense. I saw Drosten's hand fall to his belt for the knife he usually wore. But there was no blade there. We had been made to leave all of our weapons in a chest at the barracks.

Unclasping my own soaked cloak, I sniffed the air and looked about me. My eyes were growing more accustomed to the darkness now. A few candles glowed along the length of the columned building, illuminating row upon row of books of all sizes. I sighed with pleasure. I had embraced the life of a warrior with gusto, but my love of books had not abated. I knew where I was standing. I recognised the dusty scent of the vellum, the acrid bite of the encaustum, the tang of the leather bindings and the wax from the polished desks and tables. This was more akin to a scriptorium than a palace hall.

Handing my cloak to the sour-faced servant, I walked slowly down the room, my hands reaching out to stroke the decorated bindings of some of the tomes. Looking down at the pages of a massive book, I saw exquisite penmanship and an ornate image of an open-winged eagle picked out in vermillion and gleaming gold leaf. I longed to halt, to read the text and to peruse the other books that were strewn about the place. Who knew what treasures lay within this astounding collection of learning?

"You must be Hunlaf," said the man at the end of the hall.

"And you are Alhwin, I presume."

"Ah, you are all here," the man said, nodding. "Long have I wanted to meet the men who defended Werceworthe. You are all welcome to my humble hall."

Hereward strode past me.

"You spoke of wine?"

Alhwin chuckled.

"Indeed, indeed. Come, sit. Are you hungry?"

He poured wine from a silver pitcher into delicate glasses.

Hereward took a proffered glass goblet, a thing of exquisite beauty. "You have a response for us to take back to Northumbria?" he said, examining the fine workmanship of the glass before sipping the liquid.

"Not so hasty, my good man," replied Alhwin. "We will come to my response, but I would talk a while with you first. Now, let me see you all."

Gwawrddur, Drosten and Runolf joined Hereward and me in the pool of light from the candles on the desk. A bronze brazier, filled with coruscating embers, glowed nearby, giving off a pleasant heat after the blustery weather outside.

Ahmad, standing proudly tall, hung back.

"You too, young Ahmad," Alhwin said, signalling for the black-bearded man to approach. When Ahmad hesitated, Alhwin said in the man's own tongue, "Peace be upon you. You are welcome. I mean you no ill. I have need of your knowledge."

I marvelled at the old monk's grasp of al-Arabiyyah, the tongue of Ahmad's people. Ahmad had been teaching me, and despite my natural ability with languages, I still faltered over the more complex sounds and some of the nuances of word construction.

Ahmad stepped forward.

"Ah, the heroes of Werceworthe," said Alhwin, offering glasses of wine to everyone.

"I was not at Werceworthe," said Ahmad, declining the glass with a frown.

"No, no. Of course. And there were other heroes who fell. But perhaps you are yet to be the hero God intended you to be, eh? And without you, would not the quest for *The Treasure of Life* have ended in Hǫrðaland?"

I spluttered, choking on my wine.

"You wonder how it is I know so much of your past," Alhwin said, fixing me with a gleaming stare. "It always amazes me what one can learn by reading and listening."

My mind reeled. Few lived who knew of the book's existence and even fewer what had transpired in Hǫrðaland. The number of people who knew of Ahmad's role in all of it was tiny indeed, and I could not begin to fathom how Alhwin had heard tell of any of those things.

I had underestimated Ahmad for a long time. He was a thrall, and I had mistakenly believed him to be little more than a beast of burden. But then he had translated the swirling script on the scrap of paper I'd snatched from the flames of Ljósberari's hall. Ahmad spoke of a world of riches and learning far to the south; the kingdom of al-Andalus, where he had once been a wealthy noble. He could read and write and was clearly a man of some consequence. Ahmad had offered to help me find *The Treasure of Life* and had demanded only one thing in return: his freedom.

The problem was that his freedom was not mine to give. He was owned by Lord Mancas, who was never one to part with his property lightly.

"How can you know these things?" I asked Alhwin, sipping the wine. It was rich and warming.

"I know much," said Alhwin airily. He waved a hand to encompass the parchments scattered over his desk and the tables around the hall. "I receive letters from all over the world. Tales of your escapades have reached me from many different observers."

"But who told you about the book, and Ahmad?"

"What hand penned such information is unimportant. We have much to talk about and time is the one commodity that even King Carolus' riches cannot buy. The only important question now is: do you still seek *The Treasure of Life?*"

My stomach tightened. When we had returned to Northumbria with Aelfwyn and, thanks to Ahmad, the new-found knowledge of the book's whereabouts, I had been filled with a zealous fire. My plan had been to request Ahmad's freedom, then we would take *Brymsteda* and sail south immediately. However, Mancas had refused to release the thrall from his service, and, even though Runolf, Hereward and the other warriors from Bebbanburg had been freed from their oaths to Lord Uhtric upon his death, it was King Æthelred's silver that had paid for *Brymsteda*'s construction, and if we wished to sail in the ship Runolf had built, we needed to patrol the shores of Northumbria and carry out whatever tasks Æthelred commanded.

As time passed, the fire that had burnt within me to search for *The Treasure of Life* had dimmed, dampened down further with each voyage, every battle at sea, and each debauched night. Now, as if a bellows had pumped air onto an ember, the flames burst into life once more.

"I do," I said simply. "But it is not so easy."

Alhwin smiled and refilled our glasses.

"Nothing worthwhile is easy, young Hunlaf. There are obstacles in every path." He smiled and the wrinkles of his face deepened, showing me that he was a man who grinned frequently. "But few impediments are insurmountable."

I was about to answer, but he turned his piercing eyes on Ahmad.

"You know where the book is?" Alhwin spoke in Englisc now, but I knew Ahmad understood him well enough.

"I know the man who bought the book from the Norsemen," Ahmad replied in his strongly accented voice.

"Abu Jafar Yusuf ibn Sa'īd al-Zarqālluh?"

Ahmad nodded.

"How many years since you last saw Al-Zarqālluh?"

"Close to ten years." Ahmad did not hesitate.

"He was your tutor?"

"He was. I studied philosophy, law, theology and alchemy in his madrasa."

Alhwin nodded as if Ahmad's words confirmed what he already knew.

"As a former student," said a voice from the shadows, "Al-Zarqālluh will give you access to his madrasa again?" The new voice startled me. It spoke Englisc with a soft, musical accent I could not place.

Apart from Heribert the servant and Alhwin, I had believed there had been nobody else in the hall when we arrived. Gwawrddur, Drosten and Hereward all tensed, as a figure stepped from the gloom into the candlelight. Ahmad was the only one amongst us who did not appear surprised by the man's sudden appearance. The Moor raised his chin and looked down his long nose at the newcomer.

"I do not see why he would not," Ahmad said. "I imagine he would be interested to hear of what I have witnessed on my long, Allah-forsaken travels."

"This is Giso," Alhwin said. "If all transpires as I think it will, Giso will be travelling with you."

We all stared at the small man. I wondered who he was. He wore a nondescript robe and none of the trappings that would mark him out as a man of noble birth. No gold glimmered on his fingers or at his neck. But he met our gaze with assurance, and the way he had been hidden within the room, utterly still and undetected until he chose to reveal himself, was unnerving.

"We are to take him back to Northumbria?" I said. "Giso is to carry your response to Æthelred King?"

Alhwin flashed his teeth at me in a wide grin. His smile made me almost as nervous as Giso's stealthy apparition.

"Giso will carry my response, but not to Northumbria."

"But we are to return northward."

"Is that so?" he asked, taking on the tone of a tutor speaking to a slow pupil. "What was it that you were commanded to do, Hunlaf?"

I thought back to the orders we had received from Lord Mancas. My eyes narrowed at the memory, again wondering at the depth of knowledge Alhwin possessed. Could he be so cunning?

"We were commanded to bring the message to you and then to wait for your response, that we might carry it aboard *Brymsteda*."

"Ah, yes, the fabled ship that Runolf constructed. I would like to see it before you leave." His smile broadened. "But I digress. You have fulfilled the first part of your king's orders. I have received his message and other letters from Northumbria.

And Giso here will bear my response. But my response is not for Æthelred or indeed anyone from my homeland. You must carry it southward. To al-Andalus."

"We cannot travel south," said Hereward, placing his empty goblet onto one of the tables.

"Why ever not?" asked Alhwin, allowing his smile to slip. "You are a free man, are you not? You are no longer oath-sworn?"

Hereward scowled.

"My lord Uhtric is dead, it is true. But Æthelred is still my king. I serve Northumbria."

Alhwin lowered himself into a chair that was dark and polished from the use of many years. Placing his hands together as if praying, he touched his fingertips to his lips, then said, "What if I told you that travelling south would not only serve my purposes and aid our young friend Hunlaf here in his search for the book that has so enraptured him, but would also bring you wealth?"

"I'm listening," Hereward said.

"Do you recall the last time you spoke to Lord Uhtric?"

Hereward bridled.

"Of course I remember. Though I do not like to be reminded."

Hereward's face clouded and I imagined he was recalling the sickly stink of Uhtric's wound; conjuring in his mind's eye the frail, dying man we had seen at Bebbanburg shortly before we learnt of his death.

"And what did Runolf promise him?" asked Alhwin, his voice again sounding like a teacher asking a boy to prove he had been paying attention.

"What seiðr is this?" said Runolf, his voice rumbling and menacing like an approaching storm. "How can you know what we spoke of at Bebbanburg?"

Alhwin held up his hands against Runolf's growing anger.

"There is no magic here." He offered Runolf his wide smile.

"Lord Uhtric and I were friends. He told me himself of your last meeting."

Runolf frowned.

"Lord Uhtric did not write," Hereward said, but I noted that his tone had grown weaker, as if he doubted his own words.

"No, he did not, but Hygebald, the good abbot of Lindisfarnae, does. Lord Uhtric dictated his letters to Hygebald, and he would read my replies back. It might surprise you to learn of all the friends I have across Christendom." He winked at Ahmad, who glowered in return. "And beyond."

Hereward was staring at the elderly scholar with an expression that said he wouldn't welcome more surprises.

"These past months," said Alhwin, sweeping both Runolf and Hereward with his gaze, "have you been able to fulfil the promises you made?"

"There has been little in the way of plunder," grumbled Runolf. "But I am no liar. I have set aside half of what treasure we have found."

"Aye, there is precious little," said Hereward, "but what there is will go to Uhtric's son, Uhtred, as was promised."

Alhwin leaned forward, resting his elbows on the desk.

"But wouldn't you rather have more to offer the son whose father you served?" he said. "What if I told you this journey to the land of the Moors would bring you great wealth? That you could keep whatever loot you might find and," he glanced in my direction, "I will pay you handsomely for the book too?"

"I would say I am more interested than I was a moment ago," said Hereward, "but you speak in riddles and offer us wealth we cannot see."

"I merely ask that you carry my messenger, in exchange for which I will pay you."

From beneath his desk Alhwin pulled a stout leather bag. Fleetingly I thought of the sack that had contained Ljósberari's head. This bag, while similar in size, seemed much heavier.

Alhwin dropped it onto his desk. It clinked, and he tugged open the drawstring, displaying the contents. The flickering light from the candles reflected from shiny silver coins.

"This silver is for Giso's passage south. When you bring him back to me, I will give you another bag just like this. And a third such bag if you return with the book, Hunlaf."

"I want to study it, not sell it," I said. The others looked at me aghast. None of us had ever seen this amount of silver in one place.

"And study it you shall," said Alhwin. "You can be my guest."

I stared about me, my eyes wide at the stacks of tomes in the dimly lit hall. My pulse quickened at the prospect of having access to them all.

"Here?"

Alhwin smiled.

"Not here," he said, his smile widening at my obvious disappointment. "These are but a few of the books I will have at Tours."

"Tours?"

"I am to be made the abbot there. I have already sent word to have the books from the library in Eoforwic sent there. There will be no finer scriptorium in all the world. We can talk all about Mani's writings, and you can read any of my other works, if that interests you." He smirked at me, judging that he had baited the trap well.

I took a large mouthful of the wine, not wishing to give away my emotions by speaking. I wondered if the others saw my hand shaking.

"And when you return, Runolf and Hereward, you can head back to Northumbria to give half of the proceeds to Uhtric's son. But I see from your expression you are still not convinced." Alhwin sighed. "Perhaps you think Æthelred will not forgive your absence. I would not worry too much about upsetting the king."

Something in his tone snagged my attention away from the thoughts of the books that lined the hall and the silver that gleamed in the bag.

"What do you mean?" I asked.

Alhwin shrugged.

"I cannot know for certain what will occur, but the messages I have received tell me that the ealdormen and thegns of Northumbria are..." He paused, as if thinking of the best words to use. "Not best pleased with the king. Long has Æthelred courted danger with his actions. Many believe it was his lack of piety that saw God send the Norse devils to desecrate the minsters."

"Is that what you think?"

He held my stare for a few heartbeats and I saw that despite his smile, his eyes were cold.

"I think it is easy for men to say they are friends and Æthelred has surrounded himself with men who profess their friendship."

"You know something?" I asked. "Is there a plot against the king?"

"There are always plots," he said, sweeping his hand, as if clearing the air of cobwebs. "Who can say which will bear fruit and which will wither? But all I am saying is that I think the king of Northumbria will have his mind occupied elsewhere. I very much doubt that he will miss *Brymsteda* for a few weeks."

"This talk sounds too much like treason for my liking," said Hereward.

"No, no," said Alhwin. "Nothing like that. I am a true friend of Northumbria and I do not plot against the king."

Hereward stared at him for a long time. Giso reached out and poured himself a glass of wine. I started, again surprised by his movement. He had remained so still I had all but forgotten he was there.

"Even if we wished to do your bidding," said Hereward, glancing at Giso as if he too had just noticed him again, "the ship is not ours to take."

"I said nothing of stealing the ship. You will return, bringing Giso and, hopefully, the book Hunlaf seeks with you."

Gwawrddur, who had been silent until now, stepped closer and poured more wine into his glass.

"And if we do not return immediately, it will be said that we were lost at sea. We could sail away and nobody would ever know of *Brymsteda*'s wyrd."

Drosten, the tattoos on his face making him appear to glower, moved close to stand beside the Welshman.

"With this ship and this crew, you think we will be forgotten? That no tales will be told of our journeys? No songs sung of our exploits?" he said, his Pictish burr strong, but his words clear.

"Anything is possible," said Hereward, giving Runolf a sidelong glance. The two men knew each other well, and over the months they had come to a mutual understanding that allowed them to command the crew both on land and at sea. There was much meaning in the look they shared.

Runolf chuckled.

"If we have such fame that songs are sung of us," Runolf said, draining the contents of his glass, "then we will also have gold and riches and we will care nought for who comes asking for the ship. My hands built *Brymsteda*. I say the ship is mine, and I say we head south."

The memory of Alhwin's hall was shattered by voices raised in alarm. Turning, I saw that we had pulled further away from the pirate ship. The vessel was clear of the mist now, rising on a wave, its sail filled by the quickening wind. They were trying to give chase, but it was clear that they had no chance of catching

Brymsteda. The stallion prow that Drosten had carved lifted high as we crested the swell and the strakes trembled as the ship galloped away from our pursuers.

I scanned the deck and the rigging, trying to see what had caused the anxious shouting that had pulled me back to the present. A flicker in the sky told me what was happening at the same instant that Gwawrddur shouted.

"Arrows!" he yelled.

The pirates had positioned a few archers at the prow of their ship and they were loosing arrows at us in desperation. We were surely out of range of their short bows and they were shooting their arrows high into the bright morning sky, for them to arc down through the last gossamer wisps of mist to land harmlessly in the surf, where they floated like flotsam in our wake.

What a waste of arrows, I thought, just as a new cry reached me, making my heart lurch. This was not a warning shout, but a scream of pain. I looked down into the Drag section and saw Revna sprawled on the deck, her hands clasping at the arrow jutting from her chest.

Four

For a brief moment, it was as if the crew held their breath. Most of their faces were turned to where Revna lay. I could not be sure how badly she had been hurt. I wanted to rush to her side, but I was held in the strange spell of stillness that had fallen over the ship, like the shocked silence of a slapped child before the wailing begins.

Even the ship seemed to hesitate, hovering on the crest of a wave.

Then another arrow fell from the sky, thrumming into the deck near the steerboard, and the spell was broken. *Brymsteda* slid down the wave, plunging into the sea with a splash of white surf.

Runolf, his face like thunder, looked from his daughter to the arrow that protruded from the splintered deck near his foot, and began barking orders. He leaned hard on the tiller and, as one, we all began to move to do his bidding. We did not need to be told twice. Each of the section crews knew what they were about. *Brymsteda* shuddered as it lurched to larboard. It was clear from Runolf's instructions what he intended. We were going to tack back towards the wind and swing round to attack the pirate ship.

I helped Scurfa, Sygbald and Gersine to adjust the sheets, all the while cursing myself silently. I had longed for the release that came with combat. It seemed I might get my wish now, but at what cost? Looking over at where Revna had fallen, I let out a long sigh. Oslaf was helping her to her feet. I saw now that the arrow jutted from high on her left shoulder, and was not buried into her chest as I had first thought.

Giso had scampered back to the Lifting section, from where Runolf directed the crew and steered *Brymsteda*. The Frankish emissary was now beseeching Runolf not to engage with the pirates. His voice was clear over the straining grunts and calls of the crew.

"Our mission is more important," Giso said. "Do not turn us about. It is too much of a risk. More of the crew might be injured. There is nothing to be gained by attacking that vessel, but much to lose."

Runolf ignored the man, as if he were a pup yapping at his ankles. The giant Norseman must have seen that Revna was on her feet, but he made no outward acknowledgement, gave no sign that he felt any relief. Content that the crew was responding well to the change of direction, he fixed his glare on the enemy ship, adjusting the tiller slightly so that *Brymsteda* would intercept the pirates.

I watched as Hereward organised the men who would throw the iron hooks into the other ship. We had practised the manoeuvre many times and performed it in battle on a handful of occasions, but it was always rife with danger. When we were close enough, each rope bearer would throw the large hooks that were tied to a coil of hemp rope. They would then pull in the slack, snagging the hooks against rigging or timber, and hauling the two vessels together. While they did this, they would be unable to protect themselves and so would rely on the warriors beside them for protection until they had managed to secure the ropes, lashing the vessels together.

Eadstan, one of Lord Mancas' men, a tall young warrior

with long sandy hair and a full beard, held one of the hook lines. He was positioned just beside Drosten in the Tack section. The Pict's plaited black hair gleamed in the morning light and the swirling tattoos on his bare muscular arms were the same hue as the sky that could be seen where the mist had broken up.

In the Foreship section, Gamal, a sharp-faced warrior from Bebbanburg, carried the hook rope. He was to be protected by Hereward, who had already placed his helm upon his head and stood, shield in hand and one foot up on the wale.

Gwawrddur also held a shield and had his sword unsheathed, but unlike the other warriors, he refused to wear his iron byrnie while at sea. On our voyage to Rygjafylki he had fallen overboard in the cold depths of the North Sea and almost drowned. If he had been wearing a shirt of iron, he would certainly have been pulled beyond reach of Eadmaer, the sailor who had rescued him. Gwawrddur had overcome his terror of the sea and sailing, but he would rather rely on his skill with sword and shield, than risk sinking like a stone, should he happen to fall into the water again. Beside him, rope coiled and iron hook in hand, was Ida, a gruff, sneering man who, despite vomiting uncontrollably on our first sailings, had since become a seasoned sailor who was better than anyone else at throwing the heavy hooks tied to the long rope lines.

Brymsteda had swung about now and we were heading directly towards the pirate ship. The pirates were shouting and rushing about. It seemed they had not anticipated this sudden change of direction and now they were panicking. Their oars churned the water and they seemed to be attempting to trim the sail, to steer away from us. But their rigging became fouled and the oarsmen lost their rhythm, cursing and shouting as their oar blades clattered together. Instead of sailing away from us, the broader pirate ship slowed, lost headway and floundered.

We would be upon them in moments.

Tugging open my sea chest, I pulled out my byrnie and wrestled it over my head, jumping with my arms in the air so that it would slide down. Gersine tugged it the last of the way for me and I smiled my thanks. I had no intention of falling overboard. I could not swim, so I trusted that the Lord would watch over me.

Quickly, I helped Gersine don his own iron-knit shirt, then we both buckled on our belts, placed our helms on our heads and snatched up our shields. The sounds of the world were muffled by the cheek flaps of my helm and my vision was limited to what I faced, but I felt safer nonetheless. Hurrying to the port side of the ship, I gripped a taut shroud, readying myself to leap into battle.

Revna was sitting with her back to the mast. Her kirtle was stained red, the arrow still lodged in her shoulder. Her face was pale and sheened with sweat. Fury swept through me, burning inside me as if I had drunk strong mead. I would like to have been the first over the side when the ships touched, but we had practised many times and we each knew our place in an assault of another ship. Still, I thought, looking at the pirates' faces, there would be plenty of men for me to slay.

A sudden flurry of arrows whistled across the deck as the archers realised they were in range. One flashed past my face, another struck the sail then rattled to the deck. Gwawrddur caught an arrow on his shield and he shouted insults and taunts in his native Welsh across the waves at the dark-skinned archers.

In the Tack section, a sailor grunted and collapsed. I saw it was Hering, the scrawny son of Heca, the old ferryman from Uuiremutha. The youth clutched at the length of wood that had pierced his stomach, breathing through his mouth like a beached fish. He had only joined the crew a couple of months before. His father had tried to convince him to stay in the small river mouth village, but Hering had been adamant. He had heard tales of our voyage to Orkneyjar and Rygjafylki, and had seen us return victorious after skirmishes with Pictish pirates. He was bored with the life his father offered him and wanted adventure. Heca had called Hering a fool, saying he would as likely be killed as find gold and fame. It seemed Heca might have been right after all.

"Turn us about," shouted Giso, pleading with Runolf. "Look, another of your crew has been struck. This is madness. This fight is best avoided."

Runolf wheeled on the messenger. Giso was braver than he looked, for despite the Norseman towering over him, rage plain on his face, Alhwin's man did not flinch.

"Those bastards have hurt my daughter," snarled Runolf, "and they will pay with their lives." Still holding the tiller firmly in his right hand, he reached out with his left, taking a fistful of Giso's robe and hauling him on to his tiptoes. "Tell me again what to do on my ship, little man," he growled, "and I will toss you into the sea as payment to Njörðr. We already have one bag of your master's silver. Perhaps that is enough. Many accidents can happen at sea. Do you understand me?"

Giso met Runolf's stare bravely, but after a heartbeat he nodded and spoke no more. He was no fool and could see the danger in the skipper's threat.

More arrows fell, but no more bit into flesh. And then we were upon them. It looked as though *Brymsteda*'s prow would hammer into the side of the pirate ship, but Runolf leaned hard on the tiller, and we swung away, smashing into the long oars that were still frantically frothing the water. There were a series of splintering crashes, followed by screams where the long looms hammered into the rowers, cracking ribs and arms.

The collision slowed us, making me stagger. But Runolf was a master seaman and as our pace lessened, *Brymsteda*'s wales and upper strakes barely kissed the side of the other ship.

The pirate ship was taller in the water than *Brymsteda*,

and a few of the men on board had got themselves prepared enough to jab down at us with spears. But the rope-throwers were ready and at such close range they could not miss. They could almost just reach up and dig the iron hooks into the wood of the corsair ship. Drosten, Gwawrddur and Hereward protected Eadstan, Gamal and Ida with their shields. Hereward somehow managed to pull one of the pirates down and onto our deck. The man shrieked, but was quickly silenced, his blood pumping over *Brymsteda*'s timbers and dribbling down into the bilge and ballast stones. A moment later the ropes were secured and *Brymsteda*'s fighting men began to scramble up and over the side.

More screams and the clash of metal came from the other ship while I waited my turn to climb up the rope. There was nothing like the exquisite terror felt just before combat. I could hear the fighting and for the briefest of moments my anticipation was overpowered by the fear that I might be killed in the action. Swallowing down my dread, I hauled myself up the rope and leapt over the sheer strake and into the chaos of battle.

Five

All fear fled, torn away like the mist by the wind of my rage at these men who had dared attack us. Revna and Hering might yet die from their wounds and I allowed my fury to overwhelm me. I welcomed it as I took in the madness all around me, barely noting the odour of blood, piss and shit overpowering the salt-scent of the sea.

The battle was over quickly, but while fighting I felt as though I had all the time in the world. This was what I had missed, the moment when I could forget myself and surrender to the fierce joy of killing. With a glance, I saw how things went. Hereward, Gwawrddur and Drosten had already formed a wedge and were pushing into the belly of the ship. Before them was a mass of pirates screaming and yelling in a tongue I did not comprehend. Their clothes were strange to me, and their aspect like no men I had seen before. Their skin was as dark and sleek as an otter's fur. They bore wicked-looking knives with curved blades. A few of them were armed with slender swords, but none wore armour, or carried a shield, so the warriors of *Brymsteda* hacked a bloody swathe through their midst, leaving behind them a trail of corpses and mewling, dying men, gasping their last breaths.

Close to me several of the rowers were trying to free

themselves from the shattered oars. One tottered to his feet, clutching at a great splinter as long as his forearm that projected from his guts. He was wide-eyed with fear and tried to run from me, but I sliced my sword blade into his back, severing his spine and sending him crashing to the deck in a jumble of limbs.

Eadstan, Ida and Gamal had rushed forward to add their numbers to the shieldwall that had formed around Hereward. Another oarsman, a broad-shouldered hulk of a man with hands like shovels, snatched up a small axe and ran at me. I caught the blow on the rim of my shield and punched the iron boss into his face, smashing his teeth. He rocked back on his heels, eyes dazed. The fight had gone out of him. I cut down with my sword into the cloth-wrapped crown of his head. Fleetingly, I wondered if he might have a helm under that black cloth, but there was no protection from my blade hidden there. Blood gushed down his forehead, into his eyes and smothering his face. He raised his axe once more, and I thought he meant to strike me again, but his eyes glazed over. He toppled back onto another oarsman, who was attempting to extricate himself from the wreckage of the broken looms, toppled benches and injured men.

The man my adversary had collided with stumbled back. Taking advantage of his lack of balance, Gersine stepped in quickly, stabbing his sword into the man's chest. Twisting the blade, he yanked it free with a spurt of bright blood. The man fell, his mouth stretched in a yowl of agony that was lost in the cacophony of the battle.

"Hunlaf! Behind you!"

Runolf's familiar booming voice reached me and I turned at the warning, raising my shield without thought. The archers had rallied, taking up spears and knives, and were now hurrying towards us, ululating and howling like devils. The sound of their cries reminded me of Ljósberari's followers and I felt a chill of dread.

"Shieldwall!" I bellowed. "To me!"

Gersine was by my side and he spun around to meet this new threat, overlapping his shield with mine.

A spear probed over my shield. I swayed to the left and the blade flickered past my eyes. I watched the man who had jabbed the spear, expecting him to dart away, or perhaps to draw back the weapon for another attack. He did neither. Runolf, unarmoured and shieldless, but carrying his great war axe, was directly behind me and, with his shocking agility and bear-like strength he lashed out his left hand to grasp the spear's haft. Without pause, he yanked it, pulling the spearman towards me. Seizing the opportunity, I raised my shield and plunged my sword into my attacker's inner thigh. As the reality of what I had done dawned on him, the man's expression changed from spiteful ire to shocked disbelief. He staggered back, crashing into his comrades, his lifeblood pouring from his severed artery, painting the deck red.

"Have you left any for me?" shouted a new voice. I risked a look over my shoulder and saw Beorn's ugly face. Beneath his crooked nose, the burly warrior wore a wide grin. He stepped beside Gersine, adding his shield to the small shieldwall that faced the now cautious archers.

Pendrad pushed in beside him, his eyes twinkling from beneath his helm.

"Well, if you will take so long to climb over the side of the ship," he said, shaking his head and laughing. "It was like following a hog up a hill."

"What I lack in speed, I make up for in brawn," said Beorn, "and more skill than you'll ever know, boy."

I noticed Pendrad's sword was already bloody and glanced towards the stern of the ship in case we had missed any of the oarsmen. But the midships were heaped with dead and Hereward was leading his shieldwall inexorably along the length of the ship, pushing the enemies before them. Soon, the slaughter at that end would be complete.

But here, at the prow of the pirate ship, there were still a dozen men before us. Strewn on the deck behind them were their discarded bows and arrows. I wondered which of them had wounded Revna. The thought of her sitting against the mast, possibly dying, perhaps already dead, filled me with a dreadful anger, and I stepped forward a pace, pushing the shieldwall towards the pirates, who seemed to have lost their appetite for combat following the quick slaying of their comrade.

As keen as I was to carry the fight to them, Runolf was even more eager.

"What are you waiting for?" he gnarred. Without waiting for a response, Runolf shouldered us apart with his great bulk and threw himself at the archers, his axe flashing in the sun.

We hurried behind him and it was over in moments. We cut them down as if we were butchers. Perhaps these pirates were formidable against merchants and traders. They would surely have terrified fishermen and sailors. But we were warriors and killers, and they were no match for us. It was a charnel house on that deck, and there was little battle-skill on display, just streaming sweat and blood, and the stink of opened bowels in the cramped heat.

At last, just one remained alive. He dropped to his knees, and threw up his hands. He babbled through tears of terror. I could not understand his words, but it was clear enough that he was begging for mercy. I knew that Christ would have wanted me to show compassion and forgiveness, but I had long turned my back on such weakness. The weeping man should have thought about his fate when he chose to loose arrows at Runolf Ragnarsson's ship.

Giso, sensing that the battle was finally over, slipped over the side of the ship and made his way towards us. He carefully stepped over the pools of blood and avoided the few wounded men who yet cried out.

"Good," he said, taking in the kneeling man before Runolf, "you have kept one alive. Perhaps this fight is not a complete waste after all. He might have valuable information."

He began to speak in the strange tongue of the pirate. The man turned towards Giso, hope in his eyes. Before he could answer whatever it was that the Frankish messenger had asked him, Runolf hefted his axe and buried it in the pirate's skull. The man's head exploded, blood, brains and slivers of bone splattering me and Giso. I was already covered in gore, so it made no difference to me, but Giso stepped back hurriedly, wiping the blood from his cheek.

"Why did you do that?" he asked, his voice surprisingly cool and calm. "I was going to question him."

Runolf shrugged.

"Your mission is too important to waste time on questioning pirates."

He spat onto the corpse of the last of the archers, turned and strode down the ship towards Hereward and the others. Sounds of fighting had abated and now the only noise was the creaking as the two ships rolled in the surf, their hulls rubbing against one another. A shriek came from above and for a fleeting moment I wondered if someone might be aloft, in the rigging or on the yard. Looking up, I saw it was nothing more than a gull. The sky was filled with them, and other seabirds too. We were not far from land, and they must have smelt the blood on the wind.

Giso glowered after Runolf. The rest of us left him there, following after the huge Norseman. I looked down at the clumped piles of corpses. The deck was awash with blood and the whole ship was foul with death. I didn't see any of our men amongst the slain. I offered up a silent prayer that Revna would recover. The thought of her dying made my stomach as sick as on my first day aboard *Brymsteda*. Then I felt a stab of guilt that I had not prayed for Hering too. I cared more for Revna, it was true, but I could almost hear Leofstan berating me for my omission. No, I thought, Leofstan would not recognise the man I had become. And if he did, I did not think he would much like him.

"Are they all dead?" called Runolf, as he neared Hereward and the other warriors.

"Not quite," said Gwawrddur.

"Well, let us not waste more time here. Kill the last of them and let's see what loot there is in this tub."

"I don't think you will want to kill these ones," said Gwawrddur, a thin smile on his face.

Runolf scowled.

"Speak plainly, man. I have no patience for riddles."

"This is no riddle."

"Then what is it?"

Gwawrddur showed him.

Six

The women huddled together, barely daring to look up at the blood-soaked men who surrounded them. There were six in all and they were as out of place on the squalid pirate ship as a rose in a turd. Each wore fine linen and silk shifts, and their heads, arms and feet were uncovered. Their skin was unblemished and pale, evidence that they were not used to spending time under the harsh sun of those southern climes. Their raiment and skin marked them out as women of worth, but there was no jewellery at their necks, wrists or ears. Four of them were slim, young and clearly terrified. One was heavier of build, with ample bosom and wide hips. She was as young as the others, close to my age, but she met my curious gaze with defiance.

The sixth woman was older. Where the younger women's hair was as black as a crow's wing, hers was streaked with grey. She stood, interposing herself before the small group. She was not a large woman, but she was brave. Standing in what appeared to be a simple linen nightgown, she pushed out her chin and squared her shoulders. After quickly surveying us, she addressed Runolf, having judged him to be our leader.

"We are captives," she said, in al-Arabiyyah, Ahmad's tongue, the language of al-Andalus.

Runolf shook his head blankly and turned to me.

"She says they were captured," I said.

"I gathered that much for myself," he said, and the men chuckled. Their laughter was overly loud, jangling with the relieved excitement of men who have fought and survived. "Where were they captured?"

I asked her, stumbling over some of the words, but making myself understood well enough. She spoke at length and I interpreted.

"She says they were on a ship travelling from Balansiya when these pirates came upon them in the dead of night. How they found the ship or had the courage to attack, she does not know, but they came like shadows and killed their guards before they could raise the alarm."

"I cannot imagine these women were guarded well if these nithings were able to best their guards so easily," said Runolf. "Perhaps their success made them think they would fare well against us." He looked about at the carnage. "If so, they were mistaken."

I relayed Runolf's sentiment and the woman shook her head angrily. These men were cowards, she said. They killed the menfolk on their ship while it was moored for the night. She had no idea how they had come so close, but before they knew what was happening the men were dead or, if badly injured, thrown overboard. The pirates took the women from their beds. She continued speaking, her voice rising. Stepping up to the nearest fallen pirate, she kicked the corpse.

"She says these men did not wish to attack us," I went on, speaking her words. "They did not see us in the – I don't know the word, but I assume it is mist."

"Yes, the word means mist or fog," said Giso, who had joined us silently.

Ahmad too had climbed into the pirate vessel and now offered the greeting of his people, touching his chest, lips and forehead, to the cowering young women and the lady who stood before us.

"Peace be upon you all," he said.

The older woman eyed him curiously, then returned the greeting, placing her hand over her heart.

"And peace be upon you."

She turned her attention to Ahmad now, realising from this short exchange that he was a native of her land. They spoke freely and I struggled to understand everything. Following their words was made more difficult by Runolf prompting me to interpret them.

"It seems," I said, "that whatever luck they had in the night when they attacked the women's ship, it fled as the sun rose. When they came upon *Brymsteda* all of a sudden in the mist, they did not seek to fight us. She says the pirates argued and some of them thought that shooting arrows would convince us to flee. They were taken completely by surprise when we turned about and attacked."

"A mistake they will not make again," said Gwawrddur.

I listened intently to the conversation between the woman and Ahmad, trying not to miss anything.

"Her name is Aminah," I said. "She is the servant of these ladies. She says she knows that such beauties could bring us much treasure in the slave markets of the Imazighen coast, but she prays in the name of the Prophet that we are Allah-fearing men and we will return them to their kin."

When he heard this, Runolf frowned.

"I fear nothing," he said. "And certainly no god." I thought of Runolf's offerings and prayers to Njörðr, his pagan god of the sea, and wondered at his words, but I said nothing.

Ahmad interpreted for Aminah. She seemed to wilt on hearing what Runolf had said, perhaps thinking they had escaped one captor only to be seized by another. She appeared defeated for a moment, then, finding new resolve, she drew in a deep breath and began to speak rapidly and furiously to Ahmad, saying the ladies' families will pay handsomely for their safe return.

I was readying myself to translate her words when Runolf stopped me.

"Enough," he bellowed.

Aminah stuttered into silence. The sound of weeping was suddenly loud in the hush. But while the crying came from the group of women, their faces were dry.

Without warning, Drosten stepped forward and the women flinched, edging away from the tattooed Pict. The heavyset woman however did not move. There was fear in her eyes now. Drosten was an imposing sight, the whorls and swirls on his face making him appear monstrous. But she rose to stand before him, glowering. The crying grew louder. Drosten made no effort to move the woman. Instead he leaned quickly to the side and peered behind her. He nodded.

"She has a child," he said. "A boy, I think. Can't be more than three or four winters old." He held up a hand below his waist to indicate the size of the child he'd seen.

The woman began to wail, as if she thought Drosten might eat her offspring. Aminah started to speak quickly again, first trying to calm the lady and then exhorting Runolf not to harm them.

Runolf sighed and held up his hands for quiet. Slowly, both women grew still. I saw the boy now, peeking around the hip of the woman. His eyes were large, dark and expressive, his cheeks streaked with tears.

"Tell them," Runolf said, "that I fear no god."

As Ahmad translated, the women began to whimper.

"But I do not enslave women," Runolf went on. "Or children."

I thought of Scomric and the slaves we had fought in Runolf's homeland, imagining what had happened to Aelfwyn and Revna before we were able to rescue them. Runolf's face was grim and I thought he too must have been thinking of his daughter.

Now, as they understood Ahmad's words, the women ceased their crying.

"We are heading for Qadis," said Runolf. "We will carry them there if that suits." Aminah looked ready to begin talking again, but Runolf cut her off. "Unless the lady would prefer to row this ship somewhere else herself?"

On hearing this, the older woman shook her head and bowed low. She spoke rapidly offering blessings on Runolf and all of us. Runolf dismissed my translation with a wave of his hand.

"She can thank me later," he said. "I must see how Revna fares. Hunlaf, organise some of the men to search the ship. Then get it cleaned and ready to sail. We are close to our destination and will be on our way soon."

"We are to take the ship then?" I asked.

Runolf sneered as he looked along the length of the craft.

"It is as fat as a mule. But sturdy enough. It will fetch a good price at port, I imagine. I will hold a tight rein on *Brymsteda*, so as to not leave you too far behind."

"Me?"

"Aye. Just try to keep up with me. And if you are unsure of anything, ask Alf. He knows what he's about."

Runolf strode away, stepping over the bodies of the pirates. When he reached the side, he shouted down into *Brymsteda*.

"Alf, get over here. You are going to help Hunlaf get this bucket to port. How is my daughter?" He swung his bulk over the wale and dropped out of sight.

I looked about me, unsure of the task ahead. On *Brymsteda* I loved to hold the steerboard, guiding the ship and seeing that the sail was trimmed correctly. Since the first time I had boarded Runolf's great ship, I had been entranced by the sensation of riding over the waves. I had ceaselessly asked Runolf questions about the ship's operation, learning the ways of the sea as I would learn a new language. But I had never skippered a vessel alone, and certainly not one with rigging I was not accustomed to. I had no idea how this broad-bellied boat would respond when under way, and I was scared I would embarrass myself before the rest of the crew.

Gwawrddur moved to stand beside me.

"I see you thinking," he said with a smile. "Do not fret about what might be. Think of the first task you need to carry out and do it." He winked. "You can worry about how to sail the thing later." He patted my shoulder and walked away.

He was right, of course. He had known me for nearly three years, we had fought side by side and he had spent countless days instructing me in the use of sword and shield. He knew me well. If I let it, my head would fill up with worries and thoughts like a winter sky swirling with snow. Looking back, I understand now that this was partly the reason I drank so much in my youth and why I threw myself recklessly into battle with such abandon. I was not only seeking to live the life of a warrior, I welcomed the ability to react and not think.

Pushing aside my worries about what might come next, I looked about the ship and began barking orders.

It took longer than I would have liked to ready the ship for sailing. Runolf had already shouted three times impatiently across the waves that separated us from *Brymsteda,* asking when we would be ready. Each time I had called out: "We'll be ready when we're ready." The reply had not pleased him and I could see his scowl even from that distance, and with the glare of the sun reflecting off the water. But I knew that no matter how angry and short tempered he pretended to be, he was truly pleased.

Shortly after returning to *Brymsteda* with most of the crew,

Runolf had ordered the lines holding the ships together to be cut for fear of the damage being done to the side of each ship by the constant motion of the sea. Not long after that he had shouted over the waves that Revna's wound was not deep and that they had already managed to remove the arrow.

He might have said that he feared no god, but I had seen him pluck a silver torc from one of the dead pirates and then toss it into the sea. If anyone else had noticed, nobody said anything. Even if they had, they would not have complained, for surely Runolf was making a sacrifice to his heathen gods in the hope they might spare Revna. All of us wished for the same, and while we went about readying the ship, I prayed repeatedly that the Almighty would save Runolf's daughter and poor Hering.

"When we reach port, I will make a poultice for their wounds," I had called back. I offered up a prayer of thanks to the Lord that Revna's wound was not more serious. I was sure Runolf believed his own intervention had helped her, and I would not point out the foolishness of his beliefs. He had been baptised years before, but it was no secret that he was no Christ follower, and no amount of talking from me would change his mind.

When Runolf called out for the fourth time, I looked over at Alf.

"Ready?" I asked.

"As we'll ever be," he replied, with a smile. I liked the man. He was a competent sailor and had travelled with us ever since *Brymsteda*'s first voyage. He went about his tasks quietly and without fuss, and when we had returned to Uuiremutha for the first time, I had been surprised that he had asked if he might continue to sail with us. When I'd questioned him about his decision, he had grinned.

"It's more interesting than fishing every day, that's for certain."

I could not disagree with that, and he was not the only erstwhile fisherman to remain. His younger brother, Mantat, had also decided to stay aboard, along with Scurfa.

I was sure that Alf had everything in place for us to raise and unfurl the sail, but I gave the ship one last look. The women and the boy had remained aboard and were now seated near the prow, where Alf had rigged a shade, using a large sheet of sailcloth he had found in the ship's stores.

At the stern, where I stood near the tiller, there were two wooden buckets. One was filled with the valuables we had found on the pirates, and the contents gleamed in the mid-morning sun. There were some silver coins, minted with the swirling text of the writing of al-Andalus, as well as a couple of necklaces, some rings and bangles. The other bucket was full of knives and daggers we had taken from the previous owners of the ship. Their swords and spears were piled in the midships. The deck was now clean.

Once we had divested the pirates of their weapons and valuables, we heaved their bodies over the side, and then set about cleaning the deck, pulling up buckets of seawater and sluicing the timbers.

Not counting the women and the boy, there were only seven of us to crew the ship. Six, if we did not include Giso, who had been conversing quietly with the women under the shade while we were looting the bodies and scouring the deck. He had not once helped on the journey southward from Aachen, so I saw no reason to expect his aid now. As well as Alf and I, Gersine, Beorn and Eadstan had joined us aboard. The last member of our tiny crew was Ahmad.

"By Þórr's hammer," came Runolf's increasingly angry voice across the water, "are you ready to sail?"

I waved at him.

"We are," I shouted back.

"Thank the gods," he yelled, then gave the orders for the

men aboard *Brymsteda* to raise the sail. With practised ease, the yard was lifted and the sail bellied out in the breeze that had picked up since the dawn.

I shouted at Alf, who in turn snapped orders at the men, each of whom was aware of his role. It was not easy with such a small crew, but Alf was one of the best sailors of our band and all of us were by this time experienced seamen. It was not the smoothest unfurling of a sail, but in short order the sheets were trimmed and the sail billowing. I felt the tremble of the tiller in my hands as we began to make headway. Gone were my nervous worries of earlier. There had been no time for such things while we were readying the ship, and now I was filled with the familiar thrill of sailing, the wind whipping my hair about my face. I could instantly tell this vessel would never reach the speed of *Brymsteda*; nevertheless, the pitching of the deck beneath my feet and the cries of the gulls, terns and shearwaters in the cloud-streaked sky brought laughter unbidden to my lips.

Seven

The joy of sailing did not last long. The ship wasn't fast, but it handled well enough and after a few minor adjustments to the rigging and the sail, I was content with our progress. *Brymsteda* had begun to pull away quickly from us, and Runolf was forced to reef the sail, but there was nothing more I could do to make us go any faster, so I'd set our course to follow in *Brymsteda*'s wake and stared at the distant horizon. During the night we had been pushed further out to sea than we had thought, and now the land was out of sight. The clouds above the horizon spoke of where the great kingdom of al-Andalus lurked just beyond vision.

I knew little of the land the Romans had called Hispania. When pressed for details of his homeland, Ahmad spoke of cities, with great stone buildings that rivalled in scale the mountains that soared high into the bright blue sky. He talked of sweet fruits, beautiful silk-clad women and riches I could barely begin to imagine. I had seen the wondrous chapel, the warm swimming baths and the palace at Aachen, and I had walked the streets of Eoforwic with its stone walls and church. I could not imagine more magnificence, so I believed Ahmad's descriptions to be fanciful, hazed by childhood memories and his yearning to return to the land of his youth. However, I was excited at the prospect of finally laying eyes on this place that he spoke of with such awe and delight.

I would later find that, if anything, the taciturn Moor had minimised the majesty of Qadis, Qurtuba and Išbīliya. I would soon see that the Moors had built fabulous constructions, carved stone edifices of exquisite craftsmanship that appeared to defy nature with their lofting turrets and endless colonnades of towering arches. And I was soon to learn that those very palaces and spired and domed houses of worship, while glimmering like the stuff of dreams, could conceal the horrors of nightmares.

The pirate ship was not as agile as Runolf's sleek-hulled vessel, and it rolled laboriously over the waves rather than riding them. Still, there was little for me to do but hold the tiller and contemplate our situation. It wasn't long before my mind had filled with concerns and doubts once more. I thought again of Revna's injury, hoping it would not become elf-shot and poisoned. Shortly before we had uncoupled the ships I had asked Hereward how Hering fared. He had shaken his head.

"It doesn't look good for the lad," he'd said.

Ever since, I had berated myself for not praying sooner for the boy. What pride I had to imagine the Lord would listen to the prayers of a sinner like me. But whatever the sense of it, now I prayed over and again for Hering. I felt sorry for the boy. He had been brave enough to stand up to his father and to seek adventure. I respected that. For him to be cut down, so soon after joining the crew, saddened me and I furiously recited the Pater Noster, hoping that God might hear my pleas.

After a time, I beckoned to Alf to take the tiller and I walked down the length of the ship, my mind teeming with worries and prayers. I looked at the spears that were piled together alongside the oars that had not been broken in the attack. Darkening blood stained one of the looms, having escaped our hurried cleaning of the deck. I recalled with shame the savage glee I had felt in the fight. I was certain that the men we had slain had deserved punishment, but a cold, trembling guilt had gripped me as we'd lifted their cooling corpses over the side, sending them splashing to their watery tomb. It was one thing to fight for a righteous cause in the defence of others, but surely it was not right to come to enjoy the killing, as I now did.

"Are you well, Hunlaf?"

Shaking my head to free it of such dark thoughts, I faced Gersine.

"Quite well," I lied, forcing a smile. I could see my friend wasn't convinced, his concern still clear on his features. "How about you?" I asked, nodding at his forearm. He had picked up a long, shallow cut in the fighting. He wasn't sure how it had happened, but when the killing was done, blood had been dripping from his sword hand. Despite the amount of blood, it had not been deep. I had cleaned it and bandaged it, and I was hopeful it would heal well.

Gersine clasped and unclasped his fist, rotating his wrist to show me he had full movement.

"I'm fine," he said.

"Good."

I swept past him and made my way to where Beorn and Eadstan stood, shoulder-to-shoulder on the port side of the ship, watching the water slide by.

"Good work with the sheets and shrouds," I said, feeling awkward offering praise to two seasoned warriors.

"When we left Uuiremutha," said Beorn, his ugly face twisting with a beaming grin, "who would have thought we would be taking orders from young Hunlaf?"

I felt my face grow hot.

"Sorry," I said. "It is indeed strange for me to be giving you commands."

"No need to apologise," said Beorn, shaking his head. "For

anything to get done, everyone needs to follow a single voice, and you are a better sailor than Eadstan or I will ever be."

"If you were to command us in battle though," said Eadstan, with a lopsided smile and a raised eyebrow, "that would be a different matter."

"I would never dare," I said.

"Nonsense," said Beorn. "I would wager there will come a time when you will lead us in battle, and I for one will be happy to follow. You have the keen mind needed for such a task. Some men are destined to lead, others to follow."

"And others to fight like a bear and sing songs like a nightingale," said Eadstan, smiling broadly at his friend. Beorn was not only a powerful warrior, he also played the lyre with nimble fingers and sang with a voice as sweet as any scop.

"And others," said Beorn, clasping Eadstan's shoulder, "to stand steadfast by the side of their friends, come what may."

"No regrets then?" I asked.

Beorn understood my meaning. He pulled his gaze away from Eadstan and looked at me thoughtfully.

"Too late for that now," he said, chuckling. He must have seen the serious mood that had fallen over me, for his smile faded. "No. No regrets, Hunlaf," he went on, his voice softer. "Besides, it is as I told you. If our lord Mancas wishes to blame anybody for us heading south without his permission, he can blame his son. It was Gersine here who chose to travel with you and I gave my oath to his father to stay by his side."

"By God's nails," said Gersine, limping up to us, "don't remind me. When we return home my father will have me flayed."

"If," said Beorn.

"If what?" asked Gersine.

"If we return home."

I made the sign of the cross.

"Don't say such a thing," I said.

Beorn shrugged. We fell silent. We all knew the truth of it. We had killed all of the pirates, but Revna and Hering were wounded, Gersine and some of the others had taken cuts and bruises. The fight could easily have gone worse for us. Returning alive to Northumbria was not a certainty.

"Very well," said Beorn, "I will not mention that which is clear, but if you are not more careful," he pointed at the blood-stained bandage on Gersine's arm, "there won't be enough of you left for your father to beat or for us to protect."

"I don't need protecting," said Gersine.

"Your arm might think otherwise," said Beorn. "Besides, it is not for you to say. I gave my oath to your father, not to you."

Gersine frowned.

"What about you, Eadstan?" I asked.

"I don't need protecting either," replied Eadstan, his eyes twinkling in the bright sunlight.

We all laughed, the sound sudden and loud. It felt good, but even laughter could not dispel my sombre mood.

"I have no regrets," said Eadstan. "What was I to do? Sail back to Uuiremutha alone? No. If Beorn's oath keeps him close to Gersine, I would be nowhere else but here, at his side."

Gersine smiled, nodding. Movement caught his attention and we all looked over to where Ahmad knelt on the deck. He had his back to us and was bowing repeatedly, and praying quietly. He did this several times a day, and we rarely paid him much heed. But now it was strange to see the ladies we had rescued, kneeling some way from Ahmad, and performing the same bobbing bows, muttering the same chanted prayers. The small boy, who Aminah had said was the brother of the lady who had defended him, mimicked the motions of the adults. To see them all rising and bowing in unison reminded us that here, in the land of the Moors, Ahmad was no longer the outsider.

Giso had his back to us too. He had walked away from

the praying Moors to stand looking over the sea to where *Brymsteda* slid through the water.

"If any of us is to worry when we go back to my father's hall," said Gersine, glancing at me, "it is you."

The others nodded in agreement.

"I gave my word to Ahmad," I said.

"I know that. But he was not yours to free."

I sighed.

"Let us pray that we return with riches enough that I might recompense Lord Mancas for the loss of his thrall."

Whatever was to happen, it was certain that Ahmad would never go back to Uuiremutha. He had longed for his freedom and to return to his homeland, and, when we had left Frankia, I had told him that once he had made the introductions that would see me able to obtain an audience with Al-Zarqālluh, he would be free. Lord Mancas would be furious, but he was far away and his anger was a worry for another time.

Giso left the side of the ship and moved towards me. Gersine and the others walked away, making it clear to the Frankish emissary what they thought of his company.

"I did not know you spoke the Moorish tongue so fluently," I said, looking down at the small man.

"There is much you do not know about me, Hunlaf."

There was a smirking quality in Giso's tone that infuriated me.

"There is still plenty of time before we reach our destination," I said. "Perhaps you can enlighten me."

He looked askance at me. His expression seemed to say he thought I was quite mad.

"I did not say that I wished for you to know my secrets," he said.

I bristled, but bit back a retort. I understood why the others were not keen on spending time with the dry, humourless messenger.

"Did you learn anything from the women?" I asked after a time.

"Not a great deal. They are feeling better now that they have been given some food and water, and they are slowly becoming convinced we do not mean to kill or abuse them. Aminah did most of the talking, but I couldn't help feel that she is not accustomed to speaking so much. She says that the boy is Halawah's brother, but something is not right about all of this."

"Halawah?"

"The woman who stood before the boy."

"Why would they lie?"

"Why indeed?" He rubbed at his smooth chin. To the crew's amusement, every morning, Giso requested a bucket of water and, using a sharp knife of the finest Frankish steel, he expertly shaved his face so that it was as smooth as that of Halawah's little brother. "I will pray on it and see if the Lord Almighty can send me inspiration. Would you pray with me?"

I tensed, ready to decline the offer, as I had so often done, but my mind was still troubled and I felt something akin to envy watching the Moors performing their religious rites. I longed for the familiarity of the liturgy I had practised so many times in my years at Werceworthe.

Looking up at the sun high in the sky, I said, "Very well. I will join you. It must be close to Sext."

If Giso was surprised by my response, he did not show it. Instead, he knelt, signalling for me to join him. After a moment's hesitation, I too knelt. The deck was hard under my knees, the wood warm from the sun. Giso had closed his eyes and now began to recite the prayers for Sext in flawless Latin. Was there no language he did not know? I wondered if he had been a monk, for why else would he know the offices of the *Regula Sancti Benedicti*? I vowed that one day I would prise his secrets from him. But first, I would pray.

I joined in the recitation of the psalms, my lips moving as my mouth remembered the liturgy without conscious thought. The familiar shapes and sounds of the words soothed me almost as much as their meaning. As I muttered the words of the Fifty-Third Psalm, I felt God's peace wrap about me like a cloak. Why had I been so stubborn? What prideful sin had made me refuse to pray? Did I not still believe in the Lord? Of course I did not doubt the Almighty's existence, but it would be a lie to say my faith had not been shaken. Why had God allowed His servant Leofstan to be killed so foully at the hands of the madman, Scomric? Why had the Lord permitted the destruction of the minster at Lindisfarnae, and the attack on Werceworthe? So many had suffered and died.

All of these questions, anxieties and angry thoughts swarmed in my mind like locusts, but as the words of the office flowed from me, it was as if the hand of the Lord smoothed my furrowed brow. I closed my eyes and I could hear Leofstan's voice, whispering to me, as though he knelt close by my side.

"It is not for you to comprehend the Almighty's plan," Leofstan's voice said. "Have faith. Accept God's will. Be His instrument." So clear was his voice that I was certain my old mentor was there on the ship. I could feel his breath on my cheek and I pressed my eyes closed, terrified to look and to discover the truth that he was still dead, consumed by the flames of Scomric's hall. Tears trickled from my closed eyes and I continued to recite the office, praying fervently. I had listened too long to the voice of Satan, now I must once more listen to the word of God.

Such was my focus on the prayers and so intent was I on imagining Leofstan's presence that at first I did not comprehend the raised voices. Soon there could be no ignoring them. I could make out Gersine and Beorn both calling my name, their voices tinged with excitement.

Or fear.

I did not wish to open my eyes. I knew the moment I did the holy communion I felt would be lost, shattered in the stark sunlight of the open sea. Leofstan would not be there and I would need to confront the future alone.

"You are not alone," whispered the voice in my ear. Could it be Leofstan? Was it perhaps Giso?

The voices clamoured for attention now, and I could ignore them no longer. I stood, cuffing the tears from my cheeks, and opened my eyes.

Beorn and Gersine were standing near the prow, where the women were once again sheltered in the shade of the sail. Both men were pointing south and east. I peered into the bright light, shielding my eyes with my hand and blinking in the brilliant sunshine. I thought they might have spotted land, but I could see no tell-tale shadow on the horizon.

"There!" shouted Gersine. "Do you see them?"

I squinted and then, suddenly, I did.

Over the horizon rose up the sails of three ships.

Eight

The ships were not as long and fast as *Brymsteda*, but it soon became apparent they were fast enough that we would be unable to outrun them. The wind had veered into the south-west, and I shouted to Alf to steer us northward. Beorn and Eadstan trimmed the sail. The women cried out, perhaps fearing yet another attack.

Runolf must have spotted the ships too, and seen our change of course, for he swung *Brymsteda* to larboard, mirroring our trajectory. We were too far apart to communicate, so all we could do was set our sail to catch as much of the wind as possible, and pray.

We ran before the three ships for a time, but they drew ever closer. *Brymsteda* could have escaped them, but there was no way that the bulky, cumbersome ship I skippered would be able to get away.

For a time after praying with Giso, I had felt serene, my head devoid of the fears and worries that had plagued me. But that tranquillity was short-lived. I could see that the vessels were going to overhaul us. Even if Runolf was able to bring *Brymsteda* close and join the fight, I did not reckon our chances against so many.

Ahmad came to my side. I had seen him talking to the women, and wondered what he had learnt.

"Halawah says those are her kin's ships," he said.

"Who are her kin?" I asked, looking at the three large ships incredulously.

Ahmad scratched at his beard nervously, but did not answer my question.

"We cannot outrun them," he said, stating what I already knew. "It would be best for us to allow them to board us."

"We have their women," I said, "and we are in a pirate ship. You think they will listen to us before they kill us all?" I could hear the note of anxiety in my voice.

Ahmad shrugged.

"We will find out one way or another. Running will only further anger them and make us appear more guilty, I would say."

I glanced at the women sheltering under the sailcloth.

"The women will vouch for us?"

"We have done them no harm," Ahmad said. "Why would they lie about that?"

I thought of Giso's words following his conversation with the women.

"Why indeed?" I said, pondering my possible courses of action. I looked at the approaching ships, their sails taut, prows plunging through the surf. I saw Runolf alter *Brymsteda*'s course. He meant to intercept the ships, but even if he had the full crew aboard, I could see no way he would be able to halt three enemy vessels. Besides, were they actually our enemies? Runolf did not know what the women had told us, though he might suspect the reason these ships came at us with such determination.

There was nothing for it. I shouted to Eadstan and Beorn to furl the sail.

"Ahmad," I said, "help them."

I thought he might refuse me. Ahmad had always hated being told what to do, and now that he was no longer a thrall, he was rebellious and resentful of any order. But, after hesitating briefly, he grunted and ran to help with the rigging.

"Alf," I called, "we are going to let them close with us."

Alf nodded, adjusting the tiller and making no comment.

I waved to *Brymsteda* and bellowed as loudly as I could over the waves, but we were too distant for them to hear us. I prayed that they would understand what we were doing and not seek to come to our rescue with swords and axes.

Now that I had made the decision and given the order for the sail to be furled, the pirate ship slowed and the three ships coming from the south sped towards us.

They reached us in short order. Their wales were lined with archers. The sun glinted from polished helms, armour, swords and arrow points. Again I wondered who Halawah, Aminah and the other women were, but there was no time to ponder such questions.

Whoever commanded the ships had noted the danger posed by *Brymsteda*, and had placed two of their vessels between the stallion-prowed wave-steed and us. The third ship rowed to within an arrow shot of us and a man cupped his hands to his mouth and called over the water. His hands and face were darkly tanned, contrasting with his bright white clothes that shone in the light of the early afternoon sun.

His voice was thin and vague with distance, but Ahmad appeared to understand him and shouted back. The exchange went on for some time until Ahmad signalled for Halawah to approach the wale. She came to the edge of the ship, the small boy by her side. There followed more shouting, during which Halawah informed the captain of the ship that all the captives were well.

I got the gist of most of what was said, but in case I was

in any doubt, Ahmad said, "Their captain is called Rifat al-Haidar. I have agreed that they can board us. But we must give up our arms and armour."

I took a deep breath. I had expected this.

"Tell him I do not agree to be boarded."

Ahmad looked at me sharply.

"This is not something they want to discuss," he said. "They suspect a trap, I think. If we show any sign of resistance, we will all be killed."

"I think not. They have come all this way after those women and the boy. They will not risk attacking."

Ahmad frowned. Giso was looking at me with a hint of a smile on his face. He rubbed his smooth cheeks pensively.

"They will not like it," Ahmad said.

"No," I said, "but they will have no choice. Tell them."

Ahmad shouted over the surf. Even from this distance, I could see Rifat's face darken with rage.

"Tell Rifat that they can escort us into Qadis," I said before the captain could reply. "*Brymsteda* too. When we are safely at port, the women and the boy are his."

Rifat shouted back angrily, cursing us for barbarian infidels.

"Tell him we might be barbarians, but we wish no harm to befall the women and the boy. If he has his ships keep their distance, they will remain safe."

The Moorish captain hurled more insults at us, but I could see that, like a summer storm, his anger had quickly blown itself out.

"One last thing," I said to Ahmad. "Tell him we must be allowed to sail close enough to *Brymsteda* for us to relay what has been agreed. There is none aboard that understands your tongue and I can all too easily imagine Runolf deciding to attack the three ships himself."

Ahmad offered me one of his rare smiles.

"Anything is possible," he said.

And so it was that we set sail for the coast once more, but this time accompanied by the three new ships. When we sighted land, Rifat led us southward.

"That was well done," said Giso, who had come to join me at the tiller while Alf took control of the sail and rigging.

"I could not let them aboard," I said. "It could all too easily have gone against us." I looked down the length of the ship at the women and the boy. Aminah scowled back at me. Did she believe I would order them harmed? It did not matter. I had done what was needed. It was not the first time I had threatened an innocent to ensure our safety. I recalled holding a blade to the throat of young Lambi on Orkneyjar. The memory of the disappointment and hatred in his sister Thurid's eyes stabbed me with regret and shame. But that was in the past and could not be changed now.

"What about when we reach Qadis?" he asked. "You think Rifat will have taken kindly to this?"

"We'll have to take our chances and pray that God watches over us."

Giso stared out at the ships that escorted us and said nothing more.

When we finally got our first glimpse of Qadis, with its stone fortifications and watchtowers, the sun was low in the sky. I could see that the city appeared to be built on an island at the end of a long spit of land. To the west was the open ocean, to the east a great bay, and then the mainland of al-Andalus. The sea around us was not the slate grey of the North Sea. The water here was a vibrant, pale green, like a polished emerald.

The handling of the pirate ship had become familiar to me during the afternoon, and I pulled the tiller slightly to reset our course as I felt the keel shudder as we hit a tidal current. One of the other ships was ahead of us, *Brymsteda* was not far behind. The final two Moorish ships brought up the rear, ready to intercept us should we decide to attempt to flee.

I was tired after the day's exertions, but I could feel myself growing more alert at the sight of the city looming before us. Everyone aboard was looking ahead where the ruddy light of the setting sun made the rocks of the walls and towers gleam like burnished bronze. On a jutting promontory was a high mound topped with a stone structure. Its edges were hard in the evening sunlight, its shadow stark. We followed the lead ship as it turned to pass beyond the island city into the shelter of the bay. Ahmad stared in silence at the city and the smudge of mainland behind. This was the first time he had seen his homeland in ten years and there were tears in his dark eyes.

The only one of us not looking ahead was Giso. I glanced over at him and saw he was gazing at the ships behind us.

"They look like they're on fire," he said, his tone strange and distant.

I looked and saw it was true. The sun had turned the sea aflame and the shimmering light dappled and reflected on the hulls of the Moorish ships. Frowning, I turned back towards the land of al-Andalus and the great port of Qadis.

I could see now that on the eastern side of the city there was a broad channel, bordered with jetties, wharfs and piers. Many ships were moored there, their masts scraping the warm sky. The ship we followed swung about, heading for the channel. Seeing that this was our destination, I tensed, gripping the tiller more tightly. I would need to concentrate. It would not be easy to manoeuvre this clumsy ship into dock with our small crew.

Alf clearly had the same thought, for he hurried back to the mast rigging, from where he had been observing the city from the prow.

"Look lively, lads," he said, his voice uncharacteristically loud and sharp. "We don't want to embarrass ourselves in front of our hosts, do we?"

Nine

"But we have done nothing wrong!" I said, my voice rising in anger.

"So you say," said the tall man before me.

His tone was smooth and measured, further irritating me. I clenched my fists at my side. Gwawrddur patted the air gently with his hands, signalling for me to remain calm. The Welshman could not understand the words I said, but my increasing frustration was clear.

The man I spoke with was Rifat al-Haidar, the captain who had conversed with us in shouts over the water. Now, standing on the stone dock, his voice was calm. "But you were sailing in a known pirate ship and aboard were the women and child who had been taken from one of our vessels under cover of darkness." His face hardened and he jutted out his bearded chin at me. "During that attack, a dozen of my men were killed."

Behind him, a score of white-robed warriors stood to attention. They were well disciplined and did not move, but I could sense the hatred coming off them like a stink. I wondered how many of them had friends amongst the men the pirates had murdered.

I took a deep breath, in an attempt to compose myself.

"It was not us who attacked your ship," I said, biting off the words, "or took your women. We came across this ship and killed the crew when they attacked us. We rescued your people."

"So you say," repeated Rifat.

"Did not Halawah and Aminah say the same?" My voice was rising in pitch again and I forced myself to breathe slowly.

"They did." Rifat inclined his head. "And it is for that reason alone that I have allowed you to remain free."

"Free?" I spat. "You have forbidden us to leave these docks."

"You are not in chains. But you are strangers in our land. When I have reported to the wazir and we are satisfied you are not enemies, you will be permitted to travel into the city and beyond."

"And if you are not satisfied?" I asked.

Unsmiling, Rifat met my gaze for several heartbeats.

"For your sake, I pray to Allah you are not found guilty of any crime."

The implied threat hung in the night air.

"But for now, you are free to remain on your ship or the docks. If you are in need of anything, speak to the commander of the guard, Nadir ibn Mahfuz." He nodded at a flat-faced man with a thick, full beard. Nadir's lip curled in what might have been a smile, but seemed more like a snarl.

Rifat was turning to leave when he paused.

"What is your name?" he asked, looking suddenly at Ahmad, who had said little since we had moored. It seemed to me that now he was once again standing on the ground of his homeland, Ahmad was in awe.

He stepped out of the shadows and bowed low. It had taken some time to get all the ships docked and it was dark now. The flames from the torches dotted along the wharf glimmered in Ahmad's eyes.

"Peace be upon you," Ahmad said.

"And upon you," replied Rifat instinctively. "Your name?"
Ahmad swallowed.

"My name is Ahmad ibn Ibrahim."

"And where are you from, son of Ibrahim?"

"A small village on the coast. Near Malaqah." Ahmad sighed. "It is many years since I have been home."

Rifat stared at Ahmad as if trying to find him in his memory, then, with a small shrug, he turned on his heel, and marched away, his white cloak and robes clearly visible in the gloom until he reached the end of the docks and was swallowed by shadows.

A dozen guards followed Rifat in two ordered lines. The twenty warriors under the command of Nadir remained on the docks eyeing us with barely concealed disdain.

"You are known here?" I asked Ahmad.

"I doubt it," he said, his tone thoughtful, perhaps thinking of the home he had left behind and whether he would ever see it again. He walked back to *Brymsteda*.

"We are prisoners?" asked Gwawrddur.

"Rifat says we are free, but these friendly men are here to stop us leaving."

Gwawrddur scanned the glowering faces of the white-robed guards. Nadir met his gaze, hawked and spat onto the stone before us.

"Perhaps you did not understand his meaning," Gwawrddur said. "This seems a strange type of freedom to me."

"My thoughts exactly."

"Still," said Beorn, who was walking past towards the pirate ship, "better to be prisoners than the alternative."

"The alternative?" I asked.

"You're a clever lad," he said. "And brave, but how do you think we would fare against all those warriors? Any alternative to this that I can think of is not pretty."

"He's not wrong," said Gwawrddur. "And perhaps now is

not the best moment to lose your temper with the captain of the guards of the place."

I sniffed.

"You're right," I said. "I know you're right." But the reality was I could barely hold my anger in check. Nothing had gone well since Qadis had slid into view, its stone walls picked out against the green sea in the afternoon sunlight.

Alf had trimmed the sail and I had felt in control of the ship. We had sailed slowly into the port, past the numerous barges, cogs and wherries and I was painfully aware of the staring eyes of their inhabitants and the men who sat in the warm rays of the dying sun, talking, sipping drinks, and mending ropes and nets. The local sailors and fishermen were intrigued by our foreign clothing and pale faces and I felt acutely the pressure of the responsibility Runolf had placed upon me. Gone was the calm that had enveloped me after praying. Once again I was filled with anxiety. All I needed to do was to bring the ship in without incident, but the more I thought of it, the more I became convinced I would do something wrong. Of course, as is so often the way with such things, by thinking too much it was as though the very thing I least wished to happen became inevitable.

I miscalculated the angle of approach to the stone dock, and despite a shouted warning from Alf that saw me lean all my weight on the tiller, the side of the ship scraped along the rough-hewn rock of the wharf before the bow of our ship ploughed into a small fishing boat. The onlookers laughed as Alf and Ahmad had thrown ropes to a couple of waiting sailors who had already disembarked from the first of our escort vessels. They had expertly caught the lines, looped them about great stone bollards and brought our ship to a halt.

The old owner of the fishing boat had rushed forward and climbed into his boat. After a brief check of his property, he had grinned up at me and said no damage was done. I was pleased for him, and glad he was gracious about my mishandling of the ship, but my pride was sorely hurt.

Under Runolf's expert command, *Brymsteda* had fared much better. They had lowered and furled the huge woollen sail and unshipped several pairs of oars. Under the power of the rowers, *Brymsteda* had slipped gracefully to its mooring, the men lifting their oars at the last moment. The locals had watched on, open-mouthed at the beauty of the ship's lines and the intricately carved prow beast.

The sun had set by then, the sky still aglow, the western horizon as bright as a sword blade pulled from the forge. While the last two ships came into port, full dark fell and men trudged down the docks lighting torches in sconces.

I had climbed down from the ship, and the women and the small boy had been delivered into Rifat's custody long before *Brymsteda* was moored. We had been ordered to relinquish our weapons and we had obeyed, watching with dejected envy as Mantat jumped gracefully from *Brymsteda*'s Foreship section and secured the longship.

My mood had soured further as we'd waited, my previous worries multiplying in my mind.

"How is Revna," I'd called up to Runolf.

"Ask her yourself," he replied, grinning.

Scanning the faces on the ship, I spied Revna's golden hair. Her skin was pallid, but she waved at me with her right hand. Her left arm was bandaged and in a sling that looked to be made from a cloak.

"Hering?" I asked.

Revna shook her head.

"He sleeps," she said, "but he has a fever and mutters all the while. He is in terrible pain."

I was more uncertain than ever about our prospects, but I had vowed I would do what I could to help Hering. Now, I made my way to where the guards were gathered.

Touching my chest, then lips, then forehead, I addressed Nadir, being careful to keep my frustration hidden behind a warm smile.

"Peace be upon you all," I said, emulating the greeting of Ahmad's people.

Nadir frowned, and did not respond with the expected reply. Instead, he glared at me as if I were an insect that had crawled out of his pottage.

"Rifat said I should ask you if we needed anything," I said, choosing to ignore his taciturn demeanour.

Still he said nothing, so I continued.

"Two of our number were injured in the fighting. Is there a healer who could attend them?" Ahmad had told me that his people had the finest healers, men who could apply all manner of knowledge and medicine to their patients. I had seen him bring Gwawrddur back from the brink of death, and Ahmad did not profess any great skill in the arts of healing. I hoped there might be someone in Qadis who might alter the dark path that Hering appeared to be on.

"No," said Nadir. He sniffed.

I had expected this. Undeterred, I took a deep breath.

"Very well. I can treat them," I said. I had some knowledge of healing, and, with the correct herbs I might yet be able to draw out the poison from Hering's elf-shot wound. "Perhaps you could send for some things that would be of use to me." Nadir did not speak. I realised then that I needed Ahmad to help me with the words for some of the items I required. I called over to him. After hesitating, he approached, albeit somewhat reluctantly, it seemed to me. "Please ask him for honey, vinegar, garlic, springwort..." I hesitated, biting my lip as I tried to remember all I had been taught of leechcraft. I could not recall all of the wyrts needed. What I could remember would have to do. "Groundsel, wormwort, and some clean linen for bandages."

Ahmad made the request, struggling to think of the names of the plants and asking me to describe them. Nadir waited in silence for us to finish, then shook his head.

"Rifat told me to ask you if I was in need of anything," I said, hearing the tone of my voice rise in pitch as my ire grew.

Nadir grinned, his teeth bright in his thatch of black beard.

"But he did not say I would get you what you asked for," Nadir sneered, "did he?" His eyes narrowed slyly. "Not without paying a price."

I could feel my rage bubbling up within me. Gwawrddur, sensing my anger, placed a hand on my arm.

"Hunlaf," he whispered.

I shrugged him off. I was unsure what I meant to do, but I knew the anger I felt could not be contained for long. I took a step closer to Nadir, my fists bunched at my side. He smirked and did not flinch from my furious glare, which only served to make me angrier. I shook with the pent-up rage inside me and I might have struck him then, no matter the consequences, had it not been for the sudden shouting behind me.

Breaking my stare with Nadir, I looked to see what the source of the commotion was. Beorn was surrounded by half a dozen of the white-garbed Moorish guards. He had his back to the side of the pirate ship and the guards had lowered their spears at him menacingly.

"Let me past, you heathen devils," Beorn bellowed, and for a heartbeat I thought the stocky warrior might charge into the thicket of spears, even unarmed as he was. His face was ruddy and sweat-sheened in the torchlight, his eyes glaring with an anger that appeared to match mine.

On the edge of my vision I saw Eadstan leap from *Brymsteda* and run towards the group of spear-men to help his friend. We had been forced to give up our weapons and we could not win a fight against these well-trained warriors. If we were not careful, we would all be slain before sunrise.

"Eadstan, halt!" I snapped, my voice cutting through Beorn's shouts and the snarled insults of the guards surrounding him.

Eadstan glanced at me, slowing his pace, but still moving towards the huddle of warriors around Beorn.

"Halt!" shouted Hereward from *Brymsteda*'s deck. "Both of you!"

Eadstan stopped running instantly. Beorn ceased shouting. I felt a needle of frustration that my voice held little sway with these men. But the truth of it was I was yet young, and Hereward's voice carried the heft of years of leading men in battle. Its power could not be ignored.

I hurried over to Beorn. Nadir followed behind at a leisurely saunter, his callused palm resting on the pommel of the sword that hung from a sash at his hip.

"Beorn, what is the meaning of this?" I asked. "We cannot risk a fight with these people."

Beorn raised an eyebrow and shook his head.

"And you would tell me this?" He snorted, clearly thinking of the irony in what I was saying. "Were you not prepared to do just such a thing, with the leader of the guards no less?"

"I was wrong," I muttered. "He goaded me."

"All these whoresons do is insult and taunt us. They refuse to let me take what is rightfully ours. First they imprison us and now they mean to rob us too."

In his hand was the bucket containing the treasure we had taken from the dead after the battle. The torchlight made the gold and silver glimmer.

Nadir arrived. He spoke quickly to his men and one of them replied in such a rapid flurry of words I was unable to follow their meaning.

"The ship is—" he said to me, finishing with a word I did not understand.

I turned to Ahmad. He had not followed us, instead remaining back in the pool of light beneath one of the torches.

"I do not understand," I said to Nadir quietly, hating the bitter taste that came from showing my ignorance to this bully. "What is that word?"

He chuckled, pleased to see me squirming after my show of anger. He repeated the word, louder this time, so that Ahmad could hear. I was suddenly very aware of the silence that had descended on the wharf, and the glimmering eyes that watched this confrontation from the shadows.

Far off in the distance I heard music. It sounded like nothing I had heard before. It was haunting and strange, and I suddenly wished I could walk away from the docks and find the source of that enchanting melody. But I could not leave, and if I was not careful, we might never escape this place with our lives.

"It means that you do not own the ship any longer," said Ahmad. "It has been taken."

"Taken?" I asked.

Guessing at the meaning of our conversation, Nadir smiled.

"The ship is now the property of the Wazir of Qadis," he said.

"But we fought for that ship. We rescued your people. Some of our folk were wounded in the fight."

Nadir nodded, feigned sympathy on his features.

"Yes, yes," he said. "It is a sorry tale. Now, tell me once more the items you wanted."

I repeated the words Ahmad had used for the request as well as I could remember them.

Nadir nodded thoughtfully, as if going through each item in his mind and thinking where they might be procured.

"Shouldn't be too hard," he said. "For a price."

I sensed the way this was going. Swallowing down the sour taste of defeat, I sighed.

"There is much treasure there," I said, indicating the bucket in Beorn's meaty hand. "That would pay for what I need and much more besides."

Nadir smiled and held out his hand. Beorn did not move. I could see the tension in his shoulders. The muscles of his jaw bulged. He looked as if he was about to launch himself at the smirking guard.

"Beorn," I said, keeping my tone calm, "give him the bucket."

For a long while Beorn did not move. He met Nadir's gaze with open loathing.

Nadir snapped his fingers impatiently.

"Beorn," I whispered.

At last, the ugly warrior raised his hand and proffered the bucket to Nadir. Taking it, the guard began to sift through the items we had looted. His thick, warrior fingers turned over the bracelets, necklaces and coins. The torchlight caught on the metal, reflecting on Nadir's face as he nodded appreciatively. At last, seemingly satisfied, he handed the heavy bucket to one of his men.

"You are right," he said. "That is good treasure. My lord will be most pleased."

I let out a long breath. I was not happy to have given up our plunder, and I knew Runolf and the others would be furious, but at least I could now help Hering.

"Good," I said. "Now please hurry for the items I have asked for. Our man is grievously ill."

Nadir stared at me blankly for a time, his brow furrowed in mock confusion. A scratch of unease ran down my spine.

"Perhaps you did not understand me, barbarian," Nadir said at last. "You must pay a price. With what will you pay for these things?"

"We just gave you enough gold to buy a hundred times what we ask for."

"But that was not your property to give. That belongs to my lord the wazir. What is it you can offer me to bring the things you require?" At first he maintained an expression of earnest compassion, as if he wanted nothing more than to aid me. But after a moment he was unable to keep up the pretence and his teeth flashed white as he grinned. "I am sorry, little man," he said. "I fear you have nothing to interest me. I think it best if you get some rest. You look tired. I know I am."

Spinning on his heel, he strode away, laughing quietly to himself. More of his men had joined the six who had surrounded Beorn and now they closed ranks behind their leader.

My anger was such that I advanced towards the spear-men, fists raised. Now it was Beorn who pulled me back.

"We cannot hope to win that fight," he said, his tone grim.

"He's right," said Gwawrddur. "Try to ignore that nithing. It seems to me he wishes for nothing more than to provoke us to fight." He stared after Nadir, his expression unreadable. "You gain nothing standing here. Go and help Hering with what skill you have."

Shaking with anger, I slowly made my way to *Brymsteda* and clambered over the side. Runolf came to speak to me, but I brushed past him. Behind me I heard Gwawrddur mutter to the Norseman to leave me be.

My hand trembled as I dipped the cloth into the hot water, partly from the anger I still felt at Nadir's treatment of us, but more than that, I shivered to see the state of Hering's wound.

The men who had tended to him had done their best. The arrow had pierced deeply, passing through Hering's slender midriff and breaking the skin of his back. They had cut the fletching from the arrow and drawn the shaft through his body, and bandaged the wound as tightly as they could. But it was immediately clear to me that it was elf-shot. Hering's skin was hot to the touch. He muttered and moaned as I unwrapped the bandage. He cried out when I used the cloth and hot water that Scurfa had prepared to clean the red inflamed flesh around the point where the arrow had pierced his body. Hering's stomach was swollen, bruised and blotchy, and I worried he was bleeding inside. I dabbed at the dried blood on his trembling skin, wiping it away, knowing it would do nothing to help him.

"How bad is it?" Revna asked. She had stayed close to the stricken youth as if she felt a strange kind of kinship for sharing a similar injury.

I sighed, but said nothing. There was nothing to say. We could both see Hering was dying. The others knew it too and had distanced themselves, moving to the far end of the ship where they spoke in hushed tones or slept fitfully, wrapped in their cloaks. Warriors are keen to deal death, but I have never met a man of war who will willingly spend time close to those lingering at the gates of the afterlife.

"Help me lift him," I said. "So that I can bandage him again."

Without hesitation, Revna heaved Hering up. She was strong and took most of his weight on her good arm, but I noted how she winced when she was forced to prevent him falling by using her injured left arm. I bandaged him as quickly as I could, then helped Revna lay him down once more on the blanket. Despite the heat that came from him and the warmth of the evening, Hering was shaking, as if caught outside in a blizzard on a winter's night. I covered him in a cloak and sighed.

"He is in God's hands now," I said, making the sign of the cross over him and, without thinking, beginning to recite the Pater Noster. Revna was no Christian, but she lowered her head respectfully as I prayed.

"That could have been me," she said when I'd finished. She was looking down at Hering's fevered form. The thought of seeing her like that, at the doors of death, made me shudder anew.

"Let me take a look at that shoulder," I said, eager to hide the strength of emotion that had gripped me. "Scurfa," I called quietly, "is there more hot water?"

Without speaking, as if not wishing to disturb Hering, Scurfa came to us with a bowl filled with steaming water. I rose to meet him, tossing the dirty water over the side into the darkness. The contents of the bowl splashed into the sea and the stars reflected there shimmered and rippled. Taking the hot water from Scurfa, I handed him the empty bowl with a nod of thanks.

Returning to Revna's side, I helped her remove the sling. She had replaced her kirtle with a peplos which left her shoulders and arms exposed. I could not remember the last time I had seen her in women's clothes. I didn't know she even had any dresses in her sea chest. The undergarment accentuated her curves, making it harder than normal for me to ignore her shape.

"My father ripped my kirtle to get to the wound," she said, as if she was able to hear my thoughts.

I moved the oil lamp closer. The bare skin of her arm was smooth. I barely breathed as I gently unwound the bandage from her shoulder and upper arm. As my fingers brushed her skin I felt myself tremble again, and I cursed myself for the weakness of my flesh. Pushing aside my base desire, I set about cleaning and examining Revna's wound.

The bandage was stuck with dried blood, so I dunked a clean cloth into the hot water and dribbled some on the bandage, soaking it. Gently, I teased it away from the wound. It pulled at the scab that had formed and Revna hissed.

"Sorry," I muttered.

"You didn't do this," she said through gritted teeth.

I glanced at where Hering lay shivering and whimpering beneath his cloak. No, I had not done this, but hadn't my tales of adventure encouraged Hering to defy his father and come with us? And hadn't I neglected to pray for him, instead begging the Almighty that this beautiful young woman might be saved? I knew the truth: I had thought nothing of Hering until it was too late.

I cleaned Revna's wound. The skin around it was clear of the tell-tale redness that came with the wound-rot. I lowered my face to her shoulder and sniffed. There was no scent of putrefaction, only the sweet smell of her hair, the salt and sweat of her skin.

"Do I smell good?" she asked. I heard the smile in her voice, though I did not dare look at her face.

"The wound is clean," I said, glad the darkness would hide my blushing.

I bound the wound again and replaced the sling over her head.

She made a fist with her left hand.

"Feels better already," she said.

"Good."

I didn't know what else to say. I sat beside Hering and looked up at the cloudless night sky. Far off I could hear snatches of the ethereal music I had heard before. A voice was singing to the tune now, though it was too far away to make out any of the words. Its melancholy rise and fall matched my mood. At one moment I was dismayed, aghast at the state of Hering and the grave danger we faced in this foreign land. The next I was breathless and pleased to be sitting in companionable silence with Revna, content in the knowledge that she would not die from her wound.

Above us the stars stared down with their cold light and I wondered what God must think of me. Did He still have a plan for me? I had strayed so far from what I had once been, I wondered if I could ever return. Then I remembered that afternoon when I had prayed with Giso, and I berated myself for a fool. God was love and Jesus had died to wash away my sins. All I needed to do was to ask for His forgiveness and I would be welcomed back like a lost lamb being brought back into the fold by a shepherd.

Beside me, Revna yawned. Silently, she took her cloak, wrapped it about herself and lay down near Hering. I stared down at the two of them and vowed to watch over them and pray for them both as they slept.

I recited first the Pater Noster and then the Ave Maria, repeating each prayer over and over in a murmur. After a time my eyes grew heavy and I stretched out near Revna. Without further thought, sleep enveloped me in its calm, healing embrace.

Ten

I emerged slowly from a deep, restful sleep. The air was cool on my face and I opened my eyes to stare up into the lightening sky. Stars still glimmered there, but the dawn was not far off. All was still and calm and I wondered what had awoken me. A dog barked far off in the city of Qadis. One of the guards on the dock coughed. Runolf snored at the far end of *Brymsteda*'s deck. Perhaps it had been one of these sounds that had pulled me from my slumber. I sighed, wishing I had slept longer, but knowing that with the brightening day and Runolf's snores rattling the rigging, I would not find sleep again.

Recalling the vow I had made, I cursed myself again for the fragility of my flesh. I had not meant to sleep, but slumber had found me quickly enough in the quiet darkness. I remembered when I had similarly succumbed to my tiredness in the land of the Norse. That had led to our capture and the grisly events that followed.

I sat upright, throwing off my blanket. In my mind I pleaded with God not to allow my weakness to have brought further suffering to my friends.

"No need to jump up," Revna said. Her voice sounded hollow. I wondered if her shoulder pained her. For a piercing, shameful instant I hoped that's why her voice had that echoing, empty quality.

She was sitting beside Hering. It might have been her movement that had roused me. I bit my lip, berating my shortcomings. I had said I would watch over them both. I made a fresh vow then, that I would make amends. I would clean and tend to Hering's wound again. Perhaps there was a way to take him to one of the famed Moorish healers, or at least a means to get my hands on the ingredients to make a poultice for the wound.

"How does he fare?" I asked, rubbing the sleep from my eyes.

Revna did not reply at once and I felt a ripple of unease down my back.

"Revna?"

"He's..." Her voice caught in her throat. She didn't need to say anything more. My ideas of further aid for the stricken youth crumbled into ash.

Moving to Revna's side, I looked down at Hering's still form in the cold grey light of the pre-dawn. Gone was his whimpering now. His suffering had ceased. I clung to that thought like a drowning man grasping at a shattered thwart, but it barely kept my head above the sea of anguish that threatened to smother me. Hering had come seeking adventures that I had convinced him he would find with us aboard *Brymsteda*. He had been young and foolish and filled with excitement. Not so different to me, I thought, staring at his face. It was smooth and childlike in death. Because of me, he was gone, his body as still as a stone, his spirit departed in the night.

Beside me Revna sniffed and I saw the glisten of tears on her cheeks. Uselessly I placed a hand on her good shoulder.

"I'm sorry," I said.

"This is not your doing," she replied.

I couldn't free myself of the feeling that she was wrong.

This was my fault. I had failed Hering. If I had prayed for him sooner, or if I had secured the wyrts and herbs I needed, or even if I had possessed more skill at healing, perhaps he would have lived. My eyes burnt. I wanted to cry, but I swallowed back my grief. I had not done enough for the boy, I did not deserve to weep over him.

We sat there beside Hering in silence, each lost in our own thoughts.

In the city, echoing around the stone buildings and drifting over the rooftops came an ululating, wailing cry. I thought there were words in that crying voice, but I could not discern them. It was as though the distant chanting had forged into sound the sorrow that held my heart in its grip.

I saw Ahmad rise from his blankets and understood that what I heard was the call to prayer he had told me about while teaching me of the ways of his people. Just as the brethren of Christian minsters recite offices at certain times of the day, so the devout followers of the prophet Muhammad pray at intervals throughout the day. Ahmad had told me that in the towns of al-Andalus a *muezzin*, a holy man, calls the faithful to prayer.

Ahmad knelt and began to pray. Looking over the side of the ship I saw that most of the guards were also praying, kneeling and bowing towards the light in the eastern sky. Nadir was no fool though, for I noticed that half a dozen of his men stood to attention, spears in hand, looking in the direction of the Norse longship, just in case we should choose this moment to attack, I supposed.

It was not long before the rest of the crew stirred, rising and making their way over to where Hering lay and Revna and I kept vigil. Nobody called out that the boy had died in the night, but it was as if somehow, without words, tidings of his death had carried to everyone aboard. There was sadness in the cool morning air, but nobody appeared surprised by Hering's passing.

Knowing me well, Gwawrddur squeezed my shoulder.

"You did all you could," he said in a quiet voice. "You are not to blame for this. It was not you who pulled the string that shot the arrow."

I nodded. The Welshman spoke the truth. I had not drawn the bow, but still I felt a terrible remorse. I was sure that, if not for me, Hering would yet live.

As the sun rose, gleaming off the water as if it were polished gold, I helped wrap Hering in his blanket. Revna watched, dry-eyed now, her face drawn and sombre.

"What's that in his hand?" asked Gwawrddur.

I knew what was in his grasp, even as I stooped. I shivered at the waxy cool touch of his fingers, prying them apart to reveal the sea urchin shell he had cherished.

Hering had found the shell on a beach in Frankia when we moored one night. He had marvelled at the fragile sphere, covered in small bumps and raised lines. I remembered clearly the joyous awe in his voice as he turned the hollow round object in his hand.

"Looks like it was carved by a master craftsman," he'd said.

Eadstan had peered at the fragile orb the boy held.

"That's a serpent egg," he'd said. "It will keep you free from disease and injury if you keep it close. Very rare indeed."

Hering's eyes had widened.

"It was fashioned by the greatest craftsman of them all, young Hering," Giso had said. "But it is no serpent's egg. The bumps were where its spines were in life."

"Spines?"

"Like a hedgehog," he said. "Though the urchin has no head and no legs. The flesh is good eating. They are considered a delicacy. King Carolus is partial to them. He has the flesh prepared with eggs and also in a rich soup."

I remembered that Hering had been unsure whether Giso or Eadstan were speaking the truth. The older men of the crew would often jest at Hering's expense and none of us had ever seen the living creature to which Giso said the shell belonged. Eadstan's description seemed more likely to me. But Giso's face was serious and he did not seem prone to japes or ridiculing others. In the end, Hering chose to believe him.

"Wait till I show my father this," Hering had said, placing the shell carefully in his small wooden chest. I had thought he would break the thing long before we returned to Northumbria.

"I think Hering hoped Eadstan was right about its power," I said, placing the shell on Revna's palm. She closed her fingers around it.

"It was his time, Hunlaf," she said, her eyes bright and liquid in the dawn sun. "We will take it back to Heca and will tell him of how Hering found it."

I said nothing. I thought Heca would care nothing for the hollow shell, or the story of how his son had fished it out of a rock pool after slipping over on greasy seaweed. But in this, as with so many other things, Revna was proven to understand people better than I ever could. Even to this day, decades later and Heca long in his grave, I can remember his face as he listened intently to how his only son had found and then lost the shell. Somehow, the bauble brought him comfort and when he died, it was found close to his pallet, within easy reach. That urchin shell was buried along with the old ferryman.

Scurfa fetched cord and a bone needle and I held the blanket tight about Hering's stiffening body as he sewed him into his shroud. By the time he was done, the sun had climbed into the sky and the day was already warm. Beyond the docks the city had awoken and sounds of people shouting, laughing, going about their business, drifted to us. Smells too wafted across the docks. The scent of cooking meat and baking bread made my mouth water. Despite the sadness I felt at gazing down at Hering's enshrouded corpse, my stomach grumbled.

A shadow fell over me and I looked up to see Hereward, his face serious.

"Let us see if that bastard Nadir will allow us to lay Hering to rest." He squinted at the sun rising in the east. "The day will be hot and we cannot leave him here." He looked down at the wrapped form of the boy and sighed. "After that, mayhap we can eat. I feel as though my stomach is devouring me from the inside."

I felt a flash of anger.

"Hering's not yet cold and you talk of eating?"

"Easy, Hunlaf," Hereward said, holding up his hands in a placatory gesture. "We are all saddened by Hering's passing, but we still live. If we are able to find our way out of the predicament we are in, we will need our strength. I am no seer, but I imagine we will need to fight again before we are done with these Moors."

I took a long breath. He was right, of course. And I was hungry too, but I was ashamed to think of food while Hering's body lay on the deck at my feet.

"Ahmad," snapped Hereward, "tell Nadir we need to bury our friend." Ahmad looked perplexed, but before he could respond, Hereward continued. "Hunlaf, let's carry Hering onto the wharf. Ida, Pendrad, help us."

The two warriors hurried over and helped us to scoop up Hering's shrouded body. He was light, but somehow heavier than his skinny form should be. The weight of the dead, I thought. Drosten, Beorn and Eadstan clambered over *Brymsteda*'s side, ready to take Hering from us. The rest of the crew watched us in silence, their eyes hooded and grim as they faced the death of one of our own.

We passed Hering to the three men on the dock and climbed down to join them. Beorn, Eadstan and Drosten placed Hering's shrouded body gently onto the dock.

Nadir, hand resting on the ornate pommel of his sword,

swaggered towards us. With a disdainful curl of his lip, he looked down at the blanket-wrapped corpse.

"Your man here," he said, jerking his head towards Ahmad, "says you wish to bury one of your crew."

"Yes," I said. I wanted to say more; to spit at Nadir and scream that Hering might have lived if he had sent for a healer or sought the ingredients I'd asked for last night. Sensing my rising anger, Hereward placed a hand on my shoulder.

Nadir showed his teeth in a wide grin and I was certain he knew exactly what I was thinking.

"He was *Al-Muslimun* then, this man?" he said. "A true believer?"

I frowned.

"He was a good Christian."

Nadir held out his hands.

"Ah, then I am sorry." He gave an apologetic shrug. "If he was *kafir*, there is nothing I can do."

"*Kafir?*"

"One of the *kuffaar* who reject the words of the Prophet," explained Ahmad.

I could feel my anger simmering just below the surface, barely contained within me.

"But he must be buried," I said. "Before his body begins to corrupt."

"Yes, of course," replied Nadir, "but only *Al-Muslimun* may be buried in the graveyard. I am truly sorry," he went on, with unctuous insincerity. "But do not worry, there are *Ahl al-kitab* here too."

"People of the book?"

"It's what my people call Christ-followers and Iudeisc," said Ahmad.

"You will need to speak to *Ahl al-kitab* about burying your friend," said Nadir.

I took a deep breath, in an attempt to calm myself.

"Very well," I said, my words clipped. "Please direct us to the leader of the Christians, that I might petition him about this matter."

"I cannot do that," Nadir said. "I am very sorry." His tone said otherwise, as did the smirk that twitched the corners of his mouth. I dropped my hand to my hip, where my sword would normally be scabbarded. Nadir saw the gesture and his smile broadened.

I ground my teeth together, clenching my jaw furiously.

"Why can you not help us?" I asked, my growing anger evident in my strained tone.

"I have my orders, and they are to guard you here and see that none of you leaves the dock."

"Then send for one of the *Ahl al-kitab* of the city," I said, my tone as sharp and brittle as broken slate.

"It is not my place to speak to *Maseehi*, or the *Yahud*," he said.

I fixed him with a hard stare.

"You are talking to me."

"Ah, it is so," he said with a dismissive lift of his hands. "But I have orders to do so. My orders did not include sending for the *Maseehi* holy man or the *Yahud alhabr*. Now, I wouldn't leave your friend there in the sun." He sniffed the air, wrinkling his nose. "I think I can already smell him."

"Why, you nithing whoreson," I growled, stepping towards Nadir, fists raised. Hereward and Drosten pulled me back, their combined strength too much for me to overcome.

"This is what he wants," hissed Drosten. "He has been ordered to guard us. If you attack him, he can slay you." I struggled, trying to free myself, so that I might leap on Nadir and pummel the maddening smile from his bearded face.

"You are unarmed," snapped Hereward. "And outnumbered. You cannot prevail in this fight, Hunlaf. The bastard's words cannot hurt you and they certainly cause no harm to Hering.

Step back. Ignore him. And pray that God will give you a chance to kill the goat-swiving shit-stain one day."

With difficulty, I overcame my anger. Shaking off the hands that held me, I turned away from the grinning leader of the guards. I looked down at Hering again. I wondered if his eyes remained closed beneath the blanket. Or had they opened, staring into the dark? Was his spirit with the Lord or did it linger close by, looking upon us even now, judging me for my role in his death?

A harsh sound sliced into my dark thoughts. For a heartbeat I thought it might be the cackle of some sea bird perched on one of the timber jetties, or perhaps the barking of a dog. Then it came again and there could be no mistake. This was no beast, but the laughter of a man.

Spinning around, I saw Nadir, rocking back, his hands on his hips, guffawing loudly. It seemed he was no longer able to contain his mirth at our loss. A seething rage seared through me and I launched myself at him. Drosten and Hereward made a grab for me, but were too slow this time. I bellowed my fury at Nadir, channelling all of the pain and guilt within me into my incandescent hatred of the man. In that instant I cared nothing for my safety or even my life. All I wished was to silence the brute of a guard, permanently if possible.

The warriors to either side of him had a moment longer to react than my friends. They stepped forward, crossing their spears and blocking my path. I was brought up short, panting and raving like a rabid animal. This only served to make Nadir laugh all the harder.

Strong hands grabbed me, pulling me back from the Moorish guards. I snarled and spat, momentarily devoid of reason as the fire of my rage consumed my sense.

Hereward and Gwawrddur were both shouting at me, but I was not listening. Nadir laughed all the while and I wanted nothing more than to reach him so that I could make him pay for Hering's death. But strain and struggle as I might, I was unable to break free and my companions did not release me.

The fight was beginning to leave me, ebbing slowly away as if my anger was seeping from a cracked pot. But still my friends held onto me, fearing that I would once again throw myself at the taunting leader of the guards. I considered it, but the moment was gone, and my sanity had returned. The intensity of my anger had shocked me. I accepted that I revelled in the abandon of combat, but my actions were such that I might well place my friends, my shield-brothers, in danger. I could not stand the thought of bearing the burden of more deaths upon my shoulders.

The clatter of horses' hooves echoing from the stones of the buildings around the docks made me pause. Looking beyond Nadir and his score of warriors, I saw two riders cantering along the cobbled docks. They wore brightly coloured robes of silk, cloaks streaming behind them. The morning sun gleamed from gold and silver on their belts and on their horses' bridles. Their steeds, one black and one white, were tall and long-legged, bred for speed and agility, rather than pulling a plough or waggon. Both men wore what appeared to be a large silken hat atop their heads.

At the sound of their approach everyone turned to stare. The riders brought their mounts to a skidding halt a dozen paces from the cluster of men near *Brymsteda*.

The horseman on the white horse leapt from his saddle, hitting the ground lightly and throwing his reins to his companion. Whatever sound his soft leather boots made on the cobbles was hidden by the crack of the horses' hooves on the stones. He was a tall man of slender build. His face was bearded, his cheeks angular and high. His features could have been described as noble, had it not been for the crookedness of his hawk-like nose. It appeared to have been broken in some long-ago fight, and it now gave him a roguish aspect, where once he might have been handsome.

"What is the meaning of this, Nadir?" he said.

The reaction in the brutish commander of the guard was instantaneous. His laughter ceased immediately, and all indication of a smile vanished from his face. Standing rigidly straight, he barked at his men, who brought themselves to attention with a shuffling crash as they first snapped their feet together and then hammered the butts of their spears into the cobbles.

"We were just discussing what might be done with one of the *kuffaar*," Nadir said, no trace of amusement on his face now. He glanced at Hering's shrouded body. "He died in the night."

The newcomer took in the scene quickly, his dark, intelligent eyes darting from *Brymsteda*'s crew and Hering's corpse, to Nadir and his men.

"A non-believer, you say?"

"Yes, sir," replied Nadir. "*Kafir*, sir."

"Send one of your men to Julian forthwith," the rider said.

Nadir hesitated for the briefest of moments before nodding.

"Right away, sir." He clicked his fingers and pointed to one of his men. "You heard the man. Bring Julian here as soon as possible."

The guard did not hesitate. Without a word, he ran off in the direction the riders had come from.

The dismounted horseman turned away from Nadir, dismissing him without a further word. I saw Nadir's face crinkle in anger at the casual rebuff, but the rider either did not notice, or ignored the man's displeasure.

As if looking for something in particular, or rather someone, he scanned the faces of the crew until at last his gaze settled on Ahmad.

"Ahmad ibn Ibrahim," said the rider, stepping forward. "Is it really you? I thought you dead."

The man's smooth demeanour slipped then. His eyes welled with tears and his voice cracked with emotion. The two men stared at each other for a couple of heartbeats, then, to everyone's surprise, they rushed together and embraced.

Eleven

The horseman, now seated on *Brymsteda*'s deck, tore off a piece of warm flat bread and dipped it into a pale paste. The creamy substance appeared to be made from some sort of ground-up vegetable, though neither Ahmad nor his old friend, whom he had introduced as Tayyib, had been able to explain to me exactly what it was. The closest Ahmad had been able to describe it was a sort of pea. The paste tasted nothing like any pea I had eaten before. It was smooth and oily and coated the mouth with a salty creaminess. The bread too was wonderful, crusty and firm on the outside, but soft, airy and warm on the inside. It was the perfect vehicle to lift the paste from earthenware bowl to mouth, and down the length of the ship all of the crew was ravenously consuming the great pile of loaves Tayyib had ordered Nadir to have brought to the docks.

Tayyib was evidently a man of some substance in Qadis and Nadir did not argue with him. The guards he had sent for food returned shortly after with the heap of flat loaves and bowls of the delicious paste. They'd also carried sweet dates, bitter olives, balls of lamb meat in a rich sauce and a slab of goat's milk cheese. Until then we had been resigned to eating more of the smoked mackerel and hard double-baked bread we carried aboard, sure that Nadir would offer us no help in that regard. Despite the sadness we all still felt at the loss of Hering, and the residual anger that hung over us following Nadir's treatment, there could be no denying that Tayyib's arrival had seen a lifting of our mood.

After their warm greeting, Tayyib had pushed Ahmad to arm's length and looked him up and down. I saw Ahmad then as Tayyib must see him. Where Tayyib's beard was oiled and trimmed, Ahmad's was unruly. Instead of silken robes and soft leather boots, Ahmad wore a plain woollen kirtle and breeches, stained with the salt of sweat and surf. On Ahmad's feet were the simplest of leather shoes, wrapped and laced with hide thongs.

Whatever he thought of Ahmad's clothing, seeing him clearly brought Tayyib joy. His grin was genuine and after he had snapped his orders for refreshments at Nadir, he had led Ahmad to *Brymsteda*.

Despite their obvious connection, they had maintained a formal aloofness until the food and drink arrived. Ahmad had shown Tayyib around the longship, and introduced him to the crew.

"And who is this perfumed lad?" Runolf had asked. "I have seldom seen such fine clothes. If it were not for the beard, I would think him a lady."

Ahmad had frowned.

"This is my old friend, Tayyib ibn al-Kammad, and I can assure you, he is stronger than you might think."

Runolf chuckled.

"Well, I suppose he did not break that fine nose of his spinning yarn."

Ahmad chose not to translate the Norseman's words to his friend.

"This is Runolf Ragnarsson," he said. "He built this ship."

Tayyib nodded appreciatively. Runolf grinned.

"The ship is like nothing I have seen before," Tayyib said.

"His stink is like nothing you have smelt before too," replied Ahmad with an easy smile. "When he has eaten pottage with beans and peas, he produces enough wind from his arse to fill the sail."

Tayyib looked shocked.

"Do not concern yourself," Ahmad said. "Runolf cannot speak our tongue. None of the crew can, save Hunlaf here, and Giso, the small man beside the mast."

"What did he say?" asked Runolf, knowing they were speaking about him.

"He said you are a master of your craft," Ahmad replied. "One of a kind." Then he directed Tayyib further down the deck where Drosten, Gwawrddur and Hereward awaited to be introduced.

Runolf beamed, pleased of the praise. Then, perhaps noticing my smile and sensing he might be the object of jest, he tugged at my sleeve.

"What did Ahmad say about me to his friend?"

"He said you are as skilled a sailor as you are a shipwright," I replied.

Now, Ahmad and Tayyib sat in the shade of the sailcloth that had been rigged at *Brymsteda*'s stern. Nadir had protested as Scurfa and Mantat had made their way onto the pirate ship to fetch the cloth, but Tayyib had called out to the guard, telling him to let them pass.

Brymsteda's crew were now scattered along the length of the deck, with a few sitting on the dock, contentedly consuming the provender Tayyib had ordered for them. But I had perched myself at the edge of the shade and now ate quietly in the hope they would forget my presence and talk freely. I noted that Giso, who had bowed courteously to Tayyib when introduced, also sat nearby, nibbling a loaf and sipping a cup of the cool syrupy drink the guards had brought along with the food. Also underneath the shade of the sail sat Tayyib's companion. He had introduced him as Sayf ad-Din. A few years younger than Tayyib and Ahmad, Sayf spoke little and ate sparingly. His eyes were inquisitive and I could see from his posture, the way he held his head that he was just as interested as Giso and I to hear what the two old friends had to say to each other after all these years.

Tayyib and Ahmad spoke rapidly and it was all I could do to understand them. Glancing over at Giso, I wondered if he was also struggling to pick out every word of their chatter. I doubted it. The man seemed constantly at ease and I was sure his grasp of al-Arabiyyah was better than mine. I would have to ask him how it was he could speak the language of al-Andalus so well, but now was not the moment. Now all I could do was concentrate and pick out as much as possible of what the two friends talked about. I will not deny I was fascinated to hear anything that would give me more insight into Ahmad's life. I had known him for years, but he had told me very little of his existence before finding himself in Northumbria, leaving me to chew on whatever morsels I managed to glean from our conversations and al-Arabiyyah lessons.

"I didn't believe al-Haidar," Tayyib said, swallowing the mouthful of bread he had dipped into the delightful paste. "When he told me you had returned, I accused him of lying."

"He does not strike me as a man much used to lying," replied Ahmad.

"That is just what he said." Tayyib grinned. "He was not pleased with the accusation."

"But how did he recognise me? I don't believe I have met the man before."

"You gave your name," said Tayyib. "I have spoken of you. I told him how you had sailed away and never returned." He shook his head. "I believed you dead, but when he heard your name, he thought it might be you. For there are not great numbers of our people, bearing the name Ahmad, who arrive on these shores aboard a ship manned by *kuffaar* from the north." He sighed, taking a long look at Ahmad. "Still I did not believe him until I saw you with my own eyes. I thought you dead all these years." His voice cracked and he took a drink from the cup that rested beside him.

"There were times I wished I was," Ahmad said.

On hearing the words I felt the sting of regret. I was not Ahmad's master, but I felt sorrow for the time lost to being a thrall to this educated man. But whether learned or a fool, what gives the right for one man to own another? I have often contemplated this question through the years, and I have never found a better answer than "it is the way of things" or "it is God's design". I am not so sure.

"Some days I held on to the hope you might still live," Tayyib said. "Even then, I never thought you would return."

Ahmad looked surprised by this revelation.

"Of course I would have come back, if I had been able."

Tayyib shook his head, as if he could not quite comprehend what was occurring.

"What happened to you?" he asked, placing a hand on Ahmad's arm.

Ahmad held his friend's gaze, then sighed. One of the guards on the wharf laughed, the sound hiding several of Ahmad's words.

"... into the sea," he finished.

Both men had lowered their voices now and I leaned forward, straining to hear. Ahmad's tone was flat and distant-sounding as he looked back through the haze of the years to a past he did not like to visit.

"Everyone?" asked Tayyib.

Ahmad nodded sombrely.

"Most were slain there on the deck. Of those who went over the side, only half a dozen of us made it to the beach."

"There were those who said you had made your fortune and had fled with the silver you had amassed. I told them you must be dead or you would return. It sounds as if you were lucky to live."

Ahmad scowled.

"I do not believe it was luck."

"By luck, or the grace of Allah. However you survived, I never thought I would see you again."

"Nor I you." Ahmad reached out and fingered the fine silk of Tayyib's robe. "I am glad to see you have prospered. I had worried about your lot since I left."

Tayyib pulled away, his face clouding.

"What of you?" he asked. "You say the ship was attacked off the coast of Septimania and yet you come from the islands to the north-west, not from the east and the Roman Sea."

Ahmad watched as a small fishing boat rowed past. It had nets heaped high in its belly. The six sailors who were rowing, gazed up in awe at *Brymsteda* and the strange men who manned the Norse ship.

"That is a tale I do not like to tell."

"I think you owe me that story," said Tayyib. He was serious now, gone was the warmth of their meeting. It had been replaced by a calculated coolness and I wondered about the history that bound these two together.

Ahmad suppressed a shudder, as if he felt cold all of a sudden. With a sigh, he nodded.

"I came ashore with a few of the sailors. We had managed to cling to a wooden beam that Allah had sent to us. But no sooner had we reached land than we were attacked. A couple of the crew were killed. The rest of us were beaten. Then we were enslaved..."

Tayyib's face was grave as he listened.

"You have been a slave all these years?" He sounded disbelieving.

"I have." Ahmad looked out at where the fisher boat had reached the sea. Gulls swooped down, shrieking hungrily in its wake, as if they recognised the vessel. Ahmad took up his cup and drank. "Mine is a shameful existence," he said, his voice so quiet I could barely make it out.

"There is no shame in what you cannot change," said Tayyib.

"I have had three masters," replied Ahmad. "As I tell you I have been a slave all this time, I sense your judgement."

A sad, thin smile played on Tayyib's lips.

"It is not for being enslaved that you will be judged. Who is your master now? That giant Runolf?"

Ahmad shook his head and smiled.

"No, my master is far away, in the land of the Englisc, in a kingdom called Northumbria. That is my master's son." He pointed over to where Gersine sat eating with Revna and Alf in the midships. "But I will be free soon enough, Tayyib. I will be able to make good my mistakes." He sounded eager. "Hunlaf here has promised me my freedom."

They both turned to me. I swigged at my sweet drink, swallowing the bread I had been chewing.

"If you are not Ahmad's master," Tayyib asked, "how can you make such a pledge?" His eyes were as piercing as a hawk's and I felt like a fieldmouse under his gaze.

"That is not your concern," I said, my voice firm with a certainty I did not feel. "But my word is good. I will settle whatever debt there is with his master. Ahmad will be free, when he has fulfilled his promise to me."

Tayyib's eyes narrowed. He opened his mouth to reply, but before he could speak, Ahmad blurted out, "What tidings of my father?"

Frowning, Tayyib looked from me to Ahmad. He drew in a deep breath, then sighed before answering.

"He is not well."

"But he yet lives?" Ahmad's voice was tinged with a desperate hope.

"He lived when last I visited Malaqah. But the years have not treated him well."

"Do you think he will wish to see me?"

Again the guard on the dock laughed, his voice loud and booming, muffling the quiet sound of Ahmad and Tayyib's voices. I wondered if I had understood correctly, for what father would not wish to see his son after believing him dead for ten years. I thought of my own father back in Ubbanford. I had never been his favourite son, but even he would have been glad to know I lived after so many years.

"I am sure he will be overjoyed to see you hale," said Tayyib, reinforcing my own thoughts. "But you must understand, Ahmad..." He bit his lip nervously.

"I understand that there is much to speak about, and I must make amends."

"It is not so simple," replied Tayyib, a sharpness entering his tone. "Your actions ruined him." He hesitated, biting his lip again. "And many others too."

"I have had ten years to think of what I did," said Ahmad earnestly. "I am pleased to hear that my father lives. I would ask him to forgive my youthful stupidity."

"Is that all it was then?" snapped Tayyib, anger colouring his tone. "The foolhardiness of youth?"

"I cannot take back what I did," said Ahmad, his voice thick. I had never witnessed him so emotional before and I wondered at the past that connected these two. What had Ahmad done?

"No," said Tayyib, sadly. "You cannot undo the last ten years. But it was not just you or your father who paid the price for your rashness."

"I will do all I can to make it up to you, Tayyib," said Ahmad. "You have my solemn vow."

Tayyib held his gaze for a long time.

"I never thought to see you again. I was angry with you for so long." He scratched at his beard, smoothing his moustache with his fingertips. "I thought I had forgiven you years ago, but seeing you now..." His voice trailed off. There were tears in his eyes. "There are others who have been wronged because of what you did."

Ahmad looked as if he had been punched in the stomach. He leaned forward, avoiding Tayyib's stare. Tayyib flicked his gaze to me. There was a fire in his eyes now. The day was already hot and I felt sweat trickle down the nape of my neck. My kirtle was itchy against my skin and I longed to scratch, but did not wish to show any sign of weakness.

"What is the promise you spoke of?" Tayyib asked. When I did not answer immediately, he went on. "You said you would free Ahmad when he had fulfilled his promise to you. What is that promise?"

Ahmad shifted uncomfortably.

"He has promised to introduce me to Al-Zarqālluh. I have travelled a long way to speak to him."

Tayyib's brow furrowed.

"Al-Zarqālluh?" he asked.

"Yes. Abu Jafar Yusuf ibn Sa'īd al-Zarqālluh. I believe he resides in Išbīliya."

Tayyib began to laugh then, the sound jarring and harsh after the quiet conversation the two men had shared under the shade of the sailcloth. When he was able to speak again, he said, "He has a residence there, it is true." He wiped his eyes. "But Ahmad is not the man to open Al-Zarqālluh's door to you." Tayyib shook his head. "May Allah take your soul, Ahmad, you have changed nothing in all these years. Still promising what you cannot deliver." Tayyib stood abruptly. Sayf ad-Din placed his cup on the deck and rose too.

"Perhaps you will not need to free Ahmad after all," Tayyib said to me. My confusion must have been clear on my face, for he continued. "This man has lied to you. As he lied to his father years ago. He has promised what he cannot give. Do not let his delusions ruin you as they have so many others before you."

Ahmad said nothing. His face was dark. Whether from shame or fury, I could not tell. My mind was in turmoil. Could it be that I had travelled all this way for nothing?

Tayyib strode to the side of the ship. Without pausing, he placed a hand on the wale and swung his legs athletically over the side, landing gracefully on the dock. Sayf followed a pace behind.

"The horses," said Tayyib, his tone brusque.

Sayf hurried to fetch the animals from where they had been tethered in the shade of a nearby warehouse.

I climbed over *Brymsteda*'s side. Ahmad was close behind me. I could feel the eyes of the crew and the guards following our movements. Tayyib's change of demeanour had been instant and unexpected, but now he moved with alacrity, as if he had no more time to waste at the docks.

"Can you send word to my father?" asked Ahmad.

Sayf brought the horses, their hooves loud on the stone dock. Effortlessly, Tayyib swung into his saddle. His white horse skittered nervously, apparently as ready as its rider to be gone from this place.

"Tayyib, please," said Ahmad, his tone pleading. "I am his blood. That must count for something."

Tayyib pulled his steed's head around, sawing at the reins savagely.

"I will send word to the old man that his son lives," he said. "But it is not for you I do this thing, but for him."

With that, he kicked his heels into the horse's flanks, sending the beast into a cantering lope that carried them quickly along the docks and into the winding streets of Qadis.

A low whistle came from close by. Giso had quietly joined me on the wharf.

"Not quite the welcome we'd hoped for," he said, a curious expression twisting his features as we both stared after the two riders.

Twelve

"More?" asked Hereward, as I held out my cup to be refilled. "We don't have barrels of the stuff, you know, and we're all thirsty."

I didn't answer, but neither did I lower my cup. After a moment Runolf took up the skin and poured me more wine.

"Leave him be," he said, winking at me. "Hunlaf needs a drink stronger than water after what he's learnt today."

The wineskin was large and still heavy with liquid, but it sloshed noisily now that it was only half full. Hereward had purchased it, along with some fresh green-gold pilchards, from a small boat that had pulled alongside *Brymsteda* as the sun began to sink into the west.

Hereward grunted and proffered his own cup for more wine.

"Just don't drink too much," he said, sipping his wine. "Who knows when we might need to move in a hurry? I fear we have made a mistake coming here. Perhaps we should head north." He took another mouthful. "When we are able to leave."

"If we are allowed to leave, you mean," grumbled Drosten.

Hereward scowled, but nodded.

"Aye, if the lord of this place permits us to take our leave."

"What about the money that King Carolus promised us on

our return?" asked Gersine. He was different from his father in many ways, but had inherited Mancas' good sense when it came to matters of wealth and he did not like to turn his back on a profit.

"I am not sure any amount of silver will be worth us staying," said Hereward. "We have no friends here. The price we have paid for coming to this shore is already high, and I doubt the plunder we took from the pirates will be returned to us." He scanned the faces of the crew. After the wine and food had been lifted from the small skiff and placed on the deck, we had all come to sit together, to eat, drink and to morosely pick over the remaining fragments of our plans.

The only one of our number who sat apart was Ahmad. He was slumped dejectedly at the stern, beneath the sailcloth, though it no longer gave any shade as the sun had swung around the great dome of the sky and now shimmered low in the west. Long shadows stretched out from the warehouses around the docks. The towers to the west were stark against the hot bright glow of the setting sun. Ahmad had no desire to speak to us, and nobody seemed inclined to converse with him. I couldn't blame them. I had been furious at first at what I had learnt. Now, I felt a dark emptiness that I knew I could not hope to fill. I had learnt there were few things that could distract me from such a black humour.

I glanced at Revna. Her cheeks were flushed from the heat of the dying day, her hair gleaming in the flames of the sunset. She looked back at me and smiled, but there was no passion there. No invitation to share her blankets as I would have liked. Such a coupling would have allowed my mind to drift from the pressure of the concerns that assailed it, but no matter how much I yearned for her, that was not going to happen.

Of course, I thought, in the unlikely event that Revna should deign to bed me, I would quickly have another means of distraction when Runolf found out and pummelled me senseless. A good fight would no doubt serve to pull my mind away from dark thoughts, but I did not wish to test myself against the huge Norseman. Besides, he was my friend and I was certain he would not take kindly to any advance I might make towards his daughter.

No, I would have to rely on the wine to dull the sharp edges of the thoughts that scratched inside my head. I returned Revna's smile, looking away and drinking some more wine.

I had changed the bandage on her shoulder that afternoon and was pleased with the look of the wound. It was still clean and healing well, with no sign of corruption. This was the only good thing to happen that long hot day.

The wine was good and sweet, but the taste soured on my tongue as I glimpsed the blanket-swaddled corpse that lay in the shadows of *Brymsteda*'s prow. By God, Hering had paid the highest price for the spoils we had taken. And for what?

I will not allow your death to be in vain, I prayed silently, wondering if somehow he might hear my voice from the afterlife. The hollow feeling within me grew. It felt like a great deep well, black and impenetrable; a hole pulling all hope from my mind to be lost in its dark depths.

Hering's blood was on my hands. I could not permit his death to be for nought. I must find a way to achieve the ends we had set out to accomplish. The alternative was unthinkable.

The wind shifted into the west and the light breeze blew down the length of the deck, bringing with it the faint smell of Hering's decomposing body.

Gwawrddur had been reaching for one of the small fish that had been roasted over the coals of a fire, but he halted before taking one, allowing himself to settle back with a grimace.

"What shall we do if we have no word from the wazir tomorrow?" he said, wrinkling his nose, but making no mention of the unmistakable scent of death that lingered over the ship.

"I thought Giso was an emissary from the king of the Franks," said Beorn. "I know there is no love lost between the two kingdoms, but does he have no sway here as a royal envoy?"

"He is a messenger from Alhwin," I corrected.

"But does that count for nothing?" asked Beorn. "Can he not ask to speak with the lord of Qadis? At least then they might let us ashore so we can sleep in a bed."

"And sample some of the local delicacies," said Pendrad, grinning.

"We all know what kind of delights you wish to partake of," Beorn said. "The lasses of al-Andalus had best beware with the likes of you and Hunlaf sniffing around."

I flicked a look at Revna, my face flushing. Pendrad enjoyed the company of women as much as any man of our band and I had accompanied him to brothels in Eoforwic, Quentovic and even one memorable tumbledown shack in the woods near the palace of Aachen. I had made no secret of these visits, but now I felt ashamed at what Revna might think of me.

"Eat your fill of the food," said Hereward, "and drink this fine wine. But there is to be no ploughing in the local fields. Do you understand me?"

Pendrad and a couple of the other men groaned. Revna rolled her eyes and sighed.

"Where is Giso anyway?" said Gwawrddur. "I have not seen him for some time."

"Probably taking a shit," said Runolf. "That stuff Ahmad's friend gave us to eat tasted good, but it has gone right through me." As if to accentuate his point, he leaned to the side and let out a loud fart. The men around him complained, waving their hands before their faces, and crying out in dismay. I was glad to be sitting upwind.

"By Christ's bones, man," said Drosten, standing up and moving away. His grimace twisted his tattooed face into a monstrous mask. "From that stink I would say perhaps Ahmad's friend has poisoned us all. You smell dead inside."

The men chuckled. Ahmad raised his head on hearing his name, but there was no smile on his lips.

The encounter with Tayyib had left him sullen and withdrawn. I thought of our conversation that afternoon and felt my anger bubbling up inside me again, unsure if my fury was better than the cavernous emptiness. I took another swig of the wine, but it did nothing to dampen my ire or to soften the memory of our talk.

When I had first approached him, Ahmad had refused to speak.

"I know you are angry," I'd said, lowering myself down into the shade beside him. Ahmad made no move to respond and for a long while we sat in silence. He stared over the wale at the sea where the small fishing boat we had seen was now far out in the bay, casting its nets. White specks dotted the air and sea around it, but it was too far away for us to hear the cries of the sea birds that dived for the fish around the vessel.

Time passed and I felt my rage building. My stomach squirmed and I clenched my fists.

"If you are angry," I said at last, "imagine my fury." I tried to keep my tone even, but I could hear the jaggedness of my words.

"I am not angry," he replied. His voice was as dry and desolate as a desert.

"You are not? You see your friend after ten years and he wants nothing to do with you. This does not anger you?"

Ahmad stared out at the fishermen.

"Tayyib is right to hate me."

I thought he was going to say more, but he fell silent once again.

"And what about me?" I asked. "Should I hate you?"

"Do what you wish," he said.

"Was Tayyib speaking the truth about you?"

"He did not lie."

"But you did," I said, making a fist and longing to lash out, to strike his bearded face. "You told me you could gain access to Al-Zarqālluh. By Christ's thorny crown," I spat, "you said the same to Alhwin!"

"I said what you needed to hear."

I thought on that for a while, my anger slowly seeping away. Ahmad had been a thrall for years. The discovery of the scrap of paper in Ljósberari's hall naming Al-Zarqālluh as the owner of *The Treasure of Life* presented Ahmad with a unique opportunity. When asked by Alhwin about his claims, how could he refute them without dashing his chances of returning to his homeland? What would I have done, I asked myself, if I had been in the same situation?

"But why did you want to come here," I said, "when you knew that your friends," I thought of what Tayyib had said, "perhaps even your family, would not wish to see you?"

He turned to face me and I saw then the pride I knew so well in his glare.

"I would be free," he snarled. "No longer a slave. I would rather be hated as a free man, than to be despised as a thrall."

I thought of the long evenings when he had sat with me, teaching me the language of his people.

"You were not despised."

He scoffed at that.

"I was certainly not your friend," he said.

His words stabbed at me, and I realised with a start that he had hurt me with that comment. Had I believed we were friends? Had I treated him as a friend would?

"What did you do, Ahmad?" I asked, pushing aside my feelings and forcing my voice to remain steady.

He turned away, looking out to sea again.

"I do not wish to speak of it."

"I know," I replied. "But you owe it to me. Whether you think me a friend or not, I used your words to convince them," I glanced back at where the crew lounged on the deck, "to travel here. Now we are prisoners, and I would know what manner of man you are and how much worse things might get for us because we are travelling with you."

He rubbed a hand over his beard and sighed.

"Very well," he said. "I will tell you my tale. Or at least as much of it as you need to hear." He lifted the cup of syrup-flavoured water and took a sip. I said nothing, waiting for him to recount his story.

"I led you to believe I was from a noble family," he said. "But the truth is that while we were not poor, and I was educated in the Madrasa of Al-Zarqālluh in Išbīliya for a time, I was born the son of a merchant. My father made his fortune trading in olive oil. We lived in a comfortable house, with a small garden that smelt of orange blossom in the spring and droned with the sound of bees." He sighed. "It is amazing to me now that I believed such a house unworthy. It was stone-built, cool in the summer and warm in the winter and with slaves to tend to my every need. And yet I wanted more." He shook his head at the folly of his youth. "Perhaps it is the way of those who are given too much. My father had come from the humblest of beginnings, and he wanted me to have everything he had not possessed. He had accrued enough silver to send me to Išbīliya to study and it was there where I met Tayyib. We became friends immediately. It was when I was first invited to his family's palace that I began to feel that my upbringing was inadequate. If I was going to be able to remain friends with Tayyib, I needed to improve my family's prospects. His father, you see, was one of the emir's most trusted confidants. Tayyib comes from a noble family who can trace their line all the way back to Al-Ṣaḥāba, the companions of the Prophet. And what was I? The only son of a mediocre oil merchant.

"After spending time with Tayyib and the other nobles in Išbīliya and Qurtuba, I found my father's house small and provincial." He laughed bitterly at the thought. "Little did I know that I would one day be the slave to a pig herder in Frankia, where I would be forced to sleep in the sty with the hogs. Nor that I would spend a decade amongst infidels whose greatest halls were little more than shacks made of wood with rushes on the floor. I returned home with my head filled with visions of wealth and greatness and plans for how to raise up my family's status."

I had never heard Ahmad speak so much, but it was as if the dam of his voice had been broken and now the words tumbled out.

"My father had always been a cautious man, only investing into his business what he could afford. In that way he had grown prosperous, but he would never become rich. I urged him to be more adventurous, to borrow money so that we could accumulate wealth more quickly. He refused, saying that there were more important things than gold and silver. Besides, he reminded me that Allah has permitted trade but forbidden *riba*."

"*Riba?*" I asked.

Ahmad thought of how best to answer.

"Money charged on a debt." Ahmad shook his head at his memories. "Of course, I cared nothing for that." Up to this point he had been speaking in Englisc, but now he shifted into his native al-Arabiyyah. I made no comment on this, keen not to interrupt his tale.

"I was young," he went on, "and had set my mind on riches, so I pressed ahead with a plan that I was sure would bring us great rewards. It mattered nothing to me that there were also great risks. I was certain it would all work perfectly and I would return with coffers full of silver. My father would forgive me, and we would reign over a merchant empire rivalled by none."

I thought of my own naive belief that this ill-fated quest for *The Treasure of Life* might bring me peace, and at the same time fill our sea chests with silver. Was I as foolish a youth as Ahmad had been?

He took another sip of his drink, then barked a strangled sounding laugh.

"What a fool I was! Allah is great, but he does not love a prideful man." He looked me in the eye then, his mouth curled in a sad smile. "We all learn that the hard way, do we not?" I thought of Hering wrapped in his cloak. My pride had caused much suffering in my short life.

Ahmad gave me a thin, mirthless smile. I did not need to speak for him to know my thoughts.

"I sometimes wish I was that young and sure of myself once more," he said. "But then I remember what I did and how my life was ruined. Then all I want to do is to make amends to those I hurt. I wish to ask for their forgiveness and to spend the rest of my days building back whatever trust they might again find to give me."

He stared out over the sun-glinted waves, but his eyes no longer saw the fishing boat or the wheeling and diving gulls and gannets. He was staring far back through the fog of time. He was silent for a long while.

"How did you betray your father and Tayyib?" I prodded, keeping my voice low.

He did not turn to face me, but I saw his shoulders tense as he girded himself for the rest of his tale.

"Through a friend I learnt of a trader in Byzantion who would sell silk for a fraction of the normal price in exchange for leather goods and glass ornaments that are prized in the east. So I hatched a plan to fill a ship with these things and sail to Byzantion myself. My father denied my request of borrowing money to finance the expedition, but he possessed a ship. I was sure my plan was a good one, so I devised a scheme to load the ship at night in secret and sail on the midnight tide before my father would know what was happening. Of course, I was my father's son, so it was a simple matter to gain access to the moored ship. The crew were used to seeing me and were not suspicious. All I needed to do was to bribe the ship's captain, so that he would go along with my plan. I gave him some silver and offered a portion of the proceeds from the expedition. There was only one problem."

I suspected there were many more problems, but said nothing about that.

"You needed gold," I said.

He nodded.

"I needed gold to buy the trade goods. More gold than even my greedy mind had ever imagined. The thought of so much wealth was like a dream, and when I saw the leather sacks, filled with so much of the coin that they needed two men to carry each one, it made my stomach churn. But then I thought of how much more gold I would make from the sale of the silks, and I pictured my father's face when I returned with dozens of sacks of coins."

"Where did you get the gold?" I asked, sensing this was at the crux of Tayyib's anger with Ahmad.

Ahmad cleared his throat, then took a sip of his drink.

"This is the part of the story I am most ashamed of. There are men in al-Andalus who will lend money, but these *Yahud* would not give me so much. They were too afraid of what might happen to them. They are tolerated and the *Fuqaha* turn a blind eye to loans that help a farmer buy seeds, or that aid a landowner to build a wall, a bridge, or a new house. But such a huge quantity as I was asking for could not be ignored. If found out, the *Yahud* moneylenders might be exiled, or worse, for breaking the *fiqh*. The holy law," he explained, seeing my furrowed brow as I tried to keep up with him.

"But even if they had dared to lend me the sum I sought," he said, "the *Yahud* would not have wished to take such a risk. I could see no way forward. The men who were selling me the leather and blown glass were growing restless and were threatening to sell off their goods piecemeal as they had always done. It was then that Tayyib told me he knew how to contact Aljany."

"Aljany?" I asked. I had never heard the word before.

"The *jinn*." Ahmad thought for a moment. "The demon," he said in Englisc. "Or the ghost. It is the name given to a powerful man who is said to control much of the crime in al-Andalus. There are many rumours about Aljany. That he lives in catacombs beneath Qurtuba, or in a fortress hidden in the mountains, or a cave on the coast. It is said that whenever a crime is committed in al-Andalus, a portion of the money finds its way back to Aljany. I had thought Aljany was a story made up for children, but Tayyib was deadly serious. One of his father's men would be able to put me in touch with Aljany. I knew that if any of the stories were true, Aljany might be willing to lend me the money. He was rich enough by all accounts, and he did not fear the *fiqh*."

"Was he a ghost, this Aljany?" I asked. "Or a man like any other?"

"I am sure he is a man, but I cannot tell you anything of him as I never once saw him. We dealt through intermediaries, hooded men late at night in the *souk*, the market. But whoever he is, he did provide me with the gold I needed."

My eyes narrowed, thinking of the huge quantities of the precious metal Ahmad had described.

"What was his price for such wealth?" I asked.

The day was hot, even in the shade of the sailcloth, but I saw Ahmad shiver.

"I had eight months to pay back the gold twofold."

"And if you did not?"

"The *riba* I owed would rise each month that passed after that. But that is not the worst of it."

"No?" I thought of how much he must now owe this shadow man he had never met. It sounded bad enough to me.

"As there was a chance I might not return, Aljany had Tayyib vouch for me. By not returning, my debts became Tayyib's."

So here it was. This explained Tayyib's reaction.

"He seemed to be doing well for himself," I said, thinking of his silk robes and fine, prancing horse.

"Appearances can deceive," said Ahmad. "Aljany is not a man to let such a debt pass unpaid. I can only imagine what Tayyib's life has been like since I left. Even his family could not hope to accumulate such wealth. Aljany must own him."

"If Aljany is as bad as you say, perhaps you should be giving thanks that Tayyib yet lives."

"There are some things worse than death," Ahmad said. "Besides, a dead man is of no value to anyone."

"Did I hear you tell Tayyib that your ship was attacked?"

"Pirates," Ahmad said. "They came at us in three fast boats soon after dawn. The men were brave, but we were outnumbered and the pirates were brutal. Imagine yesterday's fight, but my crew fared as well as the sailors on the other ship, and the pirates who attacked us fought like the men of *Brymsteda*."

I grimaced. The memories were still fresh and sharp. The screams, the clash of blades, the blood sluicing over the deck.

"We didn't stand a chance," he said. "They murdered all those who stood before them. The rest leapt into the sea, or were cast overboard. I don't remember how it happened, but I ended up in the water. I thought I would drown then. I can swim, but we were out of sight of land and I had been injured. My strength was waning. Several of the men around me succumbed to the water, disappearing beneath the waves, but Allah did not wish for me to have such an easy end. Just as

I thought I could swim no more, I saw a timber floating in the surf. Whether it had been part of an ill-fated ship, wrecked in a storm, I do not know, but that beam saved my life and that of five other men who managed to reach it. Together we paddled towards the west, hoping to find land."

He paused then and drained his cup.

"You know the rest of my story. I was enslaved in Frankia. When my first owner fell on hard times he sold me." His words were clipped, his jaw clenched as he raked over the coals of his memories. "After a few months I was sold again. Eventually, I ended up in the market at Eoforwic where Gersine's mother decided she needed a new thrall."

Around me the men were talking loudly, pulling me back to the present. The volume of their voices had risen as the wine worked its way into their blood. I could feel the warmth of the drink in my belly. It had gone some way to masking the sensation of emptiness and guilt I felt, but thinking back on the conversation with Ahmad had rekindled my anger. My ire had subsided for a time, washed away beneath the waves of his story. I had so often asked Ahmad about his past, and he had never ventured more than snippets. I had always assumed it was too painful for him, that he was a proud man from a noble family and he hated to look back at what his life had once been. But now I knew the truth of it. His downfall had been his own doing, caused by his youthful hubris and arrogance. I would have been able to forgive that. I was young myself and had made my own share of costly mistakes, but to discover that Ahmad had lied to me over and again, filled me with a simmering rage.

His lies had led us here and now it seemed I would never get the promised audience with Al-Zarqālluh. *The Treasure of Life* was no closer to my possession and I was beginning to resign myself to the thought that I would never see it again, and never be able to unravel its mysteries.

Perhaps Giso would be able to help in that regard, I mused. As Beorn had said, he was an envoy from the Frankish court. But if the small Frank had any idea of how to see us out of the predicament we found ourselves in, he had kept very quiet about it.

Eadstan laughed at something Beorn had said, and I looked up from my cup. The crew's mood had certainly lifted since the arrival of the wine, and, despite my conflicted feelings, I found myself smiling as I listened to the riddle Sygbald was telling. He was not as good at riddling as Hereward, but he made up for it with his exaggerated bawdy gestures and raucous delivery. Now he was exaggeratedly miming a man taking his pleasure from a woman, twisting his face into contortions of ecstasy and delight, panting and rolling his eyes. Everyone laughed.

The sun had dipped behind the towers and turrets of Qadis' walls now, sending the whole of the channel, with its wharfs, timber jetties and jostling boats, into shadow. It would be dark soon and I wondered what the morning would bring.

I looked about me at the crew and something caught my attention, or rather the absence of something.

Or someone.

I stood and made my way to the port side of the ship. I surveyed the docks. The glare of the setting sun still lit up the top of the warehouse walls, casting reflected light down onto the cobbles and the guards gathered there. Since Tayyib and Sayf left, Nadir and his men had all but ignored us. We had remained on *Brymsteda* and our guards had settled into whatever shade they could find to watch us from afar. Now they were huddled together in small groups, talking and laughing. I noted the lack of dice or other games of chance so common to all warriors I had encountered previously. Even without that distraction, they were not concerned about us. They had left two men standing on duty to watch the ship and there was nowhere for any of us to go without being seen.

Looking back into the channel that had been busy with boats and ships during the day, I thought it would have been possible to drop down into a passing vessel and escape that way. But Nadir knew we would not abandon our ship, even if we had been able to all sneak away, which seemed unlikely. I presumed they would take a closer watch of us after night fell. Even as I thought this I watched as an elderly man in a dark robe trudged along the length of the dock, placing fresh torches in the sconces.

Another couple of guards, one bearing a brazier and the other pushing a handcart laden with timber, were making their way back to Nadir and the rest of the warriors.

"You are as jumpy as a frog on a stove," said a voice beside me. I recognised Runolf's gravelly rumble.

"I don't like being trapped here," I said. "It makes me nervous."

"I know how you feel." Runolf leaned forward, gripping the wale with his huge hands. I gave him a sidelong glance. He looked tired, his features pinched, dark shadows beneath his eyes. "I should not have attacked that ship," he said. "It was foolish. And what did it bring us? Nothing." He spat. "Hering died because of me and for what?" I realised then that guilt is often a dish shared, even when you think you are dining alone.

"Hering's death was not your fault," I said. "I brought us here." I watched as the old man lit the torch furthest from us and made his way slowly along the cobbled wharf.

Runolf hoomed deep in the back of his throat.

"You have forced none of us to accompany you, Hunlaf. We each make our own decisions."

I sniffed.

"Then that goes for Hering too."

"I suppose," Runolf said, drinking from his cup. It looked tiny and fragile in his massive hand. "But perhaps he would yet live, if I had not turned *Brymsteda* about. You might have had more time to tend to his wound."

The thought that if I had spent more time with Hering he might have survived was not one I wanted to dwell upon. It was too close to what I already believed.

"Those accursed pirates made the decision to loose their arrows," I said. "When they struck Revna, what else were you to do? You are a good man, Runolf. Her father."

He scowled at that.

"I have been but a poor father," he said, "but I cannot change the past."

"No man can. But I do not believe there is any man aboard who would have expected you to do other than what you did. It was the pirates who wounded Revna and Hering. They needed to be made to pay."

"There is one aboard who did not wish me to attack." He shrugged. "Perhaps Giso was right."

"Well, it matters nought now," I said. "You cannot change the past."

Runolf snorted at hearing his own words echoed back to him.

"Speaking of the Frankish weasel," he said, "where is Giso?"

"I don't know," I said, still scanning the docks, but seeing no sign of him. "I came here hoping to see him sitting on the dock. But I can't see him anywhere. He is not aboard and nobody has seen him for some time."

Runolf frowned.

"I have a bad feeling about this," he said.

I was going to voice my own concern, but before I could say anything, Runolf had jumped over *Brymsteda*'s side and down to the dock.

"Wait," I called after him, but he did not slow his pace. He was stalking towards the nearest pair of guards, the ones set to watch our ship.

"I would ask these bastards if they've seen Giso," he called back to me, his voice slurring with the wine he had consumed. "He may be a weasel, but he's our weasel."

The men before Runolf tensed, lowering their spears at the threat posed by this red-bearded giant who lumbered towards them.

Sighing, I drained the last of the wine in my cup before tossing it aside. Then, grasping the wale, I leapt down to hurry after Runolf.

Thirteen

Runolf towered above the two guards. They bore spears and Runolf was unarmed, but he was still an imposing figure, his fists bunched on his hips, legs apart and his barrel of a chest puffed out as he stared down at them over his bristling flame-red beard.

"Ask them if they have seen Giso," he said.

The guards took a step backwards, their eyes flicking from the giant Norseman and his bellowing voice to me as I reached his side. The other guards who sat some way off had all turned towards us. A couple of them made to stand, thinking there might be trouble. Nadir waved for them to remain seated. His dark eyes gleamed beneath his heavy brows and he watched us with a half-smile on his lips.

"Go on," said Runolf. "Ask them."

"We are looking for one of our number," I said in al-Arabiyyah.

"Look to your ship," replied the shorter of the guards. He was older than the other one, stocky of build and with a fighter's face; scarred flat cheeks and a wide nose that had been broken many times. "None of your people are here."

"What does he say?" asked Runolf.

"That they have seen nobody from our ship."

"Tell them what Giso looks like."

I glanced at Runolf.

"I don't think that will help."

Runolf's face was reddened from the wine and the sun that had beaten down all day.

"Just tell them," he insisted.

"He is a small man," I said to the guards, holding my hand just above my shoulder to indicate his height. "His hair is dark. He wears plain robes."

The older guard shook his head.

"I've not seen him," he said.

"Yes, we have," said the other guard. "Remember?"

I turned my attention to the younger of the two. He was a slim, sharp-faced man, with teeth that appeared too big for his mouth. Though he looked nothing like Nadir, there was a vicious glint in his eye that reminded me of the leader of the guards.

The older guard shook his head again, frowning.

"No. We have seen nobody."

The younger guard's teeth protruded, as his mouth stretched in a wide smile.

"Yes, we did. This morning. Remember?"

He was struggling to hold in his laughter now. He was evidently pleased with himself, certain he was funny, but his comrade looked confused. The guard's demeanour rankled and I could feel my anger returning. I sensed I would not welcome the end of this jest that would no doubt be at our expense.

"Well, I didn't see his face this morning," the slim guard went on, his smile growing even wider at seeing his partner's bewilderment, "but we saw him last night. He didn't look well at all, but he was short. Well, he would be. He was lying down. And when we saw him this morning he was wrapped in the plainest of cloaks." He could hold back his mirth no longer and he let out a loud guffaw.

"The man you are speaking of was my friend," I said. My voice was as chill as the north wind in winter, but my heart hammered against my ribs as I felt all the anger that had been building within me boil up.

"He can't have gone far," replied the guard, stifling his chuckles with difficulty. "It's been a hot day. Just follow your nose and you are sure to find him."

There have been many accusations levelled at me in my long life. Thinking carefully before acting is not one of them. In that moment on the docks of Qadis, all reason left me. My anger broke through the walls of my restraint that had already been weakened by the wine. Looking back now, I can see that I welcomed the release. I could find nothing to distract me fully from the guilt I felt, but violence would liberate me from having to think for a time.

I gave no indication of what I intended to do, for I gave it no thought. If I had planned my actions, I might well have given the thin-faced guard enough warning to defend himself. As it was, my left hand snaked out to grasp his spear haft, tugging it towards me and to the left. In the same instant my right fist snapped up from my side as if of its own volition, striking the man a powerful uppercut squarely in the face. I felt the crunch of cartilage as his nose broke and my punch lifted him onto his heels.

He was dazed and no longer laughing, but he was no weakling. He swayed, but did not fall. The shorter guard, the one who looked as if he'd spent a lifetime brawling, was quick. I had paid him no heed as my fury took hold, and I saw now that had been a mistake. He swung his spear up and cracked its wooden butt into my stomach. Winded, I relinquished my hold on the first man's spear and staggered back a step.

Behind the two guards, Nadir and the rest of his men surged to their feet. Time slowed, as it always did for me in combat, allowing me to comprehend the stupidity of what I had done.

But as Runolf had said, I could not change the past, no matter how recent. All I could do was move forward and finish what I had started.

Blood gushed freely now from the thin guard's nose, painting his mouth, chin and throat crimson. I watched as he shook his head, regaining his senses. I had stopped the man's taunts and laughter, but he still stood. That was something I meant to rectify. Provided the stocky guard didn't skewer me on his spear first.

He spun the weapon around, changing his grip so that he could hold it overarm. It was clear that he meant to jab it at me, whether to hold me at bay or to pierce my flesh made little difference. In a few short heartbeats the rest of the guards would be upon us and then this fight would be over soon enough. My focus was split as I weighed up the threat of the stocky brawler against my desire to continue to beat the man who had made light of Hering's death.

Runolf took the decision away from me. With a bellowing roar like a bull he sprang forward at the shorter of the two guards. The man had been watching me and was in the process of altering his grip on the spear haft, so Runolf took him by surprise. The Norseman grabbed the guard's head between his meaty hands and slammed his forehead into the brawler's face with a sickening thud.

I grinned. Runolf did not need to understand what had been said. All he saw was that a fight had started. He needed no explanation. I was his shield-brother and he would stand beside me against any foe. My heart swelled, and with renewed energy I dragged in a breath and turned my attention back to my adversary.

He was lowering his spear, the wicked point gleaming in the last of the sun's rays. But he was slow, and I lowered my head and jumped forward, before he could bring the spear-point down low enough to stab me. I barely felt the spear's haft hit my back as I barged my shoulder into him, lifting him from his feet and driving him hard into the cobbles. I got a glimpse of Nadir's men running towards us, but then I was pounding my fists into the guard's face. His lips split, splashing more blood. My own blood mingled with his as his over-long teeth cut into my knuckles, but I felt no pain, only rage.

To my right I saw Runolf lift his opponent above his head as if the stocky warrior had been as light as a child. Runolf flung him into the ranks of approaching guards. Several toppled over in a tangle of limbs and spears.

The man I was punching was motionless now, his head lolling with each blow. I pushed myself to my feet, ready to face the new threat. From somewhere I thought I could hear someone calling my name.

Runolf had slowed the advancing guards, knocking a few down, but there were too many of them and we were quickly surrounded. They may have been complacent in their guarding of us, but Nadir had been quick to respond when needed. He was barking orders now, sending some of his men towards *Brymsteda*, where I saw the faces of my friends staring down at us. Gwawrddur was there, Hereward too, and the light gleamed from Drosten's black braid. They were shouting, but I could not make out their words.

Nadir was ordering his men not to kill me or Runolf. I wondered at that as the first spear butt struck my temple. I tried to move towards the spearman who had landed the blow, but my head was filled with fog and my legs refused to obey me.

Runolf howled beside me and I saw him wrest a spear from one of the guards and begin to lay about him with it, slicing and jabbing.

"Óðinn!" he cried. The setting sun's light caught in his mane of golden-red hair, giving him the appearance of wearing a fiery crown.

I wanted to call out to him, to tell him not to give them a reason to slay him, but my tongue felt thick in my mouth and words would not come. He would not have listened even if I had managed to speak, I thought. The joy of battle had seized him and he was lost to the frenzy of it.

He looked like some hero from legend, his head wreathed in flames as he fought with abandon. He loomed above me as if he was several times the height of a normal man, like a giant from a song, or one of the gods he worshipped, come to tread the earth. For a time I could make no sense of what I witnessed. Then, with a wrenching shock I realised I was prostrated at his feet. My mind reeled. When had I fallen? Was I dying? Had one of the spears plunged into my body? I could feel no pain. But I would welcome death. If I died I might see Hering soon. I would beg him to forgive me.

It grew dark around me and I saw that the guards had rushed Runolf all at once. Please God, I prayed, do not let Runolf die because of me. I could not endure more guilt. Yet more of my friends' blood on my hands.

Something hit the side of my head. Hard. The world burst with white light. Struggling to rise, I blinked away the bright flashes that blinded me. When at last I could see once more, Nadir's leering face was staring down at me.

"You're mine now," he snarled.

His booted foot stamped into my face and blackness engulfed me.

Fourteen

I awoke to the sound of dripping water. My body ached and when I moved a stabbing pain lanced through my neck and shoulder. Someone was wailing far off in the distance, their plaintive cries echoing eerily in the darkness. I tried to open my eyes, but they seemed to be sealed shut. Reaching up with my right hand, I gingerly touched my eyes. My shoulder screamed at the sudden movement, the muscles of my arm tingling as the blood flowed once more after what must have been a long period of inactivity.

Probing my face gently, I found the skin around my eyes was swollen, puffy and tender. Carefully, I pulled at my right eyelid. It was caked with something. Dried blood, I presumed. Tattered memories surfaced in my mind of the beating I had received at the hands – and feet – of the guards. I finally managed to prise open my right eye. After touching the left, I decided it was just badly swollen.

The ground beneath me was unyielding, cold and damp. I pushed myself up into a sitting position with a groan as my body protested.

Looking about me, at first it seemed as though there was no light, but slowly I began to make out vague shapes in the gloom. The stone walls were curved, creating a circular enclosure that was perhaps as long across the centre as the height of a tall man. The wall appeared to be unbroken, making the room impenetrable. A small aperture high up in the domed ceiling was the only source of illumination. The light that filtered down into the room was silvery and diffuse. Night-time, I thought, instinctively. I presumed that the opening was the only means of access to the prison, for that is surely what this place must be. Into the small space were crowded three other prisoners besides me.

Water dripped incessantly from the hole in the roof, making a noxious pool beneath. With each drop, the muck splattered. The acrid stench assailed my nostrils and my stomach heaved. The stink transported me back to the hut where we had been imprisoned by Ljósberari. It was the same smell of piss and shit; the stink of despair and impending doom. The only improvement was that this place was at least not uncomfortably hot. If anything, it was too cold, and I shivered, wrapping my aching arms around me for warmth. My kirtle was soiled and sodden, my breeches wet and plastered to my legs.

Another howling cry drifted from faraway, to echo down through the water-slick opening. One of the figures, slumped in the darkness furthest from me, began to shake and gibber, muttering words I could not fathom. Whether he spoke in some tongue I did not comprehend, or in the incoherent language of madness, I knew not, but the sound of his lamentations was unnerving and I shuddered again.

"Good of you to awaken at last."

The sound of the rumbling voice startled me.

"Runolf!" I exclaimed. "You're alive."

"Your mind is as sharp as ever, I see," he replied, surprising me with a chuckle in the darkness. "Yes, we both live. This is not your Christ God's heaven, or Valhöll."

My memories were confused and jumbled, like stones in a wall that has been knocked down in a storm. All the pieces were there, but I could make little sense of them. The last thing I recalled clearly was punching the lean sneering guard.

"I am sorry," I whispered. I had got us into this mess. Hearing the man's cries in the distance and the mumbling ravings of the man who shared our cell, I wondered at the fate that awaited us.

"There is nothing to be sorry for," Runolf replied, and I could hear the sincerity in his voice. "Whatever that guard said to you, he clearly deserved what was coming to him."

I lifted a new memory from the scattered pile in my mind.

"He was laughing about Hering," I said.

"I thought as much," Runolf said. "You are a warrior. Like me. We cannot stand by and ignore such insults any more than we could halt the tide."

I wondered what Leofstan would have had to say about that. But Runolf was right. Whether we were truly alike or not, I *was* a warrior.

"Hitting that bastard felt good," I said, wincing as my smile pulled at the bruises on my face.

"I don't think he enjoyed the experience," replied Runolf, a smile in his words.

He shifted his position and let out a small grunt.

"Are you hurt?" I asked.

"Just stiff from sitting in this cramped cell." I could hear the tightness in his voice that told me he was hurting, but I chose not to pry further.

"What happened?" I asked, leaning against the wall beside Runolf. The stone was chill and hard, but the Norseman's great bulk was comforting beside me.

"How much do you remember?"

"Not a lot," I said, but I could sense my addled thoughts beginning to slowly fall back into place.

"Well, you finished off the jester you hit first, while I dealt with the other guard. He was tough, but no match for Runolf

Ragnarsson." In the shadows I saw him brandish his fists and I half-imagined I saw the glint of his grin. "After that things got... interesting. Nadir got his men around us quickly. They had their spears, so it wasn't looking good. One of them caught you on the head and you fell. I got hold of a spear at the same time that Hereward, Gwawrddur and Drosten led a charge from *Brymsteda*."

I looked over at the whimpering man on the far side of the room, and the other, unmoving shape huddled beside him. Surely neither of those men were our friends. But if they had charged unarmed at Nadir's spear-men... I bit my lip and instantly regretted it. My mouth was as bruised and sensitive as the rest of my face.

"Are they..." I hesitated, not wishing to voice my fears. *Almighty God, don't let them be dead*, I prayed silently.

"As far as I know they are well enough," said Runolf, "though it has been some time since I last saw them. You have been senseless for the best part of a day."

"A whole day?" No wonder my body was stiff.

"Truth be told, I thought your brains might have been shaken up so badly you would never awaken." Runolf's tone was light, almost jaunty, but I detected the concern for me lurking just beneath the surface levity.

"My body feels as if I have been trampled by a herd of cattle," I said, "and my head aches, but I'll live." I wondered for how long, but kept my own fears from my voice. "How did the others fare against Nadir's men?"

"They didn't."

"What?"

"They never reached the spear-men," Runolf said. "Nadir got to you before I could stop him. After he had... quietened you down"—I had a flashing vision of Nadir's snarling face as his boot came crashing down at me—"he held a knife at your throat and shouted for the rest of us to surrender. I thought about killing him then," growled Runolf. I remembered him looming above me like a god of old, his head crowned in flames and I knew he could have slain Nadir if he had chosen to do so. "Luckily for us both," he said, "Hereward saw sense. He shouted at me, and I listened to his voice. I threw down the spear I had picked up and allowed myself to be bound." He sniffed, hawked, and spat into the darkness. "This is the third time I have found myself a prisoner in the dark with you for company, Hunlaf. I hope this is the last time."

"I hope it isn't," I replied, recalling how I had first met Runolf after the Norse raid on Lindisfarnae. He had been held in one of the minster's prayer cells then. It had been far removed from this noisome room. That cell had been clean, with the fresh sea air reaching us through the open roof that allowed those praying to focus on God and the sky above them.

"You wish to be held captive again?" Runolf asked. "I prefer my freedom."

"We all prefer our freedom," I said, thinking of Ahmad. "I just pray that we will have the chance to be captured again in the future. One sure way for this to be our last imprisonment is that we die here."

As if in answer to my grim words, the thin scream of whoever was suffering in the distance reached us once more. It sounded weaker now, as if the owner of the voice was nearing the end of his endurance.

"I hope that is not one of the crew," I said.

"It isn't," said a quiet voice from the dark.

"Who are you?" I asked, not recognising the speaker.

"My name is Naddoðr," the man said. With a shock I realised he spoke in the same language I had been using to converse with Runolf: the tongue of the Norse.

"You speak Norse?" I said, unable to keep the surprise from my voice.

"I should," said Naddoðr. "I hale from Hálogaland."

"While you slept," said Runolf, "Naddoðr and I have become acquainted." Was there a warning in Runolf's voice?

Another wailing yowl came to us.

"That screaming is my comrade, Ragi," said Naddoðr. "I hope the nithing doesn't die too soon."

I didn't know what to answer to that.

"How is it you are here?" I asked instead.

"That is easy," he said. "That fool who now cries like a woman in childbirth is a greedy whoreson who didn't listen to me."

My head ached.

"I meant here, in Qadis," I said, "not in this hole."

"Well, that is easy too," he replied, his voice strangely jovial in the darkness. "I have told your friend Runolf here all about it. I came here on my ship, *Visund*, a sturdy knǫrr. Nobody else from Hálogaland has travelled so far south, and the trade has been good. Certainly better than raiding those holy places in Britain. I prefer men to give me gold in my hand rather than having to fight them for it. Less chance of death, that way." He paused, cocking his head. The night was quiet now. "It should have been my final voyage. After this, I was going to beach *Visund* and settle down on my farm. But Ragi had to try to be clever."

A lingering scream tapered off to silence.

"He doesn't sound so clever now, does he?" Naddoðr said.

I said nothing. My mind was still befuddled from the beating, and my battered body ached with each movement. My throat was parched and I yearned for a drink, but I kept silent and listened to Naddoðr's tale in the darkness.

"Don't cheat the Moors,' I told him. But he was so certain he was cleverer than them. 'Don't you worry,' he said. 'I'm the one with the brains.' For once he should have listened to me. Always underestimated others. Like a blindness. But I'm no fool." He hesitated, perhaps listening to hear if his comrade would scream again, but now the darkness was silent, apart from the whispered moaning of the fourth man and the dripping of water. "I should have known he would do something stupid." He fell silent for a long time. "Now I think I will be killed," he said at last, "for what Ragi did. I wonder what they have done to him."

"It didn't sound fun," said Runolf, brutally.

"No," Naddoðr muttered, "no, it didn't. Perhaps they'll give me a clean death. But I doubt it. Vicious bastards, these Moors."

"What did he do? This Ragi?" I asked.

"The oldest trick there is, the pig-brained fool. He showed them the finest mink furs, convincing the Moors the whole shipment was of the same quality, when the rest were hare, fox and wolf pelts. Once they had thrown us in here he admitted he had done it before with a single bale of pelts, as a kind of test, like. It had worked then, so he only went and did it again. But on a larger scale." He sighed and his mood shifted. "I wonder if he's dead." His voice was small and fearful now. "When do you think they'll come for me?"

Neither Runolf nor I had any idea when our gaolers would come for Naddoðr, or what was to be our fate. When we asked him how long he had been in this dungeon, he thought for a while, then said, "I lost count of the days after the first fortnight." He cackled then and his laughter was tinged with madness.

"Is there any water?" I rasped. My throat was dry and my tongue swollen.

"Not much," Runolf rumbled, reaching forward and lifting something from the sludge beneath the opening in the roof. He handed me a small earthenware cup. I had not noticed it in the dark.

I muttered my thanks, and drank. The water was cool. There was not a lot of it, but I drained the cup. The water went some way to reviving me. I could feel it trickling down inside me. With a sudden stab of shame at my selfishness, I returned it to Runolf.

"Sorry," I mumbled.

Runolf chuckled.

"I drank while you slept. You were thirsty."

Without further comment he placed the cup back where it could again collect the drops of water that fell incessantly.

"Do you think the others are still at the dock?" I whispered.

"Perhaps," Runolf replied, his voice low, but still booming in the small cell. "I hope they are well, but they must tend to themselves. We have our own worries."

There could be no denying that. My actions had landed us in this foul-smelling prison, and I had no inkling how we might escape.

"Mayhap they are all dead by now," said Naddoðr, sounding gleeful. I thought he might be talking of his own crew, but then he went on and his meaning became clear. And with his words, my guilt began to sharpen and harden into anger.

"If your friends yet breathe," he said, "they are most likely in chains. There is no silver to be made from dead men. And there is always strong demand for slaves."

"Hold your tongue, Naddoðr," growled Runolf.

"If I do not say the words, it does not make the truth of them go away. I told as much to Ragi many times. He should have listened to me. But no. He knew best and ignored my warnings. And now where is he?"

I thought of Gwawrddur, Drosten, Hereward and the others. They were strong men all, warriors and killers. I knew they could defend themselves. But they would be powerless to stop Nadir from rounding them up and chaining them together to be dragged to some slave market, that in my imagination was dusty, hot and loud with the pitiful wailing of enslaved men and women. *Brymsteda*'s crew would fight, they might even kill some of the city guards, but in the end they would be beaten, just as Runolf and I had been.

"Just be thankful that your womenfolk are far away," said Naddoðr. "I don't know what I would do if I thought my Thora might be taken by these Moorish devils."

"Silence your flapping tongue, fool!" spat Runolf.

His anger blew on the flames of my own fear-kindled ire. The thought of Revna in the hands of the likes of the sneering Nadir made the breath catch in my throat. My frame ached and my head felt as though it had been used as an anvil, but in that instant I was ready to leap into the murky dark and batter Naddoðr into silence.

Thankfully something in Runolf's tone gave the man pause and he shuffled back.

"I meant no harm with my words, good friends," he said. His words sounded wheedling, pathetic.

Beside me Runolf settled his back against the cold wall. Slowly, I sensed the tension easing from him, like the passing of a distant cloud that had promised rain but drifts by without a downpour. My own anger dissipated quickly. It was replaced with shame.

I could hear Leofstan's whispered voice, as real as if he had been sitting beside me. "Have you learnt nothing?" asked his voice. "Violence begets violence."

I closed my eyes and prayed silently, reciting first the Pater Noster and then the Ave Maria. Gradually, the familiar words calmed me, as they had when I had finally agreed to pray with Giso.

"Where do you think Giso was?" I said in a quiet voice. I spoke now in Englisc, hoping that Naddoðr would not understand me. Whether he did indeed understand me or not, I do not know, but he kept quiet, and for that I was thankful.

"I have been wondering the same," replied Runolf.

"Do you think one of Nadir's men hurt him?"

"Perhaps. But I think not. It seemed to me they truly did not know where he was."

I pondered this for a time. My head hurt worse than ever.

"I think you're right," I said. "But he was not aboard *Brymsteda*, I would swear to that."

"Perhaps he managed to get away," said Runolf. "He sneaks about like a rat."

"But where would he go?" I asked.

"Who knows? I don't think the others will miss him, if he is truly gone."

My thoughts spiralled back to our friends on the ship and what might have befallen them. What might have happened because of my rash foolishness. Neither of us spoke, and our conversation sputtered out like untended embers.

I wondered if we would escape this place, and what would happen to us if we did. My eyes grew heavy and my thoughts wandered, flitting from one thing to the next like bats snatching insects on the wing. Images flashed in my mind. I saw Revna's hair, gleaming in the setting sun. Hering's corpse, deathly still on the deck, swaddled in the makeshift shroud. *Brymsteda*'s stallion prow beast, rearing haughtily into the sky. Then I saw Alhwin and Giso, surrounded by books and scrolls in the shadows of the hall at Aachen.

Where had Giso gone? Did he know of the whereabouts of *The Treasure of Life*? He spoke little of it, but I had sensed that Giso, like me, yearned to see the book. Alhwin clearly longed to possess it.

Leofstan's obsession with the tome ultimately led to his death. I could not put into words why the book had become so important to me, but lying there in that cold, damp cell, the stink of ordure burning in my nostrils, the long shadow cast by the book fell over all the thoughts, faces and worries that drifted through my consciousness.

If the book still existed it would no longer be enclosed in

the gaudy, priceless binding I had seen on Lindisfarnae. That had been stripped off by the Norse raiders, the gold and gems sold. I knew this, but in that shadow land between waking and slumber, the last thing I saw with my mind's eye before falling into the blackness of sleep was the shimmering, jewel-encrusted cover of *The Treasure of Life*.

Fifteen

I awakened with a start. A scraping squeal reverberated in the domed cell and a bright light made me blink. Light lanced into our dark world and I peered up, squinting to see a trapdoor had been raised in the roof. A man's head and shoulders were shadowed there. My first thought was that it must be day, but the figure in the opening shifted his position, leaning to recover a lamp from beside the hatch that now yawned open out of reach above us.

The dancing flame illuminated a bearded face, with a wide mouth like a scar and eyes that were too close together.

"You," he said in al-Arabiyyah, "take the rope."

A rope dropped into the cell, curling in the muck beneath the trapdoor and toppling the water cup. Moments earlier, the light of the lamp had seemed as bright as the sun, now I saw that it cast but a dim glow. Faint as it was, it was enough light to see that the end of the rope was tied in a loop large enough for a man to place over his body. It was secured with a slipping knot, giving it the appearance of a noose for a giant.

None of us moved.

"You," snarled the man, his tone as sharp as a blade now. "The one they call Naddod." He garbled the pronunciation of the Norse name, but we knew who it was he was summoning.

Naddoðr stirred and stared up at the man. He did not move. In the lamp light I saw what had been hitherto hidden in the darkness. Naddoðr's skin was sallow, his cheeks sharp. His clothing was tattered, dark and stiff with grime. The legs and arms that protruded from his rags were bony and withered. Naddoðr's eyes were wide and watery, the fearful stare of a man who would trade pelts, wool and wheat rather than go a-viking. I felt pity for him then. I was no pagan, and cared nought for the favour of the false gods Runolf worshipped, and yet I still prayed to the Almighty that when my time came I would have the courage to face my end with my head held high.

"Take the rope," I said, thinking perhaps Naddoðr had not understood the command.

Naddoðr did not speak. He shook his head frantically, not taking his gaze from the coiled cord, as if it were a serpent preparing to strike.

"If Naddod does not take the rope this moment," shouted the man from the hatch, "I will come down into the hole and beat all of you before we take him. Do you understand me?"

"What is he saying," asked Runolf. The fourth man in the cell was huddled and still with his back to me. He had ceased his whimpering gabble and now lay completely motionless. I wondered for a fleeting moment if he might be dead.

I translated the guard's words.

"Take the rope," Runolf said to Naddoðr. "You'll go in the end."

The trader pressed himself against the wall, quivering and crying now.

"No, no, no, no."

When it became clear that Naddoðr was not going to pick up the rope, the guard let out a roar of anger. There was a clatter as he banged the lamp down beside the open hatch.

He spoke briefly, looking over his shoulder. His voice was

muffled, but the three voices that answered him were clear enough, as were the complaints of men readying themselves for an onerous task.

"Three of us are going to come down there and you are all going to wish you'd never been born. If any one of you fights back, we will put out your eyes."

At this, the fourth inmate, who until now had remained immobile, pushed himself into a sitting position. Turning slowly, he looked up at the light and the sound of the voices emanating from the open trapdoor.

The man stared up, but he did not see. Where his eyes should have been, there were dark, blood-encrusted hollows. Blood had run down his cheeks, drying into scabby brown tears. He wrapped his arms around himself and began to rock, mumbling and muttering in abject terror. With the end of each movement, he smacked the back of his head against the wall with a dull thud.

My skin grew cold and with a shudder I made the sign of the cross.

Runolf shifted, half-rising from where he had been sitting. I made to translate the guard's words, but their meaning must have been clear enough. Before the first of the guards could begin to climb down into the cell, Runolf launched himself at Naddoðr.

The merchant let out a cry of alarm, but he had no time to react further. Runolf's massive fist smacked into his jaw and Naddoðr's head snapped back into the wall. His eyes took on a dazed look, like someone who has been awoken from a nightmare, or in Naddoðr's case, was about to enter a new one. Runolf grabbed his thin frame and pulled him into the centre of the room, squelching in the quagmire of filth beneath the door. Naddoðr regained enough of his senses to begin trying to fight back, but at the first sign of a struggle, Runolf slapped him hard around the side of the head. Naddoðr's head lolled to the side and his eyes rolled up, unseeing. Snatching up the rope, Runolf looped it over Naddoðr's head and shoulders, tugging his limp arms over the rope, so that it sat around his chest and beneath his armpits. Tugging the knot tight, he turned to me, his red beard bristling and his eyes glinting with an emotion I could not comprehend.

"Tell them to pull him up," he said.

I weighed my options, then, seeing no alternative, I called out. A moment later, Naddoðr's floppy form was heaved out of the slimy dirt. When he reached the domed ceiling, strong hands grasped Naddoðr, pulling him the last of the way and out through the cell hatch.

"Tell your friend he is not as stupid as he looks," shouted the guard. The other guards, still out of sight, laughed.

I stared at Runolf in the light that fell through the opening. His features were grim and he would not meet my gaze. I was about to speak, when the hatch clanged shut. The sudden darkness was blinding after the flame-flicker of the lamp. Groping my way, I moved to the wall. Sliding down, I sat with my back to the cold stone. My eyes were beginning to adjust once more to the gloom. The light that now filtered into the cell was even dimmer than when I had first awoken.

"How long did I sleep?" I asked, not wishing to speak of what had just happened.

Runolf grunted. Perhaps he shrugged his huge shoulders, but I could not see him clearly.

"A long time. Half a day perhaps."

"I feel better for it," I said, and realised it was true. "Everything still aches, but my head hurts less."

Another grunt. I was uncertain of its meaning.

The blinded man was silent once more. I could barely make out his shape and was glad that he seemed to have decided not to continue trying to bash his brains out on the wall.

"You should not have done that," I said at last, unable to

keep quiet any longer. I had thought I was angry, appalled at Runolf's treatment of Naddoðr, but I heard only disappointment in my voice.

"He should have taken the rope," Runolf said. "He built his ship, now he has to sail it. Too late to run now."

"He said it was his partner…" I cast about in my memory for the name "… this, Ragi, who cheated the Wazir of Qadis, not him. Must he be punished for the actions of others?"

"Men are always judged by the actions of their friends, or did you forget how we came to be here? This is your doing, not mine."

My face grew hot and I was glad of the darkness.

"I didn't tell you to follow me," I said petulantly. This was unfair, and I knew it. But I wanted to win the argument.

"No, you didn't," Runolf said. "It was my decision to join your fight. It is what friends do." I felt the sting of his words, as if he had slapped me. "Just as it was Naddoðr's decision to sail with Ragi. Why should we be beaten for something they have done?"

"Don't worry about that," I said, "I am sure we will be beaten soon enough."

The sound of movement came from above and an instant later the hatch was pulled open once more. Lamplight glared, making us squint and blink. A shape filled the opening, blocking out most of the light momentarily, then it fell into the cell, splatting into the thin smear of muck beneath the trapdoor. For a brief spell the door remained open, light spilling into our cell. Then it slammed shut, and this time I heard the scrape of a bolt being pushed home.

Before the hatch had closed, I'd had just enough time to make out the form of a man, lying half-naked, blood-smeared and unmoving in the grime.

Ignoring the aches and pains in my limbs, I moved as quickly as I was able to the unfortunate soul. I could see next to nothing in the grey light from the barred opening in the trapdoor, but what I could see didn't look good. I ran my hands over his emaciated arms and legs, probing with my fingers for broken bones or open wounds.

"Does he live?" Runolf asked.

"Barely," I replied. "And he has been sorely used." I continued to examine him as best I could in the darkness. The man's fingertips were soft and sticky. At my touch, he whimpered, even though he was insensate. "They pulled out his fingernails," I said, and Runolf hoomed deep in the back of his throat.

The man's face was bruised and puffy, his chin and lips caked in dried blood. Shifting my position so that the scant light fell on his face, I peered at him, pulling his lips gently apart.

"And they've ripped out some of his teeth." My stomach roiled. Would we soon hear Naddoðr's screams as he was tortured thus? Was this what awaited Runolf and I? Was this the future I had made for us with my actions.

"I am sorry for starting the fight," I said into the darkness. "Sorry for getting us into this mess."

"It is as I said. I made my decision, and you are my friend."

Before I could reply, the battered man groaned and tried to rise. As his hand touched the ground he yelped in pain and fell back.

"Ragi, I presume," said Runolf.

Sixteen

Runolf and I sat in silence for a long while, lost in our thoughts. I was still angry at him, but his words made me think. He was right. He had chosen to fight, but I was the one to blame for us being here. All of this was my fault. I prayed silently that the Lord, in His infinite wisdom, might yet spare me so that I could serve Him. Surely God had watched over me thus far in my life, for I had no right to be alive when so many around me had died. Leofstan had made me believe that the Lord had a role for me. Surely it was not His plan for me to languish and perish in this stinking cell. And yet, perhaps God had grown weary of my arrogance, my debauched and violent conduct. I prayed for forgiveness, vowing to be a better man should we escape this place, and yet wondering whether I would be able to keep such a promise when confronted once again with the temptations of the flesh.

I did not speak to Runolf of my fears. I had mentioned such concerns to him before and had met with a blank stare and even ridicule. My worries made no sense to him. In Runolf's eyes there was nothing nobler than a warrior fighting his enemies, standing beside his shield-brothers, blade in hand, willing to kill or to be killed for what he believed. To die in battle was rewarded with an eternity of feasting and fighting.

Ragi shivered and cried out. He lay with his back to the wall, sleeping. He had slept for a long time, but his slumber had been fitful. He had barely been conscious since falling into the cell.

"Don't speak," I'd said, when he had made a gurgled attempt at what might have been a greeting. His words were muffled and garbled, his broken teeth and swollen mouth making him sound like a man who had been drinking strong mead all day and night. "Rest now. Recover your strength."

I'd helped him move out of the worst of the ordure and moisture. The moment he lay down against the wall, he had fallen into a troubled sleep.

A distant scream drifted down into the small cell, as if in answer to Ragi's cry. At first, the screams we'd heard had been louder, and it had been possible to detect Naddoðr's voice within them. But as time passed, his cries had become weaker and more inchoate. Now they could have been mistaken for the squeals of an animal in pain. I tried to ignore the sounds and focus on my prayers.

"He was quite mad, you know?" said Runolf without warning, his voice resonant and echoing in the small stone chamber.

"Who?" My voice cracked, my throat dry.

"Naddoðr," Runolf said. "We spoke much while you slept. You were asleep for a long time and I was pleased to have found a companion who spoke my tongue."

"What did you speak of?"

"Anything. And nothing." He reached for the water cup and took a sip. "He welcomed me as though he were a king and this his great hall. Then he spoke of those who had wronged him. He spoke of Ragi and named several others who he said had betrayed him."

He offered the cup to me. The drip of water from above had slowed and the cup must be practically empty now. But I accepted it.

"Do you believe his story?" I said, lifting the cup to my lips and allowing the smallest trickle of water into my mouth. "What he said about Ragi, and what he had done?" The water felt slimy on my tongue. It held an unpleasant earthy, sour taste. I pushed aside thoughts of what the water might contain and looked around the room.

There was a hint of light in the cell now, warmer than the blue-grey glow of the stars and moon. I imagined the sun rising outside to shine into a window far off, down some long corridor. Only a remnant of that sunlight now filtered into our cell, but it was enough for me to make out Runolf's shrug.

"Who can say?" he said. "But I think his mind has been broken."

I took in the green stones and the stinking mire that caught the faint light from the hatch above. Across from us huddled the blind man and the man we assumed to be Ragi. As if he could sense my gaze, Ragi suddenly shook and squirmed before letting out a juddering, sobbing cry.

I leaned forward and carefully placed the empty cup back where it could catch any water that fell through the hatch. If the guards did not give us anything to drink, we would be glad of whatever moisture we could capture. If we spent long enough here, that foul-tasting water might even end up tasting sweet to us.

"We have only been here a couple of days and I can sense the walls closing in," I said. "God alone knows how we'll fare if we stay here as long as him."

"How long do you think he has been here?"

"Who can say? Weeks at least, but to look at him and Naddoðr, I would say probably closer to months." Both men were emaciated, their bones jutting beneath their skin.

Runolf shivered. I imagined his thoughts were of his bulk and strength wasting away, leaving him weak and at the mercy of our captors.

"He said much that was coloured with the dye of madness," said Runolf, "but there was one thing he said that might prove useful, if ever we get out of here."

I met his gaze without speaking, waiting for him to continue. He paused, perhaps hoping I would break off my stare, or ask him to carry on with his tale. I did neither. After a while, he chuckled, perhaps amused at my stubbornness. Shaking his head, he went on with his story.

"When Naddoðr spoke of the man who was responsible for them being thrown in here, he grew more crazed than ever. He could barely speak without spitting. If the object of Naddoðr's ire had come into this cell then, even as weak as he was, I think Naddoðr would have killed him with his bare hands."

"You mean Ragi and Naddoðr are never left alone together in here?"

Runolf frowned, confused at my words, then understanding dawned, softening his features as he smiled.

"He does not truly blame Ragi for them being here. From what he said I believe he knew full well what Ragi was about. In fact, I wouldn't be surprised to learn that it had all been his idea, and now he is trying to justify his cowardice by blaming Ragi for his actions. The man he is truly angry with is the man who caught them cheating."

Runolf grew silent and I knew he wanted me to ask who he was talking about. I longed to hear the answer to that, but I refused to give him the satisfaction of pleading. Runolf looked at me quizzically, but when it became clear I was not going to speak, he smirked.

"Turns out we know the man responsible for Naddoðr and Ragi languishing here." He paused, again giving me a chance to ask my questions. I said nothing. "It is Ahmad's friend."

"Tayyib?" I asked, blurting the name out despite all my efforts to remain aloof and quiet.

"The same," Runolf replied. There was a gleam in his eye now. I let him enjoy his petty victory. My mind was abuzz.

"You think his friendship with Ahmad might provide us with a way out of here?"

He shrugged, but I could see from the smile tugging at the edges of his lips that he had been thinking as much.

"Tayyib is clearly a man of influence," he said. "If he can see men thrown into prison, perhaps he can see them pulled out."

I frowned, thinking of Tayyib's meeting with Ahmad.

"I don't know. Whatever love existed between them is long vanished, I think."

"And yet he came to the docks to see Ahmad the moment he heard of his arrival."

I thought about this.

"Whatever Tayyib feels for Ahmad, I am not certain it will be enough to have us released."

Runolf held his massive hands palm upwards in the shadows. I could see his teeth gleam in the dark, reflecting what scant light there was dribbling down from the hatch. I knew what he was going to say before he uttered the words, and I could not help but return his smile with a shake of my head.

"Anything is possible," he said.

Seventeen

Anything is possible.

I can hear Runolf's sonorous voice saying those words as clearly now as if it were only days and not decades since we were imprisoned in that dank dungeon in Qadis. His frequent use of the phrase irritated Drosten, but many times in my long life Runolf's words have proven true. Just today, shortly after Sext, he was proved right again.

It has been weeks since Abbot Criba's death. He now lies entombed in the crypt beneath the chapel, but still each day the brethren pray for his soul. In the first sennight after his passing, the prayers and singing had been incessant as the minster was gripped in a fervour of grief I had never witnessed before. I have known many good men and women lose their lives. At such times, it is easy for sorrow to engulf you, making even the smallest of tasks appear insurmountable. I have wept at the deaths of kin, beloved friends and lovers, but I have never known such an outpouring of grief as I saw in those days after Criba's death. The abbot had not been popular. He had made many of the brethren suffer with his peevish nature and his willingness to punish, rather than teach. I was sure that some of the other monks felt that such a show of emotion for

Criba was unnecessary, mawkish even. But who would be the first to voice such sentiment?

Not I, for sure. I ignored most of the constant prayers and songs, instead choosing to write. But even I could not avoid attending the funeral service for the abbot. I stood there, my fragile bones aching from the passage of the years and the many wounds I have suffered, and I looked about me at the weeping, solemn countenances of my fellow monks. Did they truly feel such passionate grief? Not for the first time in my life, I felt I did not belong. I did not believe Abbot Criba had been a good man, but even if he had been worthy of beatification, such a display of emotions would still have felt hollow and false to me.

I did not voice my thoughts. But when Ordric, an odious toad of a man, let out a dramatic wailing sob before Criba's casket, I almost laughed out loud. Criba never had a kind word for the chubby monk and had often derided Ordric for a fool, and yet here he was, weeping as if he had lost his closest kin.

I held my laughter in check, but caught Coenric's eye and raised an eyebrow. The boy looked down at his feet, but not before I saw a smile play across his features. As soon as the casket holding Criba's rotting corpse had been carried down into the crypt, we had hurried back to my cell.

These past weeks, I have kept my head down and written faster than ever before, allowing the words to flow onto the page with little worry as to their quality. I rush to complete this story. Before, I lived in fear that whatever illness gnawed at my guts would claim me. I felt death's cool breath on the nape of my neck as each day saw me closer to my end.

The demon deep within me still ravages at my insides with its claws and some days I can only take up my quill after I have dulled the pain with the cunning woman's brew. And yet, I have become more frightened of something else. All through these long days bent over my writing desk, I lived in the certain knowledge that soon a new abbot would be appointed and would surely order me to either move on to a new task, or show him the book that had kept me occupied all these months. What my punishment would be for such disobedience, I did not know. Nor had I truly cared.

I have suffered many chastisements in my long life. I feared no abbot's punishment. No torment could compare with the time I was staked out over an ants' nest on the plains where the people of the Yiwa tribe dwelt. Then my skin had blistered red from the sun and the ants' stinging bites had all but driven me mad. I had believed I would die then, allowed to perish of thirst under the burning sun. And that would have been my fate if it had not been for the Khagan's daughter. She came to me in the night and cut my bonds. The beautiful girl had not even spoken to me before. To do this thing must have placed her life in terrible danger, for her people were not quick to forgive and they held great store in torturing their enemies to death. To be denied taking my life must have filled them with fury. But I never knew what befell her as a result of her actions. When the sun rose, I was far away on a stolen mount. I had been convinced then that my death was imminent and had made my peace with it as well as I could. But, as so often before, against the odds, I had lived.

Anything is possible.

And so it was today once again. I had heard shouts from the open window of my cell and had sent Coenric to see what the commotion was. I had grown accustomed to hearing the offices being sung, the sound of psalms and prayers drifting to me on the breeze, but Godstan, as acting abbot, had continued to allow me special dispensation not to attend. Quite what the other monks think of this, I am not sure, and I care even less. Godstan has never asked to see what I am writing, instead sticking to the story that it is a copy of the *Life of Saint Wilfrid*.

But if I was in any doubt before, I am sure now that he knows what it is that I scribe.

Two weeks ago he came quietly into my sparsely furnished cell. It was dark and I was using one of the expensive beeswax candles that should have been saved for the altar. Even with the flame, it was almost too dim for me to continue, and I was contemplating asking Coenric to take over. His eyes are young and keen, but his penmanship is like that of a small child, clumsy and irregular, and I could not bring myself to dictate and wait for him to laboriously scratch out each letter. And so I was persevering, dabbing at my tired, watering eyes. I had been writing since shortly after dawn.

"I am pleased to see that you are working hard on your life," Godstan said.

"Not mine," I replied quickly, my throat suddenly dry. "Wilfrid's life."

He held my gaze.

"Of course." He eased himself down onto a stool with a grimace.

"Still troubling you?" I asked.

"Yes," he said, rubbing the small of his back. "It means I will travel on foot like Saint Aidan of old. I do not know if Saint Wilfrid would have approved, but riding does so aggravate the ache. I find walking much less painful."

"Less strain on the back," I said, and he nodded. "You are heading for Eoforwic tomorrow then?"

"Aye," Godstan replied. "We have mourned long enough and now I have been called to visit the bishop. When I return, the newly appointed abbot will have been chosen. He may not be content for you to continue your current work. As interesting as Wilfrid's life may be, the abbot may find something more pressing for you to attend to."

"I understand," I'd replied and he'd nodded. Looking over at Coenric, whose eyes were wide and frightened, I could see that he too had garnered the obvious message from Godstan: *finish your book before I get back.*

And so it was that I had been dreading the moment when I heard the return of Godstan and the new abbot. I have been writing as fast as my old hands and eyes allow, but still there is much of *The Treasure of Life*'s tale to tell.

But as Runolf was so keen to remind me, anything is possible and I should never have doubted the Lord's hand in this.

Shortly after Godstan and the other brothers arrived from their journey, there was a gentle rap on my cell's door. I had been attempting to write, but my mind was no longer in that dingy, shit-stinking cell in al-Andalus. I stared at the page before me and listened with my ageing ears for the approach I knew would come; the steps outside that would presage the arrival of the abbot, come to put an end to my work.

With a sigh, I set aside my quill, careful not to allow the ink to drop onto the sheet of vellum that was half-filled with neat text. Perhaps if I pleaded with the abbot, he might allow me at least to finish this tome. I prayed that Godstan would not be punished for his part in allowing me to continue with what the new abbot would surely see as, at best, an extravagant waste of resources, and at worst sacrilegious, heretical and anathema to the teachings of Christ.

The door opened and Godstan stepped into my room. From the moment I saw the glimmer in his eye, I knew that Runolf was right once again. Anything was possible. God is great and, whatever His plan was for me as a young man, it is clear what His purpose is for me now.

"It seems the Lord wishes you to finish your work, Hunlaf," Godstan said, his smile broadening as he closed the door gently behind him.

"The new abbot will allow it?" I could scarcely believe what I was hearing, but Godstan's face hid no deceit.

"He will."

I was stunned. My hands shook and I grimaced to see the spots of age on my thin skin as I gripped the edge of my writing desk to avoid losing my balance.

"These are good tidings," I said. "But tell me, Godstan, how can you be so sure he will allow it?"

Godstan smiled and pulled open his travelling cloak to reveal a golden bejewelled cross that hung on his chest.

"That's Abbot Godstan, to you, Brother Hunlaf."

Eighteen

And so it is that I return to my tale with a lighter heart, though I must not be complacent. I sense the Almighty will call me to His side soon enough and there is still much for me to put down on parchment before I am done. Still, it is with relief that I know that my new abbot is excited to read the fruits of my labour. Godstan has given me freedom to continue. He has said he would very much like to see some of my previous work, but I have so far deflected his request, saying that Coenric was still busy with binding the tomes. I do not know if he believed me and I have no reason to doubt his sincerity, but after so long keeping my writings away from Criba, it is difficult to relinquish my hold on them now. A small voice whispers to me that it would be best to finish the story of *The Treasure of Life* before any of it is read. I ask myself why I am worried. What is it that I think Godstan will do to my writings? Then I think of the tome we sought in al-Andalus all those years ago and I know what it is that I fear.

For now, though, Godstan is busy with the running of the minster. There is much for him to do, what with harvest coming soon, and I am sure I will be left alone with Coenric to carry on my work for the time being.

And so I will forge ahead as fast as I am able. I left the story with Runolf and me lying in filth in the dungeon of Qadis, and it is there I will pick it up once more.

Days went by, how many neither Runolf nor I could say. It was difficult to discern day from night, the only indication of the passage of time being the slight change in the light that filtered down into our dark prison. We were not held long enough for our wills to be broken, but we were both scared that if we stayed there too long we would become shattered husks of ourselves, just like the blind man, who jabbered and moaned from time to time, but in no other way sought to communicate with us.

Ragi was not much better. He came to after a long, troubled sleep, and he spoke to us, but he said nothing of consequence. When we tried to question him about what had happened, he cowered against the rock wall, as far from us as he could go, quivering and weeping. The sight of him and the sound of his pitiful crying was distressing, a stark reminder of what might happen to us, should we be tortured as he had been.

We never saw Naddoðr again. If Ragi missed him, he never said, and I wondered how far his mind had retreated from reality.

Every now and then, perhaps once a day, but it was hard to tell for sure, the hatch was opened and food was thrown down to us, along with a waterskin.

"A good sign," said Runolf. "They do not mean to kill us."

"They at least wish to keep us alive long enough to torture us," I muttered one day, as I chewed a piece of stale flat bread in the darkness.

"Anything is possible," he replied, leaping up to grip the bars of the small opening in the hatch. He proceeded to pull himself up, touching his head to the trapdoor, then lowering himself until he hung with arms straight. He repeated this process several times, his muscular arms bulging, until at last he dropped to the ground. I could see sweat gleaming on his face, despite the coolness of the cell. "If we are to die," he said, "I will be strong enough to fight so that Óðinn will see me, and welcome me to his hall."

The food they provided for us was sparse and often mouldy, but we forced ourselves to eat. It was not enough to maintain our bulk, and the strength that had been created with shield and spear, and from pulling at the oars and ropes aboard *Brymsteda* began to slowly wane despite our efforts. Nevertheless, it felt good to have a focus, and so we swallowed what meagre fare there was, and we trained as well as we could while Ragi watched us from beneath hooded eyes.

We would lie on our backs in the cold slime, sitting up repeatedly until our stomachs burnt with the effort. Then we would pull up our weight to the bars, first me, with Runolf's help to reach them, then Runolf, who could jump up without aid. After that we would squat, over and over, until our legs were as weak as a newborn lamb's.

The cell was cramped and cold, and the lack of substantial food made it difficult to keep up our strength. After the first week or so, I was sure that I was weaker than I had been. But in the gloom, Runolf was still imposing and when I touched my arms and legs, the muscles there were still as hard to the touch as the stones of our prison. But in the darkest part of the night, when everyone slept and sometimes screams of pain emanated from far-off torture chambers, or the blind man whimpered and cried out, I wondered how long we would be able to maintain our fortitude and not lose our minds to the tedium and terror of being abandoned down there forever.

The blind man seemed oblivious of everything until the food was dropped down each day. Then he would scrabble forward like a spider to pounce on the provender. The first time he did this, Runolf cuffed him, pushing him back against the wall. But I tore a flat loaf in half and handed a piece to the pitiful prisoner.

"Don't hurt him," I said, and Runolf released him.

I pushed the bread into the man's hand and whispered that we would share the food.

"We mean you no harm," I said, but he ignored me, shoving the bread into his toothless maw and retreating to his habitual place against the wall.

After that we divided the food evenly each day. I think Runolf believed we should have eaten as much as possible to keep up our strength, but he never said anything to contradict me.

Sometimes we would sit and torment ourselves with conversations about what we thought our friends might be doing. Were they still being held at the docks? Did they yet live? We had no reason to believe they had been killed, but it was impossible not to fear the worst when surrounded by darkness for day after interminable day.

Runolf, I knew, was most worried about Revna.

"She'll be fine," I said, thinking of the touch of her smooth, pale skin. "Her wound was clean."

"It is not her wound I worry about," he said.

"Revna will live," I said. "She is strong."

We both fell silent and I thought of how she had given herself to Chlotar, the Frankish warrior, in order to survive.

"But what kind of life?" said Runolf, and I wondered if he was thinking the same.

We had just finished exercising and were sitting close together, taking turns to sip from the waterskin we had been given sometime before, when they came for us.

The hatch opened and bright lamp light spilled into our dark domain, making us blink. The guards dropped down the rope, just as they had for Naddoðr, and the voice we knew well by this point shouted down for Runolf to tie it under his arms.

I grew cold. So the time had finally come. They would torture us and they meant to start with Runolf.

"Tell him I can climb up," Runolf said.

My mind raced. I had thought often on this moment and what would be our best course of action. We would be tortured, of that there could be no doubt, but perhaps there was yet a way that I could avoid Runolf being slain. Without hesitation, I stepped into the loop of the rope and yanked the knot tight beneath my arms.

"What are you doing?" said Runolf, stepping forward.

"This is my fault," I replied. "I will tell them to allow you to live. It is I who should be punished, not you."

He spat.

"You are a fool."

The rope bit into my flesh as the men above heaved me from my feet.

"It is possible," I replied, speaking with difficulty as the rope constricted my chest. I forced a smile.

Runolf roared with rage as the guards' rough hands grabbed me and pulled me through the trapdoor's opening. The light from several oil lamps blinded me after so many days of darkness. I squeezed my eyes shut against the glare. Strong hands pulled the rope loose, tugging the loop over my head. Other hands gripped my arms and shoulders firmly, pulling me away from the opening. I stumbled, barely able to see in the brilliant light. I could just make out several figures around me. Their hands pushed and pulled me through them, ever further from the trapdoor.

And Runolf.

A grunt came from behind, followed by a shouted warning. I turned back, blinking away the tears that filled my eyes. Before the guards had closed the trapdoor behind me, Runolf had leapt up to grasp the stone lip and now proceeded to pull himself up and out of our cell in one smooth movement. The guards had clearly not been prepared for an attack and, as I watched, my eyes adjusting to the bright light, I saw one of the warriors instinctively swing a punch at the red-haired giant. Runolf swayed away from the blow, took hold of the man's arm and flung him down through the opening into the cell. The man hit the muck-slathered flagstones with a squelching thud. This was followed by a scream of rage from Ragi, then the unmistakable giggling gibber of the blind man.

Runolf surged forwards, hurdling the open trapdoor.

"Óðinn," he bellowed, his voice deafening in the stone corridor.

The guards, taken by surprise, fell back, jostling me further away from Runolf. Reaching forward, Runolf grasped the closest guard whose movements had been hampered by his comrades. The man scrabbled at his belt for a wicked-looking knife that was sheathed there. Runolf slapped the hand away, jerking the man forward with brutal strength and smashing his forehead into the guard's nose. The guard went limp, and Runolf tossed him disdainfully through the open trapdoor behind him without a glance.

The other guards had fallen into some sort of order now as their leader barked commands. They had left their spears propped against the walls while they lifted me and evidently had not expected such a spirited onslaught from either of us. Seeing the error of their ways they now snatched up their weapons and lowered them at the approaching Norseman.

Runolf laughed, kicking one of the oil lamps at the guards. Oil spilt across the stone paving stones, catching light with a soft sighing *woosh*, like an intake of breath.

"Óðinn!" Runolf shouted again and I knew he was trying to goad them into killing him quickly. This is how he wanted to die. Fighting in a flame-licked battle against many foe-men, not strapped to a chair to have his fingernails pulled out and his teeth extracted while he fought against screaming out and displaying weakness.

The burning oil splattered against the feet and legs of the nearest guard. Small flames clawed their way up his linen breeches and he shrieked, lowering his spear and slapping at the flames with his left hand. Without pause, Runolf seized the opportunity, springing forward and wresting the spear from the guard's grip.

My eyes still streamed with tears, but I could see clearly now. There were six guards remaining in the corridor, with two dispatched into the cell we had inhabited until moments before. Screams and cackling howls came from the open trapdoor and I imagined Ragi and the blind man exacting their revenge on the men who had tormented them.

Fury rushed through me then, as hot and quick as the searing oil that burnt between Runolf and the guards. The guards had yet to fully compose themselves and Runolf had their full attention. If I were to join the fight, perhaps we could defeat them and find our way out of this accursed place.

Anything was possible, I thought, and found myself laughing. The sound was all too similar to the braying cackling of the blind man in the cell and I shuddered to think of what I had become. I would fight, and if I died, it would be a warrior's death. A death of my choosing. With dignity.

I tensed, ready to throw off the hands that held me, when a cold hard length of steel pressed into my throat.

"Tell him to stop," hissed the voice of the gaoler that I recognised so well.

I felt a stinging pain as the sharp blade broke my skin followed by the warmth of my blood as it trickled down my neck.

Runolf was jabbing the spear at the guards, but they held their own blades lowered at him, keeping him at bay. If I did not call out, he might yet find the death he sought, one worthy of song and battle-fame.

"Tell him, or I will open your throat." The knife cut deeper and I gasped. The leader of the guards could take my life in a heartbeat and faced with this reality, I felt my rage extinguished, doused in the water of the truth of my mortality. I did not wish to die there, in that echoing stone corridor far from the land of my birth.

"Runolf," I shouted.

He heard his name over the echoing tumult in the corridor and hesitated, halting his attack. Our eyes met and I understood the unspoken plea in his gaze to let him fight on.

"Hold," I said, "or I die." Even as I spoke the words I felt a new emotion grip me: shame. I had believed I was brave enough to face death without fear. I was wrong, and that truth stung worse than any wound.

For what seemed a long while, nobody moved. Runolf stared at me, and I could imagine how his thoughts whirred inside his mind. At last, with a sigh, he threw the spear down with a clatter.

At a snapped order from their leader, the guards rushed forward, bludgeoning Runolf with their spear butts, pushing him away from the flaming slick of oil and shoving him against the wall as they bound his hands tightly behind his back.

The knife was removed from my throat. I lifted a hand to my neck. My fingers came away sticky with blood.

"Fool," Runolf growled.

"What does he say?" asked the gaoler. I spat onto the flagstones, as much trying to rid my mouth of the taste of my shame as out of a sense of defiance. "Get them out of there," the gaoler barked and his men set about rescuing their comrades from the cell.

Stepping away from me, the gaoler sighed, shaking his head.

"Come now," he said at last. "What does your big friend say? It is not much to ask."

I met Runolf's sullen stare. He glowered back at me. I had already betrayed my friend, what difference would this make? Besides, Runolf spoke the truth.

"He says I am a fool."

The gaoler chuckled on hearing my translation. The sound of his humour was grating against the muffled sounds of violence that came from the cell. I did not like to imagine what fate had befallen Ragi and the blind man.

"He is not wrong, you know," the gaoler said at last. "You are a fool."

His words meant nothing to me. But Runolf's angry glare stung more than the knife that had cut into the skin beneath my chin.

"You are both fools. Our orders are not to harm you, though you have made that more difficult than it should have been."

"You are to take us to the chamber where the prisoners are tortured," I said, all defiance fled now. "Better if we are uninjured, I suppose."

He snorted.

"Perhaps that is so. And mayhap there is pain and torment in your future, *kafir*, but not at my hands or those of anyone in this fortress."

"What do you mean?" I suspected he was toying with me, giving me false hope, but I could not remain silent. Perhaps, I thought, this was where the torture started.

He said something then that confused me even further. I could make little sense of his words, not least because they were so unexpected. I asked him to repeat them and he did, grinning this time, no doubt amused by the amazement on my face.

"What are you two wittering about?" snarled Runolf. "If

they are going to start slicing bits off of us, why don't they just get on with it?"

"He says they do not plan to harm us," I said.

"Well, they would say that, wouldn't they? To keep us quiet." He sounded less than convinced though. His hands were tied and I was once again restrained by two strong warriors, so there seemed no reason to lie to us about this. Unless it was all part of the torment as I suspected.

"I don't think he is lying," I said.

"Well, you are a fool. What does he say then?"

"He says we are to be brought before the Emir of al-Andalus." Runolf frowned.

"Is that their king?"

"Their ruler."

"Wonderful," said Runolf with a sigh, "so we are to be killed before nobility."

"No."

Runolf stared at me then and I think for the first time since escaping the cell he truly saw me. Something in my expression gave him pause and he tilted his head to one side as if trying to see me from a better angle.

"What then?" he asked. "Where are they taking us?"

"He says we are to be taken to Qurtuba. Not as prisoners, but as guests of the emir."

Nineteen

I stared out over the wide river, taking a deep breath of the clean, warm air. The sun was high in the sky and I revelled in its heat and brightness, even though I knew I would not be able to remain under its glare for long. Hereward had told us we had been held prisoner for close to a month. Long enough for our skin to grow pallid and our muscles thin, despite our best efforts to maintain our strength. It was certainly enough time for both Runolf and I to relish every moment in which we could be outside, beneath the open sky.

Since we had been freed, I had avoided the stone buildings of Qadis where possible, only spending the time necessary in the hall of the wazir to hear what awaited us. I could still scarcely believe the change in our fortunes. The night after we had been pulled from the cell, I gave thanks to the Lord and offered up a prayer for Leofstan's soul. He always said that the Almighty's ways were mysterious, and what had happened to us was no exception. We still had no idea what had provoked this decision, or even how the emir had heard of our plight, but no doubt we would discover what God had in store for us when we reached our destination.

A sudden movement at the river's edge drew my gaze and I watched as two moorhens, disturbed by a small rowboat, burst out of the thick stand of reeds that lined the waterway. They flapped across to the far side of the river, where they alighted to glare at the young boys in the boat. The children ignored the birds. They were much more interested in the royal barge that transported us inland on the wide river Ahmad had told me was called al-Wadi 'l-kabir, which meant simply "the Great River". The name was apt. The river was broad and from what Ahmad said, it would carry us all the way to the great city of Išbīliya and then beyond to the capital of al-Andalus, Qurtuba. He said it would take us several days to reach our destination and I marvelled at the size of the kingdom through which we travelled.

The barge was long and shallow-hulled. It was powered by two dozen broad-shouldered slaves who heaved silently at the looms, pulling the boat smoothly against the current of the wide river as it wound its way past rockroses, sweet-smelling rosemary and mastic bushes. We had left the ocean behind but apart from a few low scrub-covered hills in the distance, the land was flat all about us. Oaks grew close to the river. To the north were flat expanses of floodplains and marshes and I marvelled at the crowds of cranes, plovers, ducks and other exotic birds. The fields to the south were verdant with growth, but further afield I could see expanses of cleared ground that were dusty and dry.

"It is too hot."

I turned at the voice, recognising Drosten's burr. I smiled to see the Pict who looked incongruous in the linen robes he had been given by our hosts. To protect himself from the blazing heat of the sun, he had wrapped a long scarf about his head in the manner of some of the men of al-Andalus. Midsummer was still weeks away but the heat was stifling. I could barely imagine that it could grow yet hotter, despite Ahmad's assurances that in the height of summer the temperatures would rise considerably.

"It feels like the heat coming from a smith's forge," I said, wiping beads of sweat from my brow.

Looking at Drosten, I wondered if I should wear one of the cloths about my head, but for the time being, I chose to keep my head uncovered. The thought of swathing my head in cloth brought back memories of the dark cell and how the walls had seemed to press in on us. The cloth was too much like a shroud. Despite the heat, I shivered to think of how close to death we had been.

Soon after we had been freed, I enquired as to Ragi's condition and was informed he had been killed by the guards, along with the blind man who had apparently been in the cell for so long nobody could remember what crime he had committed. I prayed for their souls, adding them to the long list of those who had died because of me. It was I who had caused Runolf and me to be imprisoned and if Runolf had not fought the guards, they would not have taken out their vexation on the powerless captives.

I thought of Hering then. Hereward had told me his body had been laid to rest in a graveyard for Christians. At the news my shame bubbled up to the surface and I fretfully asked about the prayers that had been recited.

"Julian, the local priest, said all the right things," Hereward had assured me. "It was a fitting ceremony for the boy."

How did he know the priest had said the correct words? Hereward could not understand Latin. But I had kept silent, swallowing the angry words that threatened to burst from my lips. Hereward was not to blame for Hering's death, nor for me missing his funeral.

High-pitched chattering brought me back to the hot day. The children in the rowing boat had swung their small vessel out close to the barge. They waved and pointed at Drosten, open-mouthed at the swirl of inked lines that adorned his face and bare arms. Drosten snarled at them playfully, raising his hands like claws, as if he were a savage beast.

The children shrieked with laughter and veered closer for a better look at the strange painted man from the north. They were in danger of colliding with the long oars that dipped with relentless monotony into the dark water, and the barge's captain, a stout man called Faruq, shouted at them to get out of the way. There was a gleam of defiance in the boys' eyes. They whispered to each other, giggling, and I wondered if they might disobey the angry skipper. But another furious bellow from the brawny Faruq saw them decide it might be wise to retreat. With skill and the effortless abandon of childhood, they steered back to the rushes, avoiding the dripping blades of the oars by no more than a hand's breadth.

Drosten laughed aloud and waved at the boys. They waved back, whooping and laughing.

"You're happy," I said. It was true. He seemed happier than at any time I could remember.

"It is not in my nature to be cooped up for so long," he said.

I gave him a sidelong glance.

"I know how you feel," I said, a thin smile on my lips.

He grinned ruefully.

"You know my meaning. It feels good to get out of the city. To have open skies above, wind in our hair and more than anything, new sights to see."

"I cannot argue with you on that," I said.

We both fell silent as we stared ahead into the north-east. The horizon was hazy, as if with smoke or clouds, and I wondered whether I was detecting the first ghostlike glimpse of the mountains Ahmad had told us we would encounter.

While Runolf and I had been imprisoned, the crew of *Brymsteda* had been confined to the ship. They had been fed well, but not allowed any further than the docks, apart from

Hereward and Gwawrddur, who had been permitted to attend the ceremony at Hering's graveside.

The crew's continued detention was due in part to the mayhem caused by me and Runolf, but also because of Giso's disappearance. The Frank had not been seen since the second night in Qadis. By all accounts, when Nadir had found out the small man was missing, he had been furious.

"Do you still not know why we are being taken to the emir?" asked Drosten.

I shook my head.

"Nobody will say. I am just glad to be free."

Drosten glanced at the armed guards and raised his eyebrows. I shrugged.

"Well, they *say* we are free at least, and this certainly beats where Runolf and I spent the last month."

"Aye, I'll take this over that dungeon any day. I can think of little worse. Still, I would rather have a weapon on my belt and *Brymsteda*'s deck beneath us. That would be true freedom. But this is not so bad. And I have to say," he stretched his arms out and looked down at the robes he wore, "I like the clothes. Though I do feel more like a monk than a warrior."

He fingered the fine linen of his long white robe. I ran my hand over the fabric of the clothes I wore. Like the rest of those aboard, I had been dressed in local clothes of lightweight linen and muslin. Before we had been clothed, Runolf and I had been escorted to a communal baths. There we had been stripped naked and washed by slaves, scrubbed clean with water almost too hot to bear. Our skin had been oiled and scraped with sticks, then our muscles massaged, kneaded and twisted until we felt as light-headed as drunks, our arms and legs weak and feeble, as we were led back through the winding streets of the city. I was uncertain what was to happen to us, and even though it felt good to be clean and we had been offered plentiful food and drink before leaving the Wazir of

Qadis' dwelling, when we had been clothed in the lightweight robes my mind had spiralled back to when Leofstan and I had been forced to wash before being dressed in clean robes and taken before Ljósberari.

A snatch of laughter reached us and I looked back to where the rest of our band, or at least those who were coming with us to Qurtuba, sat beneath the shade of an awning that had been erected in the midships on a platform above the heads of the rowers.

Revna's golden hair caught the sun. I was thankful that she was well. Her wound had healed, leaving only a small scar. Beside her, protectively close, sat Runolf. He had insisted that she come with us. Hereward had thought it might be too dangerous.

"There is danger everywhere," Runolf had replied. "Revna stays at my side."

Revna had not offered her thoughts on the matter. Hereward had merely nodded and no more had been said.

Drosten followed my gaze and placed a hand on my shoulder.

"He will come around," he said.

It had been two days since I had been dragged from the cell and Runolf had surged up out of the pit to fight the guards. In that time Runolf had not spoken a word to me. I could not blame him, for so much of what had occurred had been my doing, but his disdain cut me like a seax beneath the shieldwall.

Gwawrddur, perhaps sensing my eyes upon the group sitting in the shade, looked in my direction and raised a hand in greeting. Hereward turned and waved too. Ahmad, more sombre and sullen than ever, did not look up from where he sat, head down, dejected. Tayyib had not returned to see him since that first day, and Ahmad feared he had made a terrible decision in returning to his homeland. He might have his freedom from thralldom, but to what end, and at what cost?

Slowly, Runolf turned his head, his huge red mane flashing in the dappled sunshine that reflected from the water. Pushing himself to his feet, he walked towards me. Drosten clasped my shoulder.

"I will leave you two to talk," he said, and walked past the Norseman.

I turned back to stare out over the river and the land sliding slowly past on the banks. Runolf took the place at the rail where Drosten had stood. For a long while neither of us spoke and I began to think he would not break the silence that had fallen between us.

"I am sorry," I blurted out at last, unable to keep quiet any longer.

"I am sorry," Runolf said at exactly the same moment.

We both smiled.

"It appears we are both sorry," he said.

"I was a fool," I said. "You were right."

"You are often foolish, Hunlaf," he said, not looking me in the eye. "But you blame yourself for much. I know you think you were craven."

"I should not have called out to halt you. I knew what you wanted."

"Ah, but I too am a fool," Runolf said, a sad tinge to his tone. "As Hereward reminded me today. I longed for a brave death, a bloody slaying that would arouse the interest of the All-Father himself."

"I know," I said. "And I denied you that."

"If you had not spoken out I might well have got what I desired." He glanced over his shoulder at where the others sat. "And I would never have seen Revna again. Or seen these trees, or this river. Who knows what else I would have lost, and for what?"

"I was frightened." I reached up and touched the scab from the gaoler's knife cut. "Nothing more."

"We are all frightened, Hunlaf. But you have stood by my side when all appeared forsaken. I know you are no coward. You are my friend." He looked me in the eye then and grinned. "Fool or not."

Twenty

"By Christ's bones, it has been three days!" Drosten paced across the room as he had done dozens of times already that morning.

"Your anger gains us nothing," said Gwawrddur, sipping from an elaborately fashioned silver goblet. "But your constant pacing makes my head throb."

"It is not my pacing," Drosten grumbled. "It is your drinking."

The Welshman smiled and held up his cup.

"I have drunk but sparingly," he said. "It is Runolf who has emptied two pitchers already. And it is not even midday."

"Come and sit down," said Runolf. He belched loudly, and patted the cushions beside him. "Try some of these dates. They are as sweet as honey. And if the emir means to kill us, better to be drunk when the time comes."

"He does not mean to kill us," said Hereward in the tone he would use to explain something to a slow child. He had repeated himself many times before over recent days.

"How can you be so sure?" asked Drosten.

"Why would he bring us all this way and feed us with such delicacies, if he only meant to have us slain?" Hereward held up a small syrup-glistened pastry stuffed with almonds and pistachios, examining it briefly before popping it into his mouth.

"Perhaps he wishes to make our deaths all the more shocking for us when the moment comes," replied Drosten, but without much conviction. "If I have to remain in this room much longer, I will save him the trouble and take my own life. I thought we were done being held prisoner."

Giving up on his pacing, he threw himself down onto a pile of the soft cushions that dotted the cool tiled floor. Revna handed him a cup, which he accepted with a nod.

I didn't like being confined to these quarters either, but there were worse places to be kept prisoner. The rooms we shared were large and airy, with windows that looked out over well-tended gardens and the sprawling city of Qurtuba beyond. Past the jumble of buildings and the thick stone slabs of the old Roman wall, hills rose, clouds draping over their dark summits.

The distant murmur of the bustling city wafted on the breeze, carrying with it a rich melange of smells; cooking food, spices and herbs, and the undercurrent of manure that permeates all such conglomerations of people. When the wind shifted, the altogether more pleasant scent of orange blossom reached us from the tiered terraces of the gardens.

Looking back at my comrades sprawled about the room, I caught Runolf's eye. He drained his cup and smirked.

"Stop your complaining, Drosten," he said. "There are many worse things than to be fed and clothed and kept in luxury."

"We still don't know why we are here," said Hereward.

"We will find out soon enough," said Runolf. "If there is one thing I have learnt about kings it is that you cannot rush them. They like to feel their own power. Making us wait is all part of that dance." He stifled another belch and held out his goblet to Revna. Dutifully she filled her father's cup from a pitcher.

I turned to look out the window once more. If I could not move freely about the palace grounds, I would at least allow my eyes to wander. The morning sun glinted from the waters of the al Wadi 'l-kabir and I thought of our journey along the great meandering river.

It had taken us the best part of a fortnight to reach Qurtuba. The land had remained flat, dotted with olive groves, fields of wheat and orchards until we reached Išbīliya. The great river was wide and green-brown, lined with waxy-leaved trees and beyond them, several soaring towers from where the priests called the faithful to prayer. Išbīliya was like nothing I had ever seen before. It seemed that each city we visited was grander than the one before, and I realised then that Qadis had been a provincial settlement. Of course, this was long before I had visited the Madīnat as-Salām or the gleaming jewel that is Byzantion. If greater cities exist on this earth, I have not seen them.

We were taken ashore at Išbīliya and quartered in what appeared to be a barracks for the city guard. The warriors posted there stared at us with open interest and I was surprised to see several of their number with fair hair and skin as pale as Runolf's. After we had eaten at the table provided for us, one of the blond guards had approached us. I'd half-expected him to address us in Norse or Englisc, but he had spoken first in a tongue I did not comprehend and, when I shook my head, in al-Arabiyyah.

"Do you play at the dice?" he'd asked.

We had become bored with nobody but our small band for company. Faruq, our guards and the barge crew kept apart from us, so when I translated this fair-haired man's words to my friends they let out great whoops of joy. I have seldom met a fighting man who does not like games of chance and the men from the Išbīliya Watch were no exception.

We spent a loud night of gambling and drinking wine

with them. The man who had first spoken to us was called Leander and was a Christian. It turned out that many of the city guard were Christian men and they appeared to have more in common with us than merely the colour of their skin. The games they played were familiar to us, as were some of their riddles and jests that I interpreted. As the drink flowed, their speech became more relaxed and Leander was happy to answer my questions. His grandfather remembered a time before the coming of the Moors to the land, and while he was not bitter at the rulers who now governed the kingdom they called al-Andalus, he said the Christians tried to keep alive the memories and customs of their people.

I looked about the simple stone edifice that housed the warriors and thought of the timber buildings in the north. How long would the memories of Leander's people, so similar to ours in far-off Britain, remain? Like the Romans of old, the Moors built grand constructions of chiselled stone. Their legacy would long outlive the ghosts of wood and thatch of Leander and his people, I thought.

One other interesting thing I learnt during that long night of laughter, dice and wine made me think about Giso. When I mentioned that we had sailed from Frankia, Leander had whistled.

"Be thankful you are not Frankish," he'd said.

When I'd enquired about his comment, he'd shaken his head.

"The Moors have no love of the Franks. Carolus invaded the north. He took Ǧarundaḧ and besieged Banbalūnaḧ. That was in the time of the emir's father. But the son of Abd al-Rahman won't forget that in a hurry."

I pondered his words and later discussed them with Hereward and Gwawrddur.

"It seems to me," said Hereward, "that we would do well not to mention our Frankish friend."

"I wonder where he went," mused Gwawrddur.

"We all wonder that," I replied. "Maybe we will never know. Perhaps he didn't go far at all."

"What do you mean?" asked Hereward.

"If the Franks are hated so much here, perhaps Giso didn't run away. Maybe he found his way into the waters of the dock."

Hereward scowled at that. Gwawrddur looked pensive.

"Whatever happened to him, he is not our concern now," he said, "and I agree with Hereward. We should avoid mentioning Giso, or who he served."

The next morning we had bidden farewell to Leander and continued north on our way with a fresh crew of slaves. We made good progress, but the waters, whilst still wide, flowed faster now as the land about us became hillier.

It was on the twelfth day when we reached our destination. Išbīliya had astounded me with its towers and stone buildings, but nothing had prepared me for the grandeur of Qurtuba. Centuries before it had been home to the Romans and they had left behind massive walls of cut rock that surrounded the whole city. There were ancient temples, massive archways, fine villas and palaces. We all looked up in silent awe as we glided beneath the huge stone bridge that spanned the river on its sixteen arcades. The bridge was fortified on the southern bank by a stout tower and it glowed in the warmth of the afternoon sun.

Into this wondrous collection of buildings, the Moors had built their own palaces and fortifications. The gem of the city though, and perhaps of the entire kingdom, was the *masjid*, the grand temple. We had passed one of its arched entrances as we were being escorted to the emir's palace and I had longed to enter, to see what lay beyond the courtyard in which grew slender fruit trees. I spied pillars and arches but we were not permitted to linger, and so I was left with the memory of the line of red and cream archways drifting away into the shadowed recesses of the holy building.

From the wharfs that lined the river, we were led through the narrow, shaded streets to the palace complex on the west side of the city. The stalls in the marketplace were closing, ready for evening prayers, but the glimpses I caught of the wares on offer told a tale of wealth and prosperity. There were splendid bolts of brightly coloured fabrics, and, just as vibrant, open sacks of cumin, cinnamon, pepper and ginger, and small casks of the most precious spice, saffron. The pungent smell of the spices hung heavy over the surrounding streets. At the end of one alley we passed, I saw the glint of polished silver trinkets dangling beneath an awning. An old, leather-faced man saw me looking and beckoned to me. In the shadows beside the stall stood a burly man with the craggy face of a brawler. He leant on a massive cudgel the length of my leg. I had paused to look, but one of the guards who escorted us pushed me forward.

There was so much about the city that intrigued me and I was disappointed not to have been able to explore its secrets. But, sniffing the air now and detecting the merest hint of the aromatic spices on the breeze, I reminded myself once again that this was not so bad.

Once within the palace walls, the guards who had been with us aboard the barge, handed us over to a lean man who introduced himself as Hafiz, steward of the palace. Accompanied by a dozen armed guards in case we had any ideas of attempting to escape, Hafiz led us through the gardens and to a large building. The sun had been low in the sky and the stone of the building gleamed in the golden light. The polished armour and helms of the guards glimmered.

"Everything you require will be brought to you," Hafiz had told us, as he'd ushered us into the suite of rooms that were to be our home for the next three days.

Trays laden with food awaited us. There was spiced chicken, flat breads, oily dipping pastes, and bowls of bright, shiny fruit, the like of which we had never seen before. Beneath the tough skins, they were sweet and filled with juicy flesh that tore off in neat segments. There were large pitchers of water and wine too. That first night we had all drunk too much, glad to be off the barge. After several cups of wine, Runolf had pushed open the door that led to the gardens, intending to piss into one of the bushes. The guards stationed outside had crossed their spears, preventing him from leaving.

"Where am I to piss?" Runolf had shouted drunkenly.

My head was already swimming from my own overindulgence, but I was keen to avoid a fight that might break the fragile balance we had found with our captors.

"There are pots," I said. "In that small room. Use them."

Runolf had blinked at me.

"What if I need to shit?" he asked.

"Then use the largest pot!" shouted Hereward, which made the others laugh.

Runolf frowned for a time, but eventually joined in with the laughter.

The following morning, servants came to remove the trays, platters, cups and jugs and replaced them with fresh provender. They also removed the pots of night soil, which was a great relief to us all, as the door to the small room did little to keep the smell out of our sleeping quarters. When I asked the servants about when we would be taken before the emir, they lowered their gaze and hurried away.

By midday, we had begun to get restless and, when we had seen nobody else but the servants, I went to the door and questioned the guards posted there. They stared into the distance and would not speak to me.

That afternoon, Hafiz visited our rooms and enquired as to our comfort.

"We have all we need," I said, "but when will we see the emir?"

"Be patient, for surely Allah is with those who remain patient," he replied. "You will stay here until the emir is ready to grant you an audience."

"And how long will that be?"

"Who can say?" he said with a small bow. "Perhaps tomorrow."

But tomorrow had passed, and when Hafiz came that afternoon, he repeated the same message.

"The thing about tomorrow," said Gwawrddur, "is that it is forever a day away."

The next day passed without incident. The servants came with food and drink and we gorged ourselves, lounging on the soft cushions and debating what the emir would say once we were taken before him. At intervals throughout the day, the call to prayer would drift over the rooftops of Qurtuba, and Ahmad would kneel and chant. He spoke very little, and when I asked him if he had ever met the emir before, he merely shook his head and turned away – but not before I saw the haunted look in his eyes. He was frightened, I was sure, but when I pressed him, he denied it. There was something he was not telling us, but no matter how I tried, I could not get him to speak to me.

In the evening, by the light of oil lamps that guttered in the draught from the windows, we told riddles. None was better at the telling than Hereward, but even he could not lift our spirits for long. Despite the sumptuous luxury in which we were surrounded, we were not content. We were all warriors, people of action. Even Revna was more at home at the steerboard of a ship, or standing in a shieldwall, than she would have been baking bread, brewing ale or weaving, like other women. We were all impatient for something to happen, and even though I drank more wine than was good for me, I slept badly.

As I had drifted off to sleep on that second night, I'd heard distant singing and the plucking of a stringed instrument. The sound reminded me of the music I had heard in Qadis all those weeks before. Then, just as sleep found me, another sound jolted me awake.

I lay there in silence, listening to the night for what had awoken me. I sat up as I heard it again, clear now that I was fully awake. A pitiful scream, agonised and mad with anguish, echoed thinly on the night breeze.

The room was in darkness, but I saw I was not the only one awake. Runolf was also sitting, the moonlight from the open window reflecting coolly in his eyes.

"Did you hear that?" I whispered.

He nodded, but did not speak. Without warning, despite the pliant pillows beneath me, I was back in that dank cell in Qadis. I shivered, wrapping myself in a blanket and lying back down.

I listened for a long time but heard nothing more save the snores of my companions. I would have almost believed I had imagined the cry of pain in the darkness if Runolf had not heard it too. When at last I slept, I dreamt Ragi was slumbering nearby. I sensed the presence of the blind man too, sleeping just out of reach, and far off I heard the dreadful screams of the tortured Naddoðr.

In the morning, nobody else mentioned hearing screams in the night. But when Hereward asked us if we had slept well, Runolf raised an eyebrow at me. Neither of us said anything of the screams. There seemed little point. We were all on edge as it was and to talk of such things would only further unnerve the others.

I had slept poorly at night after that, my mind filled with nightmares.

Yawning, I rose now and moved away from the window. Outside was another bright, warm day, the city bustling with life. Soon, I calculated, it would be time for the midday prayers, but until the priest's ululating cries pierced the quiet of the palace, I decided to close my eyes. There was nothing else to do and I needed rest. My body had recovered much of its bulk these last weeks since being released from prison, but still I found the prospect of sleep increasingly attractive, especially as my nights were disturbed by bad dreams.

Pulling up some of the pillows into a nest by one wall, I lay down. For the briefest of spells, I listened to Runolf's rumbling voice, interspersed with Revna's soft tone, as they discussed the merits of the different fruits that had been delivered to us that morning. Then, as if a black curtain had been pulled over my mind, I was asleep.

I must have slept more soundly than I had anticipated, for when I woke I knew instantly that midday was long past. Sunlight streamed through the windows, its beams lancing low through dancing motes of dust.

All around the room, my friends were on their feet and I sat up quickly, still groggy from sleep and wondering what was afoot. A clatter drew my attention and I saw the door was open. Hafiz was standing in the doorway, shadowed by the bright afternoon sun beyond. Behind him the armour and weapons of a score of palace guards gleamed.

"On your feet, Killer," said Gwawrddur, using his name for me that never ceased to annoy me. "It seems the moment we have been waiting for is upon us."

I glanced over at Ahmad. His face was pallid, his dark eyes wide.

"Make haste," said Hafiz, his tone clipped. "His illustrious grace the emir will see you now."

Twenty-One

I was barely awake. My mind still reeled as we walked through the gardens behind Hafiz. The scent of the white blossom was strong as we passed through the shadows of the citrus trees. I breathed in deeply, relishing the breeze on my face, but there was no time to enjoy the sensation of freedom that came from being outside.

Of course, we were no more free than a bird in a cage. A dozen sombre-faced guards marched at our flanks and several more brought up the rear. Hafiz strode briskly, giving us scant time to take in any of the details of the garden. I wanted to speak to the others, but even as I thought it, I knew there was nothing to say. We had already exhausted the conversation about the emir's purpose in bringing us here. Now all we could do was wait and see what was in store for us.

And pray that our worst fears were not justified.

We reached a set of huge double doors that opened into the main structure of the palace. I was breathing hard, not just from the brisk walk across the gardens, but also with pent-up anxiety. There was nothing to worry about, I told myself. Of that Hereward was surely right. The emir would not have brought us here merely to have us killed.

Two of the guards stepped forward and pulled open the

doors. Hafiz squared his shoulders and kept his eyes focused straight ahead as he stepped through the doorway and into a colonnaded courtyard. We followed him, hurrying to keep up.

Beyond the doors was a shaded, quiet place, surrounded by slim columns. It reminded me of part of the chapel at Aachen, an area for peaceful reflection and prayer. At the centre of the cool space, a statue of a beast stood. From its fanged mouth trickled water into a stone bowl. Stone-lined channels ran across the ground, catching the water that fell from the fountain like rain. I found myself wondering at the spectacle of the flowing water that appeared to rise without aid from the stone statue. I frowned, attempting to envisage the mechanism that could drive such a thing.

I collided with Ahmad, who had halted without warning. Behind me, Revna gasped. Turning to see what had upset her, a cold fist gripped my chest and I realised my certainty that the emir would not slay us might have been misplaced.

I had been too intent on the fountain to notice at first, but now I saw that the courtyard was not a place for quiet contemplation. It was more akin to a torturer's chamber than a cloister. The others had also stopped and were gazing about them with horror on their features. Runolf hawked and spat into one of the fountain's channels.

The guards behind us attempted to push us forward at first, then they relented, allowing us a moment to take in the gory scene.

Between the stone columns, six stout, tall timber crosses had been raised. Upon each one hung a corpse, arms outstretched, wrists bound to the cross beams. They were naked, their bodies streaked with dried blood. Great iron nails had been driven through their hands and feet. I staggered back from this obscene parody of our Lord Jesu Christ's passion. My breath was ragged, and I thought I might faint.

"Help me," croaked a voice.

Looking up into the eyes of the nearest corpse I saw he was not dead. His mouth worked and his eyes rolled in agony and torment. There was something familiar in the man's features, but for a time I could not make out what it was. Then it came to me in a rush.

"Rifat?" I asked, my voice barely audible against the rushing of my blood.

The man on the cross mewled and whimpered, as if I had struck him. I could see clearly now. Though the assured noble I had met in Qadis was far removed from this broken husk of a man, there could be no doubt that this was Rifat al-Haidar, captain of the ships that had been in pursuit of the pirates and had later escorted us to port.

"Say what you will about the Romans," said a smooth voice in al-Arabiyyah, "they knew how to build. And they knew how to punish those who failed them."

I turned to see a tall, young man step from the shadows at the far side of the courtyard. He wore a white robe, cinched at the waist with a belt of pure gold. His hair was long and gleaming, the dark-bronze locks oiled and fashioned cunningly into what appeared to be two horns over his forehead. On his brow he wore a circlet of gold and jewels.

Hafiz immediately bowed deeply. Ahmad fell to his knees. The guards snapped to attention with a stamp of feet, a clatter of armour and the thump of spear butts on the flagstones.

"Bow before his most Royal Highness," Hafiz said without raising his eyes, "Al-Hakam Ibn Hisham Ibn Abd-ar-Rahman, Emir of al-Andalus."

The steward's meaning, reinforced by Ahmad's and the guards' reaction to the newcomer, was clear enough without translation. Hereward bowed respectfully, as did Drosten, Revna and Gwawrddur. I lowered my eyes for a moment, then looked up at the emir. Runolf did not so much as drop his gaze, instead staring down defiantly at the young man before him.

I could sense the anger coming from the Norseman. We had been imprisoned and tormented in this man's kingdom and now we were surrounded by crucified men. I shared Runolf's ire. Rifat had seemed to me a good man, a man of honour. I did not know what he had done to deserve this fate. But the emir's eyes flashed with a wicked light I had seen before in men who wield great power and enjoy inflicting pain on others.

"Easy, Runolf," I whispered. This was not a man to be goaded by an insolent glare. The broken men hanging around us were testament to that.

"I see these bitter trees do not bring you joy," the emir continued, waving his hands to encompass the crosses with their gruesome adornments. "But a leader must show his people that he is to be obeyed." He looked about the men hanging pitifully from the timber frames, a sorrowful look on his fine features.

Al-Hakam stepped closer, moving past Hafiz and the others towards me. I tensed. I have met many powerful men in my life. Some are uneasy with the authority that life and circumstance have bestowed upon them, others are resigned to their lot in life. The most dangerous are certain in their power, believing they have a divine right to command, that they are superior to all others because God so wills it. Al-Hakam was such a man and the aura of his self-worth, like a physical force, made me step aside, in spite of myself.

The guards moved to position themselves between their ruler and us, but he waved them away, quite sure that we posed him no threat.

Reaching past me, he caressed Rifat's blood-streaked foot.

"By Allah," Al-Hakam said, his voice as tender as if he talked to a child, "you are a brave one, son of Haidar."

Rifat stared down at his emir, his face a mask of conflicting emotions, terror and pain giving way to a pathetic longing. And hope.

"My lord emir," I said, speaking loudly. My throat was dry and I was glad my voice did not crack and betray my nervousness.

Hafiz took a sharp intake of breath at my audacity. The guards nearest me stepped forward, ready to drag me away.

I sensed the danger in addressing the emir so boldly, but I did not stop to think of what I was saying. All I knew was that I had to speak, no matter the consequences. I could not stand by and watch such suffering in silence.

Al-Hakam turned to stare at me, his gaze withering.

"Are you the Frank?" he asked.

Confused, I shook my head.

"I come from Northumbria. In Britain." I was pleased that Ahmad had taught me his people's names for the northern kingdom and the island to which it belonged.

"And yet you speak my tongue well. There are not many who come from the north who can speak the language of al-Arabiyyah." I could smell the expensive oils in the emir's hair. His skin was smooth and unblemished. He looked me up and down, and I stiffened, suddenly conscious of how I must seem to him. My hair was shaggy and uncut, my beard straggly. Al-Hakam's nose wrinkled. I had not bathed for many days and was instantly aware of my body's stench. "I had been told you were all warriors."

I forced myself to stand tall. I would not be cowed by this imperious Moor.

"I am a warrior," I said, glad to hear my voice remained firm. "But I am also a scholar."

"A scholar and a fighter!" Al-Hakam chuckled. "Can you truly be a Christian?" He grinned as if proud of his comment. Hafiz sniggered, whether out of a sense of duty or with real humour, I could not tell.

"I was a monk, once," I said, as if that explained everything.

"A fighting monk!" He clapped his hands in delight. "I did

not imagine I would enjoy meeting you so much." He appeared genuinely surprised and pleased. Without warning, he rounded on his steward, his tone now cold and hard as granite in winter. "Hafiz, why did you not tell me that these men were so interesting?"

"I am sorry, my lord emir," Hafiz mumbled, swallowing and bowing low. His face had grown pallid and I wondered how angry this emir would need to be to give the order for a new cross to be erected for his steward.

"What is your name, warrior monk," Al-Hakam said, turning back to me with a smile as if the exchange with Hafiz had not occurred.

"I am Hunlaf."

"Do the rest of your comrades also speak the language of my people?"

"I am afraid not, my lord," I said. "Only Ahmad there."

Al-Hakam's face clouded as he glanced at the kneeling man.

"Well, Hunlaf, it is no matter. I believe you and I can speak together well enough." He smiled broadly. "But come, let us retire inside. I have had refreshments brought for us. We have much to speak of, and..." he waved his hand before his face as if wafting away a bad smell, "... the sight of these pitiful wretches does nothing for my appetite."

He turned on his heel and began to stride back across the courtyard, certain that I would obediently follow.

I did not move.

Instead I called out, causing Al-Hakam to halt. I noted the rigid tension in his shoulders. Hafiz stared at me, consternation on his face. I sensed the guards readying themselves, as if they expected a fight to ensue.

"Lord emir," I said. "Before we eat, I have a boon to ask of you."

He turned slowly to face me. Anger flicked across his features, but it was coloured with something else. Surprise, perhaps even wonderment. I could see that all of my friends were looking at me in amazement, but I dared not pull my gaze away from Al-Hakam's for fear I might lose my nerve in the face of such privileged superiority.

"A boon, you say?"

I wondered if I had used the correct word. I delved into my memories, searching for a word that would better express my meaning.

"Yes, my lord. A request."

He held my gaze for a long while. The courtyard was silent but for the burbling of the fountain. I did not blink. I had come this far and I sensed that to show weakness now would be my undoing.

"Well ask it of me, man," Al-Hakam said at last. "I wish to slake my thirst and sate my hunger."

"I know not what these men have done," I said, gesturing at the crucified wretches. "But this man, Rifat, yet lives. I would ask that he be shown clemency."

"By Allah," said the emir, "you said you were once a monk. Perhaps there is yet too much of the holy man about you. Mercy is for the weak."

"I do not agree," I said. "It is through the display of mercy that a ruler shows his true power."

Al-Hakam glowered at me. The courtyard felt all of a sudden colder, as if a cloud had passed before the sun. The evidence of this man's temper was all around me. I was a fool to question him. But Rifat had treated us with decency. Whatever he might have done to anger his emir, surely he had suffered enough.

"Hunlaf the holy," said Al-Hakam slowly. "It is true, you do not know what these men did to displease me, but I will tell you why they have been punished soon enough." His eyes narrowed. "But you are right. It is the sign of a powerful ruler to show mercy. Rifat has ever been a loyal servant. Till now.

I will spare him. Hafiz, have Rifat cut down and his wounds tended to."

"At once, my lord," said the steward, pleased to again be receiving his master's orders, rather than his disapproval. He snapped his fingers and the leader of the guards barked a command. Three of his men moved to Rifat's cross and began the task of removing him from the object of his torment.

I let out my breath, pleased that I had been able to do this much for the poor man. I turned to thank Al-Hakam, but all I saw were his swishing silk robes as he swept out of the courtyard, under the far colonnade and through a shadowed opening into the palace.

Twenty-Two

"What do you think of the food?" Al-Hakam asked. He was propped on one elbow beside a low, gilded table. Several such tables dotted the palace hall. Each of them was laden with platters and bowls of the finest foods I had ever tasted. There were delicacies I could barely comprehend. Tiny roasted quails stuffed with almonds and honey, exquisite balls of spiced meat wrapped in vine leaves, colourful desserts encrusted with pine nuts and pistachios. We had thought that the food and drink we had been supplied in our rooms had been sumptuous, but it was like animal fodder in comparison to this fabulous feast.

I sat awkwardly upon a silken cushion near the emir. He had urged me to sit beside him at his table and had enquired who had commanded the ship we had sailed to his shores. When I told him it was Runolf, he had clapped his hands together happily and ordered the giant to join us. Scowling, Runolf now sat uncomfortably cross-legged beside the low table.

The others sprawled at a separate table. They had wanted for nothing and each of the new foods that was first laid before the emir was also served to them by one of the numerous slaves and servants.

The latest delicacy, thin slivers of meat glistening in a rich gravy, had been brought in by a veiled, plump-hipped servant. She placed the ornately decorated silver tray on the table near Al-Hakam's hand. He pushed the tray towards me, nodding for me to try it.

"Lamb. One of my favourites," he said, beaming. The light from the numerous oil lamps that hung from chains about the hall reflected on his white teeth and glimmered in his eyes. "You must try it. I had it prepared especially for you, my honoured guests."

Something in his tone unnerved me. His smile was too broad, as if he was about to let me in on a jest. Tentatively, wondering if perhaps the meat might be poisoned, I took one of the small strips of lamb and sniffed it. It smelt good, sweet and pungent with cinnamon. Nodding to Al-Hakam, I placed the meat in my mouth and offered up a silent prayer that this was not some elaborate punishment.

The flavour burst on my tongue. It was savoury as well as sweet, with a deep warmth. My eyes widened. The emir, grinning now like an excited child, clapped his hands and chuckled.

"Good, no?" he asked.

"It is extraordinary," I replied.

"It is my wife's recipe."

"Then you are blessed beyond measure," I said. "You must thank her for me. I have never tasted the like before."

"You can thank her yourself," he said, his smile growing even wider. He was pleased with himself, but I was still unsure what it was that amused him so.

"She is in the palace?"

"Indeed she is." Rising, he stepped close to the woman who had served the food and pulled away her muslin veil. "You can thank her for the food and I must also thank you, and Runolf here. All of you."

I stared at the woman. Her hair was black, long and sleek

and arranged in a simple style that pulled it back from her forehead to cascade down her back. I had believed her a servant, but I saw now that her clothes were of the finest silk, and gold and silver jewellery adorned her neck, wrists and fingers.

Slowly, I realised I had seen her before. Even then she'd had the self-assurance that came from a position of authority, but when I had seen her last, it had been under the bright hot sun, and despite her poise, her eyes had held a constant suggestion of fear and uncertainty. Now she met my gaze with an open expression. She lifted her chin so that the light from the nearest lamp fell upon her face.

"Halawah," I said at last. "Peace be upon you."

She bowed demurely.

"And upon you," she replied. "I am glad to see you are well."

I thought of the long weeks Runolf and I had spent incarcerated, but now was not the time to bring that up.

"And I am pleased to see you hale," I said.

"Is that the woman from the pirate ship?" asked Runolf.

I nodded, unable to look away from Halawah.

"She is the emir's wife."

Runolf laughed loudly at that. I didn't know what else to say.

"Ask her about her brother," he said.

My thoughts felt as though they might bolt like a frightened horse and I was struggling to hold onto their reins. But I nodded at Runolf's suggestion.

"How is your brother, my lady?" I asked.

Before she could reply, Al-Hakam let out a loud guffaw.

"Abd ar-Rahman is no more her brother than I am a peasant," he said. "He is our son."

The true import of what he said dawned on me and I whispered to Runolf, explaining what had been said. The Norseman, his tongue already loose from the wine that morning and more since we had sat at the table, shouted out to the others in Englisc, his words slurred.

"The woman we rescued is the emir's wife. The boy is his son!"

Al-Hakam did not seem to mind Runolf's lack of decorum. He smiled indulgently, as if the Norseman were a boy to be humoured.

"So now you see why I have brought you here," he said. "The moment I heard you had been detained in Qadis, I sent word for you to be freed and the charges against you dropped."

I did not answer right away and he went on. "I wanted to thank you. You, *kuffaar* from the north in one ship, did what three of my vessels failed to do. And now you also know why Rifat and the others needed to be punished."

It was all clear to me now.

"They allowed your family to be taken," I said flatly.

"From under their noses!" He slapped his hand down hard on the metal-topped table. The plates and goblets rattled.

"Your son is well now?" I asked, wishing to draw the emir's thoughts away from the captains of the ships he held responsible for his wife and son's capture.

He scooped up a goblet and drank some wine. His breathing slowed and he nodded.

"He is well. They both are." Al-Hakam sat down, waving Halawah away. Without a word, she bowed and departed. "I owe you much, warrior monk. I would repay you, but first tell me of your travels, of the things you have seen."

"What does he speak of?" asked Runolf.

"He wants to hear of our voyages. And he wishes to repay us for rescuing his family."

"I like the sound of that," said Runolf, draining the contents of his goblet. A servant stepped from the shadows beneath the columns that ran the length of the room and refilled his cup.

"If he wants to hear stories, tell him what he wants. Then I would hear how he wishes to pay us."

And so I answered Al-Hakam's questions. Despite his mercurial disposition, he was clearly educated and intelligent. He asked me about Northumbria, making it clear from his queries that he had heard tell of the Norse raids there.

"You met Runolf there?" he asked. "At that first attack?"

I hated being made to recall that terrifying day of fire and blood, but there was no denying the emir.

"I did."

He furrowed his brow and looked sidelong at Runolf.

"And yet he lives."

"The lord of those lands wished to see him slain," I said. "I convinced him to spare Runolf."

"Ah, ever the merciful monk at heart," Al-Hakam said with a smile.

I bridled at his dismissive tone.

"Runolf is now a good friend, to me and to my people. He built the ship we sail and he has fought by my side many times."

Al-Hakam stroked his chin thoughtfully. Runolf leaned over and tapped me on the arm.

"What is he asking you? I hear my name spoken."

"He was asking why you yet live after attacking Lindisfarnae."

Runolf scowled, perhaps liking even less than me to be reminded of the events at the island minster.

"I am thankful for my life," he said, "but I do not think you have had reason to complain of your decision to spare me."

I offered him a smile.

"That's what I said. Now, drink some more wine and let the emir talk. I do not think he is one who likes to be kept waiting."

I turned back to Al-Hakam, who was drumming his long fingers on the tabletop.

"Apologies," I said. "Runolf wished to know what we were speaking of."

"Of course," Al-Hakam replied smoothly, as if he had not been impatient at all. "I am told the ship he built is long and sleek like a sea serpent."

I pictured the curving lines of the overlapping strakes, the billowing sail, straining against the rigging, the sweeping prow, topped with the proud, wild-eyed stallion Drosten had carved.

"It is called *Brymsteda*, which means sea-steed, and it gallops over the waves faster than any other ship."

"Your mercy in sparing the Norseman bore fruit then."

"I thank the Lord for bringing Runolf into my life."

Al-Hakam's eyes flicked to Drosten, the Pict's tattooed face appearing inhuman in the flickering light of the torches.

"Did you find that one on your travels?" he asked. "When I heard tell of the painted man aboard your ship, I had to see him. I had not truly believed what I had been told, but he is as strange as they said."

"Drosten's people come from islands to the north of Britain. He is a Pict, and their warriors paint their bodies in this manner."

"Incredible," replied Al-Hakam. "Have him approach."

"Drosten," I called out, "the emir wishes to have a closer look at you."

"He can see me well enough from there," Drosten muttered around the stuffed quail that filled his mouth.

"Drosten," I said, careful not to raise my voice, "the emir holds our lives and our freedom in his hands. You would do well to remember that."

Reluctantly, Drosten pushed himself up with a sigh. Tossing the bones he had been chewing onto a plate, he walked towards our table, licking his fingers clean of the meat juices and sauce. He was heavily muscled and walked with the light gait of a warrior. The tattoos that swirled around his features only served to make him look even more formidable.

Al-Hakam nodded appreciatively.

"And these lines cover the rest of his body too?" he asked.

"His arms and torso are painted, yes." The emir was fascinated with Drosten. His eyes glimmered, and I dreaded the next request that I was certain would emanate from his lips.

"I would see this," he said, his tone not much more than a whisper. "Have him remove his robe."

I sighed.

Drosten could not comprehend the emir's words, but he was perceptive and no fool.

"He wants me to remove my clothing, does he not?" he snarled.

I met his gaze and nodded, with what I hoped was an apologetic expression on my face.

"He does."

Drosten squared his shoulders and clenched his fists. His knuckles were knotted and scarred.

"I will not do it," he hissed. "I am no animal for any man to gawk at."

"Drosten," I implored, "do you so quickly forget what we saw in the courtyard? It would be wise to do as he asks."

Drosten glowered at me and the emir.

"I do not believe he will kill me for not stripping off my robe." With that, he turned and stalked back to his place at the other table. The others had all been listening intently. None of them spoke.

Al-Hakam's features grew dark.

"What did he say?" he asked.

I swallowed. I could think of no way to avoid the truth.

"He said he is no animal for you to look at."

Al-Hakam stared at Drosten for a long time. The silence of the room grew oppressive.

"He is a brave man," the emir said at last. "Proud too." He was grinning and I let out my breath slowly. "A warrior should be proud. There is no place for meek warriors."

The afternoon dragged into evening.

When we had eaten our fill, we moved to a different room where musicians played soothing melodies. A handsome, fresh-faced young man plucked a short-necked stringed instrument called an *oud*. An older man with a flowing beard tapped intricate rhythms gently on the stretched skins of small drums. A third man, whose bald head gleamed in the lamp light, played counterpoints to the *oud* on a flute. More wine was served, along with a sweet mint infusion.

The emir continued to question me about our travels. I recounted the tale of our trip to Rygjafylki, telling him most of what had occurred there, but leaving out mention of *The Treasure of Life*. He was most interested when I spoke of the trade agreement Mancas had brokered with King Hjorleif.

"Commerce is the blood which pumps through the veins of a kingdom," he said. "You must take word north to your king to send emissaries. We are rich in oil and many fruits of the land. We produce fine silverware, glass and leather goods, but of course, there are always items we require from other lands."

I nodded, thinking of what Alhwin had told us, and wondering whether Æthelred yet ruled Northumbria.

"Trade flows from as far away as Byzantion, ar-Raqqah, and even further to the east, but few ships come from the north. Of course, you are not traders and merchants, apart from the son of Ibrahim there." He gestured towards Ahmad, who had been silent and morose for the whole evening. Al-Hakam had ignored him until now. "Tell me, Ahmad," he called out now, raising his voice over the music, "how did you end up with these barbarians? And how do you plan on repaying the debt you left behind?" His words held a sharp edge and cut through the music and murmur of conversation in the shadowed room.

Ahmad met the emir's stare with difficulty, before dropping his gaze. His haunted expression showed that he had been expecting such questions. He had sat tensely awaiting this inevitable interrogation. Now, without looking up, he repeated the tale he had told me, of the attack on his ship and his following enslavement. In terse, mumbled phrases, he recounted where his life had taken him and how it had led him here.

"I know I can never repay my father for the years he has lost," Ahmad said at last, "or for the shame I have brought on my family. But with your leave, my lord emir, I will do whatever I am able to make things right again. I have learnt from my errors and I would follow in the steps of the Prophet as best as I am able for the rest of my days, to bring glory to his name. I will work ceaselessly to restore my family's pride and honour."

"Allah has punished you for your avarice. But your words of remorse are well spoken," said Al-Hakam at length. "I recall you were always a gifted speaker, even when we studied together. But will your actions back up the promises you make, I wonder."

I stared at Ahmad in consternation. He had told me he had studied with Tayyib, but had mentioned nothing of knowing the emir himself. Ahmad ignored me.

"I swear I will do what I can to make amends for my mistakes," he said.

Al-Hakam stared at him for several heartbeats, then, as if having made a decision, he nodded.

"Good," he said, "tell me of your visit to Frankia."

"Frankia, lord?" Ahmad said, his voice hesitant. "I was a slave there, but that was years ago. I know not what I can tell you."

"You travelled recently to the land of our enemy King Carolus, did you not?"

"Yes, lord," replied Ahmad, his tone uncertain. "We carried certain items of trade, and messages from Northumbria."

I sensed this was where Al-Hakam had wished to guide the conversation all along. I stiffened at the mention of Carolus as his enemy.

"Of course," the emir said, "Frankia trades with the kingdoms of Britain." He drank from his goblet as if done with this tack, but I still had the feeling he had not yet steered the talk to the final destination he sought. "But surely," he continued, his expression questioning, "it was not at the order of the king of Northumbria that you turned southward, sailing to my lands."

Ahmad glanced at me. He was unsure how to answer. Still reeling from the knowledge that he knew Al-Hakam, I nodded for him to go ahead. There was no reason for us to lie. We had done nothing wrong.

"I do not command the ship," said Ahmad, looking at me pointedly.

Al-Hakam turned towards me.

"We decided there was an opportunity for us in travelling to al-Andalus," I said.

"An opportunity?" The emir raised his eyebrows. "So you did not carry with you a Frank?" There was a sharpness to his tone now. This was what interested him most of all. He fixed me with the unblinking stare of a hawk and I was certain with blade-sharp clarity that he already knew the answer to his question. This was a test. Of what exactly, I was not sure. But I was certain that any attempt to hide the truth would go badly for me; for all of us. We had decided not to mention Giso for fear of annoying the emir, but now I saw that to keep secret the Frank's presence aboard *Brymsteda* might spell disaster.

"We did," I replied, reaching for an olive with forced nonchalance. "An envoy from King Carolus' court."

"And where is he now, this envoy?"

I shook my head.

"He may well be dead for all we know."

Al-Hakam frowned.

"Dead, you say?"

"He disappeared, shortly after we docked at Qadis."

"You have not seen the man since then?"

Again I thought I might mention that I had spent weeks rotting in a dungeon, but I bit my lip.

"No, lord. We know nothing of what happened to him. He was aboard the ship with us and then, the following day, he was not. We thought perhaps one of the guards might have killed him."

"Why would they have done such a thing?"

"Who can say what drives a man's actions? But that they hated us was clear. They showed us little in the way of hospitality."

Al-Hakam straightened at that, casting his eye about the plush surroundings, the soft cushions, the silver pitchers and goblets gleaming in the lamp light. The small plates bearing slices of fruit, olives and slivers of salty cheese.

"I have been told," he said with a scowl, "that it was you and Runolf here who started the altercation on the docks. Is that not so?"

"It is," I said reluctantly. "Though it was not without provocation. And unlike our over-long stay in Qadis, I cannot fault your hospitality, my lord emir." I smiled.

Al-Hakam returned my smile.

"I like you, warrior monk," he said. "And I like Runolf and Drosten. They are brave and do not back down. This is as it should be for fighters. Your crew of barbarians slaughtered the pirates who stole away my wife and son. Then with your fists, Runolf and you beat senseless half a dozen armed guards. Earlier I spoke of a reward. You have been patient in waiting to hear what that might be."

I drank some of the wine, shaking my head to clear it. I had not meant to allow myself to drink so much, but the wine was sweet and as smooth as water. My thoughts were blurry and I cursed myself for a fool. I could not afford to lose control before the emir. The Lord alone knew what he might do if he thought I had insulted him in any way. I did not speak, but met Al-Hakam's gaze expectantly.

"I had planned to give you silver and gold as a token of my thanks and my friendship."

My mouth was dry at the prospect and I drank yet more of the wine.

"But," he went on, "perhaps I can do better than that. I am always in need of strong warriors, honest men whom I can trust to do my bidding, who cannot be bought by my enemies."

"You think we would be such men?" I asked.

"I do," he said, his face serious. "I would have you join *Al-Haras*, my personal guard. I will equip you with the finest armour and arms. Pass on my offer to Runolf and the others."

I translated the emir's words. Runolf frowned. Hereward shook his head. Drosten shrugged and drank his wine. Revna said nothing, her eyes darting from one man to the next, gauging their reaction. Gwawrddur stretched his back and looked pensive. Placing his cup down carefully on the table before him, he said, "Ask him how he can be so sure we would be loyal to him?"

I asked Al-Hakam.

"I think I have the measure of you," he said. "If you swore an oath to me, I believe you would keep your word. Besides," he said, with a grin, "I would give you more silver than you can imagine."

I spoke his words in Englisc. Hereward rose to his feet.

"Please thank the lord emir for his hospitality, but politely decline. We must return north. We have already sworn oaths that cannot be broken."

"I have sworn no oaths," said Gwawrddur.

"Nor have I," added Drosten.

"If you so wish," replied Hereward, "you can stay and serve this emir. But I cannot. I will return to Northumbria and see how our king fares."

Drosten shook his head.

"I have no desire to stay in this land without my friends."

"Nor I," said Gwawrddur, "though I would like to test my blade against some of their swordsmen. The only enemies we have faced so far have been pirates who were barely worthy of killing."

"What about you, Runolf?" I asked.

He snorted.

"I will not serve such a man as this," he said. "But ask him of the reward he promised us. I imagine he is the type of man who when rejected might change his mind about how generous he is."

"I detect that the decision does not go well for me," said Al-Hakam before I could pass on their comments.

"We thank you," I said, "but we must decline your offer. Some amongst us have oaths to fulfil and we will not sunder our fellowship."

He shrugged.

"I had to ask," he said. "It is not often I have the opportunity of speaking to such heroes. And please tell Runolf that he must not worry. I will still give you the reward I promised. I am a man of my word and whatever else you have or have not done, you did rescue my wife and son from my enemies."

I wondered then how much Al-Hakam understood of our conversations. We had all spoken in Englisc and he had not needed me to translate Runolf's words in order to answer him.

Before I could dwell on this, he changed the direction of the discourse once again, as if leaning with all his weight on the steerboard of the conversation.

"You spoke of an opportunity," he said.

It took me a moment to understand his words and meaning, so sudden was the shift from the offer of becoming members of the royal guard.

"I did, lord."

"And what opportunity was it that brought you to my lands?"

"Well, first we were paid for transporting the Frank," I smiled, thinking this might have been enough of an explanation. And yet this was a chance I could not ignore. If the service we had done the emir and his family could gain us anything, I hoped it might gain me access to the man who had bought *The Treasure of Life*. "But beyond the payment I had my own reason for coming here."

"And what would that be?"

I remembered the scrap of parchment with the name scrawled on it in flowing al-Arabiyyah.

"I am in search of one Abu Jafar Yusuf ibn Sa'īd al-Zarqālluh."

"Al-Zarqālluh? The scholar?" Al-Hakam seemed genuinely surprised. "Why do you seek him?"

"I believe he has a book I seek."

"A book? He has many books. More perhaps than any other man alive."

"This is a very special book," I said. "It was stolen from the minster of Lindisfarnae. I have searched for it for a long time."

Al-Hakam grinned.

"Then Allah smiles upon you, warrior monk. For Al-Zarqālluh is here."

"In the palace?"

"In Qurtuba."

"I have wished to speak to him for many months."

"Then tomorrow, you will have your wish. He will be giving a demonstration of a new alchemical marvel. I would be delighted if you would attend as my guests. It will be a most enlightening experience, I am sure."

I thanked him for the invitation. Al-Zarqālluh was here! Was it possible that *The Treasure of Life* was also close by? Had the Lord finally brought me to where I would at last get my hands on the tome that had so filled my mind these past years?

Few things are ever simple. But that night, I fell asleep replete with fine food and sweet wine, contented and excited at the prospect that the following day I would at last meet the man who had purchased *The Treasure of Life*.

I slept soundly, for once not disturbed by nightmares. The bad dreams would come back soon enough. It would be many days before I could sleep peacefully again, after the horrors I witnessed under the glaring bright sunshine of al-Andalus the following day.

Twenty-Three

"I have a bad feeling about this," said Hereward, squinting against the glare as he stared out over the wide waters of the al-Wadi 'l-kabir. The sun was high in the sky. Its light shimmered, almost painfully bright off the river, as if it were fashioned from burnished silver.

"I feel it too," I said. Despite the festival atmosphere on the bridge, there was a hint of menace in the warm air; a pent-up excitement that reminded me of the anxious energy before a hunt.

Or battle.

"Still no idea what this is all about?" asked Gwawrddur, holding his hand up to shade his eyes as he swept his gaze along the throng of people crowding the bridge. He was on edge too; looking for signs of danger everywhere.

"I'm not sure if the guards actually know," I said. "If they do, none will tell me. Have you heard anything, Ahmad?"

The freed thrall shook his head.

"All I know is that it will be on the water."

"That much seems obvious," said Drosten, spitting over the edge of the bridge into the river below.

Ahmad held up his hands.

"Whatever will be demonstrated, the guards seem excited

that it will be on the river, as if that is important." He shrugged. "What we are going to see, I have no idea."

Ahmad had barely spoken since the previous day's encounter with the emir. As we had walked back to our rooms in the darkness I had asked him how he knew Al-Hakam.

"We studied together," he had answered.

"And you did not think to mention this?"

He avoided my gaze, shrugging off my questions. I pressed him for information about the emir. Was he a man of his word? Could we expect him to fulfil his promise of a reward? Ahmad had spun around to face me, his face flushed and angry. "He is the Emir of al-Andalus. The most important man of this great kingdom. He is blessed by Allah. Doubt my honour," he snarled, "but not his."

He hadn't waited to hear my mumbled apology, and I had watched him stalk away, wondering at his reaction and the past he shared with Al-Hakam.

In the morning, servants had come early with refreshments and clean clothes for us. Once we were dressed, Hafiz had arrived with an entourage of a dozen palace guards, their armour polished and their white robes clean and shining.

I had enquired about meeting Al-Zarqālluh, but the steward had shaken his head.

"Later," he'd said. "He is much too busy this morning to see you. After the demonstration, his Majesty the Emir has instructed me to bring you before him again. You are to meet Al-Zarqālluh then and to receive your reward."

I had passed on these tidings to the others as we'd followed Hafiz out of the palace grounds and into the city.

"The sooner we are given this reward he keeps speaking of the better," Runolf had growled.

"I hope then he will allow us to leave," Drosten had said, wiping sweat from his brow. "We have been prisoners for too long."

"You are not wrong there, painted one," Runolf had replied. "I would return to *Brymsteda* and the open sea. Let us take our reward and be gone from this land. If nothing else, it is too hot."

I said nothing for a time as we walked behind Hafiz through the winding streets. The crowds parted, making way for us and our armed escort and, as on the first day that we had traversed Qurtuba, I revelled in the sights, sounds and smells of the bustling city. But unlike when we had arrived, now our future felt less insecure. The emir had brought us here to thank us for rescuing his wife and child. We were to be rewarded. And there was a chance that I would soon be in possession of the book I had sought for so long.

We paused at a crossroads, waiting for a cart that was heavily laden with cured leather to pass. I moved close to Hafiz. We were still unarmed and it seemed to me that the soldiers who guarded us were giving us more space than previously, making it easier to believe we were guests and not captives. But as I stepped towards the palace steward, a pair of the guards quickly moved to intercept me. One placed his hand on the pommel of the short sword he wore, but the other shook his head and whispered something. I ignored them, but took note of how the two watched me as I spoke to Hafiz and then as we continued our passage through the winding streets of Qurtuba.

"How does Rifat fare?" I asked Hafiz.

"He lives," Hafiz replied, not looking at me, but watching with a sour expression the carter beating the mule that strained to heave the heavy cart over the street's dirty cobbles. The pungent stink of the tanned leather teetering on the back of the cart caught in my throat.

"God be praised," I said. I had hoped that the captain of the ship had survived the night, and yet his injuries had been grave and I was half-expecting to hear the worst from the steward. "Do you think I might be able to see him later?" I asked.

I had thought the serious Hafiz would tell me that such a thing was impossible. Instead, surprisingly, he nodded, a rare smile tugging at the corners of his lips.

"I am sure you can see him later today," he said.

At another point on our journey through the city, Runolf saw a small boy tumble from where he had been climbing on some rubble beside a ruined house. The boy wailed as he slipped and came crashing down onto a pile of broken dry-mud bricks. He landed heavily, scaring himself and also twisting his ankle, badly enough that he could not stand. Without hesitation, the huge Norseman ran over to the boy's aid, scooping up the weeping child. Two of the guards who walked alongside us ran after him, tugging their swords free as they hurried forward. When they saw that Runolf meant no harm, they slowed to a halt and awkwardly sheathed their blades.

The boy's mother came running from a nearby alley and began screaming at Runolf, who still held her injured, sobbing boy. It took Ahmad and the guards quite a while to convince the angry woman that the giant, flame-haired foreigner was not responsible for her son's injuries.

From these two encounters I deduced that, despite the sensation of being free, each of us had been assigned two guards who would step in quickly to prevent us escaping, or doing anything they deemed untoward.

I had recognised some of the streets we followed from our previous walk and thought that we must be heading for the wharf where the barge had moored. But when we reached the timber wharf with its numerous boats and barges of all sizes, Hafiz turned along the riverside.

Our trip ended on the massive bridge that spanned the great river on its stone arches. The bridge was evidently closed for wheeled traffic, but it was busy with people. On the north side, from which we approached, guards were stationed at the crumbling Roman gateway. They were preventing most of the city's populace from passing, but when they saw Hafiz, they raised their spears and allowed us entry. From the glistening, colourful silks, and the golden jewellery on display, it was evident that the men and women on the bridge were the wealthy and powerful of Qurtuba. Along the river's banks business-minded traders had set up stalls for the gathering crowds and the smells of cooking meat drifted in the hot air. On the bridge itself there were tables containing food and drink served by servants, some of whom I recognised from the palace.

In the centre of the bridge, a wooden structure of tiered seats had been constructed. Above this a cloth as large as a ship's sail had been erected to provide shelter from the heat of the sun. The whole construction was positioned so that the seats faced north-east, ensuring that the shade fell on the rich patrons lucky enough to be beneath the huge sail. Whatever was going to be demonstrated, it was evident it would be in the water to the north-east of the bridge. But peering over the edge I saw nothing apart from the green-brown waters flowing inexorably under the stone arches and towards the distant sea.

"There are no boats afloat," said Runolf.

He was right. Where the river had been busy with watercraft when we had arrived at Qurtuba, there was no movement in the water now. Again I wondered what we were going to be shown. Whatever it was, it was deemed exciting enough for all these people to watch. The banks either side of the river were packed with people now too; the common folk who were not permitted onto the bridge with the nobles and honoured guests.

Evidently our status as guests of the emir did not extend to allowing us one of the coveted seats on the platform. When we had arrived at the bridge, Hafiz had bidden us farewell and left us with our guard shadows, but he had given no indication that we would be provided with seating or shelter. I suspected the only reason we had been allowed on the bridge at all was that it made it easier for our guards to watch us and prevent us from running away.

"Enjoy the demonstration," Hafiz had said, before melting into the crowd.

The day was sweltering and as the numbers of people on the bridge increased, the heat grew in intensity until it was almost unbearable. After a time, Ahmad spoke to our guards, explaining that being from the north we were not accustomed to such temperatures. A couple of the men took pity on us and approached one of the refreshments tables that lined the bridge. Soon a servant brought us a couple of jugs of watered wine.

We thanked the guards and drank thirstily. We offered them some of the wine, but they shook their heads.

"I am glad of this thing," said Drosten, touching the cloth that was bound about his head. His skin was flushed, making the blue of his tattoos stand out even more than usual.

"Does it not make your head hotter?" I asked.

"If it did," said Gwawrddur, who had also opted for the cloth headdress, "why would the locals wear them?"

I wished I had chosen to wear one now, but I had not imagined it would be so hot, so the sun beat down on me until my head ached.

A murmuring in the crowd caught our attention and we turned as one to see Al-Hakam Ibn Hisham Ibn Abd-ar-Rahman, Emir of Qurtuba and ruler of all of al-Andalus arrive on a white stallion. He rode out of the tower gate, where he must have been waiting for the correct moment to make his entrance. He was surrounded by an honour guard of warriors who marched in close formation. The emir halted, remaining in the saddle for a time as the crowd cheered and waved. He returned their salutations with a gentle movement of his hand and a magnanimous smile. Eventually, as the cheering began to subside, he turned his mount and rode back into the shade of the tower.

"What was the point of that?" asked Runolf.

"It is all for show," said Gwawrddur. "He wishes to demonstrate to his people that he is above them."

As the emir and his guards were swallowed by the shadowy gate of the tower, I cast my gaze down to the crowd. Across the throng, near one of the stalls serving wine, stood a tall man with a dark, full beard. I squinted. There was something familiar about the flat angular face, but I could not place it. Then he turned towards me and recognition hit me like a slap.

"Nadir," I hissed.

"What?" asked Hereward.

"That whoreson from Qadis," I said, breathless from the shock of seeing the man who had allowed Hering to die. "Nadir."

"Where?"

"There." I tried to point, but at that moment the crowds about us shifted as some late arrivals made their way towards the platform. A hugely fat man, followed by several gaudily dressed courtiers and veiled women, walked behind a contingent of villainous-looking guards. The guards parted the mass of people easily as they went and I found myself shoved to one side by the crowd. I lost sight of Nadir and ended up jammed painfully against the stone side of the bridge. A hand grasped my arm and I turned to see it belonged to one of the guards who had been assigned me as their duty for the day. There was nowhere for me to go in the press of bodies, so I shook off his hand and waited for the fat noble and his entourage to pass.

"I wonder who he is," said Ahmad. "He clearly wishes to let everybody know he arrived after the emir."

"A brave man," said Hereward.

"Or a fool," said Gwawrddur, perhaps recalling Rifat and the others hanging from the timber frames in the palace garden.

As the fat man reached the raised platform and waddled his way up to his seat, so the crowd around us thinned. People were able to spread out once more, and despite the heat, the sudden open space after the crush of moments before, felt as though a cool breeze had wafted over us. I raised myself up on my toes and peered over the heads of those gathered on the bridge, but I could see no sign of Nadir.

"Are you sure it was him?" asked Runolf.

"I only saw him for a moment," I said, beginning to doubt myself.

"Where was he?"

"Near that stall," I said, pointing.

Runolf, taller than all those around us, scanned the people.

"I cannot see the nithing," he said. "Pity. I would have liked to have finished what we started back in Qadis."

"Perhaps I was mistaken," I said. There were so many people, such a confusion would be easy.

"Anything is possible," Runolf said with a grin.

The idea of Nadir being here had further unsettled me. I was drenched in sweat. I longed for this demonstration, whatever it might be, to be over, so that we could return to the shade of the palace, but at the same time, the sensation of building tension and excitement had only grown with the emir's arrival. People clearly expected the show to begin soon, for they pressed forward to the north-east side of the bridge.

Our guards were either as excited as everyone else, or their orders went further than simply watching us, for they worked together to force the onlookers out of our way, allowing us to gain access to the wall at the edge of the bridge, and an unhindered view of the river below.

Men and women shouted abuse at the guards until they saw

their burnished armour and the gleaming pommels and hilts of their swords.

The blare of horns hushed the raucous crowd and we all turned towards the sound. Looking up, I saw the emir, standing high above us all, atop the stone tower, hands outstretched, as he waited patiently for his subjects to fall silent.

"I told you," said Gwawrddur. "Above his people."

"May the peace of Allah be upon you all," the emir shouted, when the crowd had quietened enough for him to be heard.

"And upon you peace," responded the gathered people as one. It was a roaring sound that made the hairs on my neck prickle. This was the voice of Qurtuba, and it was as loud as a battle cry.

Al-Hakam smiled down on his people and held up his hands. The crowd grew quiet. The tension that had been building felt ready to be unleashed, like lightning and thunder from a dark storm cloud. All eyes were on the emir as he addressed the men and women of al-Andalus.

"Allah is great!" he shouted and was met with a riotous cheer in response. "The land is prosperous, the sun shines and the water of the great river flows, feeding the fruit and crops in the fields. Every day when we meet we ask Allah to give us peace, and each day that peace is granted to us is a blessing."

Men and women around us nodded, their faces lifted up to stare in awe at their ruler. He spoke with verve and eloquence, and the power he held over his subjects was evident in those upturned gazes, the wide eyes and open mouths.

"But we all know," he went on, "we have enemies, both within and without the kingdom. Sometimes peace is impossible. There are those who would seek to conquer us, leading their armies over the mountains to lay siege to our great cities. Against these foes we have the power of our armies, the strength of our steel and the faith in our hearts. My grandfather and my father led armies that swept aside those who stood before them, and those who refused to accept the truth of the words of the Prophet."

The onlookers had fallen quiet, raptly listening to their ruler.

"But our great kingdom of al-Andalus has many borders. There are ports and harbours. Trade comes to us from all over the world via sea and ocean and along the great rivers that flow through the realm. And it saddens me that where we have been unvanquishable on land, where our horses are faster, our steel sharper and our hearts more valiant, at sea we are ever weaker than our enemies."

A murmur of dissent rippled through the crowd.

"I like it no more than you, my people," Al-Hakam said, "but it is the truth, and I will not lie to you. Our ships are frequently at the mercy of Imazighen pirates. They prey on our merchants like hounds snapping at rabbits. Their people have grown up sailing, and their ships are faster and nimbler than ours. No matter the bravery of our sailors, we have been all but defenceless against these corsairs."

He paused, allowing his words, like stones dropped into a mere, to send ripples through the listeners. Men muttered and grumbled. Far off at the end of the bridge someone raised their voice in a shout, though I could not make out the words. Just when it seemed that the emir had lost his audience, he bellowed.

"That ends today!"

The crowd roared.

Runolf tugged at my sleeve.

"What is he saying?" he asked, raising his voice to be heard over the tumult.

I looked at my friends' blank faces and imagined what it must have been like not to have understood any of the emir's words. Cursing myself for ignoring them and allowing myself to be caught up in the passion of Al-Hakam's speech, I quickly explained what the emir was saying; that where the kingdom's sailors had struggled against pirates in the past, all that would end now.

"What does he mean by that?" asked Revna, shouting over the roaring crowd.

"I know not," I replied, but even as I spoke the crowd was growing quiet once more.

The emir held up his hands.

"We have gathered here today," he said, "to witness a new weapon that will make us feared by all who dare attack us at sea." He looked over the throng as if looking for something. Or someone. When his eyes finally found our small group on the upstream side of the bridge, he met my gaze and held it. It was clear this message was not just for his people. This was a threat to all who came from the sea.

After a moment, Al-Hakam looked away, once more addressing all of the people on and around the bridge.

"That most learned of men, Abu Jafar Yusuf ibn Sa'īd al-Zarqālluh," he said, "has laboured long and hard with his alchemists to provide us with a defence against those who assail us from the water. You have come here to witness the fruition of Al-Zarqālluh's labour. Would you see the miraculous weapon he has forged for us?"

The crowd screamed and yelled in assent. The emir smiled broadly and clapped his hands. The sound was lost, but he gestured to the river and everyone turned to look.

From beneath one of the great arches came a barge that had been hidden from view. It was manned with a dozen oarsmen, who pulled it steadily out into the middle of the wide river, until it was some hundred paces from the bridge. At the front of the barge three men stood behind a complicated contraption of metal. What appeared to be an iron barrel was connected to some form of pipe that could be moved on a pivot by one of the men at the prow. The end of the pipe was fashioned like the open mouth of a beast, with jagged fangs. Quite what I was seeing was unclear to me. A small flame licked up from beneath the metallic maw and I saw that two of the men had their hands resting on levers that looked like they were connected to a bellows. Heat billowed up from the barge and an astringent, burning smell hit my nostrils, stinging the back of my throat.

I shuddered. I had seen the burnt bodies of the victims of Ljósberari lining the rivers of Rygjafylki. Could it be mere coincidence that Al-Zarqālluh, the new owner of *The Treasure of Life*, had created this weapon that clearly used fire?

From the far end of the bridge, from where it too had been concealed beneath one of the huge arches, came another barge. The oars rose and fell as it pulled into the open. The crowd hushed as the two barges moved out onto the open water. When the second barge was clear of the bridge, it became apparent that it towed another smaller boat behind it. This boat was stacked with bales of straw.

The barge bearing the strange weapon with its flickering flame manoeuvred smoothly to within a couple of dozen paces distance of the boat that trailed in the wake of the second barge. At the command of the helmsman, the oarsmen began to slowly row against the river's flow, holding the barge still. The men standing behind the mysterious weapon looked up expectantly at their emir. The sun blazed from the clear sky. Sweat sheened the faces of the three men at the barge's prow. The crowd was quiet now, waiting in awed silence to see the promised power of this new weapon.

The emir raised his right hand, held it aloft for a heartbeat, then sliced it downward. Aboard the barge, the men at the bellows began to pump furiously while the other man gripped a handle at the end of the tube and stared towards the straw-laden boat. What appeared to be a stream of liquid shot from the jaws of the metal beast. The instant this liquid touched the flame that guttered beneath the spout it ignited with a whispered sigh. A heartbeat later the heat of the liquid flame reached the bridge. It reminded me of standing too close to a smith's forge, and we were at least a hundred paces away. Even at that distance, the extreme heat dried my eyes and I squinted, wondering how the sailors who manned the contraption could bear it.

The liquid spurted yet further with each pump of the bellows. At first it fell short, splashing and hissing into the water, but then it reached the boat and in an instant the straw was ablaze. Moments later the boat was aflame. Plumes of black smoke roiled up from the conflagration.

The crowd had been hushed, appearing to hold its collective breath, but now the throng began to clap and cheer. The destructive power of this liquid fire was obvious. Any vessel armed with such a weapon would be terrible to face. Fire was always a danger aboard ships. To be able to cast flames across the waves at their enemies would make al-Andalus a formidable naval power.

"Roman Fire," I whispered to myself. I had heard of such a weapon as this before. I had read a chronicle in Greek about how an artificer called Kallinikos had created what he described as sea fire. The men of Byzantion had used it against their enemies to devastating effect. I had believed the accounts to be fanciful. But my own eyes told me the truth of it. As I watched the ship burn, I realised with a start that flames flickered where the burning liquid had landed on the water.

"The water is aflame," said Runolf. Sweat beaded on his brow and the fire reflected in his eyes. Runolf rarely showed any fear. I had seen him stand before a vastly superior number of foe with a grin on his face. But at the sight of the devastation brought so quickly upon the boat, his expression was one of horror.

I could scarcely believe what I was seeing. It was said that the rulers of Byzantion guarded the secret of their Roman Fire jealously, putting to death any who might try to steal its recipe and incarcerating those who knew how to brew the deadly concoction.

The men on the barge had stopped pumping now. Drops of fire fell from the mouth of the weapon, landing in a large metal bowl beneath. The bowl was evidently for just this purpose for if the drips should fall onto the timbers of the barge, it too would run the risk of being consumed by fire.

The other barge had cut the rope used to pull the target boat, and now, flames gouting and smoke churning and smudging the air above it, the burning boat spun languidly with the river current towards the bridge. It appeared that it might reach the stone arches and some of the people watching began to panic, shouting and pushing away from the edge, so that the flames and smoke would not engulf them. But as the burning boat was some twenty paces from the stone bridge, it listed to one side and started to sink. Within moments it had been swallowed by the water. Even as it disappeared from view in the murky depths of the river, I was sure I could still see flames. And could it be possible that the bubbles that churned the surface were filled with smoke?

For a long while the onlookers cheered and shouted their praise of the emir, and Al-Zarqālluh.

Drosten shook his head. He stared at the bubbling, steaming water where the boat had vanished.

"Can you imagine," he said, "being on a ship that tries to attack one armed with that?" His tone was hollow and shocked and it was not clear who he was talking to.

"I hope we will never find out," Gwawrddur said. His face was pale. He was not a natural sailor, and it had taken all his effort and will to overcome his fear of the sea. I could only imagine what he would think of this display.

The crowd was growing quiet once more, and we turned to look at the top of the tower, where Al-Hakam again stood with his hands raised.

"You have seen the power of this new weapon. You can understand how our enemies will fear us. But would you see how it destroys more than straw?" The crowd cheered and I felt a cold finger of dread scratch down my spine. "Shall I show you how this holy fire will deal with the enemies of al-Andalus?" The throng went wild. I shuddered, suddenly certain that I did not wish to see the next demonstration of this weapon that the emir referred to as holy fire.

It is a sad truth of mankind that most people are glad to revel in the suffering of others, especially when they are surrounded by those who make them certain of their own safety. It is this that turns warriors into bloodthirsty murderers and rapists. Most men will not wish to inflict pain on others when they are called upon to do it themselves, when they are at risk of retaliation. But present a mob with a small group of outsiders, and they will scream for their blood with abandon. The individuals, feeling secure in their anonymity and safe from harm, care nothing for the suffering they cause. So it was that day, in the searing heat of al-Andalus, with the stink of smoke and whatever noxious elements made up Al-Zarqālluh's holy fire hanging in the hot air. Al-Hakam offered up the chance to see torment and death, and the usually peaceful men, women and children of Qurtuba bayed like hounds who have scented blood.

I wish I had left then. I knew what we were going to be presented with, and I should have pushed away from the edge of the bridge and refused to watch the spectacle. Later that night when I could not sleep, when the visions of agonised faces flickering in the heat of the flames filled my mind, when the howls of anguish still echoed in my ears, I told myself it had been impossible to flee. The guards would have prevented it and they had almost certainly been ordered to ensure we remained to watch. But now, as I look back over the vast distance of the intervening years, the truth of it is that part of me wanted to watch. I knew it was wrong, and yet I made no effort to turn away.

I watched as the barge made its way beneath the bridge once more and shortly after heaved into view, pulling a new target behind it. This boat was not stacked with bales of hay. On this vessel, several figures stood. Each had his hands bound to a stout timber frame that ran the length of the boat. Some of the men were slumped over, perhaps senseless, others stood, staring up at the crowd, their wide eyes flicking fearfully to the barge bearing the holy fire. They must have seen the first demonstration and those prisoners who were conscious screamed and cried out for mercy.

"These men are all criminals of the worst kind," shouted Al-Hakam, his voice somehow carrying over the cacophony of Qurtuba's populace. "Murderers! Thieves! Pirates! Traitors!"

With the emir's last shouted word, my gaze fell on the man strapped in the helmsman's position at the stern of the boat. This man's face was bruised and bloody. His eyes were open and staring, but unlike the others on the boat, he did not scream. He was too proud for that.

"Rifat!" I gasped. I had saved the man from the cross only for him to be burnt alive.

The crowd's shouts drowned out the terrified wailing of the other prisoners. I was aghast. I knew what I would soon see and I did not wish to look, but I did not have the strength to look away, even as the barge pulled the boat into range of the holy fire.

It was over in moments, but the sight of it has never left me, as if the Roman Fire burnt the images into my mind's eye. The men at the bellows began to pump furiously as soon as they were close enough to this new boat. The liquid fire spurted out, licking the timbers of the vessel and splashing onto the legs and feet of the nearest of the prisoners. The first man's screams rose in pitch as he burst into flames. The rest of the prisoners were swallowed by the fire one by one as the sailor aimed the gushing liquid death at each man in turn. The crowd had fallen into a hushed, shocked stillness now as they witnessed the devastation. The prisoners' throat-ripping screams tore at my sanity and the world tilted around me as a wave of giddiness washed over me. For a time I wondered if I might swoon and drop mercifully to the ground. But I was not to find solace in unconsciousness. I did not faint and I did not look away. I watched in horror as the flames consumed each of the prisoners before reaching Rifat.

He had held himself upright until the end, stoically keeping his mouth clamped shut even as the boat burnt around him and the other prisoners erupted into columns of fire, the burning fat of their bodies sending up great black clouds of smoke. But now, as the Roman Fire licked at his legs, even the proud captain was unable to keep from crying out. The flames surged around him in a maelstrom of fire. I thought I could hear him screaming, even as the boat's timbers blackened and it began to sink. I imagined I could still hear his wailing cries of agony as the boat sank beneath the water. And though I knew it could not be so, I was certain I had seen his face clearly, still wreathed in flames as he slid down to disappear in the depths of the river.

Twenty-Four

"You think he plans to kill us now?" Drosten's gaze flicked about the hall where the emir had entertained us the night before. We had been escorted there from our rooms by a new cadre of guards. Those guards now stood waiting silently, ensuring that we remained where we were. The large room was otherwise empty. Gone were the tables covered in rich food and silver pitchers of sweet wine. It appeared that this evening we were not invited to the feast. Through the doors into the interior rooms of the palace came the sounds of merriment: music, chatter, the clink of cups, every now and then a burst of laughter.

"You know what I would say," said Runolf. His tone was bleak and matched my own sense of foreboding. Revna was standing close and he placed a large hand on her shoulder.

"I still say it would make no sense," said Hereward. "To bring us all this way, feed us and clothe us, only to have us slain." This was not the first time he had said such things since we had returned to the palace. We had been led through the shadowed streets by the sombre-faced guards and even they had appeared shocked by what they'd witnessed at the river. When we'd arrived back at our rooms, I thought I'd detected a certain sadness in the eyes of one of the guards assigned to watch over me.

Gwawrddur sighed.

"We all know you are right, Hereward," he said, "but after what we saw today, I am not so sure we can rely on the man's sense." He looked about him nervously, checking that none of the guards understood his words. They all stood to attention, eyes staring forward. They might have been stone for all the signs of comprehension they gave. Satisfied, the Welshman went on. "The emir is clearly no fool, but he is cruel. He revels in displays of power and pain."

Moments before, we had walked through the courtyard where the fountain still burbled peacefully. All sign of the timber crosses had been removed, and the flagstones scrubbed clean of blood. Evidently the crucifixes had served their purpose, their grisly ornaments showing us what Al-Hakam was capable of when he believed men had gone against him, or failed him. If we had needed a stronger message than that, we had received it at the bridge.

My head throbbed. We had been standing in the sun for a long time, but I thought the pain stemmed more from what I had seen. The demonstration of the destructive power of Roman Fire was terrible enough, but to see it consume living men had filled me with horror and dread. That one of those men was Rifat made me despair. My request that he be shown clemency had not only been ignored, but he had been subjected to further torment and suffering. And I could not shake the feeling that it had been a message to me; that I had caused his renewed agony with my intervention, rather than alleviating his pain.

I had scarcely spoken since we had come back to the palace. My head ached and after drinking some water I had lain down in the relative cool of the room. And yet sleep eluded me. I could still hear the screams, and the stink of the smoke had permeated my clothes, reminding me with each breath of the horrific scene I had watched on the river.

I glanced at Ahmad. Like me, he had spoken little since we'd returned. His expression was grave and dejected. I sensed that he felt the same desperation that had gripped me. We would die here. Al-Hakam had shown us his spitefulness. He had enjoyed prolonging our anguish and now meant to have us killed. The sight of Rifat and the other prisoners being devoured by fire had demoralised me, making me fear the worst. I could see no way out of this if it was indeed the emir's intention to have us slain. But there was another, deeper outcome to the horrific display of destruction we had witnessed. It was as if a small drop of the Roman Fire had found its way deep down into my soul, and there it had kindled a flame that grew with each passing moment. I pushed down on the rage that burnt inside me, obscuring it from my face. I suspected the emir had dark plans for us and I could see no escape, surrounded as we were by guards and stone walls. But I nurtured the flames within me and vowed that should the opportunity arise, I would be ready to unleash the full searing strength of my ire and bring it to bear on whatever enemies stood before us.

The doors to the inner rooms swung open, interrupting my thoughts. Hafiz stood there, limned by the lamplight behind him.

"His Royal Highness will see you now," he said, stepping to the side to allow us entry.

None of us spoke as we passed through the doors. I glared at Hafiz. He had known the fate that awaited Rifat and had led me to believe the man would survive. The steward met my angry glower without expression.

Unlike the previous evening, the guards followed us into the chamber where we had reclined to drink, talk and listen to music. Gwawrddur, Hereward, Drosten and Revna watched the guards file in behind us. The muscles in Drosten's jaw bunched and bulged. His hands were clasped into fists, but the Pict was no fool. He knew there was nothing to be gained from trying to fight our way out of this.

Hereward's features clouded in a scowl. Whatever he said, there could be no denying the signs for our future were not promising. We had not been invited to eat with Al-Hakam; instead we had been sent a plain meal of bread and ewe's milk cheese to our rooms, and now we were left to stand, surrounded by armed warriors.

Drawing in a deep breath, I squared my shoulders and looked about the room. Al-Hakam lounged at the table where Runolf and I had sat with him the night before. Beside him was a man with a long, thick beard, dark, but streaked with silver. He watched us closely, his eyes sharp and intelligent. Half a dozen other sombre-faced men sat at the low tables. None of them spoke. There was no sign of the musicians I had heard earlier, but their instruments lay on the cushions where they had sat the previous night. They must have been dismissed just before we were allowed entry. In the shadowed recesses, several servants lurked. The guards moved to stand beside them in the arched alcoves, leaving us exposed in the middle of the room.

Gwawrddur moved near to me.

"Easy now, Killer," he whispered. "Hold tight the reins of your anger."

Nothing got past the Welshman. He was ever good at reading my moods.

"What does it matter?" I hissed.

"Things look bad, it's true," he said, his voice barely audible. "But there may yet be a way out of this for us."

"How?"

"I do not know," he admitted with a sigh. "But if you allow your temper to get the better of you, we may never have the chance to find out."

I took a deep, calming breath.

"Don't worry about me."

I knew Gwawrddur was right, and I would try to contain my anger, but I was not sure how long I could stand to be in the presence of the emir without speaking out against the savagery of what he had ordered.

"Ah, my honoured guests," Al-Hakam said with a wide grin. He made no effort to rise and made no offer for us to sit. Awkwardly, we remained standing in the centre of the room, all eyes on us. "May the peace of Allah be upon you."

Ahmad mumbled the expected response to the greeting, touching his chest, face and forehead. I remained silent, unable to bring myself to speak of peace with this man. Al-Hakam seemed not to notice my rudeness.

"Allow me," he went on, "to present to you one of the sharpest minds in all of *Dār al-Islam*, the man whose efforts have helped ignite the holy flames of loyalty and allegiance in my people, Abu Jafar Yusuf ibn Sa'īd al-Zarqālluh." He gestured towards the man with the long beard, who inclined his head in greeting. Al-Zarqālluh surveyed each of us in turn, taking in the details of what he saw and coming to his own conclusions. At last his eyes settled on me.

"You must be the warrior monk," he said.

I met his gaze defiantly, but did not reply.

"What did you think of the display today?" Al-Zarqālluh asked.

I remained silent for a moment, fighting against the anger I could feel rising up inside me. But the pressure to speak grew too much.

"I wondered how you managed to obtain Kallinikos' recipe?" I said, my tone dripping with disdain. "Did you steal it?"

I knew it was foolish to taunt him, but I took pleasure at the flicker of surprise and anger that passed across his features. He quickly controlled his expression once more, forcing a smile.

"You were right, my lord," he said. "He is an intriguing young man."

Al-Hakam let out a barking laugh. The two of them were amusing themselves at my expense and I dug my fingernails into my palms, recalling Gwawrddur's words of caution.

"I knew you would enjoy meeting him," Al-Hakam said.

Al-Zarqālluh stared at me for a time, his eyes narrow as if he was trying hard to make out something difficult to perceive.

"His Royal Highness says that you wished to meet me," he said at last.

I did not wish to talk to this arrogant man, but I had travelled too far, sacrificed too much to turn away from my path now. The thought of *The Treasure of Life* within my reach after so long made the nape of my neck prickle.

"I have come all the way from the lands of the Norse to speak to you," I said.

"I am flattered," he said. "But why travel so far? Do you wish me to teach you at my madrasa? It seems to me you have had good teachers. You speak al-Arabiyyah well and you have clearly read widely."

"I do not come in search of a teacher. I have had the best and as you say, I have read many books. But there is one that I seek."

"Indeed?" Al-Zarqālluh raised his eyebrows questioningly. Reaching for a goblet that rested on the low, metal-covered table, he took a sip. "I have many books."

"Not like this one," I said. "One of your servants bought it from the master of a hall in Rygjafylki. The Norsemen had stolen it from the minster of Lindisfarnae in my homeland of Northumbria."

He took another sip of his drink. He gave the impression of being bored with the conversation, but his eyes gleamed as he watched me over the rim of his cup.

"And what book is this?"

"It is called *The Treasure of Life*," I said. "Scribed in Latin, translated from the original Syriac Aramaic of the writings of Mani."

He sniffed.

"It sounds interesting. And why do you seek this book over all others?"

I did not wish to speak of my reasons to this man, and even if I did I would not have been able to put into words my obsession, not in any way that would make sense.

"A friend of mine – my teacher – read it and told me something of its contents. I wish to study it for myself."

"Cannot your teacher tell you what this..." he hesitated, as if the name was unfamiliar to him. "What this Mani wrote?"

"He is dead," I said, my voice hard and sharp. "Murdered by a man driven mad after reading the book."

"*The Treasure of Life* – that is what you called it, no? – sounds dangerous. So it is just as well that I cannot aid you. I do not possess it."

"But there was a bill of sale," I said, "with your name on." The pleading tone that had crept into my voice angered me. I turned to Ahmad. He stared at the ground, clearly not wishing to be drawn into this conversation. "Ahmad, you saw it. Tell him."

Ahmad sighed, then nodded.

"It is as he says." Ahmad's voice was quiet, but clear in the still of the room. "Your name was upon the receipt."

Al-Zarqālluh raised his hands and shrugged.

"Well, that is strange. I do not recall ever having seen such a book."

My heart sank. Could it be true? To travel so far for nothing. There was something about the way Al-Zarqālluh spoke of the book, his feigned disinterest that needled me and made me question the truth of his words. And yet, even if he was lying, what could I do? I had nothing to sway the man. The Lord alone knew if we would even be able to leave the palace with our lives.

"What is he saying?" Runolf asked.

To my surprise, before I could gather my thoughts, Al-Zarqālluh answered the Norseman.

"Your friend has asked about the book he seeks," he said in heavily accented, but perfectly intelligible Englisc. "He is not pleased to find I do not possess it."

If Runolf was shocked that Al-Zarqālluh could converse with him, he did not show it.

"I can imagine," he said. "Hunlaf thinks of little else apart from that book."

Al-Zarqālluh chuckled.

"And what is it that *you* think of, my friend?"

"I think of kin," Runolf replied, placing his arm about Revna's shoulders. He looked about him at the shadowed alcoves and the guards that stood there. "And freedom. The deck of a good ship beneath my feet, the wind in its sail." He nodded to himself, as if judging his own words to be good. "And I think of plunder," he concluded.

"Plunder?" Al-Zarqālluh asked, sounding out the word that seemed unfamiliar to him.

"Gold. Silver. Jewels." Runolf looked at me sidelong, but spoke to Al-Zarqālluh. "Has Hunlaf asked about the reward yet, or just his precious book?"

Al-Zarqālluh laughed then, but held up a hand.

"If you wish for your reward, it would be best that I speak with the emir. I fear he does not speak your tongue and he is not a man accustomed to being ignored."

Runolf nodded, seeming to understand that one such as Al-Hakam should not be slighted. As Al-Zarqālluh began to interpret what had been said to the emir, Runolf turned to Hereward, Gwawrddur and Drosten, raising his eyebrows. His meaning was clear: perhaps there was hope after all.

"Before speaking of your reward, his Royal Highness wishes to know what you thought of the display today."

Runolf frowned, thinking before opening his mouth to speak.

"The sea fire is truly a mighty weapon," he said at last. "It will be feared by all your enemies." His expression grew stern. "But I did not enjoy watching men burnt to death." He shook his head. "There is no honour in such killing."

Al-Zarqālluh hesitated for a heartbeat, then translated Runolf's words. Al-Hakam's face darkened.

"Criminals do not deserve an honourable death," he said. Al-Zarqālluh spoke his words in Englisc, then continued to interpret.

"The message would not have been as clear without Rifat and the other prisoners," he said. "Their deaths were the bearers of the light, so that you would see and comprehend the power of the holy fire."

My breath caught in my throat.

"You have the book," I blurted out, my anger making my voice sharp and strident.

Al-Zarqālluh turned to face me.

"I tell you I do not," he said, his smile haughty.

"You have read it," I said. "I am sure of it. Why else would you speak of light bearers?"

He shook his head.

"It was merely a way of speaking, Hunlaf. I am not as fluent in the language of the Englisc as you are in al-Arabiyyah. And yet the words seem apt to me. Did not the burning men produce great light? And did not that light bear all the better the warning of our new power?"

He stared at me unblinking, daring me to question him further. I clenched my fists. Gwawrddur reached for me, but I shrugged off his hand. My fury was burning up within me, ready to burst forth.

"You would goad me with your words—"

The emir cut me off.

"Silence!" he snapped. He pushed himself to his feet. "I am done listening to your voice, monk. And your accursed *kafir* tongue." His face was hard, his tone flinty. The guards tensed, perhaps at some prearranged signal or sensing that their ruler would soon call on them to strike us down. As the mood in the room soured, Gwawrddur, Drosten and Hereward shifted their positions so that they faced the guards nearest them. My shield-brothers would not be struck down without a fight, even unarmed as they were.

"What is the king saying?" asked Runolf.

"That he is done talking," I replied. Turning to Al-Hakam, I spoke in the language of his people. "So now you will kill us?"

"Kill you?" he replied, his tone incredulous. "If I had wanted to take your lives, why would I have brought you out of the dungeon of Qadis? Why would I have fed and clothed you?"

Shaking his head at my stupidity, Al-Hakam clapped his hands together loudly. Two servants stepped from the shadows carrying a bronze-bound chest, which they placed on the table before the emir. At a nod from Al-Hakam, one of the servants opened the coffer. The lamplight glimmered and danced on the silver coins heaped there. The box was large and the discs of burnished silver were piled high.

"Here is your reward," Al-Hakam said. "Tell your comrades that I am a man of my word."

I repeated what the emir had said in Englisc. The hoard of silver reflected in my friends' eyes. Runolf licked his lips.

"Take this silver and be gone from my kingdom," continued Al-Hakam, his face cold. "You are not welcome here. And do not forget the message I send with you."

"What message?" I asked.

"Tell King Carolus and his spies what you have seen here. Tell him that if he sends his ships against me, they will be destroyed, consumed with holy flames, for the secret of Roman Fire is now ours!"

Twenty-Five

"At least we are alive."

I turned to see Revna. I was standing at the side of the barge watching Qurtuba slide ever further into the distance. The city's tall walls hid the sprawl of buildings, the jumble of narrow roads and winding alleyways, but I thought I could still detect the scent of spices on the warm breeze.

I had not heard Revna approach. My cheeks grew hot. I wondered if she knew the effect she had on me. I suspect she did. In my experience, most women, especially those blessed with beauty, are not oblivious of their power over men. And Revna was no fool, her mind as sharp as her face was comely. She was strikingly beautiful that morning, her brushed hair shining in the sunlight. I looked away from her, back to the river and the receding city.

"Your father would say all that matters is that we have a chest full of silver." I glanced back to where the chest, sturdy oak bound in metal strips, rested on the deck near Runolf and the others.

None of us had truly believed the emir would allow us to leave with the treasure, but whatever else he might be, Al-Hakam appeared to be a man of his word. The morning after the demonstration of Roman Fire and the presentation to us of the casket of silver coins, guards had come to our rooms at first light. We had been led through the awakening streets and down to the wharf, where we had found Faruq waiting on his barge. Two of the guards had carried the heavy chest and they deposited it on the deck. It was secured with a cunning lock and Hafiz had handed the key to Runolf before we left the palace.

"Silver is important," Revna said, moving to stand beside me.

Faruq shouted an order to the oarsmen and the barge changed direction slightly. We were navigating past green islands that dotted the river to the south of Qurtuba. Brambles and shrubs grew on them, rising high above the water and the sandy islands. I peered back at Qurtuba and the great stone arches of the bridge. The city would be lost to view soon, obscured by the foliage on the islands and then by distance and the bends in the river.

My eyes were drawn to the bridge. The raised platform had been removed and there was no sign now of the fire that had spat from the beast-mouthed syphon on the barge, or the men that the Roman Fire had consumed. But when I closed my eyes I could still see their agonised faces, and hear their pitiful screams. I rubbed at my gritty eyes and stifled a yawn. I had scarcely slept the night before. When I had managed to find sleep, it had been filled with nightmares of flame and death.

"Many things are important," I said.

"I know that," said Revna. "So does my father."

I thought of the long weeks Runolf and I had spent together in the dungeon. He had only been there because of me. I sighed.

"He is a good man."

She stared out at the barge's wake in the murky water.

"I did not always believe it to be so," she said.

I imagined how she must have felt living all those months

with the escaped thralls, the followers of the deranged monk, Scomric. I thought of the sacrifices she'd needed to make. Her father had not been there to protect her when Ljósberari and his madmen came to her family's steading.

"But you do now?" I asked.

She was silent for a long time, perhaps thinking of all she had done, or maybe of what Runolf had done since they had been reunited. A coot slipped from the rushes in the shallows of one of the islands.

"Yes," she said, watching the bird as it paddled towards us through the water, letting out its cheeping call. "I believe it now. He is a good man. Or as good as any man can be."

I wondered what she meant by that, but before I could speak, she asked me a question.

"Why is the book so important to you?"

I breathed in deeply of the fresh air. Any lingering smells of the city were gone now, replaced by the mud and plants that lined the al-Wadi 'l-kabir. I remembered how Revna's skin and hair had smelt when I had tended her wound, and I wished to move closer to her.

But I remained where I was, thinking about how to answer her question.

"It is not easy for me to explain," I said.

"Try."

I smiled.

"Very well," I said, frowning. "I feel that somehow that book is linked to me. To my past and my future. Leofstan read it for one day and from that moment on he wanted little more than to be able to study it fully. You did not know Leofstan, but he was a great man. Truly, he was like a father to me." I realised with a start I had never voiced that thought before, but as I said the words, I knew them to be true. "I feel in part I need to continue that which he wanted to do in life. To find the book and study its contents."

"You are not frightened for what you might find in its pages?"

I thought of Scomric, his mind twisted after reading *The Treasure of Life* until he believed he needed to burn those who were filled with darkness, putting out their eyes so that they could not see the light.

"I would be lying if I said it did not concern me. But Leofstan said it is only a book. Mere pages of vellum and ink cannot have any power of their own."

"You do not fear the book's magic?" She spat into the water and made the sign with her fingers to ward off evil spirits.

"It is only a book," I repeated. "It is not magic."

But I thought of how Al-Zarqālluh's eyes gleamed as he spoke of Rifat and the others being the bearers of light as they burnt with holy fire. I shuddered.

"I am sorry the book is lost to you," she said. "But as I said," a sudden smile lit up her face, "at least we are alive."

"And we have the silver," I replied, unable to keep from returning her smile, despite my tiredness and sorrow.

We made good progress all that day. The slaves who manned the oars were fresh and they were pulling us in the direction of the sea. The river's current propelled us ever forward and I could feel my spirit lightening as we travelled further from Qurtuba. The dungeon of Qadis seemed like a bad dream now and I hoped that in time, the memories of the suffering caused by the emir and Al-Zarqālluh's Roman Fire might also fade.

That evening, we moored at a small settlement. The river was lined with fig trees, their broad, dark leaves providing shade from the warmth of the setting sun. Revna and the rest of the men had gone up to the large, whitewashed farmhouse where we would spend the night. Runolf had carried the chest with him, and I was sure he would sleep with it later. The *Al-Muslimun* from the boat had all knelt beside the river for their evening prayers. I had sat beneath a tree and watched them as I murmured the words of Vespers to the Almighty, the one true God.

At that moment I felt keenly how far I was from home, from the brethren I had lived with for years, and from my kin. I missed Aelfwyn. I missed my brother, Beornnoth. I even longed to see my stern-faced father at Ubbanford, which was strange, as normally I had no inclination to spend time with him. Of course, I had a new family now, warriors and sailors who had shared with me dreadful and wonderful moments alike. But the truth was they were not of my blood and, sitting there in the shade of a fig tree beneath the hot sun of al-Andalus, that suddenly mattered to me. The conversation with Revna had made me think about Leofstan too. Until then, I don't think I had fully understood how much I had relied on his guidance and wisdom. Nor had I comprehended how much I had loved the old monk.

When the men had finished their prayers, the crew and half a dozen of the guards had followed the others up to the house. The smells of a spiced lamb stew and fresh bread being prepared drifted down to the river and my stomach grumbled. It had been a long time since we had broken our fast and we had eaten little during the day.

The oarsmen and six guards remained on the barge. I watched as Ahmad made his way into the trees and sat with his back against a trunk. He stared out over the river. None of the guards seemed interested in him or me. In fact Hereward had commented earlier that the guards seemed altogether indifferent to us now that we had left the city.

"As long as we get aboard *Brymsteda* without causing any trouble," Gwawrddur had opined, "I am sure they are more than happy to spend a couple of weeks on the barge as our nursemaids. I am certain there are worse duties they have to perform at times."

I pushed myself up and wandered over to where Ahmad sat. "Can I sit with you a while?" I asked.

He jumped, startled by my voice. Squinting at the sun's glare, he nodded. I sat down beside him and followed his gaze. He was watching the men on the barge. They were preparing their blankets. No doubt food would be brought down to them soon. Beyond the barge, the river's water shimmered in the late afternoon sunlight. Three ducks flew overhead and landed near the far bank with a series of splashes and beating wings.

"I had thought you might choose to stay in Qurtuba," I said.

"There is nothing there for me," Ahmad replied. "The emir has no love for me. I think it will be best if I am not so close to Al-Hakam's palace."

I wondered at the enmity there, but I sensed that if I pried, Ahmad would cease speaking and I would learn nothing new. For a long time now, he had been quiet and withdrawn, even more than I was used to.

"What are your plans?" I asked.

He shrugged.

"First, I will go with you to Qadis. It is not far from there to my father's home. Then I can begin to repay my debts."

"I am sure your father will be overjoyed to see his son. That will be recompense enough."

"Perhaps." He did not sound convinced. "But my debts are many. And large."

"Tayyib?"

He let out a long breath.

"I owe him more than I can hope to repay. But I must try." He rubbed a hand over his black beard. "Once he was my closest friend."

"Then I am sure he will forgive you your mistakes."

Ahmad said nothing. Digging around in the earth by his feet he pulled out a pebble. He weighed it in his palm, then tossed it far out into the river. It disappeared with a plopping splash. The nearby ducks flapped their wings in annoyance.

"I have been meaning to say something to you," I said.

He turned to look me in the eye. His shoulders were tense, his jaw clenched as if he was readying himself to receive bad tidings.

"What is it?" he asked.

"This has not been the homecoming you had wished for."

Ahmad snorted.

"I know not what I had expected, but you speak the truth. I had wished for a friendlier return than this."

"I cannot solve your problems," I said, "but perhaps there is something I can do to soften the pain, even if just a little."

Ahmad did not speak now. He just stared at me with his dark eyes.

"You are a thrall no longer, but a free man." I paused, but if I had expected him to thank me, I was disappointed. "Each of the free men of *Brymsteda* receive a portion of whatever riches we plunder," I pressed on. "It will not be enough to pay off your debts, I am sure, but when we reach Qadis, you will be given your fair share."

He scowled.

"The others will allow it?"

"Of course, you are one of the crew."

Ahmad raised his eyebrows.

"Even Runolf? He sets much store by silver."

"Runolf is a good man. I will see to it you receive what is yours by right."

He bit his lip and his eyes gleamed. For a time I thought he would say nothing. But then he reached out and grasped my arm.

"I give you thanks, Hunlaf," he said. "For everything."

I felt my face grow hot. I had wanted his thanks before, but now that he offered it, I felt ashamed.

"You do not need to thank me. I just wish I could do more. At least you are back here, in al-Andalus once more."

"Yes," he said, "and for that, and everything else, I offer you my thanks." From the house, a couple of the guards carried down trays of food. They were accompanied by two women who I guessed had prepared the meal. The smell of it reached us, reminding me how hungry I was.

Ahmad grew sombre.

"I am sorry," he said, frowning.

"For what? None of this has been your doing."

He chewed at his moustache, seeming to struggle to find the words he was seeking.

"You never got your book," he said at last.

"You are not to blame for that."

"Still," Ahmad said gravely, "I am sorry."

"I am sure Al-Zarqālluh is lying, but I know not what else I could do." I sighed. "I fear I will not retrieve the book. But, as the others keep reminding me, at least we have our lives and the silver."

"Yes," said Ahmad. "That is true. It would seem that neither of us found what we were looking for in al-Andalus."

I smiled without humour.

"Perhaps that is so," I said. "But tomorrow is a page of our story that is yet unwritten. And each day is a blessing, or so Leofstan used to tell me."

The women were serving up the food to the guards and oarsmen on the barge now. The aromas coming from the bowls were warm and inviting. My stomach rumbled loudly, and I chuckled.

"This day is almost over and I would have some of that sweet-smelling food before Runolf and Drosten eat the lot." I rose, offering my hand to Ahmad. "Coming?"

He shook his head.

"I will sit here a while longer and watch the sunset."

"I'll save you a plate of food."

I walked up towards the house in the dappled light spilling through the leaves and branches of the fig trees. When I glanced back at Ahmad, I saw he was not looking out at the sun setting over the great river. He was watching me, his features in shadow.

Twenty-Six

Everyone's spirits lifted as we continued downriver. We were looking forward to seeing the rest of our friends who remained in Qadis, though we were also worried about what might have happened to them in our absence. We had been gone for weeks. But as we ate on that first night, I mentioned our concerns to the dour-faced Faruq. He waved a splintered piece of root he was chewing and told me not to worry. Word had been sent downriver already with tidings of our return.

For the most part the days were hot and the skies clear. On the third day, dark clouds rolled in from the north as the sun dipped towards the horizon and in the night rain lashed down in a constant, roaring deluge. We had been given lodging in a large house on the edge of a settlement. The hills all around the village were covered with olive trees, their gnarled, twisted limbs pushing from the ground as if in some silent torment. Although we all wanted to hurry on our way, none of us welcomed the prospect of a day on the river underneath the bitter rain and squalling wind. Neither Faruq nor the leader of the guards, an unsmiling man with small eyes, called Ghalib, appeared to be in any rush to move on, so we hunkered down inside the smoke-filled, mud-walled house, listening to the howling wind and the rain drumming on the roof tiles. The headman of the village pursed his lips when he heard we would remain for another day and night, clearly less than happy that we would consume more of his food and drink. But he did not protest, and luckily for him, the clouds blew over during the following night and the morning dawned, damp, but bright and warm.

There were no further delays and a few days later we reached Išbīliya. I smiled as first the shadow pall of the cooking fires of hundreds of homes hazed the horizon and then, slowly, the city itself slid into sight.

"It will be good to see Leander again," said Runolf, clapping me on the back. With each day that passed and we grew closer to the sea and *Brymsteda*, so Runolf's mood improved.

"Be careful not to gamble all our silver away," I said, smiling. I was surprised in myself, but I too was looking forward to seeing Leander and the rest of the local guards again. We had few friends in this land, and the Christian men of the Išbīliya Watch had made us feel welcome.

When we entered the barracks, there was no sign of Leander and I recognised none of the faces of the men who watched us as we made our way to a corner of the room.

"It looks like we will not have to worry about the gambling tonight," Gwawrddur said with a forced smile. Like all of us, the Welshman had been looking forward to a repeat of our previous visit, but instead we sat and whispered in an awkward morose hush as the guards in the barracks eyed us suspiciously.

After a time, a horn sounded and the room was filled with noise as men within the building rose as one, buckling on sword belts, lifting helms and spears, and calling out to one another. Quickly they filed out of the barracks and shortly after, servants brought food and drink, placing it on the boards. The servants left without a word and Runolf stood.

"Perhaps this will not be such a memorable night as last time," he said, "but at least we will be fed." He reached for a piece of unleavened bread, dipping it into a thick sauce. "It is good," he said, smacking his lips.

From outside came the sound of dozens of marching feet, then the door swung open.

"Leave some for the rest of us!" shouted a familiar voice in al-Arabiyyah.

Grinning, I watched as the speaker tugged off his helm and strode towards us. His long, fair hair was drenched in sweat and plastered to his head. His face was flushed.

"Leander!" I said. "We thought we would not see you."

"And miss the chance to win back my coin?" he said, grinning. "Never!"

Runolf moved close and grasped Leander's forearm in the warrior grip.

"Tell him I hope he is ready for some serious drinking," he said. "I have a thirst on."

I interpreted the Norseman's words and Leander laughed.

"We have finished our watch and will not be called to duty until the morrow. I just hope for Runolf's sake his luck has improved. Otherwise he will be leaving Išbīliya with nothing more than the clothes on his back."

Runolf laughed, but I noticed he made sure that the chest filled with our silver was close to hand, pushed against the wall in the corner of the room where it could not be approached without any of us noticing.

We settled down to eat and drink with the men whom we had befriended on our previous visit and as the evening turned to night, the atmosphere in the room reminded me of a mead hall far off in the north. In the flickering light of rushlights, there was laughter, songs, games, riddles and drink.

Lots of drink.

My head was spinning when I stepped outside in the hope that the cool night air might clear my head somewhat. I thought to walk down to the river, and stumbled down a dark alley in what I believed to be the right direction. The raucous sounds of the men within the building grew muffled and distant. Looking up at the strip of sky that was visible between the buildings, I saw thin clouds lit by the ghostly glow of the bright crescent moon. I wondered if Aelfwyn, far away in Northumbria, was looking up at the same moon. Of course not, I chided myself. It was late and she would be abed with her new husband, Eadmaer. I hadn't thought of the fisherman for a long time and I wondered if he was happy now. Why wouldn't he be? He had risked everything in search of the woman he had secretly loved, and when he'd found her, she had accepted him. I had searched for Aelfwyn too, of course, but in the end it felt as though it was more Eadmaer's victory than mine when we had rescued her. Even though I would not admit it to anyone, I supposed I had been more fixated on finding the book. And in that, I had failed terribly. And now it seemed I would never find the object of my obsession.

I turned another corner, my foot squelching in something soft on the cobbled ground. Where was I? My steps were unsteady and I needed to piss. I sniffed, hoping my nose would lead me to the latrine, but I could detect nothing apart from the smell of whatever manure I had just stepped into. I looked up at the sky again and cursed. For the first time since we'd left Qurtuba I wished our guards were keeping a closer watch on us. Then I would not have been allowed to wander off alone into the labyrinth of alleys and streets beside the docks. But there could be no denying it now. I was lost, and the pressure from my bladder was too much to ignore any longer.

Cursing again, I staggered into a dark corner of the narrow street, pulling at my breeches. The sour stink of old piss told me I was not the first man to use this particular spot to relieve himself. Tugging my breeches down I pissed into the darkness, letting out a long sigh.

My head still spun from the wine, but I felt much better

for having emptied my bladder. I couldn't be a great distance from the barracks. I had not walked far. Turning back in the direction I thought I had come from, I picked my way along the dark alley.

Far off in the city, someone cried out. I halted, tilting my head to better listen to the night. The sound came again and I chuckled quietly to myself, feeling a small stab of envy. Someone was enjoying themselves. It was the unmistakable sound of a woman in the throes of lust. Another sound drifted to me and I thought I could make out the muted laughter from the barracks. I pressed on into the gloom.

The attack came without warning. I did not see my assailants, but they must have been stalking me, or lurking in the shadows. The first I knew of their presence was a thudding blow to the back of my head. Bright lights flashed before my eyes and my head and face took another cracking hit from the muck-covered cobbles as I hit the ground.

My senses must have left me for a time, for the next thing I knew I could feel hands tearing at my clothes, searching my belt for a pouch or anything of value.

"Have you killed him?" hissed a voice in al-Arabiyyah.

"What does it matter if I have? He is *kafir* and a stranger. Nobody will miss him."

Strong hands rolled me onto my back, patting my kirtle that was now damp and clung to my skin. The cool moon stared down from the heavens, hiding the men's faces in shadow. There were two of them. The larger of the two was close to me and I could smell garlic on his breath. The other jostled nervously from one foot to the other.

"Has he got any silver?" he asked, looking up and down the narrow lane for sign of anyone who might stumble upon us.

My mind was clearing somewhat as the larger man tugged and probed my clothes for hidden valuables. My head throbbed and my face was simultaneously hot from the blow against the cobbles and cool as the moisture from the mud came into contact with the night air. The man's hands became increasingly frantic in their searching. I knew he would find nothing worth stealing. And when the men realised that, they would either flee, leaving me where I lay, or decide that it would be best if I was silenced in case I could identify them.

I was not going to wait and see which choice they would make. I had fought bloodthirsty Norsemen, vicious Imazighen pirates, and brutal Pictish warriors. I would not allow two cutpurses to end my life in this noisome alleyway.

"Son of a dog," said the big man, turning to look up at his slender companion. "He's got nothing."

This was as good a chance as I was likely to get. Without warning, I lashed out and seized the man's right wrist. Before he could react, I grabbed his fingers and bent them backwards. There was a sickening snapping and he flung himself away from me with a scream that echoed in the night. His hand wrenched free of my grip, but I did not care. He would not be punching me with that hand again, or wielding a weapon, if he had one.

Scrabbling away from the men, pushing with my heels across the mud-slick stones, I sprang up as quickly as I was able. I tottered on my feet, still drink-dizzy from the wine and groggy from the blow to the head.

"My hand," wheezed the man who had been searching me. "My hand!"

The slimmer of the two hesitated, unsure what to do. I did not need any further encouragement. Fights are usually won by the person who strikes first. In this case that was not going to happen. This fight would be won by the combatant who did not hesitate. I had been assaulted without warning. I was outnumbered, unarmed and drunk. There was nothing for it but to move forward now, taking the fight to them before they could rally.

The big man got his left hand under him and pushed himself up. I did not pause. Before he could stand, I sprang forward and kicked him hard in the face. His head snapped back, cracking into the wall. He slumped there, half-sitting in the shadows, unmoving.

Seeing his friend knocked out appeared to spark the other would-be thief into action. He pulled something from his belt and the moonlight glimmered from steel. I could make out little in the darkness, but I could see the flicker of a blade as he moved a knife back and forth. Still hesitant, he jabbed the knife at me. I saw the movement in his shoulders and registered the scrape of his shoes as he lunged, but I was not thinking now. This was no time for thought, or for doubt. I unleashed the fury that had been simmering within me for so long and I became lost to it. With a roar I was barely aware of I stamped forward. As the blade plunged towards my chest, I sidestepped, allowing it to whisper past. At the same instant I grasped hold of the man's wrist, pulling him off balance. He stumbled and without releasing my grip, I raised my knee and pushed down on his arm. His elbow connected with a snapping sound that was sickeningly loud in the still of the night. He howled in agony and fell at my feet. Babbling and crying now, he pleaded and begged for mercy, but I was well past the point of offering the other cheek to my enemies. Grabbing his head in both hands I kneed him in the face. He fell senseless and mercifully silent to the damp cobbles.

My head throbbed and I thought I might be sick. Sucking in deep breaths, I calmed myself, and the nausea passed. I found the man's knife in the mud, and I stuck it in my belt. There was nothing else of value on him. I found a small pouch sewn inside the robe of the larger man. I could feel a few coins inside, so I tore it free, coins and all. The man groaned, and I slapped him with my open hand to shut him up. I felt a momentary guilt at stealing from these wretches, then I reminded myself that they had attacked me without provocation with the aim of robbing me, or worse. With a final kick in the ribs for the knife-man, I staggered off in what I hoped was the direction of the barracks.

Soon I saw the light of torches ahead and I recognised where I was again. The sound of laughter and chatter was loud now and I wondered how I had not been able to hear it only a few alleys away. There were two sentries on duty at the entrance. I did not recall seeing them before, but they nodded to me, evidently unsurprised by my arrival.

Shaking my head against the hammering pain in my skull, I pulled open the door. The smoky warmth of the interior engulfed me and I felt another wave of sickness.

"Hunlaf!"

The sharp cry made me wince. Then I saw it was Revna who was rushing towards me, and I felt a small sliver of pleasure.

"What happened to you?"

She made me turn my head to the side and I grimaced as she touched my scalp, probing for wounds. The laughter in the room had vanished now. Runolf, Drosten, Gwawrddur, Hereward and Leander all hurried to my side, crowding about me.

"Who did this to you?" asked Drosten.

I looked down at my clothes. My kirtle was torn and smeared with mud and muck, my breeches were likewise soiled. Reaching up, I touched the back of my head. My hair was wet and my fingertips came back stained with blood.

"You are hurt," said Gwawrddur.

"You should see the other two," I said with a pained grin.

Twenty-Seven

"There's no sign of them," said Leander. "But we found this." He held up a length of wood, almost as thick as my wrist, and as long as my forearm. Leander had listened to my account and then led half a dozen of the City Watch into the night in search of my attackers.

He placed the cudgel on the nearest table. One end, thinner than the other, was polished smooth by use and I could imagine the man whose fingers I'd snapped holding the weapon and swinging it in the darkness. The lamplight shone on the drying blood that smeared the stout end of the club.

"God must have smiled on you this night," said Leander. He raised his hand as if to clap me on the back, but thought better of it when I tensed in anticipation.

"I don't feel blessed," I said. My head was pounding and sickness washed through me like waves sliding up a beach, to retreat again with a whisper, leaving me feeling weak and shaken.

Runolf picked up the cudgel and examined it. He swung it a couple of times, feeling the heft of it. It looked small in his massive hands, but he nodded gravely.

"You're lucky this did not cave in your skull," he said.

"He has a thick skull," said Gwawrddur. "I have told him so many times."

"Or the man who wielded that club was a weakling," said Drosten, with a twisted grin. "If I had struck a man with that, he would not be getting up to fight me."

Hereward took the cudgel from Runolf and slapped it against his left palm.

"Let us be glad that God was watching over our thick-skulled friend," he said. He offered me a smile. "Or that his attacker had the strength of a babe in arms." He put the club back on the board and winked at me. The others laughed, but I could not find it in me to be amused. Despite remaining conscious, I felt I might puke at any moment, and if I moved my head too quickly, darkness threatened to engulf my vision.

"What are they laughing at?" Leander asked.

"They say I have a hard head or a very weak enemy." I winced as Revna pressed a wet cloth against the wound in my scalp. "Or both."

Leander chuckled and shook his head.

"Whatever the reason that you are still amongst the living, I would thank God for it. It is not uncommon for men who stray in the streets of Išbīliya at night to be found floating in the river in the morning."

Leander was right. I was bruised and aching, and the cut to my scalp stung and had bled badly, and yet I had seen many men die from lesser wounds. I offered up a silent prayer of thanks to the Lord, wondering if, even now, having strayed so far from the path of righteousness, the Almighty still had plans for me. I had failed to retrieve *The Treasure of Life*, but it seemed God had not forsaken me, despite my sinful ways. I felt an intense moment of shame at my lack of faith, but this was quickly burnt away by my vengeful anger at those who had attacked me.

"If you should see a pair of men," I said, turning my head

and rolling my neck with a grunt of pain, "one with a broken arm and the other with broken fingers, please see that they pay for their crimes."

Revna tutted and touched my head, pushing it straight again so she could continue ministering to me.

"Be still."

Leander was sombre faced.

"If I see them, I will make sure they are not able to waylay others from the shadows." I nodded my thanks, immediately regretting moving, as Revna cursed quietly and pushed my head straight again, more forcefully and less patiently than before. "Now," continued Leander, "when the lovely lady has finished with your head, come and have another drink. I have some wine from my village that will dull any pain."

"It will dull your pain tonight," said another of the fair-haired guards, laughing. "But tomorrow you will feel as if that cudgel really did crack your skull."

Leander called for the flask of this special drink to be brought out. Unstopping the leather bottle, he began pouring small measures into the men's proffered cups.

"Sit still," hissed Revna. She was wrapping a bandage about my head. The pressure on the swelling bruise at the back of my skull was painful, making me flinch and tense. But after careful examination, she was certain that the bone had not been cracked.

"I don't know if your God watched over you," she said, "or if you just have a strong head." Her face was close to mine as she tied off the strip of linen that Leander had given her for the purpose. "Whatever the reason, I am glad you are not badly hurt." Her breath was warm and sweet. A wave of giddiness washed over me and I wondered if it was from the blow I had suffered, or the sudden realisation of Revna's proximity and the gentle touch of her fingers. As she tightened the bandage, the pain jabbed into my head like a knife, but I made no sound, not wanting to show weakness. My nerves still jangled from the fight, and I clenched my fists in my lap to avoid shaking.

"Come on, you two," shouted Hereward, "when you have finished making eyes at each other, come over here and drink some of this. It will take your mind off your headache."

Runolf glanced over at us, and I stood quickly, stepping away from Revna.

"Thank you," I muttered, my face burning, as my stomach churned and my head throbbed.

She nodded, but said nothing further.

Staggering over to the men, I sat at the long bench and accepted a cup of Leander's wine. I sniffed it. It smelt potent, with a peppery undercurrent. The warriors were watching expectantly, waiting to see my reaction to the drink. All but Ahmad. He was sitting in the corner, near the chest, his face serious. I knew he did not approve of drunkenness and he seldom drank, and never to excess. Truly I did not wish to drink more, but if this foul-smelling concoction of Leander's could make me feel any better, I would give it a try.

Putting the cup to my lips, I hesitated, then drained the contents in one quick swallow. The liquid was cool, and yet it burnt my throat as if it were on fire. Coughing, I put the cup back on the table.

"Better already," I gasped, barely able to make a sound through my spluttering. The room erupted with laughter and merriment. Leander and the others did not seem overly concerned with my health. The interruption to the evening's merrymaking when I had come in from the night, pale, shaken and dirt-streaked, seemed all but forgotten now.

"How's your head?"

Ahmad had come to sit beside me. He lifted the flask and poured a little more into my cup.

"Well," I said, surprised that he should be condoning partaking of such an intoxicating drink, "it feels as if someone tried to crack my skull with this." I picked up the cudgel. My eyes were drawn to the dark stain of my blood on the wood.

He smiled.

"Does the drink help?"

I picked up my cup, grimaced at the smell, and emptied it.

"Well, it doesn't make my head feel any worse."

"Not yet, anyway." He grinned.

I wondered at the change that had come over him. Perhaps it was that he had made peace with his decisions as we approached Qadis, where we would part ways and he would return to his home to seek his father's forgiveness. It was a noble endeavour and I hoped he would be received with open arms and an open heart. Whatever he had done in the past, it seemed to me that Ahmad was a good man. He was not a Christian, and I knew that a believer in the teachings of the prophet Muhammad would not be permitted to enter the kingdom of heaven. But there was yet time for Ahmad. God was all powerful and if He willed it, Ahmad could still find salvation.

The ache in my head was actually growing weaker and I marvelled at the power of Leander's drink. Ahmad refilled the cups of Drosten, Hereward, Gwawrddur and Runolf. Having been a thrall for so long, I knew Ahmad hated serving others, and I took this gesture of pouring drinks for us all as a sign of contrition on his part, for the untruths he had told us about the extent of his influence in al-Andalus. But I could not blame him. He had only done what he had deemed to be necessary to obtain his freedom and return to his homeland. I might have done the same in his position.

"You're a good man, Ahmad," I said. The pain in my head had reduced to a dull ache, as if the sharp throbbing had been wrapped in a warm blanket.

He looked at me sharply, a strange expression on his face.

"I am not good," he said with a sigh.

"Nobody is perfect," I said. "All we can do is try to do our best with each moment we are given. To take the best decisions available to us."

"I am sorry," he said, his face sombre once more, almost sorrowful.

"You have nothing to apologise to me for," I said. "Make amends with your father. And Tayyib, and all will be well."

He shook his head slowly.

"I hope you are right."

"I am," I said, my words slurred now from the drink and a sudden exhaustion that had enveloped about me in a warm embrace. "I am sure of it." My head swam and I could barely keep my eyes open. "I am going to sleep now."

I moved as if in a dream to where we had left our blankets. I had difficulty shaking out my bedding, such was my torpor. A small voice whispered to me that something was wrong. Had the blow to my head split my skull after all? Was this exhaustion a symptom of the damage done by the cudgel? But I was too weary to investigate these questions. The pain in my head had been muted by Leander's drink, and I welcomed the numbing of my senses as I pulled my blanket around me and lay down, head pillowed on my arm.

I remember no more of that night, for sleep engulfed me in an instant, and I did not dream.

Twenty-Eight

I awoke to the sound of shouting. My neck was stiff and my arm numb from where my head had rested on it all night. My head pounded as if my assailants of the previous night had crept into the barracks and proceeded to beat me over and over with the cudgel Leander had found in the alley. My mouth was dry and sour tasting. I wanted nothing more than a cool drink of water, then perhaps I could find somewhere quiet to lie down once more.

But there was no chance I would find sleep again. Men were yelling, fury and outrage in their strident tone.

Runolf's booming voice, louder than the rest, was clear over the others.

"By Óðinn," he roared, "I will kill him!" It took me a moment to realise he was speaking in his native Norse, rather than the Englisc he used most frequently to communicate with me and the others.

I could just make out the softer sound of Revna's voice, but her words were lost in the tumult of the hall.

With a groan I sat up. Forcing my eyes open, I winced as bright light from the unshuttered windows lanced into the room. The lamps had long been extinguished, the air cool and sour with the breath of sleeping men. Judging by the light spearing the haze of the hall, it was well past dawn.

"What has happened?" I croaked, scarcely making a sound.

Nobody heard me, so I pushed myself to my feet, looking about for something to moisten my parched mouth and throat. There was a ewer on a nearby table. I picked it up. Liquid sloshed within and I sniffed it. Ale. I would have preferred water, but my mouth was so dry, I did not hesitate. Lifting the large jug to my lips, I took a long draught.

"I do not think more drink is the answer," said Gwawrddur. He moved close and took the pitcher from my hands.

"Answer to what?" I asked.

"To anything on this morning, I would say," he answered cryptically.

I tried again, now that the ale had cleared my throat.

"What has happened?"

Runolf spun to face me.

"What has happened?" he bellowed. "What has happened?" His face was crimson with fury, his beard and hair jutted from his head like flames. "I'll tell you what's happened. We've come all the way to al-Andalus, where we've been attacked by pirates, one of our crew has been killed, and my daughter wounded. You and I have been locked in a hole in the ground for weeks. Then we have been forced to watch men burnt alive, and for what? You still haven't got your precious book, and now the silver we were given, the one thing that went some way to making this worthwhile, is gone."

"Gone?" Stupidly I looked down at the corner where the chest had been the night before, as if I expected Runolf and the others to have made a terrible mistake. The coffer was not there. "How?"

"That treacherous rat Ahmad took it, that's how!"

★

The barracks were chaos for a time as we pieced together what had happened. Runolf overturned benches and stools, as if he hoped to find the chest of silver hidden somewhere in the cluttered room. He bellowed like an angry bear and Revna followed him, talking quietly in an attempt to calm her father's ire.

My head reeled and pounded, from the blow I'd received, the drink, and now also from the shock of losing the treasure. It had been the only thing alleviating the feeling that this had been a disastrous journey, and now that too had been snatched away.

Judging from the pinched expressions and wincing groans, I was not the only one that morning with a headache. Most of those in the barracks had awoken with dry mouths, thoughts clouded and fuzzy, and heads throbbing.

Drosten, lifting his hand to shield his eyes from the bright daylight, staggered out of the building. I called after him, but he did not respond.

"He's gone to check on the barge," said Hereward, rubbing his hand across his eyes. He looked old and tired in the stark morning light. "Ahmad is not the only one missing," he went on. "Ghalib is gone too. And a couple of his men." I thought back to the previous night and recalled Ahmad kneeling next to the sour-looking captain of the guards at evening prayers. Had they been plotting together, whispering as they'd bowed low to the ground?

The rest of the warriors who had been sent to watch over us from Qurtuba now sat dejected and sombre, no doubt imagining the punishment they would face because of their failure to protect us and the treasure we carried.

Drosten clattered back into the barracks.

"The barge and all the crew are still there," the Pict said, breathless from hurrying to the river and back.

Faruq was close behind Drosten. The thickset skipper looked about the hall, taking in the confusion and anger.

"Did you see anything last night?" I asked him, leaning on a board still covered in cups from the night's feasting.

"I saw many things," he said. "It was a warm night, and clear."

"Did you see Ahmad? Ghalib? Anyone else?" I picked up one of the cups and sniffed at it absently.

"I saw nobody," Faruq said. "The river was quiet, apart from the noise from this hall that I could hear until well after midnight." He shook his head disapprovingly. "What has happened here?"

Picking up a second cup, I sniffed the residue of drink coating the inside.

"We have been robbed," I said, knowing with a flash of certainty how they had done it. I slumped down onto a bench. I didn't have the strength to shout and rave like Runolf. Besides, I saw no point in doing so. The silver would not miraculously come back to us, no matter how furious we got.

Gwawrddur, his face grave, sat beside me.

"It saddens me that Ahmad would betray us thus," he said. Ahmad had saved his life when Gwawrddur had almost drowned and, while they had never been overly friendly, the Welshman had always treated the Moor with respect. "Men seldom fail to disappoint."

My head ached and I sighed.

"I fear there can be no doubt." I held up the two cups from the board before me. "See for yourself."

"On another day, Killer, perhaps I would welcome trying to understand your meaning." He shook his head and I noticed how drawn and sorrowful his face was. "But not today."

I handed one of the cups to him.

"Can you smell it?"

He sniffed the empty cup, frowning. His nose wrinkled and I knew he had detected the acrid scent I had noticed.

"Now smell this one."

He raised the second cup to his nose, then handed it back to me.

"I smell nothing in this one. The first has a bitter stink."

"The first cup was used by one of the guards there." I indicated to where the warriors from Qurtuba sat with their heads in their hands. "None of them drank of the wine, ale or Leander's special brew, and yet they all slept while the chest was taken."

"And the second cup?"

"Ghalib's. At first I struggled to discern the scent in our own cups, for Leander's brew was potent and masked it, but it was easier to make out in the sweet lemon water the guards drank."

Gwawrddur frowned.

"What is it?"

Before I could answer, the horn sounded for the changing of the guard. Leander and the warriors groggily pulled on their armour, strapped on their weapons and bade us farewell.

"I am sorry that this has happened," said the fair-haired warrior of the watch. "Attacked and then robbed. Some welcome in Išbīliya for you." His face was pale, his eyes dark-rimmed, as if bruised.

"It is not your fault," I said, offering my hand.

He grasped my forearm.

"We slept while your silver was stolen."

"All of us slept," I said. "We were..." I struggled to think of the right words in al-Arabiyyah. "We were given a drink to make us sleep."

His face darkened.

"What drink?"

"I know not the name for the substance in your tongue," I said. "It is like a milk squeezed from a flower." I recalled reading about the tears of the poppy in the *Herbarium Apuleii Platonici* at Werceworthe.

"And your man, Ahmad, did this?"

I glanced over to where Runolf had raised a stool above his head and looked set to smash it against the whitewashed wall. As I watched, Revna placed her hand on Runolf's arm and his anger appeared to finally ebb away. Placing the stool back on the flagstones, the giant Norseman sat down with a sigh.

"Ahmad is not my man," I said. "I doubt he ever was. But yes, I believe he did this, along with Ghalib."

"And all they took was the chest?" Leander asked, accepting with a nod a shield and spear that a passing warrior handed him.

"There was enough silver in that box to make them both rich men."

"And," said a voice from the doorway, "perhaps enough to pay off certain debts."

We turned to look at the speaker. The guards of the new watch were trudging out, heads down and weary. The sentries, perhaps still groggy from the sleeping draught, must have been distracted, for they had not stopped the newcomer, and now a stranger stood in the barracks hall. He was a short man in long black robes. His head was swaddled in dark cloth. I squinted at him, trying to make out his features, but his back was to the door, his face in shadow.

"Peace be upon you," I said.

"And upon you," he replied smoothly.

I could still not see his face, but there was something familiar about his voice.

"You spoke of a debt," I said, my mind racing. I recalled Ahmad's tale of the shadowy figure who had loaned him the riches he'd needed to put his plan into action. There seemed only one explanation for the man's sudden appearance and his words, though I could make little sense of his purpose. "Do you come from Aljany?"

The man laughed quietly.

"In a manner of speaking," he said, "I suppose I do."

Leander stiffened beside me, taking a step forward. The name of Aljany, the crime lord, was known and feared throughout the land of al-Andalus. The man held up a hand, stilling Leander's advance.

"Do not fear, brave Leander," he said, "I am no friend of that evil man. And, Hunlaf, the substance used to induce sleep in you all is the milky tears of the poppy; here it is known as *al-afion*." At the mention of my name, I suddenly knew who this stranger was. He stepped into a pool of light beneath a window and I heard Gwawrddur's sharp intake of breath.

"Giso," he whispered.

"The same," replied the small man. His face was darkly tanned beneath the black cloth that wrapped his head, and his chin was covered in a dark beard. "Now, despite how it might appear," he said, "everything is not lost. But I have travelled far and my horse has been lame these last days. I am weary and need sustenance before we can go about retrieving that which has been stolen from you."

Twenty-Nine

I leaned back, watching a large flock of sparrows wheel overhead in the pale sky. The sun was high, the bright light hurting my eyes. Far off, I could hear the wailing cry of the *muezzin* calling the people to their *Dhuhr*, midday prayers.

My head still ached terribly, but whilst the others had not been beaten with a cudgel the night before, their movements were also tentative and they winced at sudden noises. The after effects of the *al-afion* tears of the poppy had made us all lethargic and sick. I wondered at the state of the city's defences with so many of the guards on duty coming from Leander's men who must have been feeling as bad as us.

The barge that had carried us from Qurtuba rested at the wharf. Faruq and his men were on the dock, performing the ritual motions and chants of their prayers.

Faruq was waiting to hear our plans. He was devout and gave the impression that he believed our debauchery was partly responsible for our plight. He disapproved of drinking and even when he'd been told that Ghalib's men had abstained from any intoxicating drink, but had been drugged against their will, he displayed little sympathy. He did however let us know that his orders had been to carry us to Qadis and then to return with our warrior escort to Qurtuba.

"Ghalib's treachery is nothing to do with me," he'd said, when he heard of the theft. "But as we have not yet reached Qadis, if you choose to go in search of the men who stole your treasure, I would have to wait for you." His face had remained sombre and censorious, but there was a glimmer in his eye which spoke of the man's sense of justice more loudly than words.

For a short time after Giso's arrival, Runolf had pushed for us to leave at once in pursuit of Ahmad and Ghalib, but it had quickly become clear that we were in no state to travel.

"I have walked for most of the night," said the Frank. "I must rest. But even if I could continue, I don't believe you could. Look at you."

Runolf had grumbled, but the truth of Giso's words were clear to us all, so we did not protest further when he had suggested we take some food and water and sit beside the river to talk of the past and what the future might bring.

Runolf, the heat gone now from his earlier fury, was propped against a timber mooring post. He sipped from a waterskin, then passed it to Revna.

"First thing we need to know," the Norseman said, his voice rumbling like a far-off rock fall, "is who on middle earth you are."

"You know who I am," replied the Frank. I recognised his voice and the gleam of his eyes, but it was still difficult to think of this man as the pious Frankish envoy with whom we had sailed south. His skin was darker than many of the locals, and where he had taken such care to shave off his whiskers each morning, now most of his face was covered by a thick wiry beard.

"I know you say your name is Giso," said Runolf. "Perhaps that is true. And we know why Alhwin said he sent you here. But who are you really, and why did you come to al-Andalus?"

"You know all you need to know—" Giso said in his smooth voice, but Hereward cut him off.

"Enough!" he snapped. "The time for games and riddles is over, Frank. Where have you been these past weeks? We thought you dead."

Giso smiled, as if Hereward's words amused him.

"I did not lie to you, and certainly Alhwin told you the truth. He is a great teacher and a man of true piety. I said I wished to have an audience with Al-Zarqālluh, and your man, Ahmad, said he would be able to help in that regard."

"Ahmad was not my man," said Hereward, echoing my earlier words.

"Be that as it may," said Giso, "I had believed he spoke in good faith when he said he could open certain doors for me."

"We all trusted Ahmad more than we should have, it seems," said Hereward, flicking a glance at me. I wondered if he somehow blamed me for Ahmad's duplicity and felt my face grow hot. Perhaps I had been rash to believe him. It seemed obvious to me then that he would have said and done whatever he needed to obtain his freedom. And yet I had spent many months with the man, learning the language and the customs of his people, and I could still not believe he was evil. Desperate perhaps, but not truly bad.

Giso went on, paying no heed to Hereward.

"When it became clear at the docks in Qadis that Ahmad would not help me to gain access to Al-Zarqālluh, I decided I had more chance of success alone. An opportunity arose to slip away and I took it."

"You speak of success," I said. "What is your true mission here? The book I seek is important to Alhwin, but that is not the main reason for your journey here, is it?"

Giso turned his shining eyes towards me. He broke off a piece of the flat bread we had brought down from the barracks, and dipped it in olive oil. Popping it into his mouth, he chewed in silence, taking the time to think of his response.

"You are right, Hunlaf," he said at last, having made up his mind how to proceed. "And I owe it to all of you now to reveal the true nature of my quest."

Revna touched my arm, the gesture startling me. She held the waterskin out. I accepted it gratefully and took a long pull, relishing the sensation of the cool liquid trickling down my throat. I said nothing and did not look away from Giso.

"You have all already seen the power that brought me to al-Andalus," he said, his voice little more than a whisper now, as if he thought he might be overheard, though he spoke in Englisc and the nearest people were the sailors praying down by the barge and they were well out of earshot.

For a moment, I did not understand, then the truth of it hit me like a searing spout of flame.

"You speak of the Roman Fire," I whispered. "You know of it?"

"Everybody knows of it now," he replied. "But few have seen its true power unleashed. Fewer still have watched as it consumes the flesh of living men."

"You were there? In Qurtuba?"

He took a deep breath and looked out over the wide waters of the river. I wondered if he was imagining the prisoners burning like great torches as the boats' timbers charred and blackened beneath huge plumes of smoke.

"In many ways I wish that I had not seen the horror of that day," he said, his voice sounding thin and less assured, "but yes, I was there. And now it must be clear to all of you why my mission must not fail."

"You keep speaking of your mission," said Gwawrddur, "but still you have not told us what it is."

Giso nodded.

"Several months ago, we received word that the secret of Roman Fire had been stolen from the great city of Byzantion."

"We?" I asked.

"Whispers came to Alhwin. He hears much and this was

something he felt he must act upon. I had hoped to steal the secret away from the emir before his alchemist artificier, Al-Zarqālluh, had deciphered its recipe. Clearly, I am too late for that."

"You speak of stealing as if it means nothing," I said, aghast. "I thought you a Christian, and an emissary of your king. You speak like a brigand."

My youthful sense of honour and outrage washed over Giso, but rather than upset him, he smiled.

"I am a man, Hunlaf. Just a man who serves his king as best he can. I am as good a Christian as I am able, though I am a sinner and do not deny it. But then aren't we all?" I thought momentarily of the women I had lain with, drunken nights of wagers and brawling, the men I had killed. My face grew hot, but if Giso noticed my discomfort, he did not show it. "Alhwin and I," he went on, "believed it would be a disaster if the Moors had the terrible power of Roman Fire at their disposal."

"You wanted it for yourself then?" asked Drosten, tearing off some bread. He seemed to be recovering from the night's excesses and the tears of the poppy more quickly than the others.

"Not for myself. No. For my king, Carolus. Such power should be in the hands of Christian men. A Christian ruler."

Runolf made a guttural noise that sounded like laughter, but when I glanced at him his features were taut and serious.

"How is it you were at Qurtuba?" I asked.

"Ah, that is easy to answer," said Giso. "I followed an old friend of yours."

"An old friend?" I repeated, confused.

"Well, perhaps not a friend." He grinned, his teeth bright in his dark beard. "I followed Nadir."

I turned to Gwawrddur.

"I told you I'd seen that bastard on the bridge!" I cried.

"What can I say?" replied the Welshman. "Sometimes you are bound to be right, though it is not a common occurrence."

I waved away his attempt at humour. The pain in my skull was making me light-headed, the bright sunshine drilling into my eyes like thorns.

"But why was Nadir in Qurtuba?" I asked.

"It transpires that Nadir is a man with more than one master."

"Who is it he serves?" asked Gwawrddur.

"None other than the man who is responsible for the weapon of Roman Fire falling into the hands of Al-Hakam Ibn Hisham Ibn Abd-ar-Rahman, Emir of al-Andalus."

"Al-Zarqālluh?" I said.

Giso offered me a thin smile.

"In a manner of speaking."

He scratched at his beard, then dipped another piece of bread into the oil, before flicking it into his mouth. He chewed appreciatively. The small Frank's answer was obtuse. His sly manner annoyed me and I felt my anger rising. I was in more pain than ever and my impatience grew with the intensity of my headache.

"Let me understand this," I said, my tone sharp, "Nadir serves the emir's alchemist and scholar, which is why you followed him to Qurtuba."

"I followed him other places first. He is an interesting one, Nadir. He led me along many interesting paths, and not once did he see me, or even imagine that anyone might be shadowing his steps. If his master should learn of his lack of care, I fear Nadir will suffer terribly." He smirked cruelly, as if the thought was amusing.

I wanted to ask many questions about Nadir, and how Giso's travels had led him to Qurtuba and now here, to Išbīliya, but there was something I wanted to learn first.

"You have been away from us for several weeks, and you

have not been discovered. How is it that nobody has unmasked you for a stranger in these lands?" It was hard to believe. I spoke the language well, but if I had been left alone I was sure the locals would recognise an imposter in their midst immediately.

Giso reached for the waterskin and Drosten passed it to him. He took a swig and wiped the back of his hand across his bearded mouth.

"I never said that nobody had caught me out," he said.

"But you are here," I said.

"Yes, I am here." He smiled his strange smile. I met his gaze. There was no humour in his eyes now. They were dark and hard as flint. For a time neither of us spoke and I wondered at the silent message he was giving me. Then, as suddenly as a cloud moving away from the sun, his face lit up and he grinned. "But you have it wrong. You said I might be unmasked as a stranger. Yet I am no stranger. I may be a Christian, but I learnt the language and the customs of these people on my mother's knee as a boy."

"Your mother was a Moor?" I said. "I thought you were a Frank."

Giso's expression was wistful.

"She died many, many years ago, God rest her soul," he said, making the sign of the cross over his chest, "but some things can never be forgotten. What she taught me serves me now. And while I serve King Carolus, I was not born of Frankish blood." He seemed ready to stop speaking of his past, but seeing the pained expression on my face, he snorted and relented. "My father was a merchant from Lombardy. My mother taught me of the Moors, my father taught me languages, commerce and the ways of men."

"All this is touching," said Runolf, "but I care nothing for your family or your past. I want to know how it is you arrived here today, and how we can retrieve our silver."

Giso chuckled.

"Ever as direct as a knife to the throat," he said. "But you are right, Runolf. Time is against us, so I will tell you these things and then we can begin to make preparations. To answer your first question, I came here today to warn you."

"Warn us?" said Revna.

"Yes, that Nadir had plotted with Ghalib and Ahmad to steal the silver the emir had given you."

"Well, you arrived late," Revna said.

"As direct as your father, I see, and your tongue is as sharp. Though," he said with a wink, "I would much rather feel the lash of your pretty tongue than your father's."

"You are as likely to get a taste of my tongue as I am to shit gold," Revna replied without hesitation.

"Charming," Giso said, apparently not flustered by her rebuff. "And you are right. I was late. I took a mount at Qurtuba, but the rain a few days back brought down some rocks onto our path and the wretched creature managed to injure his leg. The lame beast could not bear my weight, so I had to walk much of the way. Otherwise I would have been here before you. I had planned to be sitting on the wharf as you arrived. I was so looking forward to seeing your reactions at seeing me again."

"Now that you have arrived late, little man," snarled Runolf, "what about my second question? You said all was not lost. That we could yet recover our silver."

"Yes, and it so happens that I believe the silver will lead us to the goal of my own quest too."

"Speak plainly."

"If we find the silver, we will find the secret of the Roman Fire, and," he turned to look at me, "we may well discover that *The Treasure of Life* is there too."

"How can that be true?" I asked. "Surely Ahmad has taken the silver to help pay his debts to Aljany. You yourself implied as much. Why would the Roman Fire or the book be wherever Ahmad is taking the silver? Not that we have any idea where that is. Half the day has passed and with so much silver Ahmad and Ghalib could have paid for a boat, or even bought a house in the city and now be holed up surrounded by hired guards."

"Ah, but there is still much of my tale you do not know, and there are certain facts you are missing."

"Speak straight, man," snapped Hereward. His dark-rimmed eyes were bloodshot. He was clearly in no mood for this story to be dragged on further.

Giso nodded, acknowledging that the time had come to reveal what he knew.

"Ahmad and Ghalib are taking the silver to Aljany, but I have learnt much these last weeks and I know where Aljany's fortress is."

"Very well," mused Hereward. "So we can follow the silver to Aljany's hall, but why do you think the Roman Fire and Hunlaf's damned book will be there?"

Giso laughed and clapped his hands. He was clearly enjoying himself and I wondered how a man so keen to show off had managed to remain hidden for weeks.

"Aljany is just a name used by none other than Abu Jafar Yusuf ibn Sa'īd al-Zarqālluh."

I pictured the bearded noble we had spoken to in the palace of Qurtuba.

"Al-Zarqālluh is no criminal," I said. "He is a learned man." I cast about for stronger arguments to support my case. "He speaks Englisc," I said at last, hearing the weakness of my words.

"He is learned, of that there is no doubt," replied Giso. "But the sad truth is that teaching and madrasas do not pay nearly as well as crime. There is more gold in piracy, protection and moneylending."

"And the book? You believe he has it still?" I thought of

Al-Zarqālluh's words in Qurtuba, how they had echoed those of Scomric, the malevolence and hint of madness in his glare.

"I am certain of it."

"Then our course is clear," I said.

"As long as it involves retrieving our silver, count me in," said Runolf.

"Oh yes," said Giso. "I feel the Lord Almighty has brought us together here and we will be able to find everything we seek. I know where Aljany's fortress is. I have the means to get us inside, and together we can retrieve the treasure, the book and the secret of Roman Fire."

Thirty

"By Óðinn," whispered Runolf, "how are we going to get in there?"

None of us uttered a word. We stared up at the fortress in awe and disbelief. An insect buzzed close to my face and I swatted at it absently, but I could not pull my gaze away from the stone structure perched impossibly high on its rocky crag. The sun was low in the west, the valley where we crouched already in shadow. We had left the horses further down the valley, out of sight of the towers and walls of Aljany's mountain fastness.

"Even if by some miracle we get inside," said Hereward, his voice giving away his own sense of despair, "how can we hope to find what we seek and escape with our lives."

"How many men do you think there are in there?" asked Drosten, holding up his big hand to shield his eyes against the glare of the sky that was still bright.

"Giso says he has a way in," I said, hoping my tone did not betray my own unease. "We have trusted him this far."

"The little man has got us here," said Gwawrddur, "it is true. But can he truly deliver what he has promised? I cannot see us storming that place. I have never seen the like before. God alone knows how they managed to build it up here."

I squinted up at the castle. The Welshman was right. The building was huge, constructed of great slabs of cut stone. The walls, golden in the light of the setting sun, were the height of three men. Dark shadows picked out the crenelations and small windows. The tower behind the walls was even taller, looking out over the jagged, broken landscape of the mountains that surrounded the fortress. The walls would have been formidable by themselves, but the whole edifice was built atop a steep rocky outcrop that could only be approached by a narrow winding track. Anyone travelling up that path would be seen long before they reached the imposing gates set into the tall wall.

I could see figures on the ramparts, and I imagined them looking down and spotting us hiding beneath the bent branches of one of the scrubby oaks that covered the mountains.

"I care not how the Moors built this place," said Revna. "I only hope our faith in Giso is not misplaced. I am not sure I trust him."

She wore the same robes as the men, the loose clothing hiding the curves of her body. But her fair hair cascaded from beneath the head covering she wore. Despite the long, hard days of travel and sleeping beneath the stars, she had managed to comb her hair to a shining lustre, and I thought the sentries on the wall would be sure to spot the sheen of her locks, even from so far away.

"Well, he has got us here," I replied, moving further into the shade of the tree, and hoping Revna would follow me.

"He has," she replied, unmoving. "But was it wise to come here?"

"Since when have we followed the path of the wise?" said Runolf with a chuckle.

Hereward began to push himself backwards under the trees and towards the track we'd climbed to get here.

"Let's head back," he said. "I don't want to be out on this mountainside once darkness falls."

The others started to shuffle in the direction we'd come. When they were sure they were out of sight, they rose and moved down to the goat path we'd followed to get up here.

I hesitated when I saw that Imad, the leader of the eight guards who had accompanied us from Išbīliya, had not moved. He still stared up at the fortress, his mouth clamped tightly closed. I could see the muscles of his jaw working beneath his black beard.

"What do you think?" I asked, aware that he had not understood our whispered conversation as we gazed up at the fortress.

He did not speak for a time. When he turned to look at me, I saw doubt and fear on his features.

"I think this is madness," he said. "I pray to Allah that Giso knows what he is doing."

I nodded. There was nothing else to say. We had all placed our faith in Giso.

After the initial shock had worn off, the despondency of the warriors from Qurtuba who had been drugged and abandoned by their captain had been replaced with anger. Imad had approached us and offered his and his comrades' service to seek out Ahmad, Ghalib and the other guards who had betrayed us all.

We had been unsure whether to accept their offer at first. It was Revna who had convinced us.

"They were deceived as much as us," she'd said. "Look at their faces. They truly wish to help. It may be that it is more for their own sake than ours, but should we turn away aid when it is offered?"

I thought of how we had placed our trust in Ahmad and had not perceived how he was plotting against us. These guards might not be trustworthy, but deep down I believed Revna was right. Imad and the men from Qurtuba were honest in their motives. After a brief discussion, the others had agreed.

We had not regretted our decision as we had travelled south. The guards still kept themselves apart from us, but they were helpful and their presence made the journey safer. Giso told us the hills and mountains were thronging with outlaws who would attack unwary travellers, but there were few brigands who would attack a party of fifteen armed warriors.

We moved as stealthily as we could back down to the trail. Nobody spoke, as if frightened that our voices might carry to the men on the ramparts, even though that seemed impossible. Surely they were too far away. And yet noise travelled far in the mountains and the afternoon was still and silent, making the scuffing of our feet on the stones seem loud and echoing. I stepped on a twig as we passed beneath a gnarled ash and the sharp snapping sound made us all flinch.

Not for the first time, I wondered what Giso had planned. He had told us to keep out of sight and to wait for him when he had left, but that had been at mid-morning, and we had neither seen nor heard from him or the two guards he'd taken with him since then.

It had been Hereward's idea to climb up the slope and see our destination for ourselves. He hadn't said as much, but I was sure he was concerned that Giso had somehow led us into a trap, though to what end I could not say. The small Frank was certainly mysterious and made no effort to dispel any notions we might have that he was not telling us the whole truth about our situation.

At midday, with no sign of Giso or the others, Hereward had led us onto the goat track that climbed up the side of the nearest mountain. Imad had joined us, ordering the remaining five guards to watch the three mules we'd brought with us from Išbīliya. We had hoped to procure mounts for us all in the city, but after the theft of our silver, we had little to trade. Leander, feeling responsible for our plight, had seen that we were armed, pulling together an odd assortment of weapons, shields and armour from his men. He was unable to abandon his post, but we were thankful for his assistance. He also found us some supplies, some dry cured ham and flour that we added to the provisions Giso had bought from the market, along with the three pack animals.

Despite our desire to be on the road and in pursuit of Ahmad and Ghalib, it had taken Giso the best part of the day to arrange the animals and provisions. In any event, none of us had truly felt able to set off until the following morning. By then, my head only ached dully, but that was from the blow I had sustained and no longer the aftermath of the effects of the poppy tears. The others had all refrained from drinking that night and in the morning light they had been alert and ready to leave.

As we trudged silently down towards our camp, my mouth dry and feeling caked in the dust of the mountains, I wished I'd carried a water skin, but we had left all the skins back with the mules and the five guards.

Sweat trickled into my eyes and for the first time in days, my head started to ache. It had been over a week since we had left Išbīliya and most of the days had been dry and hot. The first days we travelled through flat, dusty land, dotted with green islands of crops that erupted from the crumbling earth around farms and hamlets. Every now and then we would see a line of foliage that would signal a stream or river, but for the most part, the land was a parched, pallid brown, the roads straight and white, the fine dust from the ground clouding in our wake and covering our clothes. The sun had shone down relentlessly from the clear sky and we had all taken to wearing the cloths wrapped about our heads in the way of the Moors.

We had all been frustrated with the delay to our departure and in those first days the discontent had grown as we neither saw nor heard of any sign of Ahmad and the other men. Had they stayed in the city, or perhaps travelled in a different direction? We grumbled and muttered about Giso and his secretive ways. The questions about his true motives grew in number and I overheard some of the guards even murmuring that perhaps he worked for Aljany; that this was all some elaborate ruse to lead us to our doom.

In the afternoon of the third day, we came across an old man driving before him a sizeable herd of scrawny-looking goats. The traffic on the road had been thick close to the city, but here, in the low hills of the mountains, with the ghosts of the higher peaks rising like mist in the distance, there were few travellers. The goatherd was evidently interested in hearing any tidings we might bear, for he waited beside the road for a long time, watching our slow approach from the scant shade beneath a spindly oak.

"Peace be upon you," he said with a perfunctory nod and a touch of his chin.

"And upon you," replied Giso, assuming the status of leader of the group.

The old man squinted at the rest of us, taking in our mismatched clothing and weapons. His eyes widened when they settled on Runolf, who stood at least a head taller than anyone else. The Norseman's head was wrapped in cloth, but his shaggy beard bristled and his unruly red-gold hair jutted from beneath the head covering, catching the sun's rays.

"Travelled far?" the goatherd asked, dragging his eyes away from the giant Norseman.

The goats milled about us, staring at us with their strange, slitted eyes. *Eyes of the devil*, I thought, recalling something my friend Seoca had said to me years before. I made to push the animals aside and one snapped at my fingers. The old man laughed. I shuddered.

"Far enough," said Giso. "All the way from Išbīliya."

The man sniffed, then scratched his neck beneath his beard. Finding something there, a tick perhaps, he examined it briefly before crushing it between his nails and flicking it into the dusty grass that sprouted beside the road.

"Never been," he said. "They say it's full of thieves and whores."

Imad snorted.

"You've got the first part right at least," he said. "Have you seen anybody else travelling this way?"

"What sort of anybody?" asked the man, his eyes narrowing. "I've been up in the hills till this morning." He motioned with his chin at the scrub-covered slopes that rolled into the dust-hazed distance.

"So you've seen nobody on the road? We're looking for four men. Most likely on horseback, perhaps with a pack animal too."

The old man shook his head.

"Nobody on the road."

Imad looked disappointed. He cast a dark glance at Giso. Still nobody they had met had seen Ahmad, Ghalib and the two guards. Imad started to shove the goats aside, preparing to pass the goatherd and continue on our way, but the old man reached out and caught his robe. Imad turned angrily, not taking kindly to this peasant laying a hand on him. He may have been disgraced, but he was still one of the emir's guard and a proud man.

"Forgive me," croaked the wizened man, pulling his hand away quickly. "I said I had seen nobody on the road. I've been in the hills. But I did see four men riding southward not two days ago."

Giso stepped close, a triumphant smile on his face.

"So, they are not travelling on the road," he said.

"I don't often see riders in the hills," said the old man. "Those I see, I know." He hawked and spat into the dust. "I didn't know these men. They were riding as hard as they could push their animals."

Giso turned to Runolf and the others who did not understand al-Arabiyyah.

"He saw them less than two days ago. Riding off the road, heading southward."

"You're sure it was them?" asked Hereward.

Giso raised an eyebrow.

"Well, they didn't stop to give their names, but I think it more than likely. They were avoiding the road, which makes sense if they thought they might be followed."

"Can we catch them, you think?" said Gwawrddur.

Giso shook his head.

"Even with them in the hills and us on the road, we are on foot and they are mounted. We won't catch them unless they were to halt. But," he went on, "now we can be certain as to where they are going. And with any luck they will believe they have escaped without anyone on their heels."

Without warning he grinned and clapped his hands together.

"We will have roasted goat tonight," he said.

He bartered shortly with the old man, who eventually sold him a skinny beast for a small silver coin. There was an air of relief about Giso after the chance meeting with the goatherd that made me wonder how sure he had been of his decisions, despite the impression he gave of certainty.

That had been four days ago. Since then, we had heard of our quarry's passing a couple of times since entering the mountains, where it became apparent they had returned to the road and the paths that wound over the passes in the jumbled, boulder-strewn terrain.

"They had to come down to the path," Giso said, "unless they wanted to risk their horses."

A couple of young men had told us they had seen the men riding past on the track we were following. The wiry youths had been breaking up the thin, rocky soil in a secluded valley watered by a river that came tumbling down out of the looming mountains. They had skin as brown as tanned leather and hair as black as night. They leant on their hoes and watched us for a long time with their dark eyes as we trudged away and up towards the steeper peaks.

As we descended to the camp now, my legs ached from the long days of walking. I'd left the old patched padded shirt, or *perpunt*, that Leander had given me back at the campsite. I had set out wearing it on the first day, but quickly decided that I could not bear it in the heat. I did however carry the sword that Leander had provided, strapped in a plain scabbard at my hip.

It was not a bad blade, well-balanced, with a leather-bound grip and a narrow guard. It was a little shorter than the sword I was used to, but it was forged of good steel and would serve its purpose. Each night I practised with Gwawrddur, ensuring that skills I had not used for weeks had not rusted too much.

Some of the others joined in the sparring on a few occasions, but most nights they were too tired from walking. I was exhausted too, but as we travelled further south towards danger, my insecurities grew and I began to feel increasingly like a fraud. I trained hard until the sweat streamed from me, to strengthen my muscles and hone my sword-skill, but also to convince myself of who I was. I had fought many times, and killed several men. But still, when I lay awake staring up at the splash of stars in the velvet sky, my mind turned to God and His teachings. I had chosen the path of the warrior, and when called upon to fight, I was gripped by a savage abandon that made me deadly. And yet, I did not think Runolf or Drosten lay awake after an encounter fearing for their immortal souls.

Revna it seemed wished to practise too. She had not used a weapon in combat as much as me, but she was lithe, strong, quick and fast-witted. Perhaps she also sensed that she would be called upon to rely on her skills soon enough. She had been given a short sword by one of Leander's men. It was double-edged, but not much longer than a seax. Gwawrddur made us each repeat the movements he had drilled into me for years and it brought back memories of standing beside Cormac as we both thrust, lunged and parried against invisible foe-men. When it came time to face Revna in a mock bout, the Welshman cut two staves from an ash tree and tossed them to us.

Revna had swished the wooden stick in the warm evening. It sang in the air and Revna flashed her teeth at me in a wide grin. Her shoulder had fully healed now, and she was as fast as a cat when Gwawrddur gave the command to commence. Without hesitation Revna leapt forward and rapped her practice sword against my blade, forcing it to the side and then snapping it back to dig me in the ribs.

I stumbled backward, rubbing my side, my face hot as the watching men laughed.

"A woman with a sword will kill you just as quickly as a man," said Gwawrddur.

I frowned and rubbed a hand on the back of my skull.

"My head still hurts," I lied. The truth was I did not wish to strike Revna, but I could feel Runolf's eyes on me, so lowered myself back into the fighting stance.

Revna crouched and raised her wooden blade. I watched her closely, poised and ready to respond to her attack. Just as Gwawrddur had trained me, I concentrated on my opponent's eyes and shoulders; they would signal Revna's intentions. I saw her tense, her shoulder dropping slightly. But the instant before she moved to close with me, she licked her lips and winked. For an eye-blink, my attention had been on her shining lips and the sunlight gleaming from her eyes. She sprang forward and was almost able to strike me again. It took all my efforts to parry her lunge, then step to the side and, as she carried on forward off balance, I touched her lightly on the thigh.

She rounded on me and her eyes were full of anger. She

charged at me, scything her wooden sword at my head. I stepped back quickly, parrying her blow. She did not halt, but came on again with renewed energy. I parried each strike she aimed at me. I did not wish to hurt her, or shame her, but I could see that by treating her differently than the others, I had enraged her. The only way to halt this was to let her win, or to hit her myself, thus ending the bout.

Suddenly, I changed my direction of travel. Closing with her, I grasped her sword arm. Sticking out my leg, I forced her backwards until she tripped and fell into the dust. Releasing her, I winked and stuck my tongue out.

The onlookers laughed. Revna's eyes blazed as I held out my hand to her, then her features softened and she allowed me to pull her to her feet.

After that, we practised every evening while food was being prepared. I wore the padded armour that was now greasy and stained with sweat, while Revna wore a woven and braided shirt that Imad called a *jidla*. We were both glad of the protection, for after that first confrontation, neither of us held back with the wooden practice staves, and without the thick shirts we would have both been a mass of bruises.

I was not sure how much defence they would provide against steel, but I would don the padded armour when the time came for real action. Giso had assured us that would be soon, but I could not understand how that could be. The fortress was a gigantic stone monolith on the crest of a soaring peak and I could see no way we had any hope of entering it. And even if we were able to gain access to the building and later escape, we would be several days' travel away from safety.

All I wanted now was to reach our camp, where I could rest my weary legs and wash the dust from my throat.

When we stepped out of the gloaming and into the small camp we had made beside the trickle of a stream dribbling from a rocky cleft, we saw that Giso had returned.

"I told you to wait here," he said, rising from where he'd been sitting. "You should have listened to me and rested." He drained the water from his cup. "Now there is no time."

Scanning the camp, it was quickly apparent that the men who had accompanied Giso that morning had not returned with him.

"What is the meaning of this?" asked Imad, his tone sharp. "Where are Labib and Daud?"

"They are well," replied Giso smoothly. "And they are going to help us get into the fortress, if we do not waste any more time."

Imad had more questions, but Giso waved them away.

"There is no time," he said. "I swear to you on the bones of Christ they are well. But now prepare yourselves. Say your prayers and ready your weapons. For we enter the lair of Aljany this night."

Thirty-One

I knelt beside Giso as the dusk closed around us. At the other side of the clearing, I could hear the murmured prayers of the Moors. Since Giso had returned in Išbīliya, I had taken once more to praying with him, as I had done aboard *Brymsteda*. I wondered if this was what had caused my renewed unease and confusion about my chosen path in life. But I could not deny that reciting the familiar offices, psalms and prayers brought me comfort. Evidently I was not the only one in need of comfort that night. Whenever Giso and I had prayed before, it had just been the two of us and I had felt uncomfortable as Runolf and the other warriors watched us from the flickering glow of the campfire. But on this evening, as the mountain shadows thickened into night, and the cool of darkness rose from the stones, we were not alone. Gwawrddur, Drosten and Hereward all knelt beside us. They did not know the Latin prayers, but they added their "Amens" at the end of each oration and they spoke the words of the Pater Noster, each in his own tongue, lending a strange, confused, almost dreamlike quality to the whispered prayer.

Runolf, though he had been baptised in Eoforwic, stood aside in the shadows, close beside Revna. Over the muttered prayers of the kneeling men near me, or the murmured chanting of the Moors, I could not hear whether Runolf and Revna were speaking. But I recalled how Runolf offered a sacrifice to Njörðr, god of the sea, before each voyage, and I wondered whether he now prayed to Óðinn, the Norse god of battle, victory and death, before we embarked on our quest into the darkness.

When we had finished commending our souls to the Almighty, and the others had finished their prayers to whatever gods they worshipped, Giso stood rapidly and beckoned for us all to gather close. He dropped a small sack onto the ground. Into this he dipped a hand. Pulling out a dark powder, he poured a few drops of water from a skin into his hand.

"Ash," he said, and proceeded to smear it across his face and hands.

"We must be shadows tonight. Cover your skin. And don't forget the blades of your weapons." He repeated the instructions for Imad and the guards, and after a moment, we each did as we were told.

The paste was gritty and cool against my skin.

"This will rust our blades," grumbled Gwawrddur as he slathered the dark mixture onto his borrowed sword.

"You can clean the blade when we are safely away from here," hissed Giso. His tone held the edge of nervous energy as darkness fell. "A rusted blade is a small price to pay for life."

"And for our silver," rumbled Runolf.

"Yes, your silver too," said Giso. His teeth glimmered in the dying light as he grinned unexpectedly. I had thought him anxious about the night's mission, now I wondered if his energy was borne from excitement.

I said nothing of the fact we were also in search of *The Treasure of Life*. But now that we were close to our destination I was sure Giso was right; the book was here, in the fortress. How I knew, I have no idea, but the air of the night felt abuzz with power, as if lightning was about to strike from the cloudless sky. *It is only a book*, I heard Leofstan whisper from my memories, and yet the closer we came to it after all this time, the less sure I was of that. Could it not be possible that this tome held an unholy power?

"Guard your voices from here on," whispered Giso. "Sounds travel like birds on the wing in the silence of the mountains. I will get us inside the castle, but if we are seen or heard on our way up there, all will be lost."

I wanted to ask him about his plan, but the moment for questions had passed. The small Frank led the way into the darkness and we followed close behind in a single line threading its way into the night.

High up on the western ridges the last memories of the sun still glowed red in the sky, but here, deep in the valley, it was true dark. It was difficult to make out the figures of the others, and soon we took to walking so close to each other that we could reach out and touch the person ahead of us. Gwawrddur went before me. He walked with quiet, stealthy steps, climbing up the steep incline of the path. Like Giso, the Welshman made barely a sound, but others struggled in the gloom. A hushed curse. The scrape of a stone. The slap of a scabbard against one of the gnarled trees that clung to the rocky soil. Every sound we made seemed amplified, louder than it should have been. Surely the men on watch at the fortress must hear our clumsy approach.

But when we stepped out into a starlit open area, I saw that the straight-edged silhouetted castle was still far off. Giso had led us along paths only he could follow and I prayed that he would be there to lead us back to the mules we had left tethered beside the small stream. Pausing to catch our breath, we all stared up at our destination. Torches burnt on the walls of the castle, illuminating the men there and picking out the stark shape of the crenellated battlements.

"Good," whispered Giso. "With brands up there, the sentries

will be blind to the shadows out here. But keep your steel covered. And watch your step. They may not see us, but they are not deaf." He moved into the shadow of a huge boulder that shielded us from sight of the fortress walls. "Step close." We shuffled quietly to surround him. Sweat trickled down my neck, the quilted *perpunt* I wore, heavy and sweltering. I could smell the breath of the others in the still air. Someone stood on my left side, so close that our arms touched. Without looking I knew it was Revna. Her fingers brushed the back of my hand and I trembled, despite the warmth of the night.

"When next we stop, we will be too close to the fortress to talk. There is a deep cleft beneath the northern wall. Imad, there you will wait for our return with your men."

"No, Frank," Imad said, his voice as sharp as a blade being drawn across a whetstone. "We did not come all this way to stand in the dark. That bastard Ghalib is in there, and I will make him pay."

Giso hesitated.

"You cannot all go inside. We will be seen or heard. No," he cut off Imad's protestations, "don't argue further. It simply will not work. You can come, Imad, and one other. The others must wait outside the fortress. But tell them they must remain prepared for a fight. Aljany will not give up his treasures easily. There is a strong chance we will come out in a hurry and will be in need of their swords."

"Then it is a pity we are missing Daud and Labib." There was an accusation in Imad's hushed words.

"They are not missing," said Giso. "Without them, we would not be getting inside tonight. But there is no time for this. If we do not move now, we will miss our only chance."

I could hear Runolf's growl in the shadows. Even when whispering his voice carried and Giso made a hissing sound to quieten him.

"What is it?" he asked. He sounded exasperated and tense.

"Revna will stay here with the guards," Runolf said.

"I will not," she snapped.

"It is too dangerous," Runolf said.

"If you wanted me to be safe, Father," Revna said, her whispered voice cold, "perhaps you should not have brought me to al-Andalus."

Runolf sighed.

"I am your daughter, Runolf Ragnarsson," Revna went on, her tone softer now. "It is not my lot to stand in the shadows while the men fight."

"If anything happens to you," Runolf grumbled, "I will kill you."

"Enough of this," whispered Giso. "We can tarry no longer. Nor can we debate further. Imad, choose your man. Revna is coming with us."

"She is quieter than her father," whispered Hereward, "so perhaps we should leave him to guard outside."

We continued into the darkness in silence now. The sound of our breathing and the scrape of our feet on the gravel and stones of the path were loud in the dark, but we moved more slowly, conscious that we were getting closer to the castle. The glow of the torches flickered through the twisted boles and boughs of the stunted oaks and thorny bushes and each time I looked up, I imagined one of the sentries spying my upturned, soot-streaked face. But we made it without incident to a shadowed cleft in the rock a few dozen paces away from the base of the rocky crag upon which the fortress was built.

I sensed Giso moving to tap Imad on the shoulder. I heard the quietest of whispers, soft as the wings of a butterfly, as Imad leaned in close to murmur into the ears of his men, and then we were moving on, leaving four guards behind us in the black night. From the shadowed form beside Imad, I saw he had chosen to bring Wahid with him. He was a good choice. He was a slim, wiry man with hard eyes. He spoke little, but acted without hesitation or complaint when called upon to do so.

Slowly, we stalked into the darkness, trusting that Giso knew the way. Looking down I could see nothing but blackness. I had not gazed up at the fortress for some time, allowing my eyes to once again adjust to the night, but no light filtered down here in the lee of the rocky outcrop. I began to pray silently, placing my faith in God that I would not unsettle a pebble, or snag my clothes on a bush. From high above us came the sound of men laughing, the sudden barking noise of their mirth terrifyingly loud in the stillness. We halted. I held my breath, listening to the night. Far off, down the valley, came the howling, growled shriek of a night creature. I had heard nothing like it before, and the sound filled me with fear. I thought of the mules, tied near to the stream. If wolves or other beasts of prey scented them, they would be defenceless. Revna, who walked behind me, touched my shoulder, and I pushed thoughts of the animals from my mind. We had more pressing matters to worry about.

I reached ahead, but touched only air. Giso had begun moving again. Hesitantly, I continued up the dark path into blackness.

A sliver of moon had risen above the mountains by the time we reached the place Giso was looking for. The moon shadows were an impenetrable inky darkness, but the pale light seemed bright after our long walk, the silver glow limning the rocks and shrubs around us, making our last paces easier to navigate after so many tense steps in complete darkness. The Almighty must have been watching over us, for we had come this far without alerting the sentries on the walls and now we huddled in a tight group in what appeared to be the end of a narrow ravine.

We had climbed partway up the rocky crag, but were now so close to the soaring slope we could not see the ramparts. The sky above us glowed faintly with the light from the torches.

Men were talking up there, their voices carrying clearly. I let out a long breath and wiped away the sweat that beaded my brow. Beneath the padded armour my body was slick. What in the name of all that was holy had Giso done? Why had he brought us here?

I heard the quietest of whispers, and thought I detected Hereward's voice replying. Perhaps he was asking the very questions that fluttered in my mind. But I could not ask what was being said. To be overheard here would be to give away our position to the guards. I tried not to move, tilting my head this way and that, to better hear the sentries above us and for any indication of what was happening around me.

After a while, someone startled me by tapping me on the shoulder. It was Gwawrddur, and I leaned in close to him, my heart hammering against my ribs.

"Giso says we wait here," he whispered into my ear.

I nodded, before realising he would not see the gesture.

Turning to Revna, I touched her lightly on the arm and moved my head close. The scent of her filled my nostrils; her hair, the sweat on her skin. Swallowing against the dryness of my mouth, I whispered the news, aware of how close we were to the castle walls. My lips brushed her ear.

By way of answer, Revna gripped my arm and squeezed gently, before turning away to pass on the message to Runolf.

Once the tidings had gone along the line, we stood in silence. A long time passed. An owl screeched in the darkness and again, further off this time, I heard the wailing howl of the animal that hunted in the night. The white curve of the moon slid slowly across the sky. The sweat cooled and dried against my skin and the cold of the night began to wrap itself about me. I shivered, wishing for a fire and to be far from this place. This was madness. A couple of times, Hereward enquired of Giso what his plan was, but each time, the small Frank replied that we must wait.

As the time passed and birds began to awaken in the trees down the valley, anticipating the approach of dawn, the tension in our party intensified. I had not spoken to Giso since we had left the camp, but I could sense his nervous anxiety growing in the darkness. We had all become tired of standing, and now sat on the hard ground. But we were unable to relax. For what seemed the hundredth time I reached for the hilt of my sword, reassuring myself that it was still at my side. Gazing up at the sky, I frowned. The soot on my cheeks had dried now. It felt tight on my skin, cracking and flaking as I moved.

How much longer could we remain here and hope not to be seen? It would yet be some time before the sun rose over the peaks, but dawn was ever nearer, and if we were on the mountainside when the sun shone, it would be impossible for the men on the castle walls not to see us as we headed back down towards our camp.

I was just about to push myself to my feet and approach Giso, when a new noise reached me. Rocks scraped, metal squealed impossibly strident in the hush of the night. At first I thought one of our group had risen and stumbled in the darkness, but then a flash of bright light glimmered, making me blink.

Giso hissed something, and the light was covered, leaving only the after-images of what I had seen glowing in my vision. A man had appeared at the end of the ravine, a lantern in his hand. There had been the shape of a door, that appeared to have opened from the rock itself, and then the light had been smothered, plunging us back into the dark before the dawn.

Thirty-Two

We had no need to be given orders. This was clearly what Giso had been waiting for. We rose silently and made our way as quickly as we could along the ravine and through a low doorway. A sliver of red light escaped the lantern's hood, giving us more than enough light to see by after the lengthy wait in the darkness. The door was solid and bound in iron, set in a low archway concealed behind a boulder and shrubs. I needed to bow my head to enter. Runolf had to practically crouch to pass beneath the threshold.

When we were all inside, the man who held the lantern pulled the door closed once more, shutting out the night. He removed the cover from the light, and the brilliance of the single flame after so long in the dark made me gasp. We were crowded into a narrow corridor or tunnel that appeared to be hewn from the rock itself. All around me blinking eyes gleamed from faces dark with soot.

The man who held the lantern was dressed in simple dark clothes. He was perhaps thirty years old, with angular features and a close-cropped beard. His eyes darted, taking in all of us.

"You did not tell me there would be so many," he hissed. His voice wavered. He was clearly terrified. "If you are discovered, I will be slain."

"Then you had best hope we are not discovered," said Giso, his tone sour and cutting. He pushed his face close to the man. "For if I do not send word to my men by midday, you know what will happen to your pretty wife and those lovely daughters of yours."

The man shuddered and his face clouded with rage. I wondered if his fury and hatred for Giso would overcome his fear. Imad sensed it too, and reached out a hand to restrain him. On feeling Imad's touch on his arm, the man spun around.

"Do not touch me," he spat. His eyes held the glimmer of madness as he looked about the stone tunnel and our faces in the dancing shadows. "I would see you all killed for this," he said. His words were strangled with pent-up ire, but his voice was rising as his anger built. "I should call on the watch," he said. "I should—"

Without warning Imad grasped the man's hand that held the lantern and in the same instant brought down the iron pommel of his dagger hard on the man's head. Letting out a gargled moan, he sank to the damp stone floor of the tunnel. Imad coolly took the lantern from the man's numb fingers and handed it to Wahid.

"What in the name of Allah have you done?" said Giso.

Imad dropped down beside the insensate figure, patting the man's clothing; checking him for possessions that might prove valuable or useful, I presumed. Finding a slender dagger, he unbuckled the man's belt and removed the sheathed blade.

"I thought he would give us away," he whispered, as he stuffed the sheath into his belt and proceeded to tie the man's hands behind his back with the slender leather belt.

"He was not going to—" Giso could barely speak, such was his incandescent anger. With a force of will, he took a calming breath. "That man was not going to give us away. I have taken steps to ensure that."

Imad looked up at Giso, holding his gaze for a long moment.

"Daud and Labib. Yes, I heard." The light from the lantern made his soot-stained face look as if it were carved from the stone of the tunnel. Without further comment, he tore a couple of strips from the man's robe, wadded one into his mouth and tied it in place with the second. "Well, he won't give us away now," he said, standing and brushing dust from his hands.

"He alone knew the ways within this fortress."

"What is happening?" asked Runolf. "If I need to remain much longer bent over like this I will be stooped for life."

"Giso says that only the man Imad struck knew the way inside."

"Well," said Hereward, "we cannot undo what has been done, and I don't think any of us wish to remain within the walls for any longer than we have to."

Gwawrddur pointed into the darkness, where the tunnel continued beyond the limits of the lantern's flame.

"There is only one way from here. I say we continue with caution and go find our treasure."

"That's why we're here," said Runolf.

"What are we waiting for?" asked Drosten, pulling the sword he had been given from its sheath. The blade's edge caught the lantern light, but most of the steel was dulled with soot.

Giso sighed.

"I do not know how many men are in this place, but I am sure there are more than we can beat in an open fight." He raked us all with his glare. "Even the heroes of Werceworthe. So be careful."

Runolf chuckled, the sound like boulders crashing together in the enclosed space. Without warning, I thought of the weight of the mountain and the fortress piled above our heads. I shuddered.

"I am always careful," Runolf said.

And with that, Wahid raised the lantern and by the dim light of its flickering flame we made our way into the gloom.

Thirty-Three

We shuffled forward, our shadows jostling. The scrape of our shoes was loud in the tunnel, the sound of our breath reflected back to us from the unyielding stone. Unbidden, the image came to me of Jonah, swallowed by the great fish after he had turned away from the path that God had set for him. I could not escape the sensation that we were creeping along the throat of a huge beast towards its stone belly where we would be consumed.

The tunnel cut a straight path for some twenty paces. It was cool here, surrounded by rock, but drops of sweat tracked their fingers down my back beneath the padded armour and I cuffed at my forehead that was wet with perspiration. We moved slowly, unsure what we would encounter as we progressed further into Aljany's lair. The lantern's flame was bright in the enclosed space, but our eight bodies cast many shadows. I watched Wahid's hand and the lantern he held. I was suddenly overcome by a dread that the flame would be blown out, plunging us into utter blackness.

My breath began to come in short gasps. Runnels of sweat streaked the soot on my face. I thought of the long weeks I had spent imprisoned with Runolf. I could not bear now to be enclosed. Panic swelled within me, threatening to overwhelm me. I had never felt such terror before, not even in the heat of battle. This was a horror from nightmare, something cloying, overpowering and all-encompassing; a fever dream I could not hope to escape.

Revna placed a hand on my arm. "Breathe," she whispered.

I looked into her eyes. She held my gaze, nodding slowly.

"Breathe," she repeated.

I forced myself to slow my breathing and attempted a smile of thanks. I was sure it was more of a grimace and I was glad of the poor light, that I might hide some of my shame.

The men around us must have witnessed my discomfort, but none of them chose to mention it. For this too I was thankful, though it made me aware of how tense they all must be if they did not wish to make a jest at my expense.

We carried on, and soon, praise be to the Lord Almighty, we reached a stout timber door.

"I have never been inside this place," whispered Giso. "But the man who Imad so helpfully silenced told me some of what lies beyond this door. There should be a storeroom, and then some steps leading up. What we are looking for should be behind the first door we come to on the steps."

"The silver is there?" asked Runolf, hunched and uncomfortable in the low tunnel.

Giso shrugged.

"Most of the fortress will yet be sleeping. Keep quiet and with God's grace, we will be able to find what we have come for and leave without being detected."

He whispered hurriedly to Imad, repeating what he had said to us, then pushed the door open. For a moment it would not move and I felt my alarm begin to return. We would be trapped down here, in the bowels of the earth beneath an incalculable mass of rock.

But then the hinges creaked, and the door swung outward.

We stepped out into a stone chamber. The ceiling was higher

than the tunnel, allowing us to stand up straight. Runolf groaned as his back and neck popped and cracked.

The lantern's light illuminated a small room, full of barrels, bales and sacks, leaving scant room for us. A large timber box was pushed to the side and it looked to me as if it was usually placed against the door, concealing it.

"What is this tunnel?" I asked.

"Aljany trusts no one," Giso said. "It is an escape route, should the fortress fall. Few know of its existence."

"More know of it than Aljany would like, it would seem," said Gwawrddur sardonically, raising his eyebrows. "For here we are."

"Let us hope it is not known to many of the guards and we can remain quiet," said Giso. "For it will provide us with the very thing it was designed for: a means of escape."

No other light shone here. Giso clicked his fingers impatiently at Wahid, who looked to Imad. Imad nodded and Wahid gave Giso the lantern. Holding it high, the Frank pushed through the huddle of people and made his way further into the storage chamber.

"Careful," he hissed, halting and pointing to the side of the room where a dark gap showed that no provisions were piled there.

We filed past, each glancing into the shadows. There was barely any light when I reached the place, but I spied a black pit in the stone floor, yawning down into darkness.

"A well," whispered Hereward. "There is one like that hewn into the rock at Bebbanburg. So high in the mountains, with provisions and water, I cannot see this fortress being taken by force."

Like Hereward, I could not imagine how this fortress could be conquered in an open assault. But we had crept into the very innards of the beast and I realised the castle's exterior aspect of solid security was misleading. All that was needed was to know its weakness.

Like a frontal attack on the fortress, the mission upon which we were embarked appeared impossible. For nine of us to sneak into Aljany's stronghold and retrieve our stolen silver, *The Treasure of Life,* and the secret of Roman Fire. And yet there we were, deep beneath the castle itself. Runolf had been proven right before, I prayed that this night would be another time that the barely possible became a reality.

Giso listened at the door of the storeroom, gesturing for us to be silent. None of us moved and I held my breath. Satisfied that all was quiet beyond the door, Giso gingerly pushed it open.

Beyond, a narrow passageway disappeared into darkness. To our left, stone steps rose upward into shadow. All was quiet. Giso turned towards the steps, but Gwawrddur pulled him back.

"What's down there?" he said, pointing into the blackness of the passage.

"Cells," Giso replied. "If there are prisoners, they are not our concern. What we seek lies up the steps."

"Perhaps," replied Gwawrddur, "but I would not like to leave an enemy at our back."

Giso looked as if he were about to protest, but after a moment's hesitation, he nodded curtly.

"Wait here," he said to us, then led Gwawrddur along the passage. As they walked away with our only light, I felt my stomach clench. But they did not go far, perhaps only a couple of dozen paces, and they were both still clearly visible, the lantern's light shining on their soot-dark faces and on the chiselled stone walls of the passage. There were darker openings down there, and Giso and Gwawrddur peered into them before returning.

"Two cells," whispered the Welshman. "Both empty."

Without speaking, Giso turned and began to make his way up the steps. As if at some secret signal, we all drew our weapons. Holding my sword tightly in my sweaty hand, I followed Giso and the others up. The stone ceiling was low again. Behind me, Runolf cursed quietly as his head cracked against the stone lintel.

"Hush," hissed Giso, looking back down the stairwell. Runolf rubbed his head and glowered up at the Frank. His lips were pulled back from his teeth in a snarl, but he made no further sound. Bowing his head, the Norse giant started up the stairs.

After a score of steps, there was a flat area, and the direction of the stairs turned, doubling back. Peeking round the corner, we could see the pale glow of a lamp pooling at the next landing, where the steps changed direction again. Giso paused to allow Runolf to reach us, then continued stealthily up the steps. We were moving as quietly as we were able, but if there was anyone around the next bend in the stairs, they would have to be deaf not to hear us. And our caution meant we were going slowly. I wondered how long we had been underground. It seemed like an age, but I supposed in reality it had not been so long. I tried to imagine the passing of time outside. Was the dawn now colouring the sky? Had the first rays of the morning sun licked the crests of the mountains? Even now, was sunlight reflecting brightly from the flat surfaces and angular edges of the castle walls? Surely it must still be night, but I could feel the pressure of passing time, weighing on me now like the stone pressing down above us.

Giso poked his head around the next bend and I saw his shoulders relax slightly. Nobody stood in the light that came from the next landing. Joining him and looking up I saw a solid-looking wooden door, studded and bound with iron. The door was secured with a thick timber locking bar that ran across the width of it and slid into deep grooves in the stone itself. In a small recess in the wall nestled an earthenware oil lamp. Its naked flame flickered as we disturbed the air of the subterranean stairwell with our movement towards the door.

"The secret of Roman Fire should be in there," whispered Giso. "There will be at least two men inside. They must not be harmed. But we must keep them quiet." He flicked a glance at Imad, perhaps thinking of how the Moor might keep the prisoners quiet. "You and Wahid," he said, "watch the door. We cannot risk being locked inside."

Imad was about to protest when Gwawrddur stepped forward.

"I will stay with Wahid," he said in passable al-Arabiyyah. I did not know he had learnt any of the tongue, and I raised an eyebrow. Catching Giso's quizzical glance, Gwawrddur said in Englisc, "I told you, I do not like the idea of leaving enemies behind us."

I wasn't sure if he truly thought that Imad and Wahid were our enemies. I thought not. They had done nothing to indicate as much. But none of us contested Gwawrddur's decision to keep guard outside the door. It made sense not to rely too much on the emir's guards. Who could say where their allegiances might be if we should be discovered down here and the sword-song of battle should start? Imad looked from Gwawrddur to Giso, then nodded.

Minds made up, Giso moved close to the door.

"We must enter quickly," he whispered, "and secure whoever is inside with as little fuss as possible. Revna, take the lantern. Hunlaf, you will pull back the beam. The rest of us will enter as quickly as we can. Drosten, take the left. Runolf, the right. I will go straight on with Hereward." He looked about him to check we each understood our roles.

Revna pressed her lips together when he handed her the lantern and I sensed she was going to complain. She was a match for most men with a blade and would not take kindly to being given such a menial task, but she accepted the lantern in her left hand and raised her sword, ready for action. I felt a pang of resentment that after all of my evening training sessions, I was relegated to being the man to drag the locking bar from the door, but, like Revna, I swallowed my pride. Now was not the moment for dissent.

Propping my sword against the wall, I placed both hands on the thick plank that ran across the door.

"Ready?" I whispered, looking at the waiting men. The faces that looked back at me were crusted with dried soot, cracking and peeling like old whitewashed daub. The light from the lantern gleamed in their expectant eyes.

"Ready," replied Giso.

I took in a great lungful of the musty cool air, tightened my grip on the smooth timber, and heaved it quickly out of the way of the door.

Giso already had his hand on the door's handle, and the instant the bar was clear, he tugged it open and rushed inside.

Thirty-Four

The small room behind the door was cluttered and the men had to negotiate objects in their path. The light from the lantern Revna held was blocked by the bodies of the men hurrying through the door. Their shadows leapt and sprang about the walls and furniture, further confusing what was happening inside. Dropping the locking bar with a clatter, I snatched up my sword and followed Revna through the doorway.

A lamp flickered on a table in the centre of the room, providing more light and enough to see clearly everything within the chamber. The table was strewn with loose parchments, scrolls and books. There were small pots for mixing copperas, vinegar and oak galls to make encaustum, a cup holding several feathers and a small knife for cutting nibs. I was instantly transported back to the minsters where I had spent so much of my youth. The biting scent of the ink ingredients, the dusty pounce and the tang of the vellum were as familiar to me as the words of the Pater Noster. But there was another smell in the room, one that brought back stark memories of a more recent past; horrific recollections of men screaming, consumed by flames that would not go out, even as they sank beneath the waters of the great river. The astringent stink of the substances that made Roman Fire scratched the back of my throat and made my eyes sting.

Hereward and Giso stepped around the table, heading for a door at the far side of the room.

A voice, still blurred from sleep, called out in alarm to my left. I dragged my gaze away from the table and saw a pallet against the wall. An elderly man, hair and beard white and wispy as gossamer, was sitting up, holding his blanket beneath his chin. His face was stretched into a rictus of terror as Drosten loomed over him. The Pict, the dark lines of his tattoos seeming to writhe in the lamplight, growled for silence. The old man whimpered, but fell quiet when Drosten grabbed him by the neck with his callused left hand and held the blade of his borrowed sword to his throat.

On the other side of the room, Runolf had reached another straw-filled mattress. In that bed cowered a younger man, his dark eyes wide beneath his tousled shock of brown hair. Runolf leaned over him, prodding gently with his sword blade into the man's chest, keeping him flat on his back. Runolf placed a thick finger to his lips. The meaning was clear and the young man made no sound. He stared up at the Norse giant, possibly wondering whether he yet slept and this was some terrible nightmare.

"What's behind this door?" snapped Giso in al-Arabiyyah.

Neither man spoke and Giso repeated the question, this time in Latin.

The old man, fully awake now and taking stock of the situation, replied in the same language.

"There are stores of naphtha, sulphur and quicklime for our work. There is nobody else there, and no egress from the storeroom."

Giso's eyes narrowed. He beckoned to me and Revna.

"Open it and check what's back there," he said.

Revna handed him the lantern and I placed my hand on the leather loop that served as a door handle.

"Wait!" cried the old man.

I hesitated, turning to look at him. His face held a new fear.

"Do not enter with a flame," he said in Latin. "There is a chimney to allow fumes to escape, but we could all die if you are not cautious."

I weighed his words.

"I can smell it," I said to Giso. The acrid bite of caustic compounds lingered in the air. "If behind those doors are stores of whatever they use to create the Roman Fire, it would be best if we proceeded with caution."

Giso was wound up as taut as a bowstring. He bit his lip, then nodded in agreement.

"I will hold the lantern up from the doorway. Be careful."

I checked that Revna and Hereward were prepared, then pulled the door open. Its timbers scraped against the stone floor. Beyond the doorway was darkness. Giso lifted up the lantern and we peered inside. The smell was strong and it rolled out of the open door.

"Looks like he was telling the truth," I said, wiping at my watering eyes and stifling a cough.

I could see barrels, crates and boxes stacked in the shadows. There was no sign of anyone else in there and no door was visible. Stepping to the closest box, I examined it in the dim light that reached from the door. It was unusual in construction, seeming to be fashioned from beaten slabs of iron, riveted together at the seams. It was closed with a tight-fitting lid that was also forged from iron.

I tugged at the edge of the lid with my fingertips, but it would not budge. Seeing how closely it slotted over the metal box, I thought to use my sword's blade to pry it up. Raising my sword, I placed the tip into the narrow groove between the side of the box and its lid.

"Desist!" cried the old man from his bed. "If you make a spark, we will all die."

I thought about his words for a heartbeat, but could think of no reason he would lie about this. Placing my sword atop one of the barrels, I used both of my hands to pull up the metal lid of the box. It resisted, and I wondered if I would be unable to open it, but then, with a squeak and a sucking sound, it came free. The lid was surprisingly heavy. I set it aside and looked into the box. I could make out some straw, but not enough light reached inside to discern anything else. But I could not turn away now, even if I had wanted to. The same curiosity that had driven me to search for *The Treasure of Life*, drew me to the unknown contents of that box. I had to know what was inside.

Taking a deep breath, I lowered my hand into the straw.

"Careful," hissed the old man.

Beneath the straw, my fingers brushed against a smooth, cool curved surface. Tracing the shape, I found it to be spherical and about twice the size of a large apple. There were several of the objects inside the box, surrounded by the straw. Using both hands, I teased one of the items out and held it up to the light, turning it this way and that.

It was an earthenware orb, with a small hole at one end that had been plugged with what appeared to be wax.

"What is it?" I asked in Latin.

The young man spoke for the first time, his voice quavering with fear.

"Do not drop it. It is filled with what you call Roman Fire."

The orb instantly felt dreadfully heavy and I became aware of how slippery the smooth outside of the thing was. A fleeting image came to me then, of me dropping the globe at my feet, and the noxious compound inside splattering my legs and igniting with a spark from the lantern. I could almost feel the heat of the fire licking up my shins and beginning to char the padded armour I wore. Gingerly, I returned the earthenware ball to the box.

"There is little time for talk," Giso said to the two men, who had dressed hurriedly and were now perched on stools, pulling on their shoes.

The door to the steps stood ajar. Hereward and Imad had told Gwawrddur and Wahid what we had found and now the two stood anxiously on guard just outside, listening for the approach of feet that would surely come all too soon.

While the two inhabitants of the room were getting dressed, I had riffled through the papers on the table, and opened the books and scrolls that were piled there. For a fleeting, heart-pounding moment, I thought the largest of the books might be the very tome I had sought all this time, with a new, simpler cover than the bejewelled one that had been stripped by the Norse raiders. But as I opened the plain leather cover, I saw it was actually a treatise on the nature of fire by Herákleitos. The sheets of parchment were covered in scrawled diagrams, formulae and instructions.

"Is this the recipe for Roman Fire?" I asked in Latin. It had quickly become clear that while the two men understood rudimentary al-Arabiyyah, their knowledge of Latin and Greek was far superior.

"Some minor alterations," said the old man, whose name he had told us was Gallienus. "We have been working to make the substance more stable. Easier to transport."

"For those earthenware balls?" I asked, nodding towards the door to the storeroom.

"Amongst other things," replied Gallienus, looking up from where he was finishing tying his laces. "We are making progress."

"You will bring your notes with you," said Giso. "But nothing more. There is no time and we must leave."

"But you have come to liberate us, no?" asked the young man, who Gallienus had introduced as Praetextatus. His voice was filled with fear and his eyes flitted from the face of one of us to the next, as if trying to ascertain which one of us was going to kill him.

"Yes," replied Giso smoothly. I knew him well enough to see that he was forcing himself to give off an aura of calm. This made sense to me. The two alchemists were both on edge. It would be better for us if they did not panic. "We have a way out of here, but you must do as we say. The night is not over and there will be many dangers before the sun rises."

The two men nodded sombrely.

"Did Staurakios send you?" asked Praetextatus. "I have prayed many times that we would be rescued."

"And your prayers have been answered," said Giso. "But quickly, before we leave, tell me, have you divulged the secret of the fire to any others here?"

"No," said Gallienus. "That is what we have been doing there." He indicated the book and parchments. "Under duress, of course." He looked abashed and I wondered how much convincing he had needed to cooperate. "We have been forced to scribe what we know so that the men of al-Andalus can replicate the dragon's breath."

"Dragon's breath?" I said.

"Yes," Gallienus smiled. "The men of Byzantion have called it thus since its discovery by Kallinikos all those years ago."

"The name is apt."

"Indeed it is," he said. "It is like a thing of myth. And once seen, the dragon's breath can never be forgotten."

I thought of the screams, the intense heat, the stink of the same compounds that were heavy in the air of the small room.

"I know," I said, and something in my tone gave Gallienus pause.

"You have seen it?" he asked. "Where?"

"Qurtuba. A few weeks ago. A demonstration was held."

Gallienus clapped his hands in delight.

"They tell us nothing down here, but we worked tirelessly to produce what they needed."

He said something quickly in Greek to Praetextatus that I wasn't able to make out. Praetextatus nodded, but seemed less happy than the old man.

"Enough," snapped Giso. "There is no time for this idle chatter. Nobody else holds the secret of the dragon's breath? You are certain?"

"We have taken as long as we can to create the instructions," said Praetextatus. "We have lied about mistakes, and how certain elements need to be added to the mixture for optimum effect. But we cannot delay for ever. Our writings are almost complete, and when they are finished, I fear the Moors will have no more use for us."

"Nonsense," said Gallienus. "We have much knowledge that could benefit them. All we would have needed to do was to keep ourselves of use to them." He grinned. "But now that does not matter, for we are to be rescued."

Praetextatus frowned. He did not seem convinced with any of Gallienus' assertions.

"Ask them where our silver is," said Runolf.

While I had gone through the writings on the table, he and Drosten had pulled the lids from all of the crates and boxes in the storeroom. They had found more of the clay balls, some empty, waiting their filling of the dragon's breath compound, others full, their openings sealed with wax, packed carefully in the straw-lined metal boxes. They had also found barrels of stinking liquids and powders that burnt the eyes, throat and nose.

But they had uncovered no silver.

Giso ignored Runolf and cut through the alchemists' conversation.

"Which of you knows most about the formula?"

The two men looked at each other and a shared memory passed between them. Gallienus chuckled, and even Praetextatus smiled despite himself. With a shrug, he pointed at Gallienus.

"He taught me all I know."

Gallienus smiled at him like a proud father.

"And you have forgotten half of what I have shown you. But you are still a good student and I could not have asked for a better companion to share my incarceration."

Giso sighed with barely concealed frustration.

"But each of you knows how to make the dragon's breath without the other's help?"

"Yes, of course," replied Gallienus. "Praetextatus here is truly a wonderful apprentice. I feel I am partly to blame for us being captured and brought here, but he has never once brought up my foolishness. If I had not been so rash, we would still be living in luxury in the great city of Byzantion, instead of here in this dismal, dark cell."

"So you can make the stuff without his aid?" Giso asked Praetextatus.

"Yes," he replied, "with the correct ingredients. I memorised the process long ago."

"Good," said Giso, and without warning, he pulled a small knife from his sleeve, leaned across the table and sliced it across Gallienus' throat.

Thirty-Five

I have seen much death in my long life, a lot of it both unexpected and violent. I did not know Gallienus, but the manner of his killing, so swift and brutal, brought back to me Leofstan's murder. The shock of it struck me like a slap, and my breath caught in my throat.

I had known for some time that Giso was not the meek, officious man I had once believed him to be. He'd prayed with me each night and every morning as the sun rose, giving every impression of being a good Christian, earnest and devout. And yet clearly there was more to the man than what he had shown me during our voyage aboard *Brymsteda*, and more recently on our journey into the mountains. Giso had slipped away from us and our guards in Qadis. He had lived in the shadows of al-Andalus for weeks, travelling the land and discovering many secrets. There was a hard, impenetrable quality to the man, but nothing I had witnessed before then had prepared me for the callous brutality with which he took Gallienus' life in that cell far beneath Aljany's fortress.

Gallienus blinked and uttered strangled gasps, unbelieving that his death was fast approaching, his life force gushing from the severed arteries of his throat.

Praetextatus let out a small cry and instinctively tried to

push himself away from the fountaining blood and the dying man. The small wooden stool he sat on toppled over and he fell to the hard stone floor. He clutched at the table for purchase as he lost his balance, sending a pot of ink and several quills clattering to the stone. But the sound was lost in the uproar from the others in the room. For a brief time, nobody had uttered a sound, now everyone spoke at once.

"What have you done?" said Hereward, his face dark with anger.

Blood spurted rhythmically from Gallienus' throat, pumping out with each weakening beat of his heart. The old man grasped at Giso, who caught his wrists and stepped to the side, avoiding most of the blood. With unusual tenderness, Giso held the old man as he died, lowering him gently to the flagstone floor. Gallienus' mouth worked, opening and closing like a beached salmon, but nothing more than a liquid gurgle emanated from him.

"I did what was needed," said Giso, looking at Hereward and the others over the dying man's contorted, horrified features. "He knows too much, and he would never keep up with us. I could not leave him here."

Absently, Giso slapped away Gallienus' hands as the old alchemist reached for the Frank's face, scratching and clawing, like a drowning man, blindly trying to grip something, anything that would anchor him to this life. The flow of his blood was slowing already. A large pool was expanding beneath him. My stomach churned and I looked away from the dying man and Giso's terrifyingly calm face to Runolf. The giant Norseman was frowning but I could not read his expression. Revna was pale, her eyes wide. Sounds of scrabbling drew my eyes down to Praetextatus who was frantically sliding away backwards from the growing puddle of blood, pushing with his heels against the cold floor.

"Wha— Wha— Wha—" Praetextatus stuttered, unable to

speak. I knew how he felt. I had stood in shieldwalls and killed men, and still Gallienus' murder had shocked me profoundly. Tears streaked Praetextatus' cheeks. His skin was as white as curds.

"Get him on his feet," snapped Giso.

Nobody moved. It appeared I was not the only one shocked by the speed and casualness of Giso's violence.

"We have no time," he said, exasperation colouring his tone. "Get him up," he said to me. With another glance at Runolf, I stooped and pulled Praetextatus to his feet. Giso was at the table now, picking up sheets of parchment and holding them to the light.

"Are all the instructions here?" he asked the whimpering young man. Praetextatus did not answer, so I shook his arm.

"Answer him," I said. I wanted to let him weep in peace, to mourn the loss of his mentor, but I could feel the pressure of time. We did not have the luxury of grieving now. That would come later, if we survived the night.

Still Praetextatus did not speak, but he nodded his head, then wiped the tears and snot from his face with the back of his hands.

Giso folded the sheets of parchment and I winced at the treatment of the expensive material. It takes many days to make good vellum, but there were more important things to worry about. Giso glanced at the books, but discarded them. Content now that he had everything he needed, he turned towards the door.

"Come," he said. "By my calculation it is not yet dawn. If we hurry we can be gone from the fortress before light and before this theft is discovered. But we must leave now."

Again, nobody moved. None of us, it seemed, wished to follow a man such as Giso any longer. My friends in that room were killers, tough and ruthless. But they were warriors, and they held dear their honour. There was no honour in slaying a defenceless old man. Runolf, fists clenched at his sides, took a step forward.

"Where is the silver?" he growled.

Giso spun back to face him. He appeared oblivious of the change that had come over us, or had decided to ignore it. I thought it a dangerous strategy to so lightly dismiss the enmity of men such as Runolf, Drosten and Hereward.

"There is no time for that now," said Giso. His face gave no indication of his thoughts, but I saw him take in the stern faces of the warriors in the small room, and his demeanour changed. Gone was the sharp commanding bluster. It was replaced with a conciliatory, hushed tone. The voice of a bartering merchant. "But that is no matter, friends," he went on in his new soft voice. "King Carolus has more silver than you can ever imagine."

"I can imagine a lot," said Runolf, unsmiling.

Giso grinned, as if this was the best jest he had heard in weeks.

"And you will receive all that you can dream of and more," he said smoothly. "I promise you. But we must leave now. The knowledge this man possesses is beyond price. You will all be recompensed for his safe passage to Aachen."

Drosten turned to Runolf.

"I don't like this either," he said, his Pictish accent making the words sound like a snarl. His eyes flicked down to look at Gallienus' corpse. "But perhaps he is right. We cannot tarry here."

The white-haired alchemist was unmoving now. His unseeing eyes stared up in horror. He seemed to be accusing us all with those eyes, and I felt the weight of guilt settle on me. I had not been able to save Gallienus any more than I had been able to save Leofstan. Both had died like beasts slaughtered at harvest time.

"I do not wish to tarry," said Runolf, his usually booming

voice little more than a whisper. "All I want is our silver, not the secret of that accursed fire."

"There is no time to argue," Giso protested.

Runolf pushed past Drosten. He stepped over Gallienus' body, careful not to stand in the blood that surrounded it. He moved very close to Giso and stared down at him, his beard almost touching the Frank's forehead.

"You are right, little man," he gnarred. "It will be daybreak soon and we must have the silver before then. I will not leave empty handed."

Giso did not retreat or look away. Whatever manner of man he was, he was certainly no craven.

He took a long steadying breath, but just as he looked set to answer, Imad stepped from the shadows behind him. Giso's words died on his lips as the steel of Imad's blade touched the soft skin of his throat.

"What are you saying?" asked Imad in al-Arabiyyah. His tanned skin looked sallow in the flame light.

Most men with a knife at their throat and Runolf towering menacingly before them would have blanched. I have seen men lose control of their bladder for less. But Giso did not so much as flinch.

"I am saying," he said, his voice as calm as if he were discussing the weather, "that we must leave now if we wish to live."

"And what does the giant say?"

"He says he wants his silver," I said.

"That is what we came for, is it not?" He glanced at the corpse beside the table. "Or did you lie to us? Did you think to dupe us to aid you in your search for something we did not need or desire?"

Giso still appeared calm, but I saw a bead of sweat trickle down his brow.

"I did not lie to you," he said. "There is no trick. I am sure the silver is here, in the fortress. But to look for it now is madness. The fortress will be awake soon."

"We came for the silver," said Imad, his voice cold. "And to make those who had betrayed us pay. We have come too far to turn back now."

Gently, almost delicately, Giso reached up to Imad's hand and carefully pushed it away from his neck.

"Do what you will," he said. "But I am taking the alchemist down the stairs and out into the night."

"What are Imad's thoughts on this?" asked Hereward, arching his eyebrows.

"He wants the silver," I said. "And to find Ghalib and the others."

"Then it is settled," said Runolf. "The little man can do what he wants, but we go in search of the treasure."

Gallienus' glazed eyes seemed to stare at me and, again, the vision of Leofstan's last moments came to me. My teacher had travelled all the way to Rygjafylki to find *The Treasure of Life*. I had looked for it ever since. It was only a book, he had said to me on more than one occasion. Leather and parchment could possess no power beyond the wisdom or heresy within the words they held, and yet I fancied I could feel the throb of the tome's dark energy. It was close.

"And the book," I said, without thinking.

Runolf spat.

"I care naught for your book," he said, "but if it is with our silver, we will find it soon enough."

"Giso is right about one thing though," I said.

"What's that?"

"We must hurry. We have wasted too much time already."

As if in answer to my words, the corridor outside the door was suddenly filled with the tumult of shouts and the clanging crash of steel on steel.

Thirty-Six

Imad shoved open the door. The wicked-looking dagger he had held at Giso's throat was still in his grasp. The small landing outside was a chaos of movement, but it was instantly clear what was happening.

Two fortress wardens had descended the stairs and caught Wahid and Gwawrddur off guard. No doubt they had been distracted by the sounds of the altercations in the cell. Thankfully for us, even when surprised Gwawrddur was faster than most men and more skilled with a blade than any warrior I've ever met.

One of the guards already lay dead at his feet. Blood darkened his robe in a scarlet bloom where the Welshman's blade had pierced the man's heart.

Wahid was not faring as well. Blood streamed down his face where his cheek had been slashed open. Having wounded Wahid, his assailant had pressed home his advantage. Now the two were locked in a struggle of brute strength. Wahid's back was to the wall. He had grasped his opponent's sword arm, but it was all he could do to prevent him from striking again. He grunted, trying to push the guard back, perhaps in the hope that he might lose his footing on the stairs, but it was no good. The guard was taller and stronger than Wahid and in moments, it was clear that he would overpower him.

But Gwawrddur did not allow the fortress guard the time he needed to best Wahid. Spinning away from the warden he had killed, he rounded on the man who loomed over Wahid. The Welshman's teeth gleamed as he grinned. Wahid's eyes widened as he saw Gwawrddur approach from behind his opponent. Wahid grunted, hope shining in his eyes as he saw the slim swordsman stalking his prey, bloody blade in hand. Wahid would live, his adversary dying on the Welshman's blade.

"Wait!" I shouted. "Do not kill him."

For a heartbeat, I thought my meaning had been lost, that perhaps Gwawrddur had not heard me, or, consumed by battle-lust, had chosen to ignore my request. But as he stepped nimbly up behind the guard, Gwawrddur did not bring his sword down on the man's unprotected skull, or drive his blade into his kidneys. Instead, he grasped the guard's collar and pulled him back. At the same time, he brought his blood-smeared sword round to press against the man's unprotected throat. Gwawrddur had taught me much over the years, and I was foolish to doubt him. He had often told me to control my anger, and while he was fast and savage in a fight, he never ceased to pay attention to his surroundings.

"Halt," Gwawrddur said in al-Arabiyyah, and again, I wondered how much he understood of that tongue now.

Even before Gwawrddur had uttered the word, the guard, eyes wide and teeth bared, had lowered his sword. After the briefest of hesitations as he weighed up his chances, he allowed it to fall. There are few clearer messages than a sharp blade held to the neck. The guard's weapon clanged on the step, bouncing from the top step, then clattering down several more. The sound was harsh, ringing like a bell in the enclosed stairwell.

Nobody spoke. The sudden hush felt thick, the panting of the fighters loud. Praetextatus sniffed and wiped at his face. Peering past me, he saw the dead man at the top of the steps and let out a moan. I thought he might faint, so I gripped his arm tightly. He didn't seem to notice.

Giso stepped through the doorway, holding up his hand for us to remain silent. We listened, straining our ears for a sign that the fighting had been overheard. But no sound reached us. No alarm, shouted from the castle walls.

"The Lord Almighty is truly watching over us," Giso said.

"Perhaps Christ can tell us where the silver is," said Runolf.

Giso glowered. I felt a sliver of unease. It was never wise to make light of the Lord's power, much less so when surrounded by enemies in a foreign land.

"Maybe He can loosen this man's tongue," I said.

Runolf cracked his fingers.

"If your god cannot, I'm sure I could convince him to speak."

Dragging the sniffling Praetextatus with me, I stepped out of the room. I pushed the young alchemist towards Giso.

"You want him," I said. "You hold him."

"This is madness, Hunlaf," he whispered.

"Perhaps," I replied, turning to the man Gwawrddur was holding. "Some men arrived a few days ago with a heavy chest," I said. The guard said nothing, but his eyes did not leave mine. There was fear there. Defiance too, I thought. "They stole it from us. Where is that chest now?"

Still, he did not speak.

Runolf took a step forward, bunching his hands into meaty fists. The guard was tall and strong, but he looked like a callow youth beside Runolf.

"We have little time," I said, "and my friends are not patient men. Answer me, or you will suffer."

He glanced down at his fallen comrade.

"You will kill me if I speak," he said.

"What is your name?" I asked.

He hesitated for a heartbeat before replying.

"Milhim."

"I can tell you one thing with certainty, Milhim. If you do not speak, we will kill you. If you help us, you might yet live to see the morning." With the mention of morning, I felt renewed the strain of knowing that time was passing quickly. "Tell me where the chest is," I urged him.

When he did not immediately respond, Gwawrddur pushed his sword blade into the man's neck, making him gasp and gag.

"Speak," he hissed into the man's ear.

Milhim's eyes bulged. He was unable to talk, then Gwawrddur relaxed the pressure on his throat. The man drew in a rasping breath. He cast a sorrowful look at his dead companion, as if apologising for what he was about to do.

"The chest is in the treasure room," he croaked. "At the top of the tower."

"And what of a book?" I asked. "Where does Aljany keep his books?"

The man looked confused.

"Books?" he asked.

"Yes, I'm looking for a large book." I held out my hands to show the size of *The Treasure of Life* as I remembered it. It was a big, heavy tome, perhaps an arm's length along its longest side.

Milhim looked as though I had asked him if the moon was made of curds.

"You will soon face dozens of my brothers in battle," he said. "They will never let you leave this place alive, and you ask about a book?"

"The word of God, and the words of the Prophet are written in books," I said. "Who are you to make light of books?"

"You see?" said Giso. "Even this Moorish heathen knows this is madness. God has watched over us thus far, but even the

Almighty will tire of this stupidity. We have the most important thing we came for." He shook Praetextatus to emphasise his point. The alchemist cowered as if he thought Giso might murder him, as he had killed his mentor.

"I will not risk losing him for this foolishness. I will take him down to the exit and wait for you there. If you are not there by dawn, I will wait no further. Godspeed."

"Go with them," Runolf said, pushing Revna towards Giso and Praetextatus.

Revna wheeled on her father. The shadows from the lamplight made her face hard.

"I will not," she said. There was no give in her tone. Shaking his head, Runolf growled in the back of his throat, but said no more on the subject.

Taking the lamp from its niche in the wall, Giso pushed Praetextatus towards the steps. None of us made a move to stop them. The glow of the lamp lit their way as they stepped over the fallen sword, then the passage was plunged into darkness as they rounded the bend at the bottom and were lost to view.

Revna brought the lantern out of the cell. Hereward, Runolf and Imad followed her. Drosten brought the lamp that had been on the table and placed it in the niche. Without a word, Runolf stooped, took hold of the dead guard's robe and dragged his corpse into the room.

"Well?" I said to Milhim, as if our conversation had not been interrupted. "What of the book?"

He shrugged, shaking his head.

"The master has a reading room. Perhaps it is there." Despite the possibility of his imminent death, his tone was mocking, incredulous.

"What does he say?" asked Hereward.

"He knows where the silver is stored. He's unsure about the book."

"And where is the silver?"

Milhim didn't need Gwawrddur to persuade him further.

"He says it's at the top of the tower."

"We'd better be climbing these stairs then," said Runolf. He pulled the door shut, scooped up the locking bar and dropped it back into place. Drosten went down the steps and retrieved the dead guard's sword. There was a dark stain on the stone where the guard had died, but nothing else to indicate what had happened there. With any luck, perhaps the door would be left shut for a while longer, giving us time enough to find the silver and escape. I hoped to find the book too before we left. I was sure it was there. The air seemed to crackle with energy and I could not believe the others did not feel it. My nerves thrummed with excitement.

We were crowded onto the landing now, the flame from Revna's lantern bright with its proximity. The light, cast up onto our faces from below, darkened our eyes in shadows. Drosten's tattooed features, so stark and sombre, could have been carved from stone.

Gwawrddur turned Milhim around and shoved him up the steps. He still held his bloody sword at the man's neck, but the guard, resigned to his fate perhaps, seemed to pay little heed to it now. He continued talking, explaining what awaited us above.

On hearing his words, I turned to Imad and Wahid to see their reaction. Imad was scowling. Wahid's face was pale. He had found a piece of cloth from somewhere and held it pressed against his cheek to staunch the flow of blood from the gash there.

Placing my hand on Gwawrddur's shoulder, I halted him as he stepped onto the first step.

"There is a problem," I said.

"Just one?" asked Gwawrddur. "Then we must be blessed indeed, for I thought this whole endeavour was madness, as Giso said."

"Then why go along with it?"

"You know me," he said with a wink. "I like a challenge. Besides, if it was easy, everyone would do it."

"What's the problem," hissed Hereward.

I sighed.

"We are not beneath the tower."

"Then where are we?"

"He says these stairs end in a doorway in the wall. To get to the tower, we will need to cross the courtyard, in full view of the walls. Then, to enter the tower, there is only one door, which is guarded by two sentries."

"Is that all?" asked Runolf with a grin. "I thought you said there was a problem."

Thirty-Seven

We stood, crowded in the doorway and looked out at the courtyard. Revna had covered the lantern, so as not to give ourselves away. There were two men standing in the shadow of the door that led into the square tower. The huge building loomed up into the lightening sky. The stars were dimming as dawn approached. The sky was bright enough in the east to imagine that out of the mountains, down by the sea, the sun might have already crested the horizon. The courtyard was still engulfed in the shadows of the walls, but time was running out.

I offered up a silent prayer that God might watch over us a little longer. Against the odds we had come this far, but could we possibly hope to enter the stone keep, find what we sought and escape without notice? I could almost hear Runolf saying that anything was possible, but as I looked out at the flat area inside the walls of the fortress, and the imposing structure of the tower that rose high above the outer defences, I could not shake the feeling that Giso was right. We had chosen to continue into the maw of the beast. Now we would receive our punishment for such hubris. And yet, even as my thoughts turned to darkness and defeat, my nerves tingled with excitement. I could feel the book was close, and I would not turn back now.

"Looks like just two guards," whispered Gwawrddur.

"And the ones on the walls," I murmured. "Let us hope they are looking outward, and not for an enemy within."

The scene appeared to be just as Milhim had told us. Evidently he had decided that his best chance of survival was to cooperate. He was right, I thought, though there was no telling what the others might do to him. Drosten, Gwawrddur and Hereward were all capable of killing him in cold blood if they deemed it necessary, and Runolf was burning with a savage fury I had not seen in him since we travelled to his homeland and discovered what had befallen his wife, Estrid. Runolf had been there with me at the end of that dreadful quest, during that night of flames and blood. Could it be that he too, no matter what he said, felt the presence of the book nearby? Was it possible that it truly exerted some arcane power over us?

Imad and Wahid shouldered their way through the tightly packed throng in the open doorway.

"We will open the doors," Imad said. He turned to whisper hurriedly to Milhim.

I relayed his words to the others while Imad asked Milhim the name of his now dead companion, and those of the men on duty at the door to the castle.

"Can we trust them?" asked Hereward.

"What choice do we have?" I asked. "It will be light soon."

At a word from Imad, Wahid stepped into the courtyard, his hand on the hilt of his sword. His cheek was dark with blood, his beard glistening, but it looked as though the bleeding had slowed or stopped. Imad turned to me.

"If he makes a sound," he whispered, nodding at Milhim, "or if he has given us false information, cut his throat."

He did not wait for an answer. Turning on his heel, he joined Wahid, and the two of them crossed the courtyard at an unhurried, ambling pace. Gwawrddur pulled Milhim back away from the doorway and into the darkness. The rest of us shuffled backwards, keenly aware of how exposed we were. None of us spoke as we watched the two men get closer to the fortress.

I expected a shout from the walls, or a challenge from the door wardens at any moment, but the first sound that reached us was Imad's voice. I could not hear what he said, but the tone was friendly as he approached the door with Wahid beside him. A questioning reply came from one of the sentries. Imad and Wahid increased their pace. Another query, louder this time, a name perhaps. They closed the last steps at a run. A startled word, loud in the darkness, was cut off almost before it could be registered.

I could barely see what was happening in the shadows at the base of the tower. I heard the scrape of feet, a grunt; saw an arm punching forward once, twice, three times.

There was a sighing, sobbing breath.

Then silence.

I was certain that we would be discovered then. How could the men on the walls have failed to hear what had seemed so loud in the pre-dawn darkness?

I held my breath and sensed that all those around me did the same. Gwawrddur tensed and Milhim stiffened, as the Welshman's blade pressed firmly against his throat just in case he had any ideas. The silence dragged on. In the distance, over the wall and far down the valley, echoed the raucous, angry crow of a cockerel.

But no alarm was raised. No shouts from the walls. Slowly, I let out my breath, murmuring my thanks to the Lord.

"Are you praying?" whispered Runolf.

"I pray that God will protect us and watch over us," I replied, expecting a scathing comment about the pointlessness of praying to "my god". Runolf had long ago ceased any pretence at being a Christian, despite having been baptised.

"Don't stop," he said, surprising me. "It seems to be working."

I could feel nervous laughter bubbling up within me at Runolf's sudden belief in the power of prayer. I swallowed down my amusement. To laugh now could undo all of our stealthy progress.

On the far side of the courtyard, Imad and Wahid had taken the place of the two sentries in the door's shadow.

"How do we cross the yard?" asked Revna, her whispered voice making her sound dreadfully young.

"We walk," said Gwawrddur. "Just like them."

"But we'll be seen from the walls."

Hereward looked up at the sky. It was the colour of steel in the east. To the west, I could still see a smattering of stars, but they would be gone soon.

"There is no time for anything else," Hereward said. "If we are not out of this fortress soon, it will be day and we will all be dead. Come on."

"Keep praying, Killer," whispered Gwawrddur. Holding Milhim close to him, his blade held ready at his side, he stepped into the courtyard and began walking deliberately towards the tower.

Taking a deep breath, I muttered the Pater Noster, and followed.

Thirty-Eight

My heart was thumping so hard that I felt sure the others must hear it. My blood rushed in my ears and I did my best to control my breathing. I was light-headed.

I could scarcely believe it. We had made it across the courtyard without being challenged. I had been convinced that at any moment a shout would split the still of the night or even worse, an archer on the ramparts would loose an arrow into my back as I walked. The skin between my shoulder blades itched as I imagined an arrow piercing my padded jerkin.

But no shout of alarm had come. No iron-tipped arrow had whistled from the walls.

Runolf pushed the heavy doors of the tower closed behind us.

"That's some good praying, Hunlaf," Gwawrddur said with a grin. I felt a stab of guilt. I had prayed all the while as we walked across the open space, so why did I doubt the power of the Lord so? Could it be the proximity to the book that weakened my faith? The book might have power, despite what Leofstan had asserted, but I knew I could not blame my faithlessness on *The Treasure of Life*. I had seen much in my short life to make me question my faith, but my decision to place my belief in the sword and not the word of the Lord was mine alone. I shook my head to clear it. Now was not the moment to be distracted.

We were in an open area inside the tower, that would serve as a place to welcome guests, or where defenders could direct all their energies on enemies should the doors be breached. I could see four doors and an archway ahead of us that led to a flight of steps. The stairs turned to the right and were lost from sight. The area was lit by a single oil lamp on a stand near the arch.

"What are we going to do with them?" Runolf asked, looking down at the crumpled forms of the sentries who now lay cooling on the tiled floor.

"Hide them as best we can," replied Hereward. "But quickly. Time is against us."

Imad, seeming to understand Hereward's meaning, or coming to the same conclusion himself, moved rapidly to the closest door on the left. Pressing his ear to it, he listened for a short time. Satisfied, he tried the handle. Pushing the door open, he peered inside. Over his shoulder I could see only darkness through the doorway. It was still and silent in that darkened room.

As Wahid and Drosten dragged the dead sentries into the room, I muttered another prayer under my breath, both for the Lord Almighty to continue to watch over us and also for Him to forgive my lack of faith.

"What about him?" Revna asked quietly, indicating Milhim. Gwawrddur still gripped the man's arm, but no longer held his sword at the guard's throat. Milhim tensed, not understanding Revna's words, but understanding he was the object of her question. He opened his mouth to speak, but before he could say anything, or react further, Imad stepped close and, without warning, brought the pommel of his sword down hard on the man's skull.

Milhim grunted and tried to pull away from Gwawrddur,

but Imad struck him again, and with a moaning sigh, the strength went out of him and he collapsed.

"He might still have been useful to us," I said, my anxiety making my voice rise in volume.

Imad had dropped down beside Milhim and I realised with a shock that he was going to cut the man's throat.

"Stop," I said, aghast.

Imad ignored me and I was too far away to reach him before he drew his blade across Milhim's exposed throat. But Gwawrddur was closer. With his unrivalled speed and the strength gained from a lifetime wielding a sword, he stooped, lashed out and caught Imad's wrist.

Imad glared up at him.

"I gave my word he would be spared," I said, moving closer.

Imad spat.

"There is no time for this," he said, glowering.

"I will not let you kill him," I said, my voice quiet now, but hard-edged and dangerous, like a seax blade.

Imad shrugged. He rose and moved away, seeming disappointed not to have further blooded his sword.

"Thank you," I whispered to Gwawrddur.

"Thank me later," he said. "Help me tie him up."

We bound and gagged Milhim with the belts of the dead sentries, then dumped his inert form in the same dark room as the corpses. From the dim light filtering in from the door I could see it was sparsely decorated, with little more than a table and some plain chairs. We pulled the door shut and turned to the stairs.

The rest of our small band was gathered there, waiting for us impatiently.

"It would have been quicker to kill him," snarled Imad.

"And quicker still to have left him be. Without him we don't know which door opens to the treasure room."

He shrugged.

"He said it was at the top of the tower, so let's climb."

Without waiting for a reply, he started up the stairs. I followed close behind, Wahid and Gwawrddur just behind me. I thought there might be a better order for us to take the stairs, but there was no time to dwell on the problem.

The tower was waking up around us. It was almost imperceptible at first. A cough behind a closed door, a hushed voice. Then someone far above us in the building dropped something with a metallic clatter. Another voice hissed at them to be quiet. These must surely be the servants and thralls who would rise before the lord of the hall, his family and closest companions. They would go about the tasks necessary for the day ahead; rekindling cooking fires, preparing clothes, collecting water, setting tables for the breaking of the fast.

All about us we could hear those who served going about their morning routine as quietly as they were able, and yet no matter how careful servants and slaves might be, and how heavily the noble dwellers of a building might slumber, the castle would soon be abustle with activity. Shortly after that, everyone would be awake and we would be doomed.

A door slammed on the storey above us. We halted on the stairs, holding our breath. The footsteps receded as whoever had stepped out of a room went up ahead of us.

We continued on up. The stair followed the outside wall of the tower. Every few paces an alcove gave access to a narrow window from where defenders could shoot arrows, or keep watch. We had entered the tower from the south and the stairs started on the north side, then following the eastern wall southward. On the first-floor landing, we passed several doors, walking quickly and quietly past.

As we reached the eastern part of the stairs for the second time I glimpsed the sky through a window. It was no longer night and I wondered for how much longer we could continue to sneak about without being detected. Surely Giso was right.

This was madness. What good would the silver do us, or indeed the book, if we were dead or captured? The thought of again being thrown into a lightless cell far beneath the earth made me shudder. We should not have pressed on into the castle. Sweat ran down my face as my doubts built towards panic. I had ceased praying, and the dark thoughts of capture and failure filled me with dismay.

I have often wondered about what happened next. At the time, I thought it was a sign that God was unhappy with my lack of faith in Him. But later, long after the events in that dark tower were in the past, I wondered if in fact this encounter hadn't also been a gift sent by the Lord after all.

A door opened just after I had passed it. A man stepped out, but faltered as he was confronted by several armed men in the passageway. Our nerves thrummed, as taut as sail braces in a gale. We were ready for any eventuality, whereas the man looked barely awake, bleary eyed and rubbing a hand over his bearded face. Hereward was closest to him. The Northumbrian warrior was ready for action and before the man could even let out a sound, Hereward had pulled out a knife and leapt forward.

He may have just risen from his bed and been caught off guard by the men outside his room, but the bearded man was quick and strong. He grabbed Hereward's knife hand, preventing him from plunging the blade into his midriff.

I thought he would cry out, bringing the rest of the tower's inhabitants rushing out of their chambers. But instead he gritted his teeth and made barely a sound as he wrestled with Hereward.

The grey-cold light of the new dawn spilt from the window in the thick wall, shining onto the two of them. I recognised the man in the doorway struggling with Hereward in the same instant that he spoke.

Thirty-Nine

"Hereward," the man said. "It is me."

He was strong from the many months at sea, I knew, from heaving on halliards and pulling oars, but despite his strength the man's voice still strained with the effort of holding the burly Northumbrian's knife away from his flesh.

I reached out, pulling Hereward away.

"It is Ahmad," I hissed.

Hereward made another lunge with his knife, but Gwawrddur lent his strength to mine and together we prevented him gutting the man who had been Mancas' thrall.

"I know who he is," Hereward spat. He was shaking with fury. "We might all die because of him." He let out a long breath, shook our hands off his shoulders and turned away.

Ahmad's eyes, tinged with fear and uncertainty, flicked over us all.

"I knew you would come," he said, his voice low. "Tayyib did not believe me. He said you would never risk coming here." He shook his head, a sorrowful smile on his face. "But I knew you would come for what had been taken from you. I know you too well."

"I thought I knew you too," I hissed. "I freed you..." My words trailed off. I knew we had never been close, but I had spent many long days and nights with Ahmad, and his betrayal had cut me deeply, perhaps more deeply than I had been aware of until that moment on the stairs in Aljany's fortress.

"I am sorry, Hunlaf," he said. "Truly, I am. But you don't understand. I had no choice. Tayyib threatened my father if I did not aid them."

"Tayyib is here?"

He shook his head.

"He left at dusk. He did not believe me, but he was nervous and led some guards out on patrol." I thought again how God was watching over us. We had seen no patrols outside the fortress in the night.

"There is no time for this," snarled Hereward.

"He is right," said Ahmad. "You must flee. Now. While there is still a chance. If you remain here, Aljany's men will find you. You cannot hope to prevail against so many."

"Don't tell me what I can hope for," snarled Runolf.

"Not even the mighty Runolf Ragnarsson can survive against a fortress full of enemies."

"Save your wind for one who listens, nithing," rasped Runolf, his tone ice-cold and deadly. "And spare us your apology. The fox cannot ask forgiveness of the wolf when it has stolen the wolf's prey. It must face the consequences for its actions. Hereward had the right idea. Let us gut the worthless whoreson and be on our way. For it is certainly the truth that if we stay here much longer, we will all be as good as dead."

"What if the fox could help the wolf retrieve what had been taken?" said Ahmad.

Runolf paused, a predatory gleam in his eye.

"You can take us to the silver?"

"I can." Ahmad's eyes met mine. "And to the book."

"The book is here?" I asked, my chest tightening.

"Come on!" whispered Imad. "Can you not see that the traitor aims to slow us down?"

"The book is here," Ahmad said, ignoring Imad and not looking away from me. I still felt the crackle of energy in the air and was sure Ahmad was telling the truth, but I could not ignore Imad's words. It was true that the longer we tarried here, the more likely we were to be discovered.

"Hereward," I said, "hold Ahmad, and at the first sign of treachery, kill him."

Hereward grunted in acknowledgement, roughly grabbing Ahmad's arm and pressing his knife into his ribs.

"Come on, you lying goat turd," he said.

We continued up the steps, halting every now and then to listen to the sounds of the tower. In the short time we had paused to converse with Ahmad, the light filtering in through the narrow windows was perceptibly brighter, less the iron grey of night and more the glowing gold of dawn. From the floors below us came the sounds of movement and voices. The sentries would be found soon, and even if they were not, how could we hope to escape through the front door? I could feel panic flapping at my mind like the wings of a trapped bird.

I swallowed down my fear. There was nothing to be gained from it. We had reached the third storey now and as we came to another door, carved with intricate designs, I heard Ahmad's voice from behind me.

"In there is Aljany's library. He does not have all his books here, many are in his palace in Išbīliya, but the book you seek is inside."

My mouth grew dry.

"And the silver?" said Runolf.

"On the floor above. The last door at the top of the tower."

"Are there guards?"

"It doesn't matter how many guards there are," said Ahmad. "You'll never get your silver."

"Why?" growled Runolf, taking a threatening step towards Ahmad.

"It lies behind an iron door that is secured with a huge, cunning lock."

Revna placed a hand on her father's chest, pushing him away from Ahmad.

"Who has the key?" she asked.

"Aljany himself," replied Ahmad, "and his right-hand man, Tayyib, are the only ones with a key. Neither man is in the fortress and without the key, it is impossible to open the door."

"We shall see about that," Runolf said. He bared his teeth, but the expression seemed more grimace than grin. "Anything is possible." His assertion, usually so confident, sounded more desperate to my ears now, but perhaps my perception was coloured by my own rising panic.

Runolf stepped close to Ahmad. Revna moved aside, no match for her father's prodigious strength. Ahmad flinched and for a heartbeat I thought Runolf meant to strike him. Instead, he grabbed his shoulder, pulling him away from Hereward and shoving him towards me.

"I don't want this scum in the way," he said. "Take him with you, Hunlaf, and get your damned book. The rest of us will get our treasure."

Without waiting for a reply, Runolf turned and continued up the stairs, taking them two at a time.

Forty

The library door was different to the others we had seen within the tower. It too was made of timber, but where the other doors were plain and functional, this one was carved with intricate decorations and motifs. It reminded me of some of the carved masonry I had seen within the palace of Qurtuba. The handle too was more elaborate. Bronze rather than iron, it was fashioned into a swirl, like the coiled tail of a serpent. Its surface was dimpled and etched with symbols and writing. The inquisitive part of my mind wanted to study the door and the handle, but I knew there was no time. Grasping the cool bronze, I twisted it. It rotated easily and I heard a small click from inside. Pushing the door, it opened on well-oiled hinges.

I could hear the hushed footsteps of my companions moving up the stairs. Taking a deep breath of the musty air of the room, I stepped quickly inside, followed by Ahmad, and Gwawrddur, who had taken over guard duty from Hereward.

"I would not like to have you turn your back on this one," he'd said, by way of explanation, as he had moved to Ahmad's side and shown him the blood-smeared blade of his sword.

Knowing that the Welshman was watching Ahmad, I did just what Gwawrddur had feared and turned my back on him to survey the room.

There was a lot more light in the room than I had expected. It was not brightly lit, but after the dingy gloom of the stairs, I was surprised that I could make out many details of the contents, furnishings and decorations, despite there being no evidence of lit lamps or candles. The light was diffuse; a warm golden glow that reminded me of the light coming in from the windows. But as none of the walls of the chamber were on the outside of the tower, I could not fathom how light was entering. My eyes were drawn to brighter points of light high up on the ceiling and finally comprehension dawned on me. By some clever trick, there must have been openings to the outside, tunnels through the thick masonry. Where the light shone through these tunnels and reached the library, polished plates of silver or some other metal had been cunningly positioned to catch the beams, magnifying and reflecting them down into the room.

Such a feat was astounding and I longed to further investigate, but Gwawrddur moved into the room, silently pushing the door closed behind us.

"Come on, Killer. This is no time for daydreaming. Find your accursed book, so we can be gone." His tone, usually languid and calm, was clipped and taut now.

He was right, of course. I dragged my eyes away from the ingenious mirrors and scanned the contents of the library. Tiny motes of dust floated in the rays of light. The air was redolent of leather and dust. The walls were lined from floor to ceiling with shelves. On our left was a wall entirely dedicated to scrolls. There were hundreds of them and my heart soared to imagine the wisdom that lurked within those tightly bound rolls of parchment and papyrus. There were three chairs, a table and a couple of angled desks, perfect for writing or reading. The shelves on the walls in front of us and to the right held countless bound tomes, from the smallest psalter-sized book that would fit in the palm of a hand, to huge, unwieldy codices or pandects that would take two men to carry. Some were piled horizontally, some standing vertically on their edges; however they would best fit the limited space available on the shelves. The books were all stored with their pages facing outwards. Some of the page edges bore symbols that must surely have signified something to Aljany and the other readers who used the library, but they meant nothing to me.

My mind reeled. How was I to find *The Treasure of Life* in here? Even using my memory of the size of the book to direct my search, it would still take me ages to go through the stacks of books on the shelves.

"What are you waiting for?" said Gwawrddur. "The book isn't going to make itself known to you, if you do not look for it."

I hurried to the closest shelf, running my fingers over the pages until I reached the first book that more or less approximated the thickness and size I recalled from my brief encounter with it on Lindisfarnae. I pulled the book free of the shelf, meaning to carry it to the table, where I could quickly look at its pages to ascertain if it was indeed the tome that had caused so much misery. I could think of no better way than this, but my heart sank as I hefted the book and turned, only to hear the unmistakable sounds of combat from outside on the stairs.

Gwawrddur opened the door, and the noise grew louder.

"Hurry up, Killer. We're out of time."

There were muffled shouts coming from upstairs. A scream. The clash of metal on metal.

Giso had been right. This had been folly all along. We had been discovered as he'd said we would be and now we would be captured or killed. To come so close was maddening, but Gwawrddur was right. There was no more time. I would not be able to study any of these books or to find the one we had travelled across half the world for. Resigned to failure, I threw the book that I was holding down onto the rug-covered floor.

The book fell open, and I stared down at its pages, praying that this might be the very tome I was seeking. But of course, it was not *The Treasure of Life*. This book was penned in the swirling lines of al-Arabiyyah, not Latin, and I had no time nor the inclination to attempt a translation.

The shouts outside were growing louder. Footsteps were running down the stairs, echoing along the stone passageway.

"Time to go," said Gwawrddur. Spinning quickly away from the door, he hammered the pommel of his sword into Ahmad's temple. Ahmad's eyes became glazed and unfocused, then rolled back into his head. Without a word or a sound, he fell to his knees, then onto his face. "No time to watch him," snapped Gwawrddur. "Come on!"

He pulled the door wide open, holding his sword before him, ready for the fight that was surely coming. Outside, a bell had begun to toll, sundering whatever peace had remained in the morning. I looked from the Welshman to Ahmad's crumpled form. The footsteps and shouts were very loud on the stairs now.

Gwawrddur glanced up the stairs. Imad and Wahid sped past, running along the landing and on down the steps. There was no more time. We had to leave now if we did not wish to be trapped here in this library. With a sigh, I gave one last look over the room.

The dawn had grown in intensity, sending more light into the room. One golden shaft fell onto the nearest reading desk. There was an open book lying there that I had not noticed before. My heart clenched and I gasped. Gwawrddur had said the book would not make itself known to me, but in that moment it became clear to me that God did not wish for me to leave without *The Treasure of Life*. Surely it had been the Lord God Almighty and not the book that had drawn me to this place, and now it was the Lord who showed me the tome. I recognised the intricate drawing of the first page; the elaborate concentric circles and interlocking streams and paths surrounding what seemed to be a tree adorned with numerous symbols and sigils. I had seen this image all that time ago in the scriptorium on Lindisfarnae. This was the book that Leofstan had searched for; the object of my quest to al-Andalus.

Slamming the book shut, I saw that the ornate cover it had possessed had been replaced with a plain, soft leather binding without adornment. I seemed to feel a jolt of energy as I touched the book, though perhaps I imagined that. Then there was no time for more thinking. I shoved the closed book under my arm and drew my borrowed sword.

Jumping over Ahmad's still form, I followed Gwawrddur into the corridor. While I was picking up the book, more figures had run past. Now I saw that Runolf and Drosten were bounding down towards us, bloody weapons in their hands.

"Fly! Fly!" yelled the giant Norseman. For an instant, his hair and beard seemed afire with the light from a window as he sped past and then he was in the shadows of the passage once more.

The two were almost upon us. Behind them, I could make out the shapes of armed warriors. There were many of them.

Gwawrddur stepped out as if to face the guards, but Runolf waved his sword.

"Fly!" he bellowed again. "There are too many. We cannot stand within the fortress. We will be trapped."

After the briefest of hesitations, Gwawrddur and I turned and joined Runolf and Drosten in a careening sprint down the steps.

Forty-One

Imad, Wahid, Revna and Hereward were ahead of us, already out of sight around the bends in the stairs. Gwawrddur was close to me, and a few paces behind him came Runolf and Drosten. The book was cumbersome under my arm, slowing my progress somewhat. But I was the fastest runner of the group and nimble. So even impeded as I was, I quickly began to pull away from the two hulking warriors who brought up the rear.

I chanced a glance over my shoulder and saw that some of the tower guards had gained on them.

"No silver?" I shouted at Runolf.

"What do you think?" he snarled, panting. "Is that the fabled book?"

"What do you think?" I replied.

We didn't speak further, instead concentrating on navigating the steps. Somewhere ahead I heard a crash and shouts of alarm over the tumult of our dash down the stairs, the cries from the guards behind ordering us to halt, and the clanging of the bell outside in the grounds of the fortress.

A door opened in the corridor before me. A man peered out. I was upon him in an instant, swinging my sword at his face.

He leapt back, avoiding the blade and tumbling backward into the room. I carried on without looking back.

"Run! Run!" yelled Gwawrddur, his words ragged. "We must not be trapped in this tower."

"You think we can fight our way out?" I yelled.

"If we can get across the courtyard and back to the steps we came from, we might have a chance."

I admired his confidence. We had been in tight spots before, and we had always managed to fight our way free, but I was not sure we would fare so well this time. I hoped it was indeed God who had called me here to find the book and that He would aid us in our escape, but I could not rid myself of the fear that it might have been some dark heretical power I had followed, leading us to our doom.

We skidded around a corner and saw Imad and the others, their backs to us, blocking our path. Two warriors with spears stood shoulder-to-shoulder on the landing, preventing them from passing. The spear-points glimmered in the light from a window as the spear-men jabbed and stabbed at our companions' faces.

"Help them," I shouted at Gwawrddur, pushing him onwards towards the knot of people. "We'll hold off the others."

The Welshman did not falter. He ran on and I turned back, knowing he would do what was necessary to unblock our path.

Drosten and Runolf both came lumbering round the corner. Seeing me, stationary before them, they came to a skidding halt. I knew our pursuers were close behind. I could hear them rushing down the steps just around the bend.

"Turn and fight," I yelled, pushing the Pict and Norseman back, and shouldering my way past them. "We must halt them."

We had fought side by side often enough to trust one another fully. We all knew that failure to act instantly when called upon could lead to death. So it was no surprise to me when both men turned and raised their swords without comment.

Expecting us to have continued our headlong rush towards the tower's doors, the first of the guards who chased us ran round the corner and onto our swords. I stabbed my blade into the mouth of a long-faced man. His forward momentum drove the blade deep and I shoved it hard, driving it through his spine. I tugged my sword free and he fell down, slain as surely as if I had severed his head.

Drosten swatted away the second man's sword, then lunged his blade into his groin. Hot blood spouted, drenching my already grubby jerkin in the guard's gore. It was a killing blow no doubt, but where my strike had felled the first man instantly, leaving him silent and twitching, Drosten's adversary was wailing and flailing, clutching at his leg as the blood fountained around his fingers. This was good. His cries would unnerve his comrades, who would stop to tend to him. And they would think twice before rushing around any other corners.

The others fell back around the bend, regrouping out of sight from us.

The sounds of fighting behind us died down, but still the bell clanged outside.

"We are through," shouted Gwawrddur. "Come!"

Drosten and I did not hesitate. We turned and sprinted after our friends. But Runolf did not move. Slowing my pace, I looked over my shoulder, wondering if he had been wounded. He was not injured. Holding a finger to his lips, he winked. There were two places where Runolf was truly at home and in his element: on the rolling deck of a ship out on the open sea, and in the storm of steel when the blood flowed.

"Go," he mouthed. I carried on, but I could not bring myself to look away. A moment later, clearly having heard our retreat and assuming we had all fled, the guards peered around the corner. Runolf was there to meet them. With a booming roar, he scythed his sword into the man who had been brave, or perhaps foolhardy enough, to be the first to look.

The man staggered back with a strangled cry. Runolf let out another roar for good measure, then turned his back, leaving behind him the dying man who still thrashed and cried out where he lay. As quietly and quickly as he was able, Runolf ran after us with his rambling, loping gait.

We hurried after Gwawrddur, who now led the charge down the steps. The two spear-men were both dead, each killed with ruthless efficiency and I could imagine the Welsh swordsman slaying them both himself, revelling in his sword-skill and the challenge of facing two men. I noticed that both of the spears were missing, snatched up by my friends no doubt. Whoever had killed them, the spear-men no longer posed a threat to us, and the men behind us were now more cautious. So, it seemed, were the servants and slaves we had heard waking up and readying the tower for the day ahead. No more doors opened, and the passageway was empty as we carried on down.

We reached the entrance without further incident and there we gathered, dragging in great lungfuls of air. It was cool within the tower, but sweat streamed down my face, and my skin beneath the padded jerkin was drenched, my kirtle sodden. Wahid's face was awash with blood where his wound had started bleeding again. Revna looked at me, her eyes wide. She was pale, but seemed unharmed, for which I offered up thanks to the Lord. I noticed her sword was smeared with blood and was glad we had practised all those evenings with our weapons.

Imad had a split lip. He spat blood onto the flagstones. Drosten was the only other one of us to have been injured, his left sleeve stained dark.

When he saw me looking at it, he shook his head and grinned.

"Nothing more than a scratch."

There looked like a lot of blood to me, but there was no time to tend to the wound. We could hear the warriors coming down the stairs behind us. They were no longer running, and they paused at each bend, but they would nonetheless be upon us in moments.

"Listen," said Hereward. "The bell has stopped ringing."

Gwawrddur hurried to the double doors that led outside.

"That can only mean all the men have been alerted that they are under attack. Each moment we stay in here, is a moment more for them to prepare. We no longer have the element of surprise, but if we allow them to form up before the doors, we are doomed."

"What do you suggest?" asked Hereward.

"We fight our way to the steps. If we can get inside there, a couple of us might be able to defend that entrance long enough to allow the others to escape."

Runolf nodded gravely at Gwawrddur.

"A couple of us could hold off this rabble, given a narrow passageway," he said.

I did not like the sound of what they were proposing, but now was not the time to argue.

"But how do we get to the steps?" asked Revna, looking as sombre as I felt.

Gwawrddur grinned wolfishly.

"Why, that is easy," he said. "We give them no more time to ready themselves. We go out there and we kill the bastards."

Remembering that moment all these years later, I can still feel the emotions that surged within me and I still marvel at the joy we felt in battle. We were surrounded by foe-men, in a fortress in a land far from our homes, and yet still Gwawrddur and Runolf took pleasure in the battle-joy, in the challenge and the chance to match their skill and bravery against others. Drosten and Hereward were no less savage in battle, but did not appear to enjoy it in the same way. Still there were few who could stand against them.

I was frightened, scared of what might happen to us,

particularly to Revna, who I knew to be as resilient as her father, but looked fragile to my eyes. And yet I can still recall how I was filled with a righteous excitement. I had found the book that Leofstan had felt compelled to seek out, and I cannot deny that despite my fears, I too felt the burning thrill of the fight to come. Men were amassed before us, men who would see us killed. But we were warriors, kin of sword and shield, and we would slay all who stood in our way.

"Now, Hunlaf," said Gwawrddur. "Tell Imad and Wahid we fight or die. We head for the doorway to the steps. And we stop for nothing."

I was still translating Gwawrddur's words when he flung open the doors. Dawn light washed into the entrance and the cacophony of many men rolled in with it. At the same instant the guards who had pursued us from the top of the tower reached the last flight of steps. Seeing us, they pulled together, pointing their weapons at us, but hesitating to descend the final steps and engage once more.

Hereward flung one of the spears he had taken. The throw was true and the spear-point found its mark. A man cried out and his comrades pulled him back up the stairs.

"No more time for talk," snarled Runolf. "Pray to your god that the book was worth it."

Without waiting for me to reply, he joined Gwawrddur in the doorway. They were silhouetted briefly against the dawn light, then together they ran out into the courtyard that thronged with guardsmen. Runolf was right, of course. This was not the time for talk, but to fight.

To kill, or be killed.

Taking a deep breath, I shoved Imad and Wahid through the arched doorway and followed them out into the early morning light.

Forty-Two

"Do not halt!" shouted Gwawrddur. "Give them no time to form up!"

He was sprinting forward with Runolf lumbering at his side, trusting that we would follow without question. I ran after them. There could be no hesitation if we were to have a chance of surviving this night. I clutched the heavy, unwieldy book under my left arm and prayed that this is what God wanted. That it was His call that had brought us here and that He would see us prevail against what appeared to be insurmountable odds.

I squinted in the dawn light, surveying the gathered warriors as we ran. It seemed the Lord was aiding us, for whoever was organising the guards in the courtyard had clearly not realised how we had entered the fortress, or how we planned to escape. If they had amassed all of the two score troops that were in the courtyard before the arched doorway to the steps leading down to the stores and cells, they would have prevented us from leaving. We would have become bogged down in the fighting and then surrounded, cut down, or captured to suffer God alone knew what unpleasant fate. As it was, the commander had ordered his men to form up between the doors of the tower and the main gates out of the walled perimeter in the east. There were still armed men standing where we needed to pass, but they made up the flank of the hastily ordered ranks. If we could move quickly enough, they would not have time to reposition themselves before we were able to reach the steps and the doorway that could, perhaps, be defended against a superior force.

I glanced up at the archers on the ramparts. There were not many of them, but their bowstrings were taut, arrows nocked. I thanked God that they did not loose their deadly projectiles, perhaps worrying they might strike their own comrades.

Wahid and Imad had been running just ahead of me, but now they faltered.

"Don't stop," I bellowed, pushing Imad onward. He was staring at the guards closest to our position. Gwawrddur and Runolf had already sped past them and were halfway to the archway. The guards, seeing their error, were now changing their position, turning and hurrying forward on a course to cut us off, wedging themselves between us and our escape route. I attempted to shove Imad forward awkwardly with the arm holding the book, but he ignored me and did not move.

"Death has come for you, you thief, you dog," he screamed, consumed with rage, seemingly oblivious of me entirely.

I followed his gaze and saw the man he was focused on in the front-most rank. Like the other guards, the man wore a long byrnie covered with a black warrior coat. On his arm there was a small circular shield and there was an iron helm upon his head. The helm had a simple nasal guard that covered some of his face, but I could see enough of his features to recognise him.

"Ghalib," I muttered.

"Come on," shouted Hereward. "Leave him."

He was right, in a few heartbeats we would be cut off from our companions and any chance of escape.

"Forget him," I shouted at Imad, once more trying to cajole

him forward. Drosten joined me, taking a fistful of Imad's robe with his free hand and pulling him along with us. Again, Imad shrugged me off. He fought against Drosten, refusing to follow. "If you stay, you'll die," I said.

"Then Ghalib will die with me," he snarled, lost to the fury of his vengeance.

His blind anger reminded me of Cormac. I have known several men like this in my life. Men for whom sense and reason are burnt away by the heat of their desire for revenge. I too have succumbed to the seductive allure of violence, too often to count, but even at such time when my blood has seemed to sear my veins and I have wanted nothing more than to strike down my enemies, I have not allowed myself to be blinded. Gwawrddur had taught me that, even though a man crazed and raving with ire can be a formidable foe, the thinking man is more dangerous than the raging savage.

And even all those years ago, I had learnt that there was nothing to be gained in trying to argue with a man when his heart was set on battle.

Shaking my head, I turned away. Revna and Hereward had waited, and now we started running again, leaving Imad behind. Wahid made no effort to join us. He watched us in silence from where he stood by his shield-brother, grim-faced, his cheek gleaming with blood.

I wondered if perhaps it was already too late, that the interruption would prove fatal, for where there had been open ground moments before, a dozen men had now congregated. More were moving to join them, Ghalib amongst them.

In that moment, as one, Imad and Wahid let out a piercing, ululating howl and threw themselves at the man they had once followed. The line of warriors trembled at the ferocity of their assault, slowing them from joining their comrades in blocking our path.

Twelve men stood directly between Revna, Hereward,

Drosten and me, and the arched door to the steps. They were armoured and their sword blades shone in the dawn light. We were formidable fighters, but even as brave and skilled as we were, we did not wear byrnies, nor did we carry shields. To face these guards head on would likely prove disastrous, and yet it seemed the Lord had not forsaken us.

Their attention was split. Some had been distracted by the sudden brutality of Imad and Wahid's assault on the other cadre of tower guards, while a few had turned towards Runolf and Gwawrddur, who had run ahead. If we struck now, without hesitation, we might still have a chance.

Hereward had also recognised the opportunity. He bellowed, lowering the second spear he had snatched up in the tower, and increased his pace.

"With me!" he roared. "Don't stop!"

A guard took the spear's steel point on his shield. It dug deeply into the hide-covered board and Hereward heaved the shield to one side. Beside Hereward, Drosten did not slow. Leaping into the gap made by the missing shield, he hacked down with his sword. The Pict's tattooed face was terrifying as blood misted the air pink about him. A blade flicked towards Drosten's head. I cried out, thinking he would be slain, but he swayed away, ducking beneath the flickering steel and delivering a crunching punch with his left hand into the swordman's face. The guard's lips split against his teeth and he toppled backwards, his mouth full of blood.

Hereward had relinquished the spear now and had drawn his sword. Together with Drosten, the two warriors forced the tower guards back. Gripping the book tightly, I entered the fray. Revna was close on my right. We were still moving quickly, following into the breach made by Drosten and Hereward. They had already killed or injured three men, but there were still too many of them. The foe-men had been before us, Drosten and Hereward shoving them back, then, without warning, we were surrounded. We had moved ahead, only to be halted by the weight of their numbers.

"Revna!" I screamed, as she disappeared, falling down to be swallowed up in the maelstrom of slicing and hewing blades.

My stomach twisted at the thought I had lost her. I parried a sword, feeling the shock of it along my arm, then flicked a riposte into my opponent's wrist. He dropped his weapon with a squeal and pulled back, giving me a moment to look for Revna. I prayed that she might only be wounded, that with God's grace I would be able to heal her. If she had fallen... I could not face the thought.

As suddenly as she had vanished, Revna stood beside me again as if she had never gone. I blinked, not understanding what had happened. A man with a thick black beard raised his sword and brought it down towards her head. I cried out a warning, but she had already seen the danger and lifted a shield up to take the blow. She pushed the bearded man's blade away on the shield's board, then with the speed I had come to respect when we trained together, she slashed her blade across his throat. The man fell back, his neck and chest streaming with dark blood before he was lost to view. All about us, the morning was filled with the clangour of battle and death. Revna grinned at me.

"I needed a shield," she shouted.

On hearing her words, I felt a stabbing pain in my left arm. I looked down. A sword had stabbed hard into the leather cover of *The Treasure of Life*, the blade cutting my forearm in the process. Without thinking, I twisted my body, yanking against the book and pulling the sword out of line. Then, without pause, I hammered a blow down on the wielder's helmeted head. The sound was as loud as the warning bell had been, clanging in the press of bodies. The man staggered back, releasing his grip on his sword and vanishing behind his comrades.

Momentarily, there was space around us. Hereward and

Drosten both stood, their swords flashing, cutting, smashing down on the guards. But the warriors we faced were no fools, they had byrnies and shields and had understood our weakness and their strength. No matter how skilled we were, they were numerous and we were few. Pulling back, they gave us room, interlocking their shields to hold us at bay until the rest of the guards could arrive and bring overwhelming force to bear against us.

"Back-to-back," snapped Hereward.

Instantly, we formed our own organised unit, each with our back to the others, looking outward at the shields and the angry, fearful eyes of our enemies. The ground was slippery with the blood of those we had killed. We had caused mayhem in their ranks, but it had not been enough. If we could not be free of this wall of shields in moments, we would be lost.

"Sorry that it ends like this," I said, speaking as much to myself as to the others.

"End?" said Revna. "Who said anything about ending? I'm too young to go to Valhöll."

I shook my head at her bravado. She did not have her father's size, but she had certainly inherited his spirit.

One of the guards lunged at me, and I batted away his blade. Men were shouting in the distance and I wondered if Imad and Wahid were dead. Had they succeeded in killing Ghalib? I hoped so, it would make this whole sorry escapade less of an abject failure.

"I can see no way out of this," I said, sorrow and grief flooding through me. There was so much I wanted to do, so many things I had yet to witness and experience.

"For a man who was a monk," Revna said with a lopsided grin, "you have very little faith."

I frowned, wondering at her words. Then the shieldwall around us shook and parted, warriors falling away to left and right as if struck with a great boulder.

Forty-Three

The boulder was Runolf. He crashed into their ranks sword in hand, his huge bulk bludgeoning men out of his way. Gwawrddur was with him, blades flashing. In his left hand he held a long knife he had picked up from somewhere. Together, the two warriors cut a swathe of slaughter through the guards.

Reaching us, Runolf offered a grin very much like Revna's of moments before.

"No time to dawdle here," he said.

We followed him and Gwawrddur at a breathless run back towards the arch that led to the steps down into the rock.

"I thought we were lost," I said, panting.

"As if we would leave you to face death alone," Runolf said. "Are we not kin?" His words warmed me, but we were still far from safety and my despair yet lingered at the edges of my mind. "Besides," he went on, "I had to come back for Drosten."

"Drosten?"

"Yes," he said, "he promised he was going to help me defend this doorway. Remember?"

Several guards were running after us. Arrows skittered across the cobbles as archers on the walls tried to pick us off. We did not slow our pace and none of the missiles hit us. One projectile flicked up from the stones and struck the ankle of the foremost pursuer. He stumbled, letting out a cry of dismay. Losing his balance, he fell headlong onto the cobbles. The man directly behind him had to dart to the side to avoid being tripped. The next warrior tried to hurdle the fallen guard, but the injured man was already pushing himself up, causing the one who was jumping to collide with him. Both of them sprawled to the ground.

More arrows fell, but the guards called up to the archers to halt for fear they might injure more of their own. In the moment of confusion caused by the arrows and the fallen men, we skidded into the arched opening.

"Down, down!" bellowed Runolf, no humour in his tone now. "We will defend this place as long as we can."

Runolf had picked up a fallen shield. Revna offered her own to Drosten. The opening was narrow enough that the two warriors would be able to hold back countless foe-men for some time. But their wyrd was written if they stayed there. In the end they would fall. A lucky spear thrust, or an arrow over the heads of their attackers would see them wounded or slain, and then Aljany's guards would swarm down the steps into the depths of the mountain after the rest of us. Runolf and Drosten would certainly slow them, but they had no hope of stopping them.

"No," I shouted, pulling them both back. "I have a plan."

For a heartbeat, Runolf stared at me, conflicting emotions playing over his features. His blood was up and he wished for nothing more than to protect the rest of us, his friends and his daughter, giving us enough time to escape.

"Are we not kin?" I asked, repeating his own words back at him. "You think I would leave you here to face death alone?"

Close by, the guards were forming a shieldwall, lowering their spears and marching forward in an orderly fashion. Behind them, I could see several archers jostling for position on the walkways that ran along the walls.

Runolf's jaw was set and I knew he had not yet made up his mind. But there was no time for debate.

"Close the door and follow me," I shouted.

They would either heed my words or stand at the doorway and fall. I prayed they would see sense, but it was in the Lord's hands now. Shoving my way past Hereward and Gwawrddur, I hurried down the stone steps into the darkness.

After a dozen paces it grew too dark for a headlong rush. I slowed, sheathing my sword. I remembered the layout of the steps and recalled that they were evenly spaced, so despite barely being able to see anything, I trusted my instincts, innate balance and God, and continued down more quickly than would have been prudent if we had not had dozens of armed men in pursuit.

The sound of the door being slammed echoed down the stone passage and complete blackness engulfed us. Perhaps not complete darkness. I hesitated, closing my eyes for a moment, then opening them again and peering forward into the inky dark. There was a faint glow ahead that had been imperceptible when the fingers of the dawn light had been allowed in through the open door.

"The lantern is where we left it," I said to myself as much as to my friends. "Make haste."

Behind us, something heavy struck the timbers of the door with a booming thud. I heard my companions speed up their pace. Hereward fell with a scrape and a clatter, followed by a curse.

"Up and onwards," said Gwawrddur, heaving him to his feet again.

My left arm ached from clutching *The Treasure of Life*. My sleeve was damp with blood and my forearm throbbed as if I had been stung by a wasp. But as I descended the stairs and the light grew ever brighter, I twisted and flexed my arm as best I could whilst holding the book, ascertaining the extent of my injury. It hurt, but I thought the wound not deep. I could move the arm and would be able to use it in a fight if it should come to that.

I rounded the corner and the light was suddenly shockingly bright. It emanated from the lantern we had left in the niche outside of the alchemists' cell. Squinting against its glare, I bounded down the steps to the door. Behind me, I could hear my friends shuffling down the first flight of steps in the dark. Behind them came the sounds of the door splintering.

Reaching the landing by the cell, I dropped the book beside the door. Using both hands I grasped the stout locking bar, pulled it from its groove in the rock and flung it aside. Pulling the door open, I hurried inside. The air was heavy with the stink of the recently killed Gallienus. The iron bite of blood, the sour stench of piss and the foetid odour of spilt bowels overpowered the smells I had previously identified that pertained to the manufacture of ink and books. But nothing could completely mask the acrid, biting aromas of the compounds stored behind the metal-lined door. It was so dark in there, I could hardly see anything. I did not wish to step in Gallienus' congealing blood, or to fall over his corpse, so I gave that side of the room a wide berth and collided painfully with the table. Feeling about in the gloom, I found what I was looking for, and hurried back to the lantern in its stone niche outside.

The others were just arriving, their faces gaunt and strange in the red glow of the lantern. The shadows were black all about us and it felt almost intimate, as if there was nothing outside of that flame's glow. Then came the crash of the door to the courtyard being forced open and the sound of heavy boots on the steps. Shouted orders and curses echoed down to us. The guards would be upon us in moments.

"Well, what's your plan, Killer?" asked Runolf.

Ignoring his use of Gwawrddur's name for me, I bent to

the lantern, lighting the candle I had taken from the table. Hurrying back into the cell, I called over my shoulder.

"Throw the table and stools at the far side of the landing." I glanced at the books and parchment on the table, feeling breathless with regret at what I was proposing. "Anything that will burn."

Without pause I moved quickly across the room. I shielded the candle flame with my hand, but its light dimmed alarmingly and I thought it might go out completely. I stopped at the rear of the room and the flame grew bright once more. Setting down the candle on the stone floor, I yanked open the metal door. I could hear shouts on the stairs and the crash of the furniture from the cell being hurled out of the door and onto the landing. But I did not turn to look. There was no time. My heart hammered against my ribs as I grasped the nearest crate. My arm hurt from the effort of lifting the heavy box down from the stack. With a grunt, I carried it out backwards, dumping it onto the flagstones of the cell floor. I was breathing heavily, my panting breath making the candle flame flap and the shadows dance. Praying that the flame would not instantly ignite the fumes from the contents of the box, I tugged open its lid.

The sound of chaotic fighting filled the subterranean tunnels now. From the corner of my vision I could see shadows locked in a struggle outside the door. Frantically, I heaved at the lid. It was tight and at first it barely budged. Grinding my teeth, I grunted and pulled as hard as I was able. Finally, so suddenly that I almost lost my balance and fell, the lid flew off and clanged to the ground. Without waiting to see if the contents would burst into flames, I rammed my hands inside and pulled out two of the spherical earthenware fire pots.

Rising up, I saw that the table and stools were gone. Feathers, pots and a few sheets of vellum were strewn about the cell. One large scroll had fallen onto Gallienus' corpse, covering his terror-stricken face as if someone had placed it there to spare us having to look upon his dull, accusing eyes.

I rushed out of the door, the two globes held high. The scant light from the lantern struggled to illuminate everything and everyone on that landing, but after a heartbeat I was able to make out enough details in the surging shapes and flickering shadows to know I could not proceed with my plan immediately.

Runolf and Drosten, true to their word, were fending off the first spear-men who had descended the steps. My friends were behind the makeshift barrier of the overturned table and stools. A book lay there too, its pages splayed open. With a lurching twist of my heart, I glanced down and let out a sigh of relief. *The Treasure of Life* was where I had left it, beside the door and far from the barricade.

"Get the candle," I said to Revna, nodding back into the cell and holding up the earthenware vessels for her to understand my purpose.

Without a word she darted inside.

A brave guard attempted to leap over the barricade while his comrade thrust forward with a spear. Runolf gutted the first man, shoving him roughly backwards to add his body to the obstruction. Drosten caught the second man's spear-point on his shield, hacking at the haft until the guard pulled the weapon back out of reach.

"When I give the order," I shouted, raising my voice above the din in the enclosed space, "fall back and go down the stairs."

Runolf stepped forward, hacking down with his sword into the body of the dying man. The Norseman made no indication he had heard me. He looked as if he might attempt to climb over the obstacles and fight his way back up towards the light. Drosten shuffled forward, sword and shield held before him, clearly meaning to stand beside Runolf no matter what the consequences.

Revna emerged from the cell. Her face was lit brightly by the candle and for the first time I noticed that her smooth cheek was spattered with blood.

"Do you hear me?" I roared, desperation entering my voice.

"We hear you, Killer," said Drosten. "Only the dead would not hear your bellowing."

I prayed that we would not soon join the unhearing dead and turned to Hereward and Gwawrddur, who both stood at the top of the steps that led down to the other cells, the well and storeroom, and the secret tunnel that, with God's grace, we might yet still use to escape.

"Go down," I said to them. "Give us room."

Nodding, Hereward made his way down half a dozen steps. Gwawrddur followed him.

"You too," I said to Revna. "Take the candle, and don't let it go out."

She joined the two men. Before me, on the other side of the barricade, more guards had come down the steps, filling the landing with their shouts and the gleaming points of their spears. Just by sheer weight of numbers they would soon push the barricade aside, even if that meant that their leaders would die on Drosten and Runolf's blades. I had to act now.

"Back! Now!" I screamed, praying that the Lord was still watching over us, for there was much that could go wrong.

Drosten flung a spear he had taken from a foe, then moved towards me. Runolf roared and swept his sword down at the shaft of a probing spear, catching another of the wicked iron points on his tattered shield. I thought he might ignore my call, then, with another great howling roar that made the fortress guards hesitate, Runolf leapt back.

As soon as they were both clear of the barricade, the guards, seeing an opportunity, surged forward, scrabbling to climb over the broken furniture. There was no time to think now. I flung the first of the earthenware pots at the advancing men who clambered over the splintered timbers of the table and the jumbled stools. The fire pot struck the leg of one of the guards and fell to the ground. To my horror, it did not shatter as I had expected. The guards did not even slow, barely registering what had happened.

Lord Almighty, I implored, *help deliver Your servant now with righteous fire.*

I was uncertain what exactly would happen when the flasks broke, but I knew enough to know that the contents needed to escape.

The first guard had cleared the debris now. Runolf made to move forward again, but I shoved him back towards the stairs, my desperation lending me strength. Taking a deep breath, I threw the second orb down at the man's feet, directly onto the flagstones. This time, the clay ball shattered into myriad pieces, spilling a dark, noxious-smelling liquid onto the floor and spattering up the guard's leg. The smell caught in the back of my throat, sending my memories flying back to the horror I had witnessed from the bridge in Qurtuba.

The guard looked down. Raising his eyes again, he stared at me. He was a tall, broad-chested man with a thick, dark beard. His nose was twisted and his brows heavy in the way of a brawler.

"You are going to die now, boy!" he spat.

He took another step closer, holding his sword and shield high. The huge red-haired Norseman and the painted Pict who had defended the barricade had both retreated and now there was nobody before him but a young man with no weapons in his hands.

Sweeping the lantern from its niche on the wall, I flung it down onto the ground. The oil within spilt out, fire running along the stone floor. The Roman Fire caught with a sighing whoosh. The warrior's expression changed from one of furious defiance to abject terror as his clothes ignited. Flames licked up his legs and over his torso. More of the thick black liquid had dribbled out of the broken ball of clay and the heat from the sudden flames was intense. I moved away, watching as black smoke began to billow up from the burning man. The men on the barricade faltered, pulling back from their companion, who screamed as his beard caught fire and his head was wreathed in searing flame.

Runolf pushed me aside. Using the leg of a splintered stool he shoved the warrior backwards onto the barricade. The man stumbled and fell, still screaming and writhing in agony as the hungry fire gorged itself on his flesh. The flames were still raging, though I thought perhaps the intensity was already dying down. There had not been a huge amount of the Roman Fire in the earthenware ball that had broken. But as I watched, where drops of the liquid touched the wood of the barricade or the pages of the books, so they flared to flame instantly. The smoke was growing thicker too, roiling up from the wailing warrior and the burning wood.

"Get back," snarled Runolf, pulling me backwards when I did not move.

As I stumbled back, colliding with the cell's door jamb, the second orb exploded. Shards of pottery peppered the ceiling, and flames spouted high into the smoke-hazed air. Such was the force of the blast, that the table and the dying warrior were both flung up from the floor. When they landed, both aflame now, it was clear the fire would not be extinguished any time soon.

I could barely see the guards beyond the barricade. They shimmered and fluttered behind the wall of flame. Their shouts were loud, but the roaring rush of the fire was louder.

I began to cough and my eyes were streaming with tears. Looking up I saw that the ceiling was already obscured with dark smoke that rolled along like a black, twisting serpent.

"We cannot stay here," I said to Runolf, sputtering. "Our only hope now is to reach the door in the mountain before they find it."

I started down the stairs, before suddenly remembering *The Treasure of Life*. I had almost left it propped there against the wall. Turning, I made to hurry back for it. But Runolf had already stooped and retrieved it.

I nodded my thanks, holding out my hand for the book. But rather than handing it to me, he shook his head, then, without warning or hesitation, he turned and threw *The Treasure of Life* onto the huge conflagration.

Forty-Four

"What have you done?" I screamed, the fury I felt at Runolf as incandescent as the Roman Fire that now consumed the book I had sought for years. I ran up the steps, meaning to snatch *The Treasure of Life* from the flames before it could be destroyed. The heat on my face was too intense and I watched in horror as the fire engulfed the book, charring the leather cover and turning the parchment pages to ash before my eyes.

Runolf placed a hand on my shoulder, pulling me away from the bonfire. Tears streamed from my eyes, as much from rage as from the stinging smoke that was quickly filling the passage. On the other side of the blaze, I could just make out the shapes of the guards. Their voices were muffled by the flames as they shouted for water to tackle the fire.

I shook off Runolf's hand and rounded on him, raising my fists to strike. He held the scored and tattered shield before him. I knew it would have been useless to attack him. He would fend me off easily with the shield, and I was no match for his strength and size.

"Why?" I asked, my ire still as hot, but my voice dropping to a barely audible whisper. "Why?" Runolf knew how much the book meant to me and I could see no reason for his actions.

"You are better off without that book, Hunlaf," he replied, his face hard and cold in the heat-glow of the flames.

"I have searched for it for years. People have given their life for that book…" My voice died on my lips. I could not put into words the anger I felt in that instant. I had thought of Runolf as my friend, my kin, and now he had betrayed me.

But if I had expected him to show remorse or regret, I was disappointed. Runolf glowered, his lips curling back from his teeth in a snarl as his own anger surged within him.

"That book was cursed!" he yelled, the power of his passion making his voice crack. "You are right. Many have died for it. Estrid was killed because of your accursed book. And Revna…" His voice faltered. "Revna…" He could not continue and I knew he was thinking of the hellish existence his daughter had endured with Chlotar and Ljósberari. He shook with emotion and I lowered my fists. Turning, he walked down the steps towards the others.

"Come on," urged Hereward. "It is only a book. Our lives are more important."

I nodded, but said nothing.

Only a book.

Only a book.

His words reminded me of Leofstan. He had said the same, that there was no magic in the vellum pages of *The Treasure of Life,* for such power only comes from God. But still this was a book filled with knowledge and teaching; pages of text and drawings that should have been studied by the keenest minds of Christendom.

It was surely nothing more than a book, a collection of scratchings on parchment. And yet Leofstan had become obsessed with *The Treasure of Life,* just as Scomric had. That obsession appeared to have contaminated all who had come into contact, or studied the tome and the teachings of Mani. I thought of Abu Jafar Yusuf ibn Sa'īd al-Zarqālluh's words in

Qurtuba and how he seemed to relish burning men alive. Was it possible that Runolf was right? Could the book have been cursed?

I suppose I can never be certain of the true nature of the book, but despite Leofstan's assertions that it possessed no magical power, as I followed the others down the stairs, leaving the tome to be destroyed in the savage heat of the fire, my rage ebbed away like acid dribbling from a cracked pot. Leaving the bitter smoke behind, the air grew fresher the further down we descended and I drew in great lungfuls of cool, clean air. I was sorrowful that the learning within the book had been destroyed, but as my anger dissipated, so it was replaced by a calm serenity I had not felt for a long time.

We were soon far from the light of the fire. Revna shielded the candle flame with her hand, the small pool of illumination guiding our steps ever downward. The sounds of the conflagration and the shouts of the guards were distant and muted by the time we reached the storeroom.

Gwawrddur opened the door, sword in his right hand. The candle flame flickered and guttered. The tears on my face cooled against my soot-smeared cheeks as a breeze blew from the doorway.

"Careful with the light," hissed Hereward. "And be ready for anything when we reach the door out onto the mountain. There is no telling what awaits us there."

None of us spoke. I drew my sword. Gwawrddur stepped into the storeroom, followed by Hereward. Tentatively, Revna, cupping her fingers around the candle, moved behind them. It felt like an age since we had travelled this way, but nothing had changed and in truth, though much had occurred, less time had passed than the interval between the offices of Lauds and Prime. We moved as quickly as we could past the yawning darkness of the well and the looming barrels and bales that were stacked high against the walls.

At the rear of the storeroom, we found the secret door partially hidden behind the timber box I had noticed earlier. The door was slightly ajar and the draught here was noticeable. Revna turned away from the door, using her body to protect the delicate candle flame, while Hereward and Gwawrddur opened the door fully.

We stood there in silence, listening to the darkness. Far off, echoing and distant, I could make out the shouts of the guards. But from down the dark tunnel there was nothing but hushed blackness.

Hereward ducked his head to enter the tunnel and turned to me.

"When we are all inside," he said. "Do your best to conceal the door. Once they get that fire under control, we don't want it obvious where we have gone."

I wondered how many of the fortress guards knew about the secret tunnel. If there were a few with that knowledge, it wouldn't matter how well concealed the door was. They would find the exit soon enough, as it would be clear we had not left via the stairs.

I nodded and did not voice my concerns.

With the door open wide, the breeze lessened somewhat, and Revna was able to keep the flame burning behind her steadying hand. After Runolf had crouched down and shuffled into the darkness, I backed in, dragging the large box as close as I could, then pulling the door closed. The cut on my forearm stung as it bumped against the door frame, but I barely registered the pain. My mind still reeled from the loss of the book.

Even to this day, decades later, I cannot say whether *The Treasure of Life* was truly cursed. I know that Leofstan told me there was no magic in it. But the scriptures speak of sorcery and idols, so could it not be that a book might indeed possess an evil power? But whatever the truth of it, the buzz of energy I had felt as we had grown ever closer to the book had vanished, like smoke in a strong wind.

We shuffled down the tunnel, Revna's candle providing just enough light for us to make our way without fear of tripping or banging our heads. After a time, Gwawrddur cursed and we halted.

"What is it?" I hissed.

Nobody answered.

"Watch your step," Hereward said, his tone hushed and sombre.

We continued on and I saw what had caused them to pause. On the cold stone of the tunnel floor lay the guard that Imad had knocked senseless. His bindings and gag were still in place, and he was unmoving. His throat had been cut from ear to ear. Blood had puddled beneath him and it was impossible to avoid it completely in the narrow tunnel.

Warily, I stepped over the man's corpse, shivering as the dancing light of the candle flame made it appear as if he was still moving in the shadows.

There was a new light ahead. We carried on towards it and a moment later, Revna blew out the candle, setting it down and drawing her sword. The door at the end of the tunnel was half open and the light of the early morning shone in, slicing the darkness like a golden blade.

We huddled there in the glow of the dawn, allowing our eyes to grow accustomed to the morning light.

"God alone knows what lies beyond this door," whispered Hereward. "Prepare yourselves, and with God's grace and some luck we will make it back to our camp. From there, we can strike out to the coast and leave this godforsaken land behind us."

He looked at each of us in turn, and I flicked my gaze over my companions. All of us were grim-faced and apprehensive. Even Revna, whose beauty could not be hidden with soot, blood and dirt, looked tense, her jaw set and hard against what might await us beyond the door.

I gripped my sword tightly and bit my lip, wondering whether the book's curse had been lifted with the coming of the dawn, or if death lurked in the morning light of the mountains.

"Ready?" asked Hereward.

Despite my misgivings, I nodded, along with the others. What else could we do?

Hereward drew in a long breath, pushed the door open and stepped out into the light.

Forty-Five

We rushed out of the doorway and into the dawn. The cleft in the mountainside was deep and narrow. The light from the rising sun had yet to reach the secret entrance, but the sky above us was pale blue streaked with bronze.

Hereward hurried along the ravine some way, making space for the rest of us outside the door. My skin prickled as I imagined men lying in wait for us, ready to loose arrows and throw spears down upon us. Waiting in that place in the darkness, unseen by the men on the soaring walls of the fortress, had made my heart pound with anxiety. Now, with sunlight painting the castle walls gold and with the slopes of the mountains all around bright, warm and clear, I felt terribly exposed. Even if no men were waiting to ambush us, surely we would be spotted by the wardens who manned the ramparts.

But no shout of alarm came. No biting spear. No deadly dart from a bow whistled down to bury itself in our flesh. I peered up at the fortress, wondering how long we could hope to go without being seen. There were enough warriors inside Aljany's stronghold that they would be able to swarm out of the gate and head us off as we attempted to flee down the mountainside.

The walls were starkly lit in the morning light, hard-edged

and imposing. I could see no sentries between the crenelations. I offered up a prayer of thanks, for surely the Lord's hand was in this. We had fought and killed several of the guards, and started a fire that would prove difficult to combat for a time, but we were still few, and our foe many. It seemed inconceivable to me that not a single pair of eyes watched for sign of us or other threats from the walls.

"There's nobody up there," I said in an amazed whisper.

"Best we don't tarry then," said Hereward.

He opened his mouth to say more, when the earth shook beneath our feet. A hollow booming thud rang out. Pebbles trickled down from the rocks all about us, and a boulder the size of a barrel teetered for a heartbeat, before toppling over and rolling down the steep slope, snapping and crashing through the scrub as it picked up speed.

Luckily the rock was some distance from us and fell away from the ravine in which we stood. I stared up at the fortress again and saw now a black plume of smoke rising from where the subterranean steps came out into the courtyard.

"An impressive explosion," said a voice behind me. "Unless I am mistaken, I would guess that was the remainder of the Roman Fire."

I spun around, nervous and on edge, but even before I saw the speaker, I had recognised the voice.

"You waited for us, then," I said.

Giso stood in the shade of a bent oak. He had the calm appearance of someone out for a morning stroll. Beside him sat Praetextatus. The alchemist was staring up at the smoke in the sky. Tracks of tears streaked his dejected-looking face.

"I would not have waited much longer," said Giso. "But I had faith in the heroes of Werceworthe." He grinned. "I was not so sure of those two Moors," he said, noticing that Imad and Wahid were missing. "The Lord God protects His own."

The man's flippant tone needled me.

"They fell in the courtyard," I said. "They fought bravely and had a score to settle. Without them, we might not have made it."

"The Lord is mysterious. He uses whatever tool is best suited to his work. Even infidels and pagans."

Another explosion made the ground tremble. The shrubs rattled as if in a sudden breeze and more stones and rocks were dislodged from the mountain.

"Ah," Giso said, holding up a finger, "I was wrong. But that must surely be the last of it now."

I noticed that his hand was dark with blood.

"You didn't have to kill that man," I said, my tone clipped.

Giso raised an eyebrow.

"What man?"

"You know full well," I said. "The guard in the tunnel."

Giso shrugged.

"Perhaps you are right," he said. "But who can say what they must or must not do? I thought it best to leave one less enemy behind me." He glanced up at the smoke darkening the sky above the fortress walls. "Have you not slain in pursuit of what you sought, Hunlaf?" He quickly flicked his gaze over us all. "Not that it seems to have done you much good. I do not see the book or the silver. At least I have killed with a purpose."

I stepped closer to the small man. His words infuriated me and I wanted to lash out at him.

"It is not the same," I hissed.

"But who are you to judge that?" he said, his tone suddenly as chill as the North Sea in winter. "I will be judged by the Almighty when I stand before His throne. As will you for your actions, young Hunlaf. Or should I call you Killer, as your friends do."

"You are not my friend."

He feigned a sorrowful expression, pushing out his lower lip.

"You sadden me."

"Enough of this," snapped Hereward, stepping between us. "There is no time for bickering now. We have a chance to escape while Aljany's men are otherwise engaged. Let us not waste the opportunity that God has given us."

I bit my lip and gripped my sword so tightly that my fingers hurt. I clenched my left hand and my forearm stung from where my bunching muscles tugged at the cut there, setting it bleeding again. Rage boiled up within me. The loss of the book was still as fresh as the wound and I was furious at Runolf for what he had done. And I felt a deep, burning loathing for Giso. I had considered the Frank a fine Christian, but now I knew that he would allow nothing to stand in his path, even if that meant placing his immortal soul in jeopardy. But more than this, I was furious that Giso had made me reflect on who I was and what I was prepared to do in order to obtain what I sought.

I have ever been driven, a man who is single-minded and stubborn in the face of adversity. I am old now, and long since have I accepted who I am and the sins I have committed. But then, in the cool dawn of that early summer's day in al-Andalus, I did not enjoy the feeling of having a light shone onto the darker side of my character.

A hand on my arm startled me out of my enraged reverie. Snarling, I spun around, ready to strike whoever had dared to touch me.

"Calm yourself, Hunlaf," Revna said, her eyes wide and gleaming. "Hereward is right. We must go, while nobody is watching for us."

Ashamed, I pulled back from her. My face was hot and I mumbled an apology. Hereward had already set off down the ravine and Giso was pulling Praetextatus to his feet. Not wishing to have the treacherous Giso at my back, I waited for them to begin walking, then followed after them.

The sky behind us was black. The pall of smoke, ever thicker, rose high into the pale morning. Looking around us as we scrambled down through the gullies and ravines, the serried peaks of the mountains vanished into the hazed distance. The sky was the pallid blue of a starling's egg. To the south billowed the plume of dark smoke from the fortress. To the north, smoke from the cooking fires in the nearest settlement smudged the horizon, indicating where others inhabited the sparsely populated mountain range.

Climbing up to the fortress had taken us what had seemed an age in the darkness of the night, but now, with light to guide our path, we made good time. Soon we stepped into an open bowl of rock, surrounded on all sides by boulders. From here it was possible to see the walls and tower of the fortress high on its crag, but also, by crouching behind the rocks it would be easy to keep hidden from the stronghold and also remain unseen from the lower slopes of the mountain.

Giso had taken the lead since leaving the secret door, handing over responsibility for Praetextatus to Hereward who held the young man's arm and trudged silently behind the Frank. Praetextatus sniffed and snivelled as he walked, making all of us uneasy. But none of us chastised him. He had lost much, his past was dark and his future uncertain.

Giso stopped, holding up his blood-stained hand for us to halt. Quickly, with apparent urgency, Giso looked about the hollow, picking up a twig here, a scuffed stone there. Frowning, he turned to Hereward and the rest of us.

"This is where we left Imad's men."

"We told them to head back to the camp if dawn came and we had not returned," said Hereward.

"Yes," said Giso, scratching at his beard, "yes, we did. Let us hope we find them there."

Without speaking further, he turned and continued down the dusty path that led between shrubs and rocks.

"What do you think he saw?" I asked Gwawrddur. I wanted to ask Giso, but after my outburst, I could not address him directly.

"I am not sure," replied the Welshman. "But something is not right. Can you not feel it? Be wary and have your sword ready."

Gwawrddur's words unnerved me, but I pressed on close behind the others. I searched the shadow-strewn slopes for signs of danger, but saw nothing save for a huge eagle that launched suddenly into the air, flapping its great wings angrily until it was high enough above the ground to soar and glide on the wind.

I shuddered, thinking of Runolf's god, Óðinn, and his two ravens that flew over the land to report back to their master. I squinted up at the eagle. It circled high above us, and I imagined it looking down upon the inconsequential actions of the tiny men on the earth far below. Was that how God thought of us? Were we akin to insects to Him? Were our actions of no true consequence?

I looked away from the bird of prey, shaking my head to clear it of such blasphemous thoughts. Behind us, the fortress burnt, sending up ever thicker clouds of smoke. We may not have retrieved our silver, and *The Treasure of Life* had been destroyed, but it seemed clear to me that once more the Lord God Almighty had helped us. There was no way that any of the men from the fortress would come in search of us now; they would be too occupied attempting to put out the fire. Besides, they might well believe we had been killed in the blasts as the reserves of Roman Fire ignited deep underground.

Reaching the small stream where we had tethered the mules, we hesitated, surveying the clearing for any signs of danger. The mules were where we had left them. Sensing our presence, one of the beasts looked up from where it had been drinking and stared at us, its ears flicking at the flies that swarmed about its head.

A small fire, mainly embers and ash, smouldered within a circle of rocks in the centre of the clearing. We had not lit a fire for fear of being seen in the night. My skin prickled.

"Where are the men?" I asked. Apart from the beasts of burden, there was nothing and nobody else within sight.

"I know not," replied Giso in a whisper. "Tread carefully."

We made our way cautiously down into the camp. All was calm, the air cool where the sun had yet to rise high enough above the mountains to bathe this part of the valley in light. Revna went to the mules and patted their necks, murmuring to them. She was good with animals and they liked her, responding well to her soft words and touch.

The rest of us looked about the clearing for signs of the men we had expected. We saw none, but Giso spotted a dark patch in the dust and he knelt to examine it more closely.

"Blood?" asked Gwawrddur.

Giso pinched the dust between thumb and forefinger. Nodding, he looked up sombrely.

"Looking for these?" said a gruff voice in al-Arabiyyah.

Giso stood up quickly, pulling his sword from its scabbard and turning in the direction of the voice.

Forty-Six

There was a deep cleft in the ground on the western side of
the camp. Out of that gorge flew a heavy, dark, round object.
For a terrible, heart-stopping moment I thought it was one of
the clay Roman Fire orbs. But when it hit the earth in front of
Giso it did not shatter, but made a dull, wet thudding sound. It
rolled for a time before coming to a halt. It was larger than one
of the Roman Fire balls, and where the orbs were smooth, this
had features. A twisted, broken nose, fleshy lips and shocked
staring eyes beneath a thick mat of black hair. I recognised
the face as belonging to Daud, one of the men Giso had left
watching the family of the fortress guard he had killed in the
tunnel. Daud's head had been severed cleanly, and some time
ago for the skin held the blue-tinged pallor of death and no
blood oozed from the stump of the neck.

Before the grisly object had stopped rolling, so a second
head arced out of the cleft and thumped into the dust near the
fire.

I stared at the heads in horror. Revna gasped. The mules
stamped and brayed in annoyance and fear. I was aware of
movement all around me, as Runolf and the rest of the men
formed into a line; a shieldwall without shields.

They had reacted more quickly than Revna and I. But even

Gwawrddur, Runolf, Drosten and Hereward had been slower than normal to respond to the sudden threat. The severed heads had done their job, shocking us into inaction for long enough to allow our enemies to ready themselves for combat. Even as Revna and I ran forward to join our companions, men were surging up out of the ravine.

They wore the byrnies and the black coats of the fortress guards. Their helms were crowned in black cloth and their shields were covered in blackened hide. The morning sun glimmered from the naked steel of their swords. I counted a dozen such warriors, all dour and grim-faced. At a barked command from an imposing figure who strode out of the gulch at their centre, they halted, raising their shields and swords as one. The man who commanded them raked us with his dark glare and I realised with a start that he was known to me.

"Nadir," growled Runolf, who had also recognised the leader of the guards from Qadis.

Beside Nadir stood a tall, slim man with a well-trimmed beard and sharp, chiselled cheekbones. He wore dark silks over his armour, and his hand rested on the intricately fashioned pommel of a finely crafted sword. He stared imperiously at us down his crooked, aquiline nose. The last time I had seen Tayyib had been on the docks of Qadis, but after speaking to Ahmad in the tower I knew he had been instrumental in much that had happened to us since.

"I apologise for the theatrics," Tayyib said. "But you were right, Nadir. The heads did make them hesitate."

Nadir's flat face twisted in an approximation of a smile.

"And the rest of the men?" asked Giso, his tone measured and calm, as if he was simply discussing the price of cheese at a market stall.

Tayyib held up his hands and replied, using the same calm, almost apologetic tone.

"The four you had left up the mountain arrived not long

before you," he said. "They stood no chance against us. They are down in that gorge. We didn't have time to prepare their heads to welcome you."

"What is he saying?" asked Hereward.

"He is boasting about killing all of Imad's men," I said.

Drosten made a growling sound in the back of his throat and I thought he might charge at the amassed warriors, but a soft word from Gwawrddur stilled him.

Giso and Tayyib ignored the muttered aside and Drosten's growing anger. Nadir showed his teeth in a sneering grin, clearly pleased at the effect the severed heads and Tayyib's words were having on us.

"How did you find them?" Giso asked, nodding at the two heads that lay in the dust near the smoking embers of the fire. I followed his gaze and immediately wished I hadn't when I found myself staring directly into Daud's unseeing eyes.

"Allah guided us to them," Tayyib said. "I thought it likely we had been followed from Išbīliya and decided to head down into the village to see if any of the local peasants had seen strangers in the mountains. Better than that. We discovered two of your men watching over the wife and children of a man who served in the fortress." He sighed and flicked absently at a smudge of dirt on his silk robe. "Before they died they told us everything they knew. We did not think we would reach the fortress in time to warn them or to intercept you, so we made our way here to await your return, in case you managed to avoid capture or death." He raised his eyebrows. "It appears you were somewhat successful in your mission," his eyes flicked first to Praetextatus, who cowered behind our line nervously, then up to the fortress on its crag, where black smoke poured up into the bright sky. He frowned, then shook his head. "Aljany will not forgive you for that," he said. "I take it the other artificer is dead?"

Giso did not reply.

"No matter," Tayyib went on. He gestured towards Praetextatus. "This one will be sufficient." His eyes roved over Revna next. He licked his lips appreciatively. "And I will take the girl for my trouble too. Hand them over and throw down your weapons. If you are lucky, Aljany might keep you alive. He does like to study things from far-off places. Then again," he said with a shrug and a sigh, "death might be preferable."

"Let me guess," said Gwawrddur, "he is telling us to drop our swords."

I nodded, but did not turn to look at the Welshman.

"And to surrender ourselves to capture," I said, "and to hand over Praetextatus."

"We'll not be handing anybody over to these bastards," said Hereward. "Tell him that."

I hesitated, wondering if there might be a better course of action, but when nothing presented itself to me, I repeated Hereward's words in al-Arabiyyah.

Tayyib shook his head in a gesture of mock sorrow that reminded me of Giso.

"I told you they would not surrender," said Nadir, a savage smile on his broad face.

"And once again, my horrid friend, you appear to be right." Raising his voice to address the black-garbed warriors, Tayyib said, "Prepare for combat."

The guards closed ranks, interlocking their shields and taking a step forward.

Runolf looked over his shoulder at Revna. His face was in shadow, but the sun had finally found its way into the hollow and lit Tayyib, Nadir and their warriors in its warming glow.

"Stay with the alchemist," Runolf said to his daughter. "Protect him."

"Father?" she replied, but he turned away from her and glowered at the warriors before us.

"Enough of this talk," he said. "I would rather die than

be thrown again into a dungeon far from the air and light." Runolf's booming voice rose in volume. "These men are all that stand between us and freedom. They have come seeking a fight, let us give them what they want."

Without waiting for our response, he sprang forward with a roar, out of the shadows and into the light of the dawn. His red hair and beard flamed in the sunlight. His sword gleamed as he raised it high over his head.

We only hesitated for a heartbeat. There was no question of standing back and allowing Runolf to attack on his own. Raising our own voices in battle cries, we ran after the giant Norseman and charged at the enemy line.

Forty-Seven

We were outnumbered two to one. For the most part we were unarmoured and did not possess shields or helmets. And yet I felt no fear as we charged their shieldwall. The strange calmness that had fallen over me like a cloak since the destruction of the book vanished in an instant. It was replaced with a dreadful fury. We had come so far, through fire and death, and I would not allow our escape to be thwarted now. I had lost the book and we had lost the silver. Now we faced losing our freedom again and I could not bear the thought of spending the rest of my days tortured in the darkness far beneath the ground in a cell.

As I ran, I took pleasure in the shock etched on the warriors' faces at our sudden, mad attack. Closing the distance to the enemy line, I focused on Tayyib. Ahmad's betrayal had hurt me more than I cared to admit. And looking at the smooth-spoken Tayyib I blamed everything on him. It had been his decision to lend Ahmad silver all those years before, and now he had led Ahmad into betraying us, the very people who had freed him and brought him back to his homeland. I recalled too the lascivious way in which Tayyib had stared at Revna, and I allowed my anger to overflow.

Ahead of me, Runolf batted aside blades and careened into

the shieldwall, followed closely by Hereward and Drosten. Each lending their weight to the wedge they drove through the guards' defence. The ferocity of our sudden attack had startled them, but I noted that Nadir had managed to step behind the line before Runolf could reach him.

But if our sudden rushing attack had unnerved the warriors, Tayyib did not appear in the least concerned. He saw that I was intent on attacking him, but, rather than retreat to be shielded behind the guardsmen, he stepped to the side, drawing his sword from its finely tooled leather and silver-chased scabbard.

Gwawrddur had always told me to keep a tight rein on my emotions in a fight, for the angry adversary is one who is rash and makes mistakes. I had always tried to heed his advice, but now I was incapable of keeping my rage in check. I bellowed my fury at Tayyib. He stepped forward to meet me. His sardonic smile and easy, lithe steps as he dropped into a fighting stance should have given me pause. His relaxed manner in the face of my anger would surely have made me reconsider my course of action, if I had not been so intent on revenge for everything I had lost and all that might yet be taken from me; for what might be done to us if we were captured and the fate that would befall Revna if we were defeated.

Like me, Tayyib did not hold a shield, and he seemed perfectly happy about that. He dropped into a crouch and beckoned for me to approach. I was too angry for fear, but a sliver of unease scratched down the back of my neck. I was fast and skilled with a blade, but I was still no match for Gwawrddur and there was something about Tayyib's fluid movements that reminded me of the Welsh swordsman. Here was a man who was born to wield a blade and who had surely trained with a sword since the moment he could walk.

And yet, despite the warning signs, I did not slow my headlong rush, hoping instead that my anger and strength would allow me to bludgeon my way through Tayyib's defences.

My anger and strength were not enough.

Almost without seeming to move, at the last moment, Tayyib parried my blade and stepped inside my guard. His sword snaked forward in a deadly riposte that would have gutted me if it had not been for the quilted *perpunt* I wore. The blade pierced the material, but I desperately twisted my body and my forward momentum carried me onward. I felt a stabbing pain, as the tip of his sword scoured along my ribs, and then I was past him, and spinning about to face him again.

He had already freed his blade and had turned to face me. I marvelled at his speed as I felt my hot blood streaming down inside the *perpunt*.

All about us was chaos now. A cacophony of shouts and grunts, swords slamming against the hide-covered boards of shields and the tolling crash of blade against blade. As I spun around, I caught a fleeting glimpse of Revna standing white-faced beside Praetextatus. The sight of her filled me with hope and a renewed desire to beat Tayyib, to prevent him from forcing himself upon her.

I lunged at him, but he parried the blow easily, stepping back quickly and counter-attacking with the speed of a striking viper. I had anticipated his riposte, bouncing back on the balls of my feet out of range. Even knowing what he had meant to do I only avoided his sword by a hand's breadth. My fury began to dissipate, as if it dribbled out of me along with the blood that seeped from the sword cut to my side. I wondered if the cut was deeper than I had imagined. Like so often in combat it barely hurt in the moment, but I had sustained enough wounds to know it was bad enough. It would pain me plenty later. If I survived.

And my survival was looking increasingly unlikely.

Perhaps sensing my thoughts, or seeing the growing despair

on my face, Tayyib stood back. The rest of my companions were still fighting, but I dared not look away from Tayyib. Someone was screaming, wailing like a woman in childbirth. I recognised the sound of Drosten's native Pictish, as he hurled unintelligible insults at his foes.

"It is not too late to surrender," Tayyib said, with a thin smile. "Aljany might well keep you alive. He always seeks knowledgeable companions." Without warning, he made a feint at my face with his blade. I flinched, parrying the strike clumsily and leaping backward. Tayyib laughed. "You are not completely unskilled with a blade," he said, "but you are no match for me. You know this to be true."

He was not wrong. I could see no way to survive this encounter. And yet, despite what I saw as my inevitable defeat, I did not consider throwing down my sword. I have many flaws, but perhaps the greatest of them all is my pride. Certainly that is what Abbot Criba, God rest his immortal soul, would have said, and he was not the first to reflect on this defect of mine.

Fear had begun to wrap its cold fingers around my heart. I would surely die if I continued to fight. But whatever my shortcomings, I have never been accused of being craven.

"If you wish to end this," I said, jutting out my chin in defiance, "cast aside your sword. Surrender and call off your men. I give you my word as a Christian your life will be spared." I had no confidence in my ability to deliver on that promise. It seemed more than likely that Runolf and my comrades would slaughter our adversaries. Even if I could convince my friends to stay their hands, Giso had already proven himself to be a cold killer. Still, this did not concern me then. I was certain that Tayyib would refuse my offer. It was more bravado than anything. As I'd expected, he threw his head back and laughed.

"I am almost sorry that I will need to slay you," he said, still chuckling.

Some way from where we faced each other I could hear

the flow of the fight subtly shift. In all battles there are such moments where morale breaks, or a chance event changes the direction of a struggle. Often it is the smallest of things that radically affects a confrontation. A chance blow injuring a leader, a patch of slippery ground causing men to stumble, even bright sunlight shining in the eyes of one side. Whatever the cause now, I could sense that things had changed. I wanted to cast a glance over my shoulder, but my initial blind fury had washed away now and I knew that to turn my attention from Tayyib would be to invite a sudden death.

I bent my legs into the warrior stance, feet apart, right foot forward. Gwawrddur had drilled it into me so often that the position was as natural as walking or breathing. I did not remove my gaze from Tayyib's eyes. With luck or God's grace, I might get the slightest of warnings before he attacked.

"Come on, if you dare," I said, forcing my voice to remain calm. Inside my stomach churned and the words of the Pater Noster tumbled unbidden over and over in my mind.

Tayyib smiled and for what seemed a long time he did not move. The screams of a dying man rose in pitch, filling my ears with their painful screech. Somewhere behind me a sword clanged against another, as loud as a bell. Was this the knell of my death? As that dark thought entered my mind, so Tayyib's eyes narrowed and his right shoulder dropped, giving me an instant's warning.

It was enough to permit me to take a step back, but not sufficient to avoid Tayyib's attack completely. I was fast, but Tayyib was faster than any man I had ever faced before. His sword flickered out towards my throat. There was nothing I could do but parry the thrust, pushing his blade off its line and away from my exposed neck. Our blades connected in a thrumming crash of steel and in that same instant I knew this was what he had intended all along. I had been tricked into the obvious defence and now he gripped my right wrist, raising my sword harmlessly above our heads. Without pause, Tayyib stepped in close, twisting my sword arm painfully, and placing his leg behind mine. He brought his pommel down hard on my head. Bright lights burst behind my eyes and for a moment I could see nothing. The strength left my limbs and I would have surely fallen without any assistance, but Tayyib helped me on my way, applying pressure on my wrist. Losing my balance, I tumbled over his outstretched foot and sprawled into the dust, dazed and half-blind from the blow to my skull.

My blood rushed in my ears, masking all other sound. My vision darkened as I looked up at his sneering face. I tried to lift my sword, desperate to make some show of retaliation, to defend myself one final time. But my hand was empty and I realised through the fog that clouded my mind that I had dropped my weapon. I reached about in the dust, frantically seeking the sword's hilt, like a pagan Norseman wishing to be holding a weapon when death approached, so that Óðinn might see his bravery and reward him with a seat in his hall of the slain. My hand flapped at my side, but I grasped nothing more than dust and pebbles. Tayyib loomed over me, his shadow falling across my face and I knew I would be empty handed when he dealt the killing blow.

Somewhere, far away and muffled as if underwater, a voice was shouting my name. I could not place it, and dimly I wondered which of my friends it belonged to, and which of them were yet alive to witness my death. Was it possible that they would avenge me when I was gone?

Tayyib's features swam above me as tears filled my eyes at the certainty of my impending doom. The sun gleamed bright as Tayyib raised his sword. I closed my eyes and started to pray. Mayhap that sounds like a cowardly act after all I have written in these pages about courage and defiance, but I do not believe it to be so. I did not wail and beg for mercy. And yet I had seen much death in my young life and, in what I thought would be my final moments, I chose to pray for my soul and not to watch the manner of my own slaying.

Whispering the Pater Noster through gritted teeth, I readied myself for Tayyib's final sword thrust.

Forty-Eight

I lay there in the dust, the blood roaring in my ears like a river in spate, and my head throbbing from the savage blow Tayyib had dealt me. As I breathed I felt acutely the sting of the stab to my ribs, the throb of the cut on my forearm. It was as if my body was reminding me of all the physical injuries I had sustained just before my life was to be snatched away.

Without thinking, I recited the Lord's Prayer and concentrated on the aches and pains of my body, of the touch of the dry, gritty dust in my right hand. The hot blood that mingled with my sweat to soak my chest beneath the *perpunt*. I relished all of those feelings, for soon I would be standing before the Lord and would never again know earthly sensations.

But Tayyib's killing blow never came.

Instead, a voice pierced my murmured praying.

"Hunlaf," it called to me. "Hunlaf!"

A hand shook my shoulder, and at last, almost reluctantly, I opened my eyes and stared up into Revna's pale blue gaze. She was close to me, her hair falling about her beautiful, soot-stained face and brushing my cheeks. I noted that blood spattered her chin, nose and forehead. Had I drifted out of consciousness? Had I been senseless for a long time, or only moments? A tear rolled down her cheek and dropped into my eye, making me blink. Revna was crying. Were her tears for me, or had that bastard Tayyib laid a hand on her?

That thought brought me to my senses, though my head still throbbed in agony. Pushing her hands away, I struggled to sit.

"Let me up," I said. I was confused, my mind trying in vain to piece together recent events. All I knew was that Tayyib meant to slay me and to force himself on Revna. That I could not allow.

Squinting from the pain in my head, I scrabbled in the dust for my sword. It lay close by and I grasped it. Groaning, I got my knees beneath me and pushed myself shakily to my feet.

"Where is he?" I asked, swaying unsteadily, sword in hand, looking about us.

Several bodies were strewn on the ground on the brightly lit side of the camp. Runolf, unmissable with his fiery hair and huge height, stood there amidst the slaughter, bloody sword in hand. Gwawrddur and Hereward were there too. They had their arms around Drosten, who sagged woozily between them. I prayed that the Pict's wounds were not fatal, but there was no time to worry about that now. I cast about for Tayyib, but there was no sign of him.

"Did he hurt you?" I asked, my tone sharp with fear for Revna.

"No, Hunlaf," she said, with a savage grin, "but I hurt him right enough." She turned her gaze downward and for the first time I noticed the dark shape there at her feet. "He never knew what hit him."

Tayyib's eyes were half closed, his mouth open as if about to speak. Even in death, his expression was still one of sneering sarcasm. Despite lying in the dust, and clearly quite dead, his features were clean and handsome. Save from the absolute stillness in his face, there was nothing there to indicate he was no longer alive. The top of his head though told a very different tale. His silken hat had been torn away and lay crumpled in the dirt. A deep gash was opened in the crown of his head, exposing bone, blood and soft pink brain matter.

Blinking in an attempt to clear my mind, I looked back to Revna. She held her sword at her side. A few wisps of dark hair and a smear of crimson clung to the blade.

"You saved me," I muttered, imagining how she must have stepped up behind the gloating noble and struck a mighty blow to his head, felling him like an ox at the beginning of winter.

"That is possible," she replied with a smirk.

I stared at her, in awe and still somewhat addled from Tayyib's blow. As I finally understood that I would not die, my legs almost gave way with relief. Revna reached for me, holding me upright. I returned her smile and felt laughter bubbling up within me to replace the fury I had felt moments before.

But before my glee at surviving was able to manifest itself, a shout cut through my befuddled senses.

"I will kill him!" came the bellowed scream in al-Arabiyyah.

I spun around, almost losing my balance and needing to lean heavily on Revna. On the north side of the hollow, far from the fighting, stood Nadir. He gripped Praetextatus tightly before him, holding the young man up on his tiptoes with a vicious-looking dagger pressed under his chin. Behind them, the mules rolled their eyes. High above and distant, the black smoke boiled up from the fortress, the sun on its walls still warm and golden with the dawn. Barely any time had passed since Tayyib had flung me to the ground.

Giso, who, like Nadir, appeared to have somehow avoided the fighting, stood with his back to us. He took a step closer, but halted when Nadir jerked Praetextatus, digging his blade painfully into the man's neck. Thin ghosts of smoke drifted up from the dying fire near Giso's feet.

Runolf walked to our side. He was limping, I saw, and there

was blood on his face and hands. Without a word, he placed an arm around Revna's shoulders, pulling her to him. He rarely showed affection so openly, but she allowed herself to be gathered into his embrace without a word. Gwawrddur and Hereward, half-carrying Drosten, reached us a moment later. Beneath the dirt, soot, spattered blood and tattoos, Drosten's skin was pallid.

Seeing my worried look, the Pict forced a smile. Blood stained his teeth where his lip had been split.

"I'll live, Killer." He raised an eyebrow. "Will you?"

I wondered how bad I looked, and smiled despite the pain. "God willing, I'll live a while yet. Thanks to Revna."

Giso was holding his hands out, palms upward.

"Go ahead, Nadir," he said, in that same calm voice he had used to converse with Tayyib. "Kill him."

Nadir looked about him. He had no allies left standing. The threat to his hostage was the only way out he could see.

"This is what you came for," he shouted, shaking Praetextatus as if he was as light as a child's straw doll. "Grant me safe passage from here, or I swear on sacred *al-Qur'ān* that I will slay the alchemist. Then you will have nothing."

Giso sighed as if bored with the man's outburst.

"I do not respect a man who makes idle threats," he said. "Kill him, or surrender. Either way, we will not let you leave here alive."

Nadir's eyes narrowed. He tightened his grip on the quivering Praetextatus, but still made no move to cut the man's throat, perhaps believing Giso to be bluffing and that he still had a way out of this.

He did not.

Giso reached inside his robes and pulled out a familiar earthenware orb. He held it in his hand, allowing both Nadir and his prisoner to see it. From Nadir's lack of reaction it was clear he did not know what the clay ball held. The young alchemist however let out a howling scream and began to thrash and fight against his captor. But Nadir was too strong for him. Pulling back his hand he clubbed the pommel of his dagger into Praetextatus' head. The young man from Byzantion ceased struggling, his eyes glazing over.

Later, I told myself that perhaps Giso had waited for such a moment, so that the young alchemist would not suffer, but the truth of it is I know Giso cared nothing for the man's suffering.

With a sharp, overarm throw, Giso tossed the earthenware ball down at Praetextatus' feet. It shattered, splattering both men's legs with the dark viscous fluid it held. The noxious smell of the potion that made Roman Fire reached my nostrils. Nadir looked down, confusion on his features.

Without pause Giso stepped forward and kicked the embers from the fire. A great cloud of ash blew up, but a few heavier shards of wood that were still glowing red landed on the dark fluid. With a whispering hiss the liquid caught. An instant later Praetextatus and Nadir's clothing was alight.

Then the screaming began.

There was nothing we could do for them. We turned our back on the two burning men as they collapsed to the ground, writhing and wailing pitifully. Their screams grew in intensity until their throats could make no further sound. The stench of the Roman Fire and their burning flesh was terrible. It clogged my throat, making me gag, and I could taste it for the rest of that long day.

When they ceased burning, there was little left of them but twisted blackened skeletons. The Roman Fire had burnt away all their flesh and clothing; everything that made them men. I recalled the charred remains of Ljósberari's victims and wondered again at *The Treasure of Life*'s role in all this.

Revna bound my wounds, then set about dressing her father's injury – a gash to his left calf. Gwawrddur used some of Tayyib's silk robes to bandage a deep cut to Drosten's thigh.

Then we went about the dead, quickly stripping them of things we could use: weapons, armour, clothing, and strapping what we wished to take with us on the mules.

All the while we did not speak to Giso. He had become like a storm crow to us, a dark, enigmatic presence. We were all accustomed to fighting and death, but there was something calculating and cold about him that unnerved even the hardest of men.

As we trudged away into the mountains, Drosten riding on one of the mules despite his protests, I found myself walking beside Giso.

"So we will return to King Carolus with nothing," I said. I hoped that my words might wound him in the way we had been wounded. We had lost all that we sought and it gave me some pleasure to think that he too, as callous and devious as he was, was also leaving empty handed after all of the perils we had faced.

Giso looked sidelong at me. He tapped his chest, then pulled out from inside his robe a wad of parchments. They were folded, but I could see some of the formula and instructions the alchemists had scratched on the vellum.

"Not quite nothing," Giso said, secreting the papers inside his clothing once more and walking on towards the rising sun, and the far-off coast.

Forty-Nine

"I will not lose my leg to a cut from one of those bastard Moors."

Drosten was drenched in sweat, even though the sun had set some time before and it was cool in the valley where we had made camp in the shade of a copse of twisted oak trees.

We had been travelling as fast as we could for close to a sennight, certain that Aljany and perhaps even the emir himself would send men after us once they learnt of what had occurred at the fortress in the mountains and of our escape.

"If we do not remove the limb, you might well lose your life to it," I said, biting my lower lip.

I was worried about Drosten. Each day he sat swaying as if drunk on the back of the mule, wrapped in a cloak despite the warmth of the sun. The wound in his leg was festering and he had been gripped with fever for days now. I was concerned that the wound-rot had set in. If it had, his only chance of survival would be to cut off the infected leg.

"I will speak no more of it," he said, his tone brooking no dissent, "until we are aboard *Brymsteda*." He had set his mind against this and I knew there was little point in continuing the conversation.

I sighed, looking to Gwawrddur for support. The Welshman shook his head. He too knew Drosten's character.

Later, when the Pict was sleeping fitfully, Gwawrddur came to me.

"We both know he is as stubborn as the mule he rides," he said.

I chuckled, though there was no mirth in me.

"More stubborn than that good-natured beast," I said. And it was true, the animal that bore him each day was as biddable as any creature I have ever known.

"Do what you can for him now," Gwawrddur went on. "If he loses his senses to the fever, we will have to make the decision for him."

"That might well be too late," I replied, terrified that Drosten might die, consumed by the sickness that could enter an elf-shot wound.

We had enough food on the mules to last us, if we ate sparingly, but now I told the others we had to pause, if Drosten was to have any chance of survival.

"We should not tarry," Giso said.

Runolf stepped close, towering over the small Frank.

"If Hunlaf says we need to halt for Drosten," he snarled, his contempt for Giso clear in every word, "then we stop. And you do whatever he asks of you."

None of us trusted the Frank after we had seen what he was capable of, but he had led us unerringly along seldom used tracks and paths over the rocky ridges of the mountains and down onto the dusty plains, dotted with orchards and fields of wheat. And now, when he understood that we would not be swayed, for we were as stubborn as Drosten, he agreed to head to the nearest farmstead in search of what I needed.

Before he left, Runolf snapped his fingers at him.

"The parchments," the Norseman said, in response to Giso's raised eyebrow. "To ensure you will return."

"Of course I will return. Your ship will bear me back to Aachen."

"There are other ships," said Runolf, holding out his hand.

Giso smiled at that.

"Indeed there are," he said.

Runolf did not return his grin.

Giso pulled the papers from his robes. To protect them from the elements he had wrapped them in an envelope of leather that he had fashioned from a satchel carried by one of the dead warriors. He slapped this leather pouch onto Runolf's massive, callused palm.

We didn't like the man, but he was true to his word and he returned before sundown with honey, milk, bread, vinegar and garlic. He also brought with him some clean cloths, of the sort used to strain curds from whey.

I prepared a small fire, where I heated the ingredients and made a poultice. I hadn't been able to find any of the wyrts that would have helped with the healing, but it would have to do. When it was cool enough to touch without scalding, I placed the mixture on Drosten's leg, securing it with one of the clean cloths.

The Pict tensed, his muscles bunching, his teeth grinding together. He moaned deep in the back of his throat at the pain. But the next day when I applied a new poultice it seemed to me that the wound had grown no worse, and might in fact be slightly less inflamed. It was still dark, bruised and the skin surrounding it was an angry red, but I could not detect the stink of rot. I prayed that the Lord would spare my friend and, still conscious of the possibility of pursuit, we carried on.

Two days later we reached the coast, following nine long, slow days of travel.

I had imagined Giso would lead us directly to Qadis, but as

we saw the sun setting over the sea in the west on that ninth evening, there was no sign of the city.

"By my calculation," Giso said, "we are about half a day's journey south of Qadis. I have thought about what we might find there and I have decided on the best course of action."

"And what would that be?" enquired Hereward, his tone gruff. He had barely spoken to Giso since the fortress, and when he did, he did not hide his dislike of the man.

"In the morning, I will set out alone." Hereward began to protest, but Giso held up his hand to quieten him. "It is likely there will be men watching the ship. If they are looking for us, where else would be a better place than the docks at Qadis to spring an ambush?"

None of us liked the idea of him heading off on his own, but nor could we deny that what he said made sense.

"But how will you get to the ship if it is being watched?" I asked.

"I managed to be free of the docks when we were under guard and then I travelled the lands for weeks without being detected." He smiled thinly. "I will have no problems getting word to the crew. Any watchers will be waiting for you." He looked pointedly at Runolf. Despite wearing the black robes we had taken from the warriors we had killed, and covering his head with a winding cloth in the manner of the local people, the tall Norseman was still terribly conspicuous. His red hair and beard were clearly visible and he was easily a head taller than the rest of us. In contrast, Giso's skin had grown tanned and dark in the hot sun. He was small and nondescript. He knew the ways and the tongue of the people and I could all too easily imagine him slipping into the city without being noticed.

"What if *Brymsteda* is no longer there?" asked Gwawrddur.

"Let us pray it is," replied Giso. "But if it is not, I will try to find another vessel. Keep yourselves hidden. Camp in those white poplars and send someone down to the cove each day at midday for a sign."

"What sign?" I asked.

"Keep your eyes open and you will know it."

"And if we find a sign?"

"If you can see *Brymsteda*, light a fire to attract us in to shore. If you cannot see the ship, come to the beach at the next high tide and we will come for you."

None of us much liked the plan, but we could think of nothing better. Before the sun rose over the hills to the east, Giso was ready to leave. He went to Runolf and without a word handed him the papers in their leather binding.

"I'll be back," Giso said.

None of us spoke for a time as we watched him make his way down from the stand of poplars to the path that led northward.

"How much do you wager he'll not return?" said Drosten from where he sat, his back against a tree trunk.

At least Drosten would get a day or two's rest, I thought. I had done all I could, and now his life was in the Lord's hands. What might help God in healing the Pict would be for him to sleep and rest. The constant travel was taking its toll on him.

"That is a bet I'd take," replied Runolf. He snorted. "But with what silver?"

He laughed without humour and we fell silent again, staring after the dark-garbed Frank, each of us lost to our thoughts.

Our camp was comfortable enough, but we were all nervous, tired and on edge. Drosten was no better, but I thanked the Lord he was no worse either.

My wounds were healing well. For the first couple of days after the fight, my head had ached terribly, but on the third day that had subsided somewhat, and on the fifth I realised when I awoke the constant throbbing had disappeared altogether.

Revna tended to my injuries as I had seen to hers when she

had been hurt at sea. I enjoyed the moments when she would remove my bandages, her fingers lightly touching my skin. We spoke little, but there was a closeness between us now that did not need words. At times I caught Runolf watching us, his eyes thoughtful and shadowed beneath his thick brows. But he never said anything about the tenderness Revna showed me, or my obvious affection for her.

For my part, I relished any attention Revna gave me, but lived with the knowledge that we could never be more than friends. Runolf was like kin and he would not take kindly to me making advances towards his daughter.

The deep cut to Runolf's leg was also healing. Revna bathed and bandaged it, and only a few days after the fight, her father was barely limping.

Each day, they sent me down to the cove in search of a sign. I even went the first day, despite there being no chance of Giso having reached Qadis, let alone enough time for him to have returned. Still, it gave me a chance to see the sand and shingle as it was, driftwood from recent storms lining the high tide mark. If I was to recognise a sign, I needed to know how the strand looked without it.

I enjoyed the solitary walks. I had toyed with the idea of asking Revna to join me, but when I glanced at Runolf, he was glowering, as if he knew my thoughts and anticipated my invitation to his daughter. I swallowed my words and strode down alone from the poplars, across the path and then the steep, rocky incline that led to the sheltered beach. There were few travellers on the path, and those I saw in the distance, I avoided, darting away from the track to hide in the scrub or behind a boulder until they had passed.

On the beach I would sit on the rocks beside the sea for a time, watching the waves and listening to their sighing passage up and down the sand. There were sandpipers and redshanks and I watched them, jealous of their freedom, as they waded in the shallows, while further out over the surf, gannets soared and dived into the water.

On the third day, as I scrambled over the rocks that led down to the beach, there was no need of a sign from Giso. Looking out to sea, I saw *Brymsteda* itself surging over the waves, the great stallion Drosten had carved rising tall and proud above the prow.

Fifty

Brymsteda slid onto the sand of the cove. I looked up, grinning madly at the faces of the sailors and warriors. They were like family to me and my heart sang to see them again. Before the ship stopped moving Gersine jumped into the surf and waded ashore to pull me into an embrace. Tears stung my eyes. There was much to talk about. I had so many questions. But that would have to wait.

"There is no time to waste," shouted Alf from where he stood at the tiller. "Fetch the others without delay."

Taking Gersine, Beorn and Eadstan with me, I led them at a jog back up over the rocks, across the path and up to the stand of poplars. The others saw us approaching and by the time we reached them, they had already packed up our belongings. Drosten still needed to ride on the back of the docile mule down to the rocky slope that led to the strand, but I was heartened to see him able to dismount and clamber clumsily over the rocks. Removing the baggage from the mules, we started to carry it down to the beached ship. Others hurried up the sand to us, lending their hands to help Drosten and to carry our swords, byrnies, shields and the last of our food supplies to *Brymsteda*.

"No room for those beasts aboard," said Sygbald.

Hereward nodded, looking at each animal in turn, before

slapping the rump of the mule that had carried Drosten all this way without complaint.

"You have served us well," he said to the animal, as it trotted away. "Godspeed."

The other mule, a cantankerous creature that had often tried to bite us when we had turned our back on it, still wore its bridle and Hereward led it down to the tide line of flotsam on the beach, picking its way over the jumbled rocks.

"How much meat is there aboard?" he asked when we were close to *Brymsteda*.

"Not much," replied Oslaf, his jowls shaking. He had not lost any of his bulk since last we had seen him. "We left in a hurry and had no time to buy supplies."

Hereward nodded and, without warning, pulled a knife from his belt and stabbed it into the throat of the unsuspecting mule. It whinnied and strained at its rope, but Hereward held tight and, as its lifeblood gushed from the deep wound in the artery, he wrestled the beast to the ground where its blood soaked into the damp sand.

"His biting days are over," said Gwawrddur with a grim smile.

Hereward summoned Oslaf and Gamal with a shout. They were both skilled at butchery, and they set about the carcass in the midday sun as quickly as they were able.

"There is no time for that," called Alf from the deck. "It seems we have been followed."

He pointed out to sea. Three sails were rounding the headland.

"You did not notice them before?" Runolf said, shaking his head.

Alf shrugged.

"They must have set out soon after us and hugged the coast." He did not wait for a response, but began bellowing orders. We rushed to obey, needing no further incentive than the approaching vessels. It was clear to all of us that if we were unable to get the ship afloat and out of the small bay quickly, we would be trapped.

Gamal and Oslaf had finished gutting the mule. Its offal steamed in the sunshine. But there was no time to butcher it on land. Working quickly and expertly, they quartered the animal and then screamed out for a line. The Moorish sails were closer now and *Brymsteda* was ready to be heaved out into the surf. The two men secured a rope around one haunch of the animal and it was rapidly hauled aboard by eager hands. They hefted another quarter onto their shoulders and between them wrestled it over the side.

"Come on!" shouted Runolf. "Leave the rest."

He was right. The sails were dangerously near now and I could begin to make out the faces of the men aboard.

Oslaf and Gamal, smeared in gore, joined us as we leaned into the strakes. Digging our toes into the soft sand, we grunted with the effort of pushing the mighty wave-steed out onto the water where once again it would be the fast, sea-riding stallion that inspired its name and not the lumbering hulk that canted on its side in the shallows.

As soon as *Brymsteda* was afloat, we climbed aboard and took our places at the oars. There was little talk. The only voice that of Alf who cried out commands from the Lifting at the stern. We laboured furiously, sweating beneath the hot sun, each stroke of the oar blades heaving the sleek ship out towards the horizon.

We sped along. The tide had turned and was on our side now, the invisible force of it sliding the water beneath our keel away from the beach. That same unseen power was exerting itself on the three ships that had swung around the headland to the north. And yet, the wind was coming from seaward, filling their sails and pushing them inexorably on a course that would see them intercept us.

We toiled at the looms, frantically watching for a sign that the Moorish ships might cut us off from the open sea. My shoulders and back began to ache. I had grown unaccustomed to the task of rowing and my muscles had not regained their full strength. I said nothing. Gritting my teeth against the pain, I fell into the familiar rhythm and prayed that God would deliver us once more from the men of al-Andalus.

Around me, my shield-brothers' faces were stern; jaws set as they pulled on the oars. We could all see we had left it too late. *Brymsteda* would not be able to outpace the al-Andalus ships, even with the help of the tide.

In that instant, like a sighing reply to my prayers, the wind shifted into the south. Now it worked against our enemies, causing them to have to tack. Runolf shouted for the sail to be unfurled. His voice merged with that of Alf who had given the exact same order. He had been commanding *Brymsteda* in Runolf's absence and now the two men looked at each other and laughed.

"We only have one sail," said Alf with a grin.

"We will only need one to beat them," replied Runolf, laughing with the joy of having the rolling deck of a fine ship beneath his feet. "We will leave those fat ducks behind, as sure as my father was named Ragnar!"

Near me, Oslaf pulled at a loom, his blood-caked hands smearing the wood red. All the while his eyes were fixed on the rapidly receding beach and the dark shape of the remaining half of the slaughtered mule.

"Damn waste of good meat," he moaned. "All that offal and blood too. We could have had blood sausage if we'd only had a little more time."

"If we had remained much longer on that beach," I said, breathless from the exertion at the oar, the wound across my ribs paining me as I pulled, "we might have ended up losing our own guts and not just those of the mule."

"True enough," he said. "Still, I hate to see good food go to waste."

With the wind in our sail and our hands to the oars, we raced away from the three ships with ease. Once clear of our enemies, Runolf leaned on the tiller and called out for the sheets to be trimmed. The wind picked up, straining against the grease-soaked wool of the sail, and *Brymsteda* bounded forward over the crests of the waves like a colt given its head.

"They won't catch us now," I said to Gersine, shipping my oar and hurrying to do Scurfa's bidding. He had called for the brace to be secured, and as he still commanded the Aft crew it felt natural to obey him without question.

I finished tying the knot and stood on *Brymsteda*'s deck, relishing the sensation of the wind in my hair and the familiar creak of the hull as the strakes flexed with the force of the waves. It felt good to once again be performing the tasks of the ship, and I marvelled at how quickly we had all fallen back into our roles aboard. There had been scant time to talk since we had boarded *Brymsteda*, but now the sail was set, the brisk southerly wind filling its belly and pulling the wool taut.

There wouldn't be much for me to do for a while, I guessed, so I rose and turned to look out over the blue-green expanse of the sea. The three sails of the Moorish ships that pursued us fell ever further into our wake. They would disappear over the horizon soon.

"I told you they would never catch us," I said to Gersine.

"Do not tempt fate," he replied, his tone a mixture of excitement and anxiety. "We've had too much bad luck to speak so rashly of escape before we are far from these shores."

I grunted, watching the distant lands of al-Andalus slide by in the haze. It would be good to leave this place behind. I wished I could have come here under different circumstances. I would have liked to have been able to study the books and scrolls in Al-Zarqālluh's libraries, to have learnt more of the teachings of the Prophet revered by *Al-Muslimun*. There was such a wealth of knowledge there. Part of me yearned to have been able to grasp some of it, as Runolf longed for his silver. And yet, I could not think of the last few months with anything other than sorrow and bitter regret. I thought of Hering's death after the pirate attack. His demise seemed to have marked the change in our fortunes. What followed had been a litany of suffering and anguish. The dank cell beneath the fortress of Qadis, the brutal demonstration of Roman Fire in Qurtuba, the theft of the silver, Ahmad's betrayal, and finally the death and chaos in the mountains, culminating in the destruction of *The Treasure of Life*.

"Bad luck?" I said, my tone bitter. "Perhaps that is what it is. Or maybe God has turned his back on us."

Gersine shook his head.

"How can you say such a thing? Has there ever been a more blessed man than you?"

I turned to him, incredulous.

"Blessed?"

"If God had forsaken you, do you truly believe you would yet live?"

I sighed. Gersine was right. Things could have been much worse. Hering's loss still weighed heavily upon me, and yet, despite all the misfortune that had befallen us and the adversities we had faced on our trip to and from Qurtuba, young Hering was the only one of our band to perish.

Stretching, I winced as the recently healed wound on my chest pulled, reminding me of how close to death I had come. But the gash had healed well and I knew the pain would subside in time.

Of course, I mused bitterly, we had also lost Ahmad. I was angry that I had not foreseen his treachery and I wondered what happened to him after we fled the fortress in the mountains. I had promised him his freedom, but he had taken so much more. I had thought much about his actions during our journey to the coast, and I had finally forgiven him. He was weak, as we all are, and I vowed to pray for him. Runolf and the others were less understanding and I hoped for Ahmad's sake that our paths would never cross again.

I looked back along the length of the ship. The Moorish sails were perceptibly further away already. With this wind, and Runolf at the steerboard, the thick-bellied ships would be no match for *Brymsteda*.

Drosten sat at the stern, close to Runolf. Seeing my glance, he raised a hand and I returned the gesture with a smile. He was wrapped in a blanket against the cool breeze, but his condition had improved with the days of rest.

Later, some time after the pale sails of our pursuers had dropped beneath the horizon, we crowded together amidships and recounted what had befallen us in the weeks since last we met.

I did much of the talking, with interjections from time to time from the others. Just as Hereward had a knack for telling riddles, so, even back then as a young man, my natural skill as a storyteller shone through. When I recounted a tale, others listened. The crew lounged about me, quiet and in awe at the pictures my words painted for their minds' eyes. I did not seek to embellish the events, or even to linger on them, merely to give a true account of our experience. But as I spoke I realised how much had transpired and I knew that the telling would not be over quickly.

Listening intently, Oslaf and Gamal each set about butchering the haunches of mule. Ida prepared a small fire in one of the earthenware pots we used for the purpose. As my story progressed from the dungeon of Qadis, to the river voyage towards Qurtuba and the meeting with the emir, the freshly cut meat was dropped into a pot along with some onions, coarse flour and water to make a thick stew.

The sun had slipped into the west and the pottage was almost ready by the time I had finished telling our story.

"And you say you are not blessed," whispered Gersine in the hush that followed.

My face grew hot. I did not wish to dwell on how much God's hand had been a part of our survival. To think of it made me question too much. I had turned the events over in my mind several times since we had fled the mountains and I was still unsure how I felt about the destruction of the book and our escape. Giso said he had been guided by God, but how could that be? Would the Lord allow one of His own to perform such atrocities as we had witnessed? If so, what separated Him from Allah, or Runolf's Óðinn?

"I have told you our tale," I said, wishing to change the subject. "Now tell us yours. What have you done these weeks since we departed?"

"Very little," Gersine said. "For the first couple of weeks we were held aboard the ship and not allowed to leave the docks. But as time went by, and after Nadir left, so our guards became more relaxed with us. They sold us food and drink, and, after a time, they even allowed us into the city, as long as we did not travel alone."

"And I thank the Lord for that," said Ida.

"That they allowed you to travel," said Hereward, smirking, "or that they went with you?"

"Both!" replied Ida, smiling broadly from where he stirred the stew simmering over the fire. "I might have died of boredom if they had not allowed us to frequent Florentina's palace. And without someone to guide us back afterwards, I would probably still be traipsing through those tangled streets." He shook his head. "No matter how many times we walked the paths of Qadis, I could never find my way. I am meant for open spaces, for this," he waved his hand over the waters around us, "or the hills and cliffs and white beaches of Northumbria. It is not natural for so many to be cooped up like hens in cities of stone. I am glad to be free of it at last."

"But you'll miss Florentina's palace!" said Mantat.

Ida rubbed a hand over his eyes, as if wiping away memories.

"Aye, that I will. And I will not be the only one, I'd wager."

"Who is this Florentina?" asked Revna, her face serious.

Ida blushed crimson above his beard. The others laughed.

"She keeps… a house…" he said, stammering and uncertain, "of girls…"

"And boys too," said Beorn with a wink to Eadstan.

"Aye, boys too," Ida said, more crimson than ever, "if that is your pleasure."

"I am sorry to have missed a visit to her palace then," said Revna sombrely. "Perhaps I could have taken a boy there." She held Ida's gaze, unsmiling. "If that had been my pleasure."

He spluttered, opening and closing his mouth, unsure what to say.

"It is not a real palace," he blurted out at last.

Revna's expression slipped to one of barely suppressed hilarity, eyes crinkling, lips pulling up in a smile. A moment later, unable to hold in her mirth any longer, she laughed loud and long. Everyone else joined in. It felt as though our laughter dispelled some of the darkness from our recollections. We had escaped near certain death and we were together again, this large, boisterous family forged in the flames of adversity and hardship.

Even Drosten, hunched over in the Lifting, chuckled, which I took for another good sign of his recovery. Runolf had not moved from his position at the steerboard and I wondered if he heard the jest his daughter had made, but when I looked I saw that he too was grinning.

We had borne tension within us for so long that the release of laughter felt like a balm, soothing our frayed nerves. Just as the honey and bread poultice I had placed on Drosten's thigh had succeeded in drawing out the poison there, so this laughter began to dispel the despair that had clung to us.

The only person not joining in was Giso. He sat apart from the rest. Sufficiently close to listen, but far enough not to be included. Whether he had chosen this separation or the rest of the crew had forced it upon him, I could not say.

I turned back to Ida who was wiping at his tears of laughter with the back of his hand.

"If you have been whoring and drinking your fill," I said, "free to come and go as you liked, why did you not escape before?"

"We most likely could have sailed away weeks ago," he said, barely able to get the words out around the giggles that yet gripped him, "if we had wished to."

"But Florentina's palace was too inviting," I said. It was not a question.

"Well, yes," he said, "but it is not just that. We were waiting for you."

"And now here we are." I glanced over at Giso. "How did the Frank get word to you?"

"You'll not believe it," he said.

"Tell us," said Gwawrddur.

"He left a message with Florentina!" He barked with laughter again before continuing. "It is just as well for you that we were frequent guests of her establishment or else you would still be waiting under those trees looking for signs on the beach."

Everyone laughed again, and soon the pottage was being ladled into wooden bowls and handed out. I took an extra bowl and carried it to Giso.

As I walked across the deck, stepping over sea chests and coiled lines, I surveyed the sea around us. We were far away from the coast now, the land almost lost from view in the sun-glare and the mist of distance. Gulls flew in the bright sky above us, perhaps smelling the pottage and waiting to snatch any scraps from the water when he had finished eating. Ahead, but close to the land, there rose a small sail. I squinted to make out details, but it was too far away for me to discern anything of note.

Without speaking, I sat down beside Giso, holding out a bowl to him. He accepted it with a nod.

"It's no threat," he said.

"What?" I had no idea what he was speaking about.

"That boat. It is just a fishing bark, crewed by four, I think, though it is hard to tell at this distance."

I had not seen him look over the side in the direction of the sail. Giso always appeared to see more and further than anyone else. It unnerved me, but I said nothing. I took a spoonful of the stew. It was bland, but hot and wholesome. I chewed in silence. When I offered him no reply, Giso sniffed the contents of his own bowl, then proceeded to eat. He ate with no sign of pleasure, as though it were a task he had been commanded to complete as quickly and efficiently as possible.

He set his empty bowl aside while I still had a couple of mouthfuls left.

"Thank you for the food," he said.

I grunted, chewing the last chunk of meat from my bowl.

"Did you come to pray with me?" he asked. "It must be getting on for Vespers."

I frowned. My soul had been unburdened by the burning of the book, but it was still heavy with grief, guilt, and the uncertainty of both the future and the past. To share in the communion of prayer would bring me some comfort, but I could not bring myself to pray with this man.

"No," I said, my tone harsh as a slap. "If I want to pray, I will pray alone."

Giso nodded and gave a small shrug that seemed to say he understood, or at least was not surprised by my response.

"We are returning to your master with little to show for our troubles," I said after swallowing the last of the pottage.

"It is true that it has not been a complete success," he said, "but still we bring much of value."

"Those sheets of vellum?"

He placed a hand on his chest where I knew he stored the leather-wrapped sheets.

"Those," he said, "and this." He tapped his head. "Alhwin deals in knowledge and we have learnt much in the land of Al-Hakam Ibn Hisham. King Carolus will reward us well for the tidings we bring."

"You truly believe so?"

"Oh yes," Giso said. "To learn of one's enemies is worth much to someone like Carolus."

"Someone like Carolus?" I said. "What do you mean by that?"

"A man destined for greatness."

"Is he not already great? He commands the people of Frankia, the Saxons and the Langobards."

"Yes, but he will rule over more before he is done. And it is not only through might that such an empire is won, but through guile, wisdom and knowledge."

"And through the grace of God," I said.

"Of course."

"And this is what Alhwin provides the king?"

"He is a most holy man, and wise beyond any other in Christendom."

"And you bring him knowledge."

"Me and others like me."

Turning, I pulled myself up to peer over the wale. We were closer to the sail now and I could make out more details. It belonged to a small fishing boat. The sun glistened on the wet net the fishermen were pulling over the side. Afternoon sunlight flashed on the silver fish that flapped and flicked in the net's grasp. We were near enough now that I could count the men aboard. There were four of them.

I slid back to sit beside Giso.

"There is something I have wished to ask you since…" my words trailed off. "Since the night of the fortress."

"If I can answer your question, I will," he replied, his voice guarded as if he expected a trap.

"When you sent Labib and Daud to watch over that man's wife and children, you told the guard in the fortress that if you did not return, they would kill his family."

"I did. Yes." He spoke in a flat tone, devoid of emotion.

"Would they have slain them?"

"Of course not," Giso replied, shock colouring his words. "I gave them the order to return to our camp after the break of day, whether they had heard from me or not. By then we would already either have succeeded or failed. Killing the woman and girls would have been for nought." He turned his head to look me in the eye. "I'm not a monster, Hunlaf."

I was not so sure of that. I recalled the dispassionate ease with which he had reached out and slit Gallienus' throat. The bound guard in the tunnel lying in a pool of his blood. The flames reflecting in Giso's eyes as Praetextatus and Nadir had been consumed by the rapacious Roman Fire.

A shadow fell on us.

"What are you two talking about?"

Runolf towered over us. He held a bowl in his massive hand. With a glance towards the stern, I saw that Alf had relieved him at the steerboard.

"We were talking of the future," said Giso, "which is always wise. There is nothing to be gained in looking backwards."

"Unless you are being chased," rumbled Runolf, lowering his bulk to sit beside us.

"Quite so," said Giso. "But we have outrun our pursuers thanks to your skill and this ship."

Runolf grinned at the compliment.

"*Brymsteda* was born from my skill too," he said, speaking around a mouthful of stew.

"Indeed."

There was a lightness in Runolf's demeanour ever since we had climbed aboard and I wondered at the toll the last few weeks had taken on us all. Was the change to the rest of us as noticeable as in the giant Norseman? I looked towards the mast where Revna was talking to Eadstan and Beorn. Of course, Runolf had carried with him the fear for his daughter. I understood this burden of dread for a loved one. I too had felt the pressure of anxiety for Revna lift as we'd sailed away from al-Andalus.

"What of the future then?" Runolf asked, wiping his mouth on his sleeve.

"I was telling Hunlaf that my master will pay you handsomely for bringing me back, for what I carry with me and what I have learnt about the state of al-Andalus and its emir."

"Everything has a price," Runolf said, with a twisted smile. "I doubt it will be as much silver as we lost though."

"Perhaps not," said Giso, "but you might be surprised at Alhwin's generosity."

"If he will pay us with coffers of silver, I will listen to whatever he has to say."

Giso held Runolf's gaze, as if weighing his words, or gauging how to respond.

"Alhwin might well have more missions for a crew such as *Brymsteda*'s. The Teacher is a God-fearing man with far-reaching interests. There are already many who act as his eyes and hands throughout the lands of Christendom and beyond. He surely has need of good Christians armed with sharp swords, keen minds and a fast ship."

"Well," said Runolf, swallowing the food in his mouth, then

showing his white teeth in a grin, "two out of four is not so bad, I would say."

Giso chuckled, but I noted how his eyes remained cold and distant.

"You think Alhwin will want thick-skulled warriors of dubious faith?" asked Runolf, still smiling and seeming not to notice Giso's cool expression.

"Anything is possible," Giso replied, mirroring Runolf's wolfish grin.

Fifty-One

When first I picked up the quill all those months ago to begin recording my story in a prideful act against the will of my abbot, I thought it unlikely that the Almighty would spare me long enough to tell of the coming of the Norsemen to Lindisfarnae and the subsequent, almost forgotten attack on Werceworthe and the heroes that were forged in its defence.

Since then, God, in His infinite wisdom, has seen fit to allow this old, withered sinner to stave off death long enough to pen the account of how *The Treasure of Life* was lost, then found once more, and finally destroyed in purifying fire in a faraway kingdom. The more I wrote of the tale, reliving dark days I have often sought to forget, I became increasingly convinced that this was the true story the Lord Almighty had wished for me to tell all along. In my hubris, I had imagined *my* story was of interest, and perhaps it will be to some. I know Coenric enjoys my tales of battle and intrigue, but despite being well meaning and devoted to me, he is little more than a child, with a boy's wide-eyed wonder for adventure.

I understand now that it was not the story of my life, but that of the book, and how it poisoned the minds of all those who touched it, that I was destined to write. And this I have done to the best of my ability, writing day and night as if the

Devil himself were chasing behind me, his hot breath on the nape of my neck. Perhaps that is not so far from the truth of it. With each passing day, as I scratched the words of the account onto the vellum, the more I came to believe that the instant I was done with this, Satan would claim me for all the evil deeds I have committed.

I do not comprehend the power *The Treasure of Life* exerted. And I cannot well explain the feeling I had when it was destroyed in the flames beneath Aljany's fortress. The closest I have felt to the strange sensation of absence following the book's sudden loss, occurred to me many years later. One of my teeth grew infected, my gum swollen and painful. It was a constant, nagging ache, making me ill-tempered and interrupting my sleep. And yet I lived with the throbbing soreness for months, until I barely registered it. One day, a visiting pedlar told me he could rid me of the bad tooth and he pulled it free from my mouth in a painful gush of blood and pus. The next day, I realised that where there had been discomfort, now my mouth felt well and all that was left was a gap where the tooth had been. My tongue would often seek out that hole, unbidden, probing there in search of the missing tooth.

Losing *The Treasure of Life* was much the same feeling. It was as if, in being rid of the book, a muted torment had been removed from my very soul. And yet my spirit remains heavily burdened after writing this tome. I have been reminded of so many evil acts that I committed. Acts that must surely lead to my damnation.

Coenric has prayed with me frequently, offering words of encouragement. But what does he know? He is but a youth. He has never known true fear or hardship such as we faced all those years ago. Coenric is a sweet boy, but he has never felt the hot blood of an enemy spray over his face. Never has he revelled in the joy of fury and killing when the blades sing and the screams of dying men sound like music. I have barely rested these last weeks, even after Godstan gave me permission to continue my work, I sensed that the time left to me was running out. Ceaselessly I have written, until my hand was cramped and I could scarcely hold the quill. Abbot Godstan has been generous with candles and has allowed me to neglect my other duties. It is as if he too knows that my days are numbered and so he has made no demand on my time. My beard has grown full, long and unkempt, in spite of Coenric's nagging for me to allow him to trim it, and if the crown of my head had not been bald these last dozen years or more, my tonsure would have become lost by now.

At times the memories tumbled out of me faster than I could write and I would mutter angrily as I had to painstakingly scribe each letter. Coenric again offered to take my place, allowing me to dictate while he wrote, but I am not so far gone yet that I would allow the boy to record my story with his dreadful penmanship. Besides, he is no faster than I and his mistakes drive me to despair.

For a time, when the sun shone in the sky, the barley waved ripe and green in the fields and bees droned outside my window, alighting on the comfrey and lavender that grow in the herb garden, I felt as if some of my youth had returned to me. I awoke with a renewed vigour, urgent to write the next pages of this book. During that time of warm pride, I began to believe that mayhap I would live for years yet. I started to think of the tales that were still locked within my mind that I could put down on parchment if the Lord continued to spare me. And there are so many memories, so many tales yet to tell.

Giso had been right. Alhwin had offered us wealth to serve him. But it was not just knowledge he sought. For that he had men of subtlety and ruthlessness, men like Giso, who could infiltrate the harem of Harun al-Rashid in ar-Raqqah without being discovered. The crew of *Brymsteda* was something else.

We were not afraid to sail where other men were terrified to travel. We would fight when attacked, and we were attacked often. And for a time, while Carolus Magnus bestrode the world like a colossus, we were invincible.

In those summer days, I recalled how, in the service of Alhwin, we had travelled the length and breadth of the world. My mind would wander to the streets of Byzantion, or the bustling stalls of the *souk* in the shadow of the Yafah Gate at Jerusalem. I remembered the faces of men and women I had known and artefacts and relics I had held in my own hands. Items so holy and possessing such power that they are now preserved in the most exquisite of reliquaries in Saint Peter's Basilica in Roma. I thought of how the deeds of a few men led to Carolus being anointed the Holy Roman Emperor by the Pope himself. Runolf, Drosten, Gwawrddur, Hereward, and beautiful Revna, all played their part in those mad years as we scoured the face of the earth for items of power to further Carolus' cause.

I am the only member of *Brymsteda*'s crew left now and it pains me to think I will not be able to complete my friends' stories. For a time I forgot the true purpose of this reprieve that God has provided me. To remind me, the day I scribed the destruction of the book, the pain in my stomach returned with enough vehemence that I wept as I wrote.

I have lived a rich and varied life, filled with such wonder and horror as few men have endured. I have written much in the three annals I have already penned, but there are still countless adventures I have not described in any detail. And yet I fear my work here is done. The summer is over. The skies darken earlier each day and already the storms of autumn have begun to strip the leaves from the alders down by the river.

These may well be the last words I write. If that is God's will, I beseech you to pray for my soul and that of my fallen comrades who were ever braver and better than I. Pray even for Runolf, who died with the name of Óðinn on his lips and a weapon in his hand. Despite his heathen ways, I have not forgotten that he was baptised, so pray for him, that God might grant his soul everlasting peace, even though I know he would have wanted to be seated in the hall of the slain beside his pagan god. And never doubt that I have recounted this tale to the best of my ability. Any omission or error in the telling should be blamed on my ageing mind and the waning memory that dims as I peer back through the decades of my past.

I commend my soul to the Lord. May His blessings be upon all who read this tome.

And thus ends the history of *The Treasure of Life* and the third volume of the Annals of the life of Hunlaf of Ubbanford.

Author's Note

Hunlaf's travels have once again taken him far from his home of Northumbria. We know from his asides and recollections that he travelled to all manner of exotic locations during his long life, and with each new locale he visits, I am called upon to dive into a new pile of research tomes, the like of which would have pleased Hunlaf, with his love of books, immensely.

As always, though the adventures of Hunlaf and his companions are fictional, the world they inhabit is based on history. Most of the places they journey to, and many of the people they encounter, existed. My imagination is responsible for most of what transpires.

Whilst I have visited some of the locations mentioned in this book and I lived in Spain for well over ten years, I am by no means an expert of the history of the Iberian Peninsula in the late eighth century, so I apologise for any historical inaccuracy.

By the end of the eighth century, much of the Peninsula had been conquered and settled by Arabs and other Muslim ethnic groups from the north of Africa. These invaders were expanding the *Dār al-Islam* ("Islamic world") through conquest. But after taking over the kingdoms of Spain through force, they allowed Christians and Jews already there to remain, living out their lives in relative peace. These were the *Ahl al-kitab*

("People of the Book"), or *dhimmi* ("protected peoples"), who were free to follow their own laws and religions as long as they acknowledged the superior authority of Islam.

There have been all manner of things written about this seemingly idyllic situation of the three Abrahamic religions coexisting in harmony. But it should not be forgotten that the Islamic Arabs were the rulers and the upper class in the societies that had been conquered. Arabic became the *lingua franca* of the region over time, and after seven centuries of Moorish occupancy, its impact on modern-day Spanish is still very noticeable, particularly in the names of things that originated from the time of al-Andalus, such as imported foodstuffs. For example, *azúcar* is the Spanish word for sugar. In Arabic, the word is *al-sukkar*. The Spanish for rice is *arroz*, derived from the Arabic word *aruzz*. The Arabic word for orange, *narang*, became *naranja* in Spanish. The list goes on.

One of the challenges I faced was deciding how to refer to the different ethnic and ethno-religious groups with whom Hunlaf interacts within the story. I wanted to be true to the time I was writing about, giving an inkling of the bigotry and division that existed, without ignoring modern sensibilities.

The term "Moor" that has been traditionally used to describe the Islamic people who settled in Iberia has become contentious in recent years, as it can be seen as derogatory. Despite this possible negative connotation, taking into consideration the word's ancient roots, I decided to use it in the story when the men from northern Europe are referring to the disparate Muslim ethnic groups who ruled over al-Andalus. Like the outmoded term, "Dark Ages", the word "Moor" has been used for hundreds of years, so many readers will instantly have a reference point. Besides, I didn't want to shy away from the fact that the Christians of the time would feel great prejudice towards Muslims and any other faith not their own. I have chosen for the Muslims in this book to refer to themselves as

Al-Muslimun. And to highlight that the prejudice was not one-sided, I have Muslims refer to those they see as non-believers or deniers of the authority of Allah as *kuffaar* (singular *kafir*).

The Imazighen pirates that Hunlaf and his friends encounter at the start of the story are from the coastal regions of North Africa or Maghreb that would later in history be known as the Barbary (or Berber) Coast. The exact derivation of the name "Berber" is debated, but it is widely accepted as an exonym, or a name given to the people of that region by others. It is also commonly viewed as pejorative, perhaps relating to the Greek word for "barbarian" or the Arab word for "babbling". The term Amazigh ("free man") is an endonym for indigenous North Africans, and Imazighen is the native plural term. While the piracy in that region would become legendary later in history, there must have been men from that coast who would be more than happy to steal the riches from the Emirate of Córdoba (Qurtuba), or perhaps even engage in some espionage under the patronage of one of the rival Islamic dynasties that abounded in the Iberian Peninsula.

AD 796 was a year of great upheaval, both in al-Andalus and Northumbria. As Alhwin (or Alcuin, as he is commonly known) implies when he meets Hunlaf, Æthelred, the king of Northumbria would soon be overthrown, murdered on the eighteenth of April by some of his nobles after a tumultuous reign. And in the south, Al-Hakam had just taken over from his father who also died in the same month.

Al-Hakam's uncles, Sulayman and Abdallah, tried to wrest him from power, and I envisaged that they might attempt to kidnap the new emir's wife and son, perhaps using pirates for some form of plausible deniability. Abdallah later travelled with his sons to King Carolus' court in order to seek the Frankish king's help in their fight against Al-Hakam. This is not the only reference of Christians and Muslims joining forces against a common enemy.

Carolus is, of course, more commonly known as Charlemagne, or Charles the Great, and as Hunlaf recounts at the end of this book, he will eventually become the Holy Roman Emperor. Alhwin was indeed a clergyman from Northumbria, who became a respected counsellor and teacher in Charlemagne's court. He famously wrote letters to people all over Christendom and amassed one of the greatest libraries of the early medieval period. He was not only a pious man and prodigious epistoler, but also a poet and scholar. As if these were not enough achievements, I have chosen to have him employing his wide web of contacts as a sort of spy master, working to help see his master, Carolus, enthroned as the head of the Holy Roman Empire of Western Europe.

Alhwin was a great lover of knowledge and books, as was the king of the Franks. It is said that Charlemagne would have soldiers bring back ancient Latin literature they might find on campaign. Carolingian monks would meticulously copy these texts into new volumes. In this way Charlemagne helped preserve works by Cicero, Pliny the Younger, Ovid and others. It was not a huge stretch to imagine that Alhwin and Carolus would be interested in a rare, heretical book by a Persian named Mani.

Roman Fire (or as it is more commonly known, Greek Fire) was developed by an artificer from Heliopolis called Kallinikos and was first used in AD 678 against the fleet of the Arab invasion that had besieged the city. Its formula was jealously guarded by the Byzantines, who I have the people of al-Andalus refer to as Romans. The men of the Eastern Roman Empire who knew the secret of the liquid that could supposedly even burn on water were kept captives, and if anyone tried to steal the recipe, they were executed.

To this day, the exact formula is not known, but it is believed to have contained some, or all of the following: naphtha, sulphur, tar and quicklime, crude oil, pine resin, turpentine and pitch.

It was used from ships, pumped from syphons as described here, very much like modern flamethrowers that later saw use in the twentieth century from the First World War onwards. In the Vietnam War, there were even boats with napalm flamethrowers mounted on them. Flamethrowers are still weapons of modern warfare, but their use is restricted under Protocol III of the United Nations Convention on Certain Conventional Weapons.

There are records of firepots being used throughout history, and ceramic grenades that would have been filled with "liquid fire" have been found in Crete dating from the tenth century. The Moors of al-Andalus used some form of incendiary liquid thrown by catapults in AD 844 against a fleet of Viking ships that raided far up the Guadalquivir River and attacked Seville (Išbīliya). It is not known if they came up with their own concoction or somehow managed to procure the recipe of the Byzantine Roman Fire.

Al-Hakam governed in a time of great strife, putting down several uprisings in the most brutal ways imaginable. In AD 806 it is said he ordered seventy-two nobles and their attendants (perhaps numbering as many as five thousand) to be massacred at a banquet. He then had their bodies crucified and displayed along the banks of the Guadalquivir. He was also known to have the heads of rebels and Christian enemies put on show at the gates of Cordoba. With such ruthless cruelty one can easily imagine what he might have done to men he believed were responsible for his wife and son being captured.

The Emir of Cordoba did indeed have a royal bodyguard made up of non-Arabs called the *Al-Haras*. These non-Arabs were seen to be free of the tribal loyalties that might otherwise compromise Arab warriors' loyalty. Similar units of bodyguards were used by several other medieval Islamic leaders.

The Mosque of Cordoba (known now simply as the *Mezquita*, Spanish for Mosque), while much smaller in AD 796, would still have been a marvel, and it is recorded as having fruit trees growing within its walls. Orange, palm and cypress trees still grow in the *Patio de los Naranjos*. Originally built by Al-Hakam's grandfather, Abd al-Rahman I, it was added to in several phases over the subsequent centuries until it became the massive building that now holds an extravagantly baroque Catholic Cathedral within its colonnaded interior. If you are ever in the south of Spain, I thoroughly recommend a visit!

Aljany's fortress in the mountains is loosely based on more than one castle and location. The architecture of Islamic Spain was revolutionary in many ways, and several castles, such as Guadalest Castle in Alicante, were constructed on difficult to access peaks, with walls running along the slopes of the mountains. The main inspiration for Aljany's fortress is the Castillo del Aznalmara, imagining it to be situated on a higher peak of the Sierra de Grazalema.

Throughout the pages of the three books written so far, Hunlaf has frequently mentioned there are many more adventures he would like to set down on paper. He has tantalisingly hinted at certain events and many faraway and fascinating locales he visited before he returned to his monastic life of peace and seclusion.

At the end of *A Day of Reckoning*, his body is ailing and it is uncertain how much longer he will be able to cling on to life. Perhaps he managed to scratch some more of his exploits onto vellum before death claimed him. If he did, we will find out another day.

And in other books.

Acknowledgements

As ever, I must thank you, dear reader, for spending some of your money and valuable time to read this book. In this modern world in which we are bombarded with entertainment in all manner of formats, I really appreciate that my writing made it to the top of your list of content to consume.

If you have enjoyed the story, please spread the word to others, and if you have a moment, please consider leaving a short review on your online store of choice. Reviews really help new readers pick up a writer they might not otherwise take a chance on.

I must give extra special thanks to Jon McAfee, Mary Faulkner and Emma Stone, for their ongoing generous patronage. To find out more about becoming a patron, and what rewards you can receive for doing so, please go to www. matthewwharffy.com.

Thanks to my friends and test readers, Gareth Jones, Alex Forbes, Shane Smart and Simon Blunsdon. As always, they are the first to read each book and I find their input extremely useful.

Thanks to Steven A. McKay, author and co-host of Rock, Paper, Swords! The Historical Action and Adventure Podcast, for giving me a sympathetic ear when I need to vent, and for helping me maintain some perspective when the crazy publishing industry gets too much. Not only is Steven a great guy, he's a wonderful writer too. Read his books!

A huge amount of work goes into every book, well beyond the actual writing. Thank you to my editors, Nicolas Cheetham and Greg Rees, for polishing the story, and thanks to all of the wonderful team at Aries and Head of Zeus for designing and producing the finished product.

Thanks to the online community of authors and readers who connect with me regularly on Facebook, Twitter, Mastodon and Instagram. It is always great to hear from like-minded individuals.

And finally, but never least, my everlasting love and thanks go to my family. To Elora and Iona, for ensuring I never believe my own hype, and to my wife, Maite (aka Maria!), for putting up with me, always listening, and for her steadfast guidance and unwavering support.

Matthew Harffy
Wiltshire, January 2023

About the Author

MATTHEW HARFFY grew up in Northumberland where the rugged terrain, ruined castles and rocky coastline had a huge impact on him. He now lives in Wiltshire, England, with his wife and their two daughters. Matthew is the author of the critically acclaimed Bernicia Chronicles and A Time for Swords series, and he also presents the popular podcast, *Rock, Paper, Swords!*, with fellow author Steven A. McKay.

Follow Matthew at @MatthewHarffy and
www.matthewharffy.com

A DAY OF RECKONING

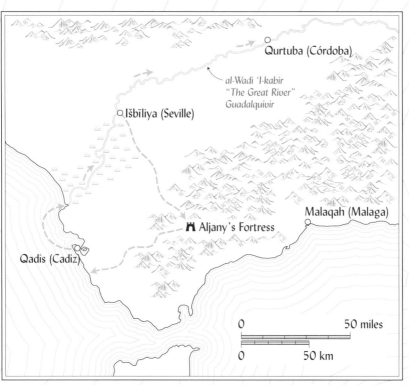

al-Wadi 'l-kabir
"The Great River"
Guadalquivir

Qurtuba (Córdoba)

Išbīliya (Seville)

Aljany's Fortress

Malaqah (Malaga)

Qadis (Cadiz)

0   50 miles

0   50 km

ATLANTIC OCEAN

Bay

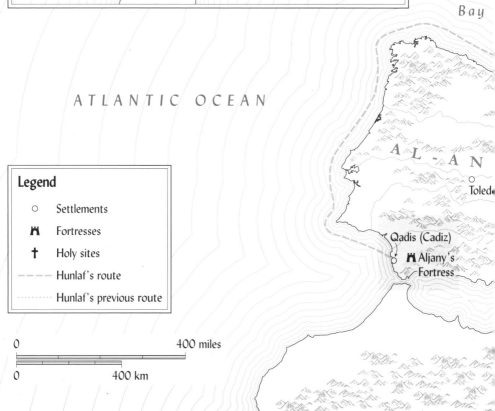

A L - A N

Toled

Qadis (Cadiz)

Aljany's
Fortress

Legend

○	Settlements
♖	Fortresses
†	Holy sites
– – –	Hunlaf's route
··········	Hunlaf's previous route

0   400 miles

0   400 km